FLY
ON THE WALL

Also by Trista Russell

Going Broke

FLY
ON THE WALL

TRISTA RUSSELL

Urban Books
74 Andrews Avenue
Wheatley Heights, NY 11798

ISBN 978-0-7394-6620-9

Printed in the United States of America

This is a work of fiction. Any references or similarities to actual events, real people, living, or dead, or to real locales are intended to give the novel a sense of reality. Any similarity in other names, characters, places, and incidents is entirely coincidental.

Acknowledgments

This book, and others, may not be filled with Scriptures, but God uses the least of us—ordinary people—to send extraordinary messages to those in need. Therefore, until my tongue lies silent in the grave, I will believe that I have a purpose in you, Lord, and that my writing is not in vain. I thank you God for Your undeserved grace and mercies in my life.

I would like to acknowledge my immediate family. My husband, best friend, and soul mate, Steve Burris, thank you for being you and supporting me, sometimes even beyond logic. I love you! My parents, Reverend Everett & Mrs. Zerlean Russell; my sister, Roslyn Underwood, and my brother-in-law, Mike; my brother, Minister Phillip Russell, and sister-in-law, Stefanie; my nieces, Raeshawnda, Philisha, and Jayla; and nephews, Phillip Jr., Ray Jr., Malik, and Javon.

Now that I am so far away from you, I know what an awesome family we truly are. I love you more and more each day—the Russells, Francises, Robinses, Mosses, Rolles, etc.... C'mon, y'all know we are a huge family. To Pastor Ferguson and the New Mount Zion Baptist Church family (Florida City, Florida) thank you for the love and for reading my work and not judging me, in spite of the subject matter.

To the entire island of Bimini, my family and friends there, thank you for your love and support. To my Freeport & Nassau family and readers: "Y'all carryin' on bad!" To all other Bahamians, or anyone who knows what "muthasick," "spry," and "potcake" are, thank you! To the elite *Fly on the Wall* advance readers and discussion committee, South Miami chapter—just kidding—to two true friends: Erica Calderon and Roshunda Slaton, thank you for keepin' it real with me, believing in me, putting up with me. Your feedback on this book was much needed and appreciated. However, if there were a fly on the wall the night the "mother ship landed" or the times we [Erica] "went to the mall," we'd be the hottest gossip ever. Hmm, maybe I should write about that. Names would be changed of course. Ha, Ha, Ha.

Other advanced readers: Chinikue, April, Nikki, and Raquel, thank you. Special thanks to all of my high-school fans who consider me a role model—keep the e-mails coming (www.tristarussell.com). I must say, "What's up," and "Thanks," to the Cutler Ridge, Florida Applebee's (bar) crew (Renee, Sarah, TJ, and Isaac) for always telling people who I was and then getting them so drunk that it made being an author very profitable. To the various authors (too many to name) that I've met during this journey: I've learned from each of you and I thank you for freely sharing your knowledge.

Sha-Shana Crichton, my agent, I am so blessed to have you and don't know where my career would be without you. Lisa D'Angelo, my editor—If it wasn't for you, people would know just what I think of "i" before "e" except after "c." Thank you for always making time for me and working so hard to keep me happy. Belinda Williams of Literary Lifestyle, you are the bomb! Peggy Hicks, I cannot say thanks enough; you did it for me.

Carl Weber and Urban Books, thank you for another opportunity to share my talent with the world. You've given me my stage!

To those who thought that this storyline was crass and tasteless, know that a truly gifted writer can turn the Declaration of Independence into a torrid and passionate affair. It doesn't take a village to believe in me, all it takes is me. Your lack of faith has ushered me to stop at nothing to succeed. Oh, and no eighteen-year-old men were molested or harmed during the production of this book.

To you, my new or dedicated reader, *Fly on the Wall* and *Going Broke* sat on the shelves with so many others, yet you saw fit to make it/them yours—thank you! I love hearing from you. Keep the e-mails coming. Visit www.tristarussell.com to write to me.

To Three Aunts, Now Three Angels

Sylvia [Francis] Davis
First page - June 1951 / Final chapter - April 2005

Grace Leona [Russell] Moss
Sunrise - June 1928 / Sunset - November 2002

Marietta [Russell] Eden
Hello - January 1950 / Goodbye - February 1997

"When peace like a river attendeth my way;
When sorrows like sea billows roll;
Whatever my lot, thou hast taught me to say,
It is well, it is well with my soul."
It Is Well" by Horatio Spafford & Philip Bliss [1873]

Fly on the Wall
By Trista Russell

You would have to be a *Fly on the Wall* to learn of the secret love affair between Paige, an English teacher, and Theo, a high school student and basketball star. You will be a fly on the sizzling hot walls when this flirtatious and lustful duo takes risks during detentions, school dances, and games. However, once in her bedroom, it is he who teaches the lessons and she who becomes the willing and ready-to-learn student.

What happens when her ex-husband, who happens to be Theo's coach, walks in on them, and also when Theo's mother learns that Paige's lesson plans include much more than just the parts of speech?

Oh, to be a *Fly on the Wall* throughout this sensual and passionate tale.

~Situation #9~

The Fly

His tongue attacked her swollen, pinkish-brown cherry like it was a boxing bag. "Oh, oh, ooh . . ." she moaned. The sensation and suction was so powerful, her back arched away from the bed, and her eyes rolled to the back of her head.

He inserted a thick caramel finger. "Oh, oh my goodness," she whispered and rotated her hips as his tongue dove deeper into her infinite pit. "Shit." She grabbed the sheets with so much force that she ripped them from the mattress.

"Stop," she begged him. "Stop." Pushing his head away, nearly out of breath, she asked, "Where did you learn how to do that?"

He offered a shy grin while crawling up her naked body. "In your class." In his answer, she smelled her bittersweet aroma.

She struggled to regulate her breathing. "That was never in my lesson plans." Still in shock, she said, "But that was . . ." She reached for and took a sip of the catalyst of this lunacy, her fifth glass of H-Squared, a mixture of double shots of Hennessy and Hypnotiq, which was sitting on the night-stand. "That was unbefuckinlievable," she said with a laugh.

His legs dangled over the edge of the bed. "So," he rubbed his nose against hers, "you're the loser . . ."

"Wait a minute," she interrupted him. "How did I get to be the loser?" She thought for a second. "I won a few times."

He tried to make her remember. "We were playing strip *and* drink dominoes. So, let's see." He paused. "You're drunk *and* you were the first one naked." He laughed. "So that constitutes me as the winner."

"Constitute?" She giggled longer than necessary. "Wasn't that a vocabulary word last week?"

"Yes." He kissed her neck. "I used it in a sentence. Do I get extra credit?"

"Nope." She blushed.

"Damn, what can a brotha do to get an A?"

"In the world today, you have to kiss ass." She added sarcastically, "Brotha."

"Ass?" He got serious. "I'm not into all of that. This brotha won't toss salad unless it's on a plate with some croutons."

"I have bread in the kitchen if it's that serious." She laughed.

When his hand touched her inner thigh, he felt her tremble. She had told him that it had been a long time, though she never specified how long. He wanted to bring her wait to an end. "What's it gonna be?" He kissed her shoulder.

"Speak proper English," she teased him. "What *shall* it be?"

"Fuck proper English." He lay beside her then scooped his hand under her to turn her on her side. "Can I?" he asked.

She looked into his eyes, unprotected, and saw what she always thought she was too strong to see in him: a full-grown man. For weeks she thought that he was sexy, suave, seductive, and although at times he didn't act like it, smart. However, she always had her shield up, causing his rays to bounce off of her, but tonight his brown eyes, thick coffee-colored lips, broad shoulders, and muscular arms caught her when her defense mechanisms were breached by intoxication. "Can you what?"

"Um." He tried to control his nervousness and struggled with his words. "I meant, can we?" He took a deep breath. "Now that I've shown you that I can, well, now that you see that I know how to . . ." His hand slid down the side of her body, from her shoulder to the tip of her fingers, then down to her thighs. "Can I show you what else I can do?" He had never asked a woman that question, but he felt he had so much to prove to her.

"No." Her flirty eyes sucked him into a realm of passion he didn't know. "I can't let you outdo me." She gently pushed his long, lean body to his back. "Why don't you let me show *you* a few things? Do you mind?" she asked, kneeling between his knees.

"Not at all." He looked at the perfect package before him and was even more aroused. She had turned the tables and he was pleased. It felt like a dream, a dream that shouldn't be coming true. He couldn't believe that he was actually in *her* bed, his tongue was still saturated with *her* flavor, and *she* was naked before him, asking his permission to bring it.

She leaned forward and quickly kissed him on the lips. Her tongue trailed him from the bottom of his neck to his smooth chest, then along the firmness of his abs. She lashed back and forth over his muscles but stopped at the tip of his shorts and untied the drawstring with her teeth. Sliding his boxers down unveiled his audacious spectacle.

"Whoa," she whispered to herself. The damn thing was big enough to have a social security number. She let her fingers walk up the side of it and counted nine steps. "Damn." She was talking to herself again. Never in a million years did she predict that she would be a part of something that so many people would consider crass, asinine, and even criminal. She had no control . . . He was the right one; who he happened to be was the mistake. She was willing to take the chance, ready for any consequence, but more than anything, prepared to make room for him in her heart.

"It may be big, but it won't bite." He joked about the way she stared at his piece. "Show me what you got." When the damp warmness of her mouth covered his skin, he muttered, "Damn," and pushed into her moisture. Within seconds, she caught his rhythm and grew to adore his feel, smell, and taste. Her mouth was a well-oiled machine, and all he wanted was to add a little more grease to her engine. "Oh, oh yeah, girl." He struggled not to bite his bottom lip too hard, but ten minutes into it, he was squealing, squirming, and groaning like there was a bomb inside of him and he was ready to explode.

"Mm," she hummed as she traveled upward on his dick and kissed its tip. "You like?" She licked her lips.

He could barely speak. "Yeah." He was breathing heavily and looked down at her. "Don't stop." She stroked him tightly, but when their eyes met, he saw concern flicker in them. "What's wrong?"

She licked her lips and looked away. "I'm thinking."

"About what?"

She hesitated. "About what we're doing."

He quieted her. "Shh. You're thinking too much. I'm not thinking about it." Still on his back, he rose up onto his elbows and took her hands in his. "There's nothing wrong with what we want to do, as long as we both want to do it." He pulled her on top of him, in a straddle position, and her legs rested outward at his sides. "Don't worry so much."

"But what if people find out?"

"Fuck people."

"You can't just have a fuck-the-world attitude about this." She rested her head on his chest. "It's possible that people could find out about us."

"All right." He steadied and positioned his flaming arrow,

aiming at the target. "I won't have a *fuck* attitude about this." He rubbed his arrowhead against her wet crease. "I'll have a let's-make-love attitude about this." He locked his hands on her waist and pushed upward, giving her no time to protest.

"Oh, ooh yes. Oh yes." She took him in and realized that there was no turning back.

"Oh shit." He closed his eyes and savored the feel of her tight, wet, hot fold. "Yeah."

She was still trippin'. "Are things going to be different?"

"What?"

"Are you going to change?"

"Why would I?" he asked.

"Just answer the question." She pushed herself down on him.

"Never." He kissed her softly and braced her back to give her more.

"Ooh shit," she moaned. "Fuck. Oh yeah."

"I'll never change," he promised her again.

She rushed down his pole like a firefighter on her way to a four-alarm fire. She rode him like he had wheels, taking him places that in his imagination had always been unreal. His toes began to curl and his sweat beaded up as large as dimes. She assumed she had taken him to school, but he put on his game face and brought it on like no other man ever had.

***

I am the narrator of the above story, someone whom you have at least once in your life said that you wanted to be. My real name is Musca Domestica, but you probably refer to me as a housefly. Don't you remember saying, "I wish I could've been a fly on the wall"? Well, you just got your opportunity. What you just read was my view from atop a picture frame hanging directly over a bed.

Imagine my shock when I flew into the bedroom in search

of cookie crumbs and stumbled upon the scene . . . the horror. Actually, it was no big shock to me. For months I've been following the two of them around, and I saw it coming. There's only so much flirtation, insinuation, and temptation that two people can handle. In a normal case of boy meets girl, I don't see anything wrong with a little bump and grind. However, in their situation, ignoring each other would've been the smart route. With them being who they are, what you and I just witnessed can only lead to heart-racing, tear-jerking, jaw-dropping, better-than-baby-momma drama.

For you to know where I'm coming from, I'll have to take you back a few months and . . . I'll let them tell the story themselves so that you can't accuse me of overexaggerating.

Bad decisions stem from every avoidable **situation.**

~Situation #8~

Theo

"Pussy is the best thing that God ever made. I know because I have one." As she spoke, she stared into my face with the same intense glare that used to terrify me as a child. However, now that I towered over her head, Mom isn't so scary anymore. She continued. "Pussy is the eighth wonder of the world . . ."

I giggled and interrupted. "Amen to that."

"Amen?" Her eyebrows moved toward each other.

"Yeah, you finally said something that I agree with."

"I didn't ask you for your opinion, Theo," she huffed.

"Why would you say something like that if you didn't want me to say anything back?" When I walked into the kitchen this morning, all I wanted was a glass of orange juice, buttered toast, and the keys to the damn car. While I was away at All-Star Basketball Camp, Mom bought a brand new Durango and promised me that the Maxima would officially be mine at the end of the summer. The summer ended on the first day of school, so today was the day. Not only was I a high school senior, but also a basketball player at West Dade Senior High, and those keys were my ticket to not having to ride the orange limousine for the entire school year. "Okay,

okay, I don't agree then." I smiled. "Why are we talking about this anyway?"

"Because that's exactly what your problem is. Pussy has become *your* main focus, your reason for living. It's like you worship it." She paused. "It's your damn god."

"My *god*?" I knew where this was going. "What makes you say that, Ma?"

She backed away and reached for her coffee mug. "Have you forgotten about last night?"

I looked down. "No, I haven't." In any thesaurus, the only words listed under *drama queen* would be *Eva Lakewood*. "We weren't doing nothing."

"Well, that was certainly a whole lot of nothing." She raised her voice. "I would call Trese kneeling in front of you and suckin' on your little pecker a big something." She tried to control her tone. "What if Kevin would've walked in there? He's only ten years old. How would you have explained that?"

"All right," I confessed. "I wouldn't have been able to explain it." I saw her point and gave her the answer she wanted. "I see the lesson in this situation."

"Do you?" She seemed pleased that I walked away with some knowledge. "What is it?"

I could barely contain my laughter. "You should've knocked."

"Knock?" She rested her coffee mug and moved a little closer to me. "Boy, I'll knock you upside your head. This is my house," she took a breath, "and I don't want her here anymore." She firmed up. "As a matter of fact, I don't think you need to be that serious with anyone right now."

"We're not serious."

"I would call her suckin' your," she paused, "your little thingy very serious, Theo." She threw whatever was left in her mug down the drain. "I'm not stupid. I know that you've had sex with her. What if she gets pregnant? Then what happens?" She didn't give me a chance to speak. "This is your last year of high school. You have an opportunity of a lifetime." Her voice started trembling and I saw tears forming in her eyes. "There are colleges and NBA teams all standing in line for you. Everybody wants a piece of Theodore Lakewood." By now she was crying. "You can't let anything keep you from your dreams."

I walked across the kitchen and wrapped my long arms around her. "I want this just as much as you want it for me." She rested her head on my chest as I rubbed her back. "Don't worry about me." I was serious. "I know that I act crazy sometimes, but I won't make the wrong decisions, Ma." I cupped her chin and made her look up at me. "I won't let you down." I would never be a disappointment to her.

After all the tears were out and the promises were once again guaranteed, she fished through her purse and dangled the keys in front of me. "To school and back."

I had driven the car many times, but this time it'd be mine. "Can I at least pick up Will?" I couldn't let my boy ride the bus.

"Pick up Will," she smiled, "but bring that car straight home after practice."

I reached out for the keys, and the moment she dropped them into my hand, I felt life getting a little easier. I bent down and kissed her on the cheek. "Thank you, Ma."

"Drive safely." She hugged me around the neck.

"Ma, I'm eighteen. I've been driving for five years." I laughed. "Well, you only know about three of 'em."

She laughed. "Boy, get out of here before you're late."

I grabbed my bookbag and made it to the front door before I remembered that I needed to correct her. "Oh yeah, and there's nothing little about my pecker." Her hand flew to her mouth in shock as the other one reached for the dishtowel that she threw in my direction.

*   *   *

I stared at the gold Maxima and whispered, "You're officially mine." It wasn't a Lexus, BMW, or Benz, but it now belonged to me. I cranked her up and Jay-Z's *Black Album* was still blasting from the last time I was in it.

Now why you frontin' on me? Is that necessary?

My timing was perfect; I pulled up to Will's bus stop right behind his bus and honked the horn. He ran over and jumped in.

"Man, you just saved my life." We knocked knuckles. "I didn't think you were coming. I called your house last night and your mom was straight buggin'." He laughed. "What in the hell happened?"

"Trese was over and Mom walked in my room without knocking."

"Oh, snap." He covered his mouth. "Moms saw you cuttin'?"

"Naw." I was embarrassed but proud at the same time. "She was givin' me head."

"Damn." Will sounded like he was enjoying the thought. "Damn." Then he snapped out of it. "I told you that Trese ain't nothing but trouble anyway. You picked the wrong one, man."

"First of all, Trese is not picked. She's not my girl."

"Oh yeah? I bet you walk her to at least one class today." He chuckled. "I guess the coochie is real nice because she has you on a leash."

"Man, fuck you and a damn leash. Trese is a booty call."

"Does she know that?"

I couldn't lie. "No." Before he could say anything, I spoke up. "But she knows that she's not my girlfriend."

"Whatever!" he said. "Congratulations on your blow job, though." He continued jokingly. "I wish I *could* get some head for someone to walk in on."

"It was good, too."

Will asked, "What did your mom say?"

"Well, we had a little talk this morning." I remembered the look on her face when she thought for one second that I'd make a mistake that couldn't be undone. "She's thinking that I'll get some chick pregnant or something."

"That's exactly what girls like Trese want, though, man," he said. "She wants a baby daddy who is somebody, so that she won't have to work for the rest of her life."

"Shit me." He was probably right about Trese. "I don't have time for that. That's the last thing I need." Girls at school had been overly generous, willing to give me whatever, whenever, and wherever, which was why Trese was at my house last night. She was trying hard, actually too hard to get on my bandwagon. Though we had sex I didn't consider her my girl. "That's the last thing that I need."

"That's right, 'cause we going to the NBA, baby," he yelled.

I still found it hard to believe that people were comparing me to Kobe Bryant and Lebron James. At eighteen years old, I stood at six foot nine and 230 pounds. In tenth grade, it was hard to believe that I was the best shooting guard in Miami-Dade County. Then the newspaper reporters started calling me the best in Florida, and now I was considered one of the best in the entire country. NBA scouts were at most of my games, and I got calls at all times of the day and night from college recruiters and coaches. I'd been offered numerous undercover gifts: jet skis, clothes, jewelry, women, vacations, and cars. If it weren't for my mom, I'd probably have three of each, but she didn't believe in bribery like I did. She was actually ruling out those schools and teams, but the choice was ultimately mine.

The only reason I picked up a basketball ten years ago was to get my sperm donor to start coming around again. By the time I realized that wasn't working, I was already in love with the court, the ball, dribbling, dunking, and the way I seemed to matter when I was playing. The fact that I had a male to depend on, my coach, and people depending on me, my team, meant more to me than I'm sure I ever meant to my father.

My mom was only nineteen when she met Theodore Brown. Within two months he had her pregnant, and within another three months he was nowhere to be found. I was seven when this strange and very tall man suddenly showed up and told my mom that he had been in jail for seven years (which we later learned was a lie) and was ready to do right by his family. Mom welcomed him in with open arms. Theodore Brown stayed around long enough to make me believe that we'd always be together. Even though he fussed at Mom all the time, he played with me a lot, and that was all that mattered.

When I was nine and Kevin was just eight months old, Dad went away to visit his family in Texas. Two weeks later when the telephone rang, Mom and I picked up the extension in different rooms at the same time. I listened as that loser told my sobbing mother that he had met someone else, wasn't ever coming back, and that he didn't believe that I was really his son. To this day she doesn't know that I heard what that motherfucka had to say. I kept it a secret. I don't know if I did it because of how much it hurt me or because I knew how much it hurt her.

One thing was for sure: I'd go to my grave and never want to see his sorry ass again. After working in fast food restaurants, hotels, and a daycare, Mom went back to college and became a pediatric nurse. I had both a father and a mother in her. She provided the best life that Kevin and I could possibly have. Because of her I was on the road to success, and when I got there she'd know that all of her sacrifices weren't in vain. Basketball and my mom were the only two certainties in my life. One day, basketball might lead me to a place where I don't want to be, but Mom would never lead me down the wrong road.

* * *

"We have history class together," Will said as we walked away from the car.

"How do you know?" I was confused. "We don't even have our schedules yet."

"I don't need a schedule. I got into the system two nights ago."

"Damn, you and that computer." He was always up to and into something. "You gonna get in trouble one day."

"Naw, I'm not one of those types of hackers. I just like to see what others can't see, but I never cause problems."

I met Will two years earlier when he transferred from a school in New Jersey. All of my other friends were on the basketball team, but I managed to have a *best* friend that dribbled like an eighty-six-year-old woman and couldn't dunk if the basket was waist high. However, Will knew the computer inside and out, had built a few from the motherboard up, and met all of his girlfriends in chat rooms. He wasn't a bad-looking dude; he was just shy, and thanks to my popularity, he, too, now had a variety of honeys. But if they didn't have an e-mail address, didn't know what a megabyte is, or don't own a computer, then he had no time or conversation for them.

"So that's the only class we have together?" I asked as we continued to make our way through the parking lot.

"Um, I think so." He thought for a while. "We have Ms. Fatrick for English, but during different periods."

"Ah, damn. I have her?" I wanted to reverse the day already.

"Yep."

"She kept George and Tyrone from graduating last year, and a few people the year before."

"Word?"

The school year just took a turn for the worse. "Yeah. I was hoping for anybody but her."

"Yeah," Will agreed. "I heard she's mean as all outdoors."

"That's because she got fat and frustrated as hell." Ms. Fatrick was the students' alias for Ms. Patrick. Rumor had it that she used to be a cool teacher and she was fine as hell, but when she lost her figure, she lost her damn mind and turned into the strictest black teacher in the school. She wasn't really fat, obese, or anything close to that, but because she was a firm, by-the-book, detention-giving English teacher who now happened to be a little on the chubby side, she earned the name Fatrick. She used to be married to my basketball coach, Coach Johnson. They divorced when I was in the ninth or tenth grade.

"Coach must've been on something when he married her mean ass."

"He was on that ass," Will joked. "But seriously, I heard she used to be real tight, though. As a matter of fact, I saw a picture of her taken a few years ago on the school website, and she was all that . . ."

"Now she's just a bag of chips." I laughed.

"Hell yeah, that's why she's so mean." He went on. "Somebody needs to give her some good lovin' so that we can pass."

I was already thinking about not graduating. "What period do I have her?"

"If memory serves me right, I think it's sixth, right after gym."

Things couldn't get worse. "Shit." We entered the building and the smell of West Dade hit my nostrils and I was on a natural high. I loved my school. I slapped fives with a bunch of dudes and hugged my female classmates from last year.

"Hello, Theo." A sexy, light-skinned girl approached me. "How come you never called me?"

Before I could form my lips to answer, a beautiful, full-chested, tall, brown-skinned girl overtook Ms. Light-Skinned like they were cars in traffic. She issued no signal light or hand gesture; she just ran the poor girl off the road.

"Hey, Theo." She wasn't nervous at all. "We went to middle school together." She smiled and flashed the letter L on her gold tooth. I couldn't stop staring at it. "You remember me?"

"Yeah, your name starts with an L, right?" I couldn't resist.

"Yeah." She gasped and looked over to her friends. "I told y'all that he'd remember me." By the time she looked back in my direction, Will and I were down the hall.

Sometimes the attention I received from girls was overwhelming. They wanted to be with me for one of three reasons: One, because of who they thought I'd be someday. They wanted to be that lucky one that I carried to the top. Two, because I was tall. They associated that with me having a big dick, which was the truth. Three, just to say that they had sex with Theodore Lakewood.

As much as I adored girls, I couldn't be a fool. Sex was here from the beginning of the earth and would be here way after I was dead and gone. I couldn't afford to get anyone pregnant, catch anything, or give anybody anything before I signed my name on somebody's dotted line. All I had to do was make it through this school year and then my life would really begin.

"It seems like everybody and their grandma is here this year, man," Will screamed as we pushed our way through the crowded lobby. "I'm putting on a protective cup tomorrow," he joked. "I've been hit in the nuts three times already."

"What are you complaining for?" I laughed. "You know you like that shit."

Instead of congregating in front of the posted sheets by the main office to find out where we went for homeroom, Will had already handed me a printed version of our schedules. "All right, boy. See you in history," he said as we parted ways on the stairway. I went to the computer wing and he went toward the math section. I was careful as I turned each corner. The last person I wanted to run into was Trese, and if I were lucky, we wouldn't have any classes together.

Don't get me wrong. Every black guy at West Dade wanted a piece of her. At five foot eight and 120 pounds, Trese was thick in all the right places, with an ass that looked like it would punch back if you smacked it. She had a flawless, medium-brown complexion, was fashionable, and could suck and fuck better than any porno video I'd ever seen. So what was wrong with her? She was too nasty, loud, and ghetto as hell.

Trese and I met at a party at the end of the last school year. She put up a nice front in order to get me interested, but gave up the goodies far too early on the third day of knowing me. As if that weren't enough, meeting her family proved that she was someone I couldn't have a future with.

She lived with her grandmother, but that was because her own mother never moved out. How in the hell could sixteen people share a small three-bedroom house and two cars? I didn't know the answer, but what I did know was that whenever I was there, somebody was always being yelled at, roaches weren't concerned about being spotted, kids ran around at all times of the day and night, and nobody had a damn job.

I managed to get through five periods and lunch before I heard "Theooooo" coming from behind me. In a time like this, being tall was a pain in the ass because no matter how crowded the halls were, I would always stand out. I sped up, pretending not to hear her calling my name. "Theo!" she screamed, and when I was about to start running, a guy tapped me on my arm.

"Yo, somebody's calling you." I never wanted anyone at school to know about Trese and me.

"Shit," I said under my breath then turned around to see her roughly pushing her way through the crowd.

"Hey, boo." She smiled.

"Hey, what's up, Trese?" I said in a less than enthusiastic tone.

"Nothing." She never got the picture. "I thought you were supposed to call me last night."

"My mom was trippin'." I wasn't lying. After Mom walked in on us, Trese was asked to leave. Mom then snatched the phone from my room and the one in the living room off of the wall. "I couldn't call anyone."

"Why was she actin' like that?" She ran her hand down my chest. "Don't she know that you a man?" As bad as I wanted to walk away, staring at her lips gave me reason to stick around another minute. She whispered, "I like suckin' your dick."

I said, "Damn," and right away I felt the blood exiting my brain. "You do?"

"Yeah, I went home and played with myself." Those words left her lips and went straight into my jeans. I imagined her tight, brown, naked body rolling around in bed, rubbing on her clit, pinching her nipples, and sliding her fingers up and down through her wet pussy lips. My heart started racing . . . then reality hit. She shared a room with her mother and her two little brothers.

"I was waiting on you to call so that I could tell you to meet me somewhere," she said.

I couldn't formulate a sentence right then if it was for a grade. "Really?"

"Yeah, I was just gettin' started." Trese had a perfect set of glossy, full brown lips. They always made my imagination run wild. She licked her lips and my beef tightened and thickened. "I can't wait to finish."

She innocently ran her hand over my growing knot as the crowd continuously brushed by. She knew how to get to me, and the sad part was that I always allowed her to. Before the blood could get back to the right organs, we were holding hands, strolling down the hall, looking like a happy couple.

When the bell rang, Trese and I were still walking. "Where's your class?" I asked.

"Don't worry. I'm going to class late," she said as she squeezed my hand. The hallways were empty, and she looked over at me, studying me up and down.

"Well, I have English this hour. I have to go," I said.

"But I want to give you something." Trese made a sharp right into the boys' bathroom. All of the stall doors were open. We were alone.

"Trese, I can't," I said, but I sure wasn't putting up a fight. "I have Ms. Patrick this hour."

"Ms. Fatrick?" She chuckled. "This will only take five minutes."

"You're crazy." I meant it.

She had a freaky smirk on her cute face. "Yeah, crazy about you."

We went to the last stall. She pulled me in, locked the door behind me, hopped onto the toilet, and grabbed my li'l man through my pants and stroked him. "Damn." Her touch was amazing.

"I want to finish what I started last night," she said as she squatted before me. "Take it out."

How could I not comply? She was sexy, freaky, and wanted nothing more than to give me any type of sex my heart desired. It was moments like this, when my dick was throbbing, that made me feel that maybe I did care for her, that maybe she should be the one. "Here you go."

She looked at my nine inches of flesh as though it were lost treasure. She teased me with little licks around the head and then slid my muscle into her mouth as she moved her hand back and forth from the shaft to meet her lips.

"Oh, man." My eyes rolled back and my right hand

quickly gripped the top of the stall. I rested my left hand on the back of her head. Trese was a pro; no teeth, all tongue, cheek, suction, and spit.

"Shit," I whispered and watched those juicy lips slide back and forth, back and forth. I closed my eyes and envisioned being inside of her. It was tight, wet, and warm. I moved my pelvis in and out of her, slowly. After a few minutes, I was screwing her in the mouth like she was on top of me. Then suddenly she stopped. I opened my eyes and she was bent over the toilet with her skirt raised up over her ass.

"Put it in," she said.

I couldn't believe that we were doing this at school. "What?"

"Fuck me."

"You have a condom?" I asked.

"No, just put it in." She reached back for my piece and pulled me by it. I couldn't think. All I wanted were her pussy lips contracting around my dick. "We don't need a condom. Stick it in and fuck me."

When my meat rubbed against the wet surface of her gates, as much as I wanted to give her my entire big, black, fat dick, I panicked. "Naw, we can't do it like that."

"Why?" I saw her roll her eyes.

"Because I'm not as stupid as you want me to be," was what I wanted to say, but instead I said, "'cause we just can't." Now I really believed what Will said was true. Trese wanted to trap me.

"What are you trying to say, Theo?" She turned back toward me. "You act like I have something."

"You should be more concerned about yourself." I stepped up. "What if I have something? Don't you care about me giving it to you?" It bothered me that she would just let me get in her without protection.

She sighed and rolled her eyes again. "Whatever." She

fixed her skirt. "We don't always have to use condoms. They take away from the feeling anyway."

I stroked my long stick with a smile. "There's no way in the hell that you won't feel this." In a world where I was king I would've said, "Shut the fuck up and suck my dick." I didn't have the nerves or the time for drama. I just took a deep breath, put my hand on the back of her head, and guided my piece back to her lips.

She grabbed my dick with an attitude. "You don't have a problem with doing this without a condom." She took me in aggressively, like she was trying to suck my soul out of me, and it was good. Her saliva covered me like a warm blanket and her lips were like fluffy pillows, but my beef was far from ready to take a nap.

"Damn, girl." When I looked down, she was staring up at me and began sucking even faster. My whole piece disappeared into her mouth. "Damn." I nearly ripped the stalls out of the walls to keep from groaning too loud. "Oh, oh, oh shit." Trese opened up wide, and as God as my witness, I passed her tonsils and spewed out what felt like my entire blood supply into her throat.

"Let's go," I said the moment I was able to think and breathe at the same time. I already regretted it.

She still had an attitude when we went our separate ways. I promised myself that I wouldn't mess with her again. She was trying too hard. The fun about being with a girl was trying to break her down; Trese was broken from the jump. I was up for a challenger, not someone that forfeited every game. I'd never been with an older woman, but Trese sucked dick like I was sure women in their forties did, which was a great thing, but also a big turn-off . . . It meant that she had plenty of practice.

"Stupid." I called myself names as I made my way to Ms. Fatrick's class. Running through the halls, darting around things, all I needed was a ball. I was already seventeen minutes late, and I might as well have fun on the way there. I thought up a lie, but from what I heard, nothing ever worked on this lady.

"Whatever," I said when I saw the room number. "I'm late. She can't kill me." I hoped that I didn't smell like I had just gotten head, and I hoped that I didn't look like it either, but I was sure that it beat walking in the room trying to hide an erection.

It was the first day of school, so if worse came to worse, I could always say that I went to the wrong class. I slung my bookbag over one shoulder, and with sweaty palms I grabbed the knob, pulled the door open, and saw Ms. Patrick standing in front of the chalkboard. "Damn," I said loudly. This year was already shaping up to be more interesting than I ever imagined.

~Situation #7~

Paige

"Excuse me." I checked my watch and couldn't believe his audacity. "Besides being twenty minutes late to my class, who you are?" He was too tall to slip in unnoticed.

"Theo," he answered and took the first available seat, which happened to be right in front of my desk. I already knew who he was. Who wouldn't? The school, local TV news, and newspapers treated him like he was the Messiah. But he wasn't getting any special privileges in my classroom. I pretended to need to look at my attendance sheet to know his name. "Do you mean Theodore Lakewood?" I spoke facetiously.

"Yes." He gave me a hint of the winning smile I'd seen on TV so much. "That's me." As he made himself comfortable in his seat, he stared at me skeptically, the same way I found most students doing today, trying to be sure that they were in the right class and with the right teacher. "I like to be called Theo, though."

Was he serious? "When you're *this* late to class, Theodore, I get to decide what you'll be called." I smiled and redirected my attention to the class as his ego shrank a little. "I was in the midst of going over the rules with your classmates who arrived on time." I panned the silent room. "Would someone like to tell Mr. Lakewood what the penalty is for being tardy to class?"

A young man, who answered earlier to the name Richard Chambers, said, "You gotta stay an hour after school, dawg."

"That's right, *dawg*." I looked at Theodore and giggled along with the students at my usage of slang.

"I apologize," he said. "But what exactly is considered late?"

"Did you think that this class began at one-fifty instead of one-thirty?" I asked.

He answered, "No."

"Then you are late."

"But what makes a person late?"

"You are late if the bell rings and you are not on the inside of that door." I pointed.

"Don't we get a grace period?"

"No, sir." This wasn't the basketball court. He was going to play my game. "You have five minutes between classes, which is more than enough time to make it to any room in this building." I tried to smile.

"But some teachers at least—"

"I am not some teachers. I am Ms. Patrick," I interrupted, giving him a grin. "When the bell rings, you are on my time, and on my time I get to call the shots." I was trying hard to tone the "mean teacher" thing down this year. "Is that all right?"

"I guess." He looked nervous. "But it's not really my fault." I could hear the lie formulating, so I paced the area in front of the class until he got it together. Before he could speak, I said it for him. "Let me guess. You went to the wrong class?" I smiled.

"No, I had an emergency." He looked away. "There was a

message from my mom in the main office. I had to call her at work." He continued. "It was an emergency."

"All right." I wanted to laugh. "Not a problem, Theodore. I'm laying down my rules today, but they officially go into effect tomorrow." I softened my look. "So you're off the hook today."

"Thank you." He flashed those pearly whites again.

"Thank *you*." Then I remembered. "Oh, and by the way, watch your language when you're in my classroom." Not only was he late, but he came in cursing.

"Oh, I'm sorry." He played up to me. "It won't happen again, teach."

"Good." I took a deep breath as I walked over to the board and wrote my e-mail address. "As all of you know, my name is Ms. Paige Patrick. I will be your English teacher for this school year." I pointed at the board. "This is my e-mail address. Use this for any homework questions you may have outside of regular school hours, and also for online assignments that you will have throughout the course of the year." I continued. "I am thirty two years young, and this is my sixth year here at West Dade High." I took a breath and went on. "I am divorced." I let students know about my divorce right off the bat. Why? Because many of them were still under the impression that I was married to Craig, and they knew that he was a ho. "I have no children or pets. My favorite color is black, and my hobbies include dancing, reading, going to the movies, and swimming. I spent my summer with friends and also used it to help me get in better shape." I looked around the room then walked over to the late-comer's seat. "Theodore, since you were the last one to sit down, let's hear from you first. Introduce yourself to the class."

"Ah, man," he sighed and mumbled a bit before standing. When he stood next to me, I was a tad intimidated. He sprung up over a foot above my head. I skimmed over many newspaper articles about Theodore Lakewood, the basketball player from West Dade, but I had only seen him from a distance. Though he had a very handsome and boyish face, there was nothing else boyish about him. He was built like a man at least twenty-five years old. Breathtaking! They didn't make boys that size when I was in high school. I stepped away from him, walked over to my desk, and gave orders.

"When you're done, pick someone else, and then that person goes and selects someone else, and so on and so forth until everyone has had a turn."

As Theodore spoke to the class, I drifted miles away. I went over my introduction fifty times in my head and wished that I had the opportunity to say more, but this wasn't quite the audience that I needed to vent to. I thought about what I really wanted to say.

Hi, I'm Paige Patrick, your English teacher. I am thirty-two years young and this is my sixth year here at West Dade High. My e-mail address is on the board; use it only for your questions and online assignments. Please don't forward me jokes, chain letters, corny-ass stories about miracles, or missing people.

I know that many of you had your hopes up about walking into this classroom today and calling me Ms. Fatrick under ya damn breaths, but the joke is on you. In a year and a half, I went from two hundred and six pounds to one hundred and thirty-two pounds. How? Well, after winning twenty-five thousand dollars in a lawsuit against a restaurant that served me poisoned fish, I had liposuction, plastic surgery to lift, tuck, and snip any area that gravity had in its jealous grasp, and enough left over to hire a personal trainer. I'm back into the body I had in college, and I love it.

Yes, I used to be married to that whore basketball coach, Coach Johnson. I met him seven years ago when I was twenty-five, and married him just a few months later. We were happily married for two years and in misery for three.

I stayed in the marriage because the man was a sexual genius . . . damn, just thinking about it . . . I need a moment. Girls, beware of a man that is fine, smart, sexy, and strong. If he seems too good of a package, that means that he is, and chances are another woman is thinking the same thing along with you. I thought that Craig could do no wrong until I visited my gynecologist two years into our marriage and walked out with a penicillin prescription for some bullshit that I, an English teacher, couldn't even pronounce.

After the explosion of an argument was over, though I didn't believe his story about picking up the 'bug' when he sat on a toilet seat on a bus to an away game, I stayed with him. I was insecure and didn't leave because I had started gaining weight. Somehow, I thought he was doing me a favor by still wanting to make love to me. At the time, I believed that walking away would be too complicated and I'd never find another man with my excess physical baggage. What I didn't know was that the only person I needed to find was myself. However, a year later, I walked out of my doctor's office broken, embarrassed, and homicidal with yet another prescription for penicillin.

Instead of waiting on him to come home, I went to the sports bar where he and the other coaches would go some Fridays after school. Craig was sitting at the bar, and the slim, blonde bartender seemed very interested in tending to his every sip, drip, and desire. I watched him flirt with her, kiss her hand, comment on her breast size, and run his hand down the side of her face for about five minutes before I made my approach. She stared at me but didn't think for one second that this tall, zero body fat, brick house of a brotha could be married to this slightly overweight, brown-skinned woman walking toward them.

"Don't bother bringing your diseased ass home tonight."
He watched in disbelief as I dropped penicillin pills into his
beer then turned to the blonde. "You might find yourself
needing these." I slammed a few of the pills on the counter
then walked away. The chances of me being arrested for mur-
der would've been high if he came home that night. Stupidly,
a part of me wanted him to come and comfort me, or pretend
to care that I was hurt beyond repair.

Thankfully things went down on the Friday before Spring
Break, so I had two weeks to get myself together. I didn't
know which way to go, but all of the signs pointed in the di-
rection of the courthouse. Our divorce was finalized two
years ago, on my thirtieth birthday. I spent the entire year
cooking and eating myself content. However, each time I
looked into the mirror, my depression got worse, and when I
got unhappier, I ate. The circle of food, depression, and guilt
was ongoing.

When I won the lawsuit, I knew right away what I wanted
to do with the money, and I did. Judge me or love me.
Anyone that says that they won't pay for a nice body just
simply can't afford it.

Ms. Fatrick was retired. My favorite color is black, and
my hobbies include dancing, reading, going to the movies,
and swimming.

I tuned back right in time to hear what the last student had
to say. "My name is Angela Porter. I'm eighteen, I'm a cheerleader, and I hope to go to the University of Central Florida.
I have two dogs, and my favorite color is blue."

"Great." I stood up. "Thank you all for the wonderful in-
troductions." I glanced at the clock. I had about a minute left
with them. "Our focus this school year will be putting together everything you've learned about the English language
from kindergarten through last year. We will be doing a lot of
writing in this class." I could hear their young minds shutting

down. "Many of you have heard that I'm mean, that I'm hard, and that I give a lot of work. But the truth is that I want you all to succeed in life. I want you to not be worried when you make it to college or into the workforce. I want you to be prepared."

I was far from the mean, sexually frustrated, fat woman they thought I would be. "This is going to be a wonderful school year." I was now a laid back but still sexually frustrated size eight. The bell rang. "I'll see you all tomorrow." Within forty seconds, the classroom was empty and the first day of school was just a memory. I kicked off my heels and erased the chalkboard.

My classroom door opened and in sauntered Doran, known by the students as Mr. Bess, the new math teacher. Doran was no stranger to me, though. We met at the gym over the summer, and I was delighted that such an attractive brother would be joining this dreary faculty.

"Well, we made it through the first day, Paige." He smiled.

"Barely," I joked.

"It wasn't so bad." He smiled again.

"Speak for yourself," I said as he lowered himself onto the chair at my desk.

Doran and I met at The Fitness Stop about a month and a half ago. I was on the Stairmaster when he walked in and struggled to get his machine working. I was tempted to laugh at his frustration, but instead helped him reset the instrument. Side by side we did our cardiovascular exercise and talked. I learned that he was new in the South Florida area, just in from Memphis, Tennessee. When he mentioned being a teacher, we discovered that we'd be working at the same school.

We exchanged cellular phone numbers for the sole purpose of informing each other if something came up and we couldn't make it to The Stop. I'd only had to call him twice: once when I had the flu and couldn't get out of bed, the other time when I had forgotten that my parents would be in town from Minneapolis for the weekend.

"You sure got out of your classroom in record time." I continued erasing the board and looked over at the clock. The bell had only rung four minutes ago.

"Sixth is my planning period." He studied me, and his look said more than *You're my workout partner and I'm checking out your progress.* A light, satisfactory moan confirmed his approval of my physique as he said, "You're looking real nice, Ms. Patrick."

I tried not to, but I blushed anyway. "Thank you." His eyes were still on me. "You're not looking too shabby yourself." Doran looked delicious enough for me to eat without ketchup, mustard, salt or pepper.

"Thank you." Then he asked, "Are you working out today?"

"Um." Doran always left me speechless. He had that Boris Kodjoe thing going on, with paper-bag-brown skin, standing at six foot two or three, medium build, broad shoulders, thick legs, and a panty-dropping voice. And yes . . . I did check out the bulk of his knot while spotting him on the free weight bench. Doran had enough to feed the needy . . . and I considered myself dirt poor and hungry. Forget eating him, I'd swallow him whole, hot and fresh out of the oven. "I don't think I'll be able to go today." I had no excuse except that seeing him in a suit for the first time was blowing my mind, and I didn't want to say anything foolish.

"Aw." He sounded disappointed. "I was going to take it easy on you today."

"Take it easy on me?" I turned toward him. "I'm the last person that you need to take it easy on and you know it." Other than preparing for the students in our classrooms over the past week, we had never seen each other outside of The Stop. "I just can't go today, but you know that I can handle it."

He stood up in front of me with a sexy grin. "What are you saying?"

"I'm . . ." I fumbled with my words. "I'm saying that I haven't had a problem keeping up with you."

"So you think you can handle everything that I do?"

"Yes." Lord, why was he doing this to me? "Everything at the gym, of course." I started cleaning the board again.

He laughed for a while before he spoke. "The real work-out happens outside of the gym." At times, it seemed like Doran was interested in me, but then two seconds later he'd turn around and leave a huge gap in our conversation to stare at another woman. "I'll have you sweatin' in places you didn't know could sweat."

I tried to regain my composure. "Doran, you are some-thing else."

"Yeah, but at least I'm going to the gym today." He smiled then walked toward one of the desks and picked up a few pieces of paper from the floor.

I watched him and giggled. "You're moonlighting as a cus-todian?"

"Whatever makes you happy, Paige."

"So, tell me." I sat down at my desk. "How was your first day here?"

"Other than seeing a young lady walk out of the boys' restroom wiping her mouth about an hour ago, this is your typical American high school," he said with a laugh.

I was in shock. "She was coming out of the boys' room?"

"Yep," he said. "I looked at the sign twice to be sure."

"Maybe it was a he-she or something."

"It was a girl." He shook his head and continued. "I know a girl when I see one."

"Oh my." There were always students who got caught try-ing to get freaky, but to start out a new school year that way was just nasty. "And she was wiping her mouth?"

"Yep, like she had just gotten through eating chicken fried in too much grease."

"You're so wrong for that." I made a face. "Yuck."

"There's nothing yucky about it if it's done right." He walked toward the door with a smile. "See you tomorrow, Paige." He looked back. "And I won't be accepting anymore copouts from our workout."

"I'll be at The Stop tomorrow," I said.

"Who's talking about working out at the gym?" He walked out of the door and left me tempted to follow. As good-looking as Doran was, there was something wrong about him, something about his sexy brown eyes I didn't trust, plus I had promised myself to never again get involved with anyone who worked at the school. But damn, Doran looked like he'd be one hell of a booty call.

I made my way from my classroom to the parking lot, and I received many interesting stares from the boys on the football team. When the short, husky player whistled at me, I stopped and turned toward the chain-linked fence.

"You better watch your mouth, Justin McGregor."

He smiled. "You look good, Ms. Patrick."

In total I'd lost eighty-five pounds. It took me a year; however, the last twenty pounds were dropped over the summer, so what the students were seeing was still more of a shock than last year . . . It just kept getting better.

I hopped into my car and hit the Florida Turnpike north. Within ten minutes, my Acura went from pushing eighty to traffic "parking lot" style, and I was in the center lane.

"Shit. I should've gone to the gym." My phone was ringing. I dug around inside my purse until I saw the flashing blue light. "Hello?"

"Don't get on the turnpike."

"Too late for that. I'm stuck." I laughed. "You should've called me fifteen minutes ago."

Toni giggled. "Sorry, I just turned to the news."

"No problem." I smiled. "What's going on?"

"An overturned tractor-trailer."

"Again?" It seemed to happen at least once a week now.

"Yep," Toni said. "Someone in another car died. I was calling to make sure it wasn't you."

"Aw, what a friend," I joked. "It's not me, but if you want to call the credit card companies and tell them that it's me, that'll be all right with me."

"Crazy girl," she said. "Are you on your way to the gym?"

I looked around to see if there was any way around or backward to get free of this mess. "No, I decided to skip out today."

"Wow! You missed an opportunity with Mr. Best?" she teased.

"His last name is Bess, not Best," I corrected her, but I knew what she was hinting at.

"Well, you damn sure act like he's Mr. Best, as in the best damn thing period." She laughed.

"Whatever." I brushed her off. "But he did flirt with me a little again today."

"I told you that the man likes you."

"I don't know about all of that, Toni."

She asked, "Then why else would he say some of the things that he does to you?"

I confessed, "I know that he'd sleep with me, but I won't say that he likes me." I added, "There's a big difference between those two things."

"Okay, he wants to do you," she said. "So, what's the damn problem? You wanna do him too, don't you?"

"The damn problem is that that's not what I'm in the market for," I preached. "Yes, I find him interestingly attractive, but he clearly just wants sex." I continued. "Doran doesn't want or know how to be anybody's man from what I've seen."

"What have you seen?" she asked, hungry for detail.

"Hmmm." I contemplated which example to use. "All right, last week while we were working out, this chick walked past us and he, without ever looking away from her ass, said 'Do you know what I could do with that?' " I paused. "Why in the hell would he say something like that in front of me if he liked me? I'm not one of his guy friends. We haven't even known one another long enough for him to be so comfortable. The man isn't ready for *me* because I'm not one of those women that tolerate that." *Well, at least not anymore.*

"Wow." Toni thought about it. "That was tacky."

"Very."

"Maybe you should tell him that it bothers you."

"What?" Was she high? "Toni, Doran is just my workout partner, that's it. I have no right telling him how I feel about him looking at other women."

"Then tell him that you're interested," Toni said. "Then he'll know that he can't say certain things around you. At least hint to him that you're attracted."

I regretted telling her so much about Doran. "Correction, I find him inter—"

"Interestingly attractive," she finished my sentence. "Bullshit. You want some action and so does he."

"So we should just fuck, huh?"

She didn't hesitate. "Yes. Like wild dogs."

I laughed. "I'm now convinced that you are insane."

"Paige, I would do anything for you to stop sleeping with Craig's diseased ass." She had to go there. "We both know that that's a sure recipe for pain and penicillin."

Once again, I regretted informing her of my occasional slipups. "Where are you?" I changed the subject with a lie. "I can barely hear you."

"At home." She paused. "Don't try to change the subject." She giggled. "Stop fuckin' Craig. When will you get enough? Paige, he gave you a damn STD." She only knew about the second sexually transmitted shit I caught from him. "Hold on." She rested the telephone down. "Boys, I'm on the phone, so please turn the video game down."

Toni Young, formerly known as Toni the Tigress in her exotic dancing days, was not only my best friend, but also the closest thing I ever had to a sister, and her twin boys, Kevin and Devin, were my godsons.

Eight years ago, I ran into Toni at a grocery store. She approached me and asked how to make seafood lasagna. Right then I knew that the poor girl needed a friend.

I was twenty-four and she was twenty. Within the time it took to gather the proper ingredients for her meal, the talkative girl told me her entire life story. In Fort Walton Beach, Toni's mother's boyfriend sexually molested her at age thirteen. At fifteen, she dropped out of high school and ran away to Miami, where she lived on the streets until she befriended an old white man named Rick. He allowed her to live in his apartment, and never asked her for anything more than a cooked meal once or twice a week.

On her eighteenth birthday, she went to The Cure, one of the most popular strip clubs in Miami, shook her moneymaker for the owner, and was hired on the spot. Within a month, she was living on her own and was earning close to three thousand dollars a week.

The day we met, she was cooking dinner for a lawyer named Marcus, who frequented the club. He spent thousands on private dances and alone time with Toni, and was surprised when she asked to see him away from the club. Her plan was simply dinner and a movie, nothing more.

After the grocery store, I followed her home and helped with the cooking. Then we tore through her closet until we found something sexy that but didn't scream, "Lap dance!"

Now, Marcus was her husband of seven years. Toni gave up the yeast-infected pole, got her GED, and was now in college working on her bachelors in accounting, and attorney Marcus Young was the father of my beautiful five-and-a-half-year-old twin godsons, who were always up to no damn good.

"What are the boys doing?" I asked.

"Thanks to you, they're driving me insane with that never-ending Dragon Ball Z game." She added, "I believe that you bought them this game to torture me."

"It was on sale." I giggled.

"Leave the sales alone, Paige."

"C'mon," I said, "if it's marked down . . ."

"Oh," she remembered, "before I forget, I'm having a small dinner party next Friday for Marcus' birthday. Nothing big, just a few people over."

"Okay." I needed to get out of the house. "Who's coming?"

"The usual, Derrick and Kim, Nikki and Nate, Fred and Melinda, and Michael and Jason."

I had changed my mind. "And me?" I asked. "Am I the only person coming alone?"

"Yeah," she tried to be of comfort, "but you won't be by yourself. We'll all be here."

"You have a husband," I said. "All the names you mentioned are couples, Toni." I hated being the token single friend now. "I'll just keep the twins that weekend so that you guys can have fun."

"They'll be at Marcus' parents' house." She added, "I know that you're not trying to get out of coming."

"Toni, I refuse to be the only single person there." I remembered the last time well. "Michael will use this as another opportunity to try to analyze me, and I don't have time for that shit." He needed to analyze himself because it made no sense for a man that damn fine to be bragging about how well he could suck a dick. "I'll pass."

"Why don't you bring Doran?"

The idea tickled me, but before it surfaced, I drowned it. "I am not asking him out."

"Not like it's a date. Just invite him over."

"Are you serious?" I couldn't even imagine it. "I'm not asking him."

"Whateva!" She sounded frustrated. "All I know is that you better be here next Friday."

"Toni, I don't think you understand how awkward it is being the only single person in the midst of four or five couples." I added, "That's hell."

"It was hell being married to that asshole, too, so make up your mind."

"I never said that I wanted Craig back." I was getting upset. "And please stop bringing him up every two minutes."

"It's every three minutes, thank you." She continued with a smile in her voice. "Paige, just find someone and invite him."

I whined, "It's not that simple, Toni."

"It's not that damn hard either, Paige. You're a good-looking woman. You're too hard on yourself . . . live a little." She paused but continued carefully. "The ball is in your court, now dunk that muthafucka." For the next ten minutes, Toni praised everything about me: my personality, intelligence, physical attributes, etc. When she was through, I touched myself to see if I would sizzle, 'cause she described me as a Red Hot Mama.

I sat silent in my car for a few seconds. "All right." I smiled and made myself comfortable in traffic. "I'll be at the damn party."

"Thank you." She blew me a kiss. "Hurry up and call him."

"Bye." I hung up and dialed Doran's number while still on that cocky high that Toni created.

"Changed your mind?" Doran said as he picked up. "Come on, let's sweat."

"Actually, I wish I was there." I giggled nervously. "Instead, I'm stuck on the turnpike."

"That's your punishment." He continued, "What's going on?"

"Nothing." All of a sudden, I needed Toni's cheerleading. "Nothing much."

I could tell that he was pondering the reason for my call. "Is everything all right?"

"Yes." I wanted to hang up. "Yes, everything is fine."

"Okay."

"Um, I just wanted to know if you would be free next Friday evening." In dropped the uncomfortable silence that I thought I could handle by doing this over the phone instead of in person.

"Next Friday?" he asked.

"Yes, next Friday." My poor heart was jumping like it was being kicked. I was biting my nails, making faces at myself in the rearview mirror, and was one breath away from saying, "You know what? Never mind." I took a deep breath.

"Why, what's going on?" he asked.

The damn question called for a yes or no answer, and he was turning my car into a torture chamber. "Well, my best friend is having a dinner party for her husband's birthday," I turned it around on him, "and I know that you still haven't met a lot of people here, so I thought this might be a good opportunity for you to do so."

He broke the silence and a chunk of my fragile ego by saying, "I was wondering how long it would take you to ask me out."

"What?" My mouth flew open. "No, I'm not asking—"

"I'm just kidding. Relax," he said. "You're absolutely right. I haven't mingled much since I've been here. Sure, I'll go."

"Great." I took a breath of relief. "I'll give you more details next week."

"Sounds like a plan." Then he added, "What else are we doing?"

"Huh?"

"Let's go dancing or something afterward. Let's maximize the evening." He paused. "I was already trying to figure out a way to turn our *workout* routine into more of a friendship, so maybe this will be the start."

"Maybe." I blushed.

"I mean, it's hard for me to watch you sweatin' on that treadmill day in and day out without—" He stopped and chuckled.

No he didn't. "Without what?" Call me George, because I was curious.

He finished in laughter. "Without knowing your middle name or your favorite drink."

He couldn't be serious. "My middle name is Danae, and for the moment, I like a glass of red wine. Now tell me what you were really about to say."

Doran asked, "Are you sure you wanna know?"

"Yeah." What the heck? "Why not?"

He hesitated. "It's just hard to watch you sweat up a storm the way you do and not wonder how much you sweat in bed." My mouth and eyes were wide open, and although what Doran had said was absolutely tasteless, I was very turned on.

Silence fell on us once more. I couldn't speak, breathe, think, or anything else, for that matter. "Are you still there?" he asked.

"Yes." I tried not playing into his game. "I'm here. A car almost hit me. I can't believe the way people drive these days."

He didn't buy it. "Did I scare you or something?"

"Scare me?" I repeated. "No. No, not at all."

"Good. I'm sure you've seen the way I look at you."

I brushed it off. "Well, you stare at every woman that walks by."

"I look at everybody," he said. "But you're the one that I want to touch."

"Touch?" I needed clarification.

"Would you allow me?"

If I said no, I'd be a frigid bitch. If I said yes, I'd be a slut. "Damn, I have another call coming in, Doran. I'll call you back."

"No problem. Drive safely, and I'll talk to you later."

In the matter of minutes that I allowed Doran to usher me into a very uncomfortable and miserable, desperate place, I suddenly wished I hadn't called. He wanted sex, nothing more, and he wasn't ashamed to ask for it.

~Situation #6~

Theo

Having a locker in high school is equivalent to having an apartment. People you don't want to see might just stop by, move in next door, or some retard could just drive by with her lights off just to see if you're home, *or* to peep out if you have company.

Trese waited in front of my locker between four consecutive class periods. However, unlike an apartment, I couldn't pretend not to be home, tell the neighbors to say that I moved, or call the cops to report a stalker. I just didn't get the books that I needed for my classes.

To say that I regretted getting involved with Trese over the summer was an understatement. Why? Because it had been confirmed that she had the impression that since we were having sex, she was going places in my life. She told one of my boys that she and I were going to the same college. How? I didn't even know if I was headed to college, and with grades like hers, she was headed back to middle school.

Ever since the bathroom incident more than a week before I'd been playing hard to find, ducking and dodging like I owed her money. However, Trese got smart. The chick staked out my locker until she got what she wanted: a crowd, a damn scene, and me.

I couldn't go to Ms. Patrick's class without my book, so I took a deep breath and made a beeline to my locker. When Trese saw me, she didn't smile like she used to. Instead, she squinted her eyes and put her hands akimbo.

"How come you ain't tell me you were driving to school?" she asked loudly. I was still fifteen feet away.

What the—? Who in the hell? I looked behind me 'cause she couldn't be talking to me, not the kid, and not like that.

"Whom are you talking to?"

"You." She had the nerve to put her acrylic fingernails all in my face. "When were you gonna tell me?"

"Hold up, shorty." I politely moved her hand out of my face and reached for my lock.

"Why didn't you tell me?" Trese got loud. "What, you drivin' some bitch to school?"

"Whoa." I smirked through my embarrassment; there were people all around. "Let's talk about this after school."

"No." She knocked my hand away from the lock as I tried to enter the combination. "I wanna know now."

I took a deep breath and looked at her. There was nothing sexy, appealing, or tantalizing about her anymore. She was played out and very close to getting her feelings hurt. "Trese, stop bullshitting. I have to go to class."

She was really upset. "Answer my question first."

"I don't have to answer a damn thing." I grabbed her hand and moved it out of my way. "So get the hell out of my face." That sure wasn't the way to talk to a lady, but I had nothing to worry about. There was nothing ladylike about Trese.

Right then, one of my teammates made eye contact with me as he walked by. I reached out to him. "What's up, son?" We knocked knuckles, and for a second, I ignored Trese like she was a useless piece of hallway junk. "Practice is gonna be a killa today, but I got something for you, boy." He mumbled something then laughed, and I joined him. "See you later, man."

"You ignoring me now?" she asked.

I was pissed. "What do you want?"

She spoke more calmly. "I'm sorry about getting mad, but I just feel like you've been pushing me away over the past week." It looked like she wanted to cry, but like most actresses, she just couldn't get the tears to come on cue. I wasn't a director, so I wasn't going to yell "cut!" She only had one shot.

"When I heard that you were driving and didn't even offer me a ride, I felt a little hurt." She continued with dry eyes. "All I want to know is why you didn't tell me that you were driving to school all this time."

I wasn't moved by her antics, and didn't feel that I owed her an explanation. "Did you ask me?" I opened my locker.

"Just answer the question." She kicked back into ghetto gear. "If you bringin' somebody, just say that." She was acting like I had stolen one of the two cars that she and her fifteen family members shared.

"Did you ever ask me?"

"No." Then along came the neck movement. "So, what you sayin'?"

"I'm saying that since you didn't ask me, there was nothing to tell." I shrugged my shoulders. "I don't report to you."

She looked absolutely stunned. "I see that."

I grabbed my English book and closed the locker. "I can't be late to Ms. Patrick's class." I looked at my watch. "I have to get going."

She grabbed my hand. "Don't you need to go to the bathroom first?" She was the queen of manipulation.

"Maybe another day." I knew that there would be no more days between us.

"Come on." She pulled herself into me. "Let's have a little

fun." She laughed. "You know you want to." She licked those luscious soup coolers then whispered, "I'll give you head."

Damn! Trese knew what to say, what to do, and how to do it. But those were the things that were turning me off because that's all she knew how to do. "Naw, I have to go."

"Okay." She squeezed my hand. "So, what time are you picking me up in the morning?"

The drama was only just beginning. "What?" I asked.

"I'm not riding the bus if you have a ride." She looked at me like I should've already known that. "Just tell me what time to be ready."

"No." I had had enough. The halls were getting clearer by the second. "Trese, I'm not picking you up in the morning or taking you home after school."

"How come?" She looked dazed.

"I can't take this." I pointed at her then back at myself. "This is over."

"What do you mean *this*?"

"You know exactly what I'm saying."

"No, I don't." The tears she was hoping for finally ran out to the stage. "What are you trying to say?"

"I'm sick of you acting like you're my damn girl."

"You saying that I'm not?" she asked.

I shook my head from side to side. "Did I ever tell you or ask you to be my girl?"

"Not in so many words, but we . . ." She looked down.

"Did I ever ask you to be my girl?" I didn't want there to be any misunderstanding when we walked away from locker number 507.

"No, but—"

I interrupted. "Then that might mean that you're not."

"Wait a minute." Then out came the girl that the hood would be proud of. "Wait a fuckin' minute." Trese rolled her eyes and her neck all at once, proving once again that she was the president of Hoochie Phi Coochie. "Are you breakin' up with me?"

"I can't break up with you if we were never a couple." I couldn't hold my tongue. Trese had put me through hell for the last week. She sent fake passes to get me out of classes, asked girls to hand me love letters from her, staked out my locker, and would call and hang up when my mom answered the phone.

The bell rang, and I was still up to my eyebrows with Trese.

"So, what the hell have we been doing?" Her inquiring mind wanted to know.

"Ah—" I tried to think of a better word, but since I was pressed for time, I just used the first word that came to mind. "Fuckin'." Right away, I felt something cold yet hot touch my cheek. "You didn't just do that."

"Yes, the hell I did," she said.

Though my anger had reached never before seen heights, I didn't have the reactionary thought of hitting her back. She didn't look scared, nervous, remorseful, or surprised at what she had done, and that bothered me more than anything else.

I sucked my lips inward to keep from calling her a few names I knew I shouldn't ever call a woman. I was still too shocked to leave. "You better never say another damn word to me."

"I won't," she sneered. "You weren't even man enough to tell me that all you wanted was to sleep with me."

"And you weren't woman enough to not sleep with me. That's just plain nasty."

Now that the halls were just about empty, her voice was echoing, but she didn't care. "Nothing was nasty about it when *you* were all up in it, though."

I could tell that behind it all, she was hurting. Trese expected me to change her life. She wanted to go with me, but she couldn't. *I* couldn't. Truth was she expected me to treat her differently than other guys did, and I tried, but she didn't let me. She threw herself on my dick before I could learn anything about her. She had no one to blame for her pain but her.

"Why did you have sex with me?" she wanted to know.

Why did she have to ask that question? I wasn't about to start lying now. "I did it because you gave it up." I didn't know how not to tell the truth right now. "You were cool, Trese, but I don't like you . . . not in a girlfriend kinda way."

She looked at me like I had just doused her with hot cooking oil. "Not in a girlfriend kinda way, huh?" She wiped her tears. "Well, you better decide in which damn way you want me, because I'm pregnant." She dropped her nuclear weapon and vacated the grounds.

In absolute shock, I heard myself whisper, "What?" as she walked away. I didn't call her back or run behind her because I couldn't stand for her to repeat those words. I was fine with believing that I needed a hearing aid.

In slow motion and much denial, I strolled to class. "Whatever." She couldn't be pregnant. We used condoms each and every time. I scratched my head. "She's lying," I said to pacify my growing desire to punch the wall. "Naw." With each step, I tortured myself with maybes and maybe nots. "She can't be." A step later, I switched. "But what if she is?" I hated to be the type of man to say this, but I had to. "If she's pregnant that doesn't mean that it's mine." I couldn't stand to hear guys lay blame on another man when push came to shove, but let's be real . . . Trese was far from the Virgin Mary, and with air pollution the way it is, the angel Gabriel wouldn't dare commute from Jerusalem to Miami.

When I made it to my English class, I stood outside for five minutes before I opened the door. I felt her eyes on me, but couldn't care less about what Ms. Patrick had to say. I didn't even look at her as I took my seat.

"Theodore, I'm sure we'll have a lot to talk about during our hour together after school today." My peers all laughed.

"Whateva," I said under my breath, knowing that now I'd have to explain to Coach J. why I was an hour late to practice.

Ms. Patrick started talking about the parts of speech, and for the next forty-five minutes, she sounded like Charlie Brown's teacher to me. "Mwa, mwa, mwa, mwa, mwa, mwa, mwa." I just opened my textbook to the page everyone else was on and flew two thousand miles per hour into my nightmarish future.

Trese would probably be calling the local news and the papers tonight to tell them that Boy Wonder wasn't so wonderful after all. Boy Wonder was now wondering what the future had in store for him. How could I deal with having a child with *her*? I thought about being connected to her for eighteen years, and nothing had ever made me feel so sick. It was upsetting to think that a child of mine might grow up in the household where Trese did.

The bell rang, and I watched the other students walk by me and out the door. I couldn't leave, but I somehow appeased myself with the thought of Trese waiting at my locker to apologize for the cruel joke.

The classroom went from being alive with whispers, coughs, and the noise of crumpling paper to just two people breathing. Forty seconds into my detention, I already felt that running down a flight of stairs blindfolded would be better. I rested my head on the desk.

Ms. Patrick said, "Theodore, this is not the time to catch up on your rest."

"I don't see why not," I mumbled.

"I'll tell you why." She paused. "You're keeping me from

helping a friend of mine prepare for her party tonight. Therefore, I intend to make your life just as miserable as she will make mine." She giggled a bit. "So, heads up."

"I'm not feeling well."

"You're a big, strong basketball player," she said. "Please sit up."

I picked up my head and saw Ms. Patrick standing behind her desk, removing her navy blue jacket. She revealed a tight white blouse. The shirt was so close-fitting that her hard nipples were protruding through the material. Damn, she was moving her mouth, but I couldn't comprehend.

"Huh?" Here I was in the middle of my crisis with Trese, wishing that whatever insect Ms. Patrick was afraid of would land on her arm so that I could kill it and then intentionally rake my hand against her breasts. "I'm sorry, what did you say?"

"You said that you were sick, so I asked if that was the reason you were late." She stepped out of her shoes and started straightening her desk.

"Oh, yes." Damn, I was in shock. I had never seen anything like that on a teacher. Now I could see exactly why Coach J. fell for her, but she was mean as hell, so I also saw why he had to step, too.

Back when I first came to West Dade four years ago, Ms. Patrick didn't look half as good. Now she was the teacher that all of the others were jealous of. Had she been fifteen years younger, she would be the embodiment of my dream girl. Or if I was fifteen years older, she'd be in danger of . . . Damn, she was facing me again. Her nipples were staring at me.

She opened her mouth. "Mwa, mwa, mwa, mwa, mwa, mwa, mwa." I sized her up, 36-28-40 . . . I was never wrong. "Are you listening to me?" she asked while staring at me weirdly.

"I'm sorry. I'm just a little out of it." I was.

"Is it a headache?"

"Yes," I lied and tore my eyes away from her chest.

"Would you like something for it?"

"Yes." I heard that breast milk does a body good. "What do you have?"

"Tylenol," she spoke softly, "but it has to be our secret. I'm not supposed to supply students with drugs."

"Well, I won't tell," I whispered back, "if you promise to go easy on the homework."

She grinned. "No can do." Then she added, "But I'll let you off of the hook for your lack of participation in class today."

"Sorry." I frowned as I thought of my reason for being in detention. "It's just been one of those days."

Ms. Patrick started walking in my direction. "Child, please. You don't have a car note, rent, or a utility bill." She smiled. "Until you have bills to pay, you don't have anything to be worked up about." She placed the red-and-yellow capsules in my hand and rested an unopened bottle of water on my desk. "Wanna trade places?"

"Thank you," I said. "I'd rather try to pay your bills than go through what I'm going through."

"Sounds serious." Her facial expression showed concern. "Is everything all right?" She sat down at a desk next to me.

I didn't know what to say or if I should say anything. "I just got some bad news."

"Oh, I'm so sorry." Her hand flew up to her mouth like she expected me to say that someone died. What she'd find hard to believe is that I was the corpse. I felt like I died when I heard what Trese had to say.

"Would you like to talk about it?" she asked.

"It's nothing tragic." I shifted in my seat and stared down at the desk. "I may have just screwed something up for myself."

Ms. Patrick went on without knowing my problem.

"Theodore, a lot of times we make decisions, and just because the result isn't something that we expected, we consider it a mistake." I wasn't looking at her, but I heard the smile in her voice. "Nothing happens without purpose." She reached over and quickly patted me on the shoulder. "So whatever it is, just know that in the end it could have a meaning that'll blow your mind."

"I don't know about that, but thanks anyway." I smiled, though I couldn't see how there could ever be a bright light at the end of my tunnel. "Thanks."

She chuckled like someone was tickling her. "Anytime." She sat back in the chair like she planned on sitting there awhile, which made me relax. "However, Theodore, if you feel that the situation you're going through is one that you can live without learning from, then do your best to avoid it in the future."

"I have a question for you, Paige," I said.

"Excuse me!" She pushed my head playfully with her index finger. "Who told you that you could call me Paige?"

"Who told you that you could call me Theodore?" I laughed. "Ms. Patrick, please call me Theo."

"I will when you start coming to class on time."

"Come on," I begged. "It takes less energy to say Theo."

"I'm not looking for an easy way out." She smiled. "Maybe I like it the hard way."

Being a man, I took her statement and ran with it. I was tempted to respond with something like, "I like it the hard way too," but I held back.

She stood up. "I'll think about it." I checked her out from the back and was extremely pleased. Her navy skirt hugged her hips, and I found myself wishing I were a stitch in the fabric. Other than Halle Berry, Angela Bassett, and the thing I have for Oprah, Ms. Patrick was another older woman who was now on my "would do" list. She was tight work.

"Hey, sexy, are we sweatin' today?" the new math teacher said as he walked through the door. He quickly covered his mouth when he noticed that she wasn't alone. "I'm very sorry."

"Hello," she said.

He looked at me through the sides of his eyes. "So, I guess we're not doing it today either, huh?"

"No." She looked over at me. "He has to be here for an hour, plus I was supposed to help Toni with the food."

"Damn." He thought he was whispering. "I wanted to see you in those shorts." I felt like the third and fourth wheel. I opened my textbook and pretended to be reading something . . . anything, but when they weren't looking at me, I was peeping at them.

She blushed. "So, how was your day?"

"It was cool. My first set of quizzes went over well."

"Good." She looked like she was faking her smile.

There was an awkward amount of silence before he asked, "Are you cold?"

"No. Why, are you?"

"I'm not complaining, but . . ." He stared directly at her chest. "It sure looks like you are."

She gazed downward, humiliated, and snatched her jacket from the back of the chair. "Thanks." I knew that she would've preferred he didn't make such a statement in my meager presence. Now she probably knew why I was staring at her so much.

She walked away from him to unplug the projector and he asked, "So, what time am I picking you up tonight?"

She answered quickly in a whisper, "I thought we'd just meet there."

"Naw, I can pick you up so that later—"

She interrupted him and shook her head. "Doran, I still have a student here. Let's talk about this in about an hour."

"Oh, okay." He finally caught on. "No problem."

"All right." She walked him to the door. "I'll see you later."

When the mathematician was out of sight, I wasted no time teasing her. "Ms. Patrick has a boyfriend, huh?"

"Mind your business." She blushed. "Mr. Bess is my workout partner."

"It don't sound like y'all gonna be working out tonight," I joked. "What's that all about?"

She smiled. "If I call you Theo and let you leave right now instead of in forty-five minutes, will you not mention this to anyone?"

"I can see where that is a possibility." I was willing to negotiate.

"You're dismissed, Theo."

"Thank you." I gathered my things.

"Have a great weekend."

"I heard the math teacher plottin'," I teased, "so don't do anything that I wouldn't do."

"You are too silly, Theo." She smacked me lightly on the arm. "Get out of here."

I smiled all the way out the door then ran downstairs and into the locker room. I was only twenty minutes late to practice, but to Coach J. that was just like not showing up. I pulled off my Rocawear gear and with no hesitation jumped into my gym clothes and hit the hardwood floor with my signature yell.

"What time is it, W. D.?" Normally my teammates would scream, "Game time," but Coach J. was still going over yesterday's practice. The look he gave me said that I would probably have twenty-five more pushups and crunches than the rest of the team, but the added exercise was all right with me. I needed to do something with my bottled up aggression.

I joined the team and listened to Coach, but my mind just

wouldn't process anything he said. Trese's news was like a ghost. It was haunting me, and this was just phase one. She wasn't going to make things easy for me. I could already imagine her with a big stomach at the home games, holding up stupid signs or booing me while I was at the free-throw line. I had seen it done to other players by baby mommas and ex-girlfriends. "Damn it," I said to myself.

"All right, boys," Coach yelled. "Let's get on the ball." He read from his clipboard. "Twenty-five sit-ups, pushups, crunches, and lunges." He flipped the page. "And let me get four suicides before we go into lay-up drill." He blew his whistle and we all knew what to do.

I tried to walk by him, but he grabbed my elbow. "Where you been?"

"I had to stay late with Ms. Patrick."

With the mention of her name, his eyes lit up, but he played it off well. He had to regret not being with her now. If he didn't, then that meant that he had someone better, and I didn't see how that was possible. "Why did you get a detention?"

"I was late." I answered his next question before he even asked. "A li'l diarrhea." I whispered the lie.

"Ah, man." He jokingly stepped away from me. "All right, Shitty Gonzalez, don't let anything loose when you doing them sit-ups."

"I'll try." I started walking away. "You got some extra trunks just in case?"

"Hell Naw." He laughed. "You better tighten them ass muscles."

I ran away, screaming, "What time is it, W.D.?"

"Game time."

"Man, I can't hear y'all."

"Game time!"

"What time?"

"Game time!" We all hit the floor and started counting off our crunches. "One, two, three, four, five . . ." Somewhere around the ninth crunch, I glanced over at Coach J. He was staring blankly up into the rafters, and somehow I felt as though we were thinking about the same thing: Ms. Patrick's nipples.

~Situation #5~

Paige

"All right, now I'm starting to think that you just want to hear my voice." I smiled into the phone as I clipped on my earrings. "My directions can't be that bad." Doran had already called three times for help navigating his way to my house.

"Hmmm." He cleared his throat. "It used to be mine, so of course I know my way to the house. Are you inviting me?"

It was Craig. "Shit," I whispered then sighed in disappointment. I felt my smile melt into my face and gave him a less than weak greeting. "Hi."

He teased, "Where did all of the flirtation go?"

"Right out of the window," I said.

"Does this mean that I can't come over?" he asked.

"My sentiments exactly."

"I miss you," he said. "Don't you have anything for me, for old time's sake?"

"Something like what?"

He chuckled a little. "You know what I like."

I blushed but didn't let him move me. "How can I help you, Mr. Johnson?"

He said, "I'm doing fine. Thank you for asking. How are

you?" I couldn't figure out if he was trying to be nice, sexy, or pleasantly annoying. Regardless of his ploy, I decided to stick to the bad attitude that he was used to getting from me.

"What do you want?"

"I believe I asked how you were doing," he repeated.

"I'm fine. But does it really matter?"

"Of course it matters," he said. "Everything about you matters."

"Whatever." Though there were days when I still longed for him, Craig would never know. "What do you want?" I had to handle him with an iron fist. He had given me not one, but two sexually transmitted diseases, so as long as hell was hot, Craig would be on my IDGF list. As a matter of fact, he was on my I Don't Give a Fuck list twice, under his first name and that last name that I had to get rid of.

"Why are you so rude today?" he asked.

I rolled my eyes. "Just not in a good mood."

"Oh, I see. That time of the month again?" he said.

"I'm not listening to this." I couldn't believe him. "Call back and leave a fuckin' message." I was about to hang up when I heard him apologize.

"Wait, wait. I'm sorry. I just called to ask a question."

"What?" This was actually our nicest exchange of words in the last three months. My hatred for him intensified during the summer months. As though temperatures in the nineties, busting my ass at the gym, and being sexually frustrated weren't enough, my ex-husband just happened to look like he walked off of the cover of a magazine. So, I was stressed and pissed by the end of the summer.

He finally asked his million-dollar question. "Did a letter from Harrison Financial come there for me?"

"No."

He asked, "Are you sure?"

I rolled my eyes and sighed without answering the ignorant question.

"Hello?"

"I'm here," I said.

"Did you hear me?" he asked.

"Yes." I applied my eyeliner. "Craig, there is no letter from Harrison Financial here for you. As a matter of fact, there is no mail here for you." I went on. "If something was here, I would've dropped it into your mail slot at the school like I always do."

"Well, I'm sorry about bothering you."

"Do you have any other questions?" I continued, when I knew that I really didn't have to. "Because I'm expecting company and would hate to be interrupted by another call from you."

"No, that's all I called for."

I smiled as I said, "Good-bye."

"Paige," he called just as I began to take the receiver away from my ear. "Wait."

"What?"

"So your company . . ." He paused. "Is it a male or a female?" "Why?" I was glad that I had tapped into his curiosity. This was exactly the kind of conversation I always wanted us to have, one where he was left wondering, and only I would know the truth.

"It's a man." I was grinning from ear to ear. Even if I were expecting Toni, I wouldn't have changed my answer. I wanted to make him think about another man's fingertips tracing my nipples. I longed for the day when Craig would imagine my innocent little lips sliding downward to the shaft of another man's dick. "Why did you ask?" I hoped that later he'd sit alone and picture a man moving his feather-soft tongue over my most sensitive spots.

"No special reason," he lied. "Just thought I'd ask."

"Well, yes, it's a man," I repeated, in case he didn't hear me the first time.

"Just be careful," he said.

"Careful of what? I think I've had every sexually transmitted disease that there is."

"Here we go a-fuckin-gain," he said.

I didn't know why I threw that in his face so much, because even after our divorce, Craig and I still got together for sex once every four or five months. It was always protected, but the meaning of it was still missing. However, the sex was powerful, and at the time, it did more for me than the psychiatrist I was paying. Craig was the snake that attacked me, so I went back to drain him of his venom. It was also the cure. Craig was the problem, and his dick was one hell of a solution.

I called these sexual gatherings DSS, short for Divorce Sex Sessions. During our DSS, I was untamed, nasty, and had the filthiest mouth in all of the southern states. I called him everything but a child of God. I wanted him to know that though I was stupid enough to be in bed with him, I wasn't silly enough to forget who he really was.

One of my favorite lines was, "Fuck me, you ungrateful, whorish motherfucka." He knew that I would never forgive him. "After you eat my pussy, get the fuck out of my house." He knew that deep down inside I wanted nothing more than his eight inches of sausage in my meat grinder. "Make me scream, you big-dick bitch."

Then there were those times, normally a few days before my period, when I got emotional. "Why couldn't you just act right?" I asked a few times, soaked in tears, and got no answer. To this day, I don't know if those emotions were from the heart or evoked by him hitting my G, H, I, and J spots from the back. "This pussy was all yours. Why couldn't you just do right?" We would sweat, grind, expand, and deflate together through the night, but the next day at school, I'd walk by him as though he was a student that never took my class.

Just as all good things must come to an end, all bad things

that we fool ourselves into believing were good, must also die. The DSS stopped six months ago, one night when I was on my knees before him and Craig answered his cellular phone. With only the whites of his eyes showing, he lied to the woman on the other end about where he was, then promised her that he'd be at her house within an hour and a half.

"Damn." I used to be her. I, the ex-wife, became the other woman.

"Get the fuck out," I cried as I stood up and wiped my mouth, ashamed by what I had allowed myself to become, all for a big dick and a smile. "Get out."

"What?" he asked.

"Leave." I pointed at the door.

"What are you talkin' about?" he asked. "Why?"

"Why?" I screamed. "Because I'm not stupid."

"Paige, what are you talking about?" He stroked himself and beckoned to me. "Come on. Come sit on it." He joked, "You can't send me out with my dick like this."

"Yes, I can." I was hurting like it was day one all over again. "Just leave."

He stood up. "What in the hell is your problem today?"

"My problem is that I'm not going to suck your dick for you to go out and fuck someone else." I walked over to the door.

"Don't you have someone that you see?" he asked, and when I didn't respond, he spoke again. "I never told you that you couldn't have sex with someone else." He added, "We're divorced."

He was right. We were divorced, and I wasn't even trying to be with another man . . . All I wanted was him. The only thing the divorce did was make it all right for him to do what he had already been doing. It made me stupid enough to believe that as long as we weren't living together, sharing the same last name and bank account, that sex was just sex. But it wasn't just sex. It was beginning to destroy me all over again.

"You didn't have a problem doing it all the other times," he said, pointing to his piece.

"What the—?" I wanted to strangle him. "The only thing that matters is that I have a problem doing it today." I opened the door and felt comfort watching him walk away.

I'm only human, so of course I'd been tempted to dip onto his chocolate cone again, but that was the last time because if I knew better, which I did, I needed to start acting like it.

I had forgotten all about being on the phone with Craig until I heard his voice again. "So, who's this guy?"

"A friend of mine," I said.

"Of course he's a friend of yours. He's certainly not my friend. I meant what's his name?"

"What does any of this have to do with your letter from Harrison Financial?"

"Never mind," he said. "Well, I hope you two have a nice evening."

"Thank you." My doorbell rang. "That's him now. I have to go." I hung up. "I'm coming," I shouted then went down my checklist. "Purse, Moët, cell phone, and keys." When all four things were in my possession, I raced to the door.

"Hey." I stepped out toward Doran in his black slacks and navy shirt. I tiptoed and pecked him on the cheek. "Hey back at you. You're looking good." He looked me up and down then took the champagne bottle from my hand.

"Thank you." I had been saving this extra-low-V-cut black top for months. It was so revealing that I had to use double-sided tape to keep me from doing a Janet Jackson wardrobe malfunction—and yes, I, too, had the sterling silver sunburst nipple shields on both breasts. I gave them as gifts to myself right after Super Bowl XXXVIII. "Does that mean that you like my outfit?"

He was staring at the ultra-high split in the front of my short, tight-fitting black skirt. He glanced back up at my top. "I love your outfit."

"Thank you," I said and pointed to his car. "Let's get this show on the road."

Toni and Marcus were overcharged with sexual energy. His hands didn't leave her body all night. He sat her in his lap, danced with her, held her hand, and I even caught him rubbing on her thighs during dinner. "I ain't mad at you," I whispered into her ear at the table and smiled.

Kimberly, Toni's other best friend, also a recovering pole addict, had a baby two months ago. This was Kim and Derrick's first night out since becoming parents. They, too, were all hands.

Marcus' younger brother, Nathan, had just returned from Iraq four days prior to the dinner party, and Nikki, his girl-friend of two years, was all smiles.

Michael was Toni's cousin, and he and his boyfriend, Jason, were just gross, not because they we're gay, but because they had no boundary of what they wouldn't do in public. I personally wouldn't want to watch a woman, sitting across a coffee table from me, shove her hand in her man's pocket and begin rubbing his third leg. Well, that was exactly what Michael was doing to Jason, and at one point, I even saw Jason's eyes roll back a little. With Doran there, I was more than embarrassed, and completely understood when he excused himself to the patio.

Fred, Marcus' best friend, and his wife, Melinda, were nicknamed the Mega-Couple. They were both lawyers, worked at the same firm, and had two children, ages eleven and eight. The surprising thing about Fred and Melinda was that they flew to Cancun once a year to a swingers' gathering. No one, including me, was supposed to know about that, but one night Marcus tried selling Toni on the idea of going. She called me and asked my opinion, and then it all came out. Fred and Melinda got their freak on by switching partners with other couples. More power to them. I wasn't strong enough to know that my man was cheating on me, so you know I couldn't *watch* him with another chick. It would be called swinging because that's exactly what I'd be doing— swinging, trying to beat the bitch down.

Throughout the night, Doran did a great job at my side, holding my hand, pouring me drinks. He didn't hesitate to pull me onto the makeshift dance floor when R. Kelly sang, "I know that there's somebody's birthday tonight, and I know that somebody's breaking out the champagne."

Everybody in attendance stepped in the name of something. I was stepping in the name of lust. Doran spun me around, dipped me, swung me, and when he pulled me into him, I felt the tempting hardness below his waist.

"I didn't know you had it in you," he whispered in my ear.

"Had what?"

He smiled. "Those types of moves."

"Please," I taunted him, "that was nothing."

"Really?" He tightened his grasp around my waist. "Please show me more," he pleaded and I delivered, all the way until it was time to go.

Suddenly, he wasn't just another teacher, workout partner, or a friend. He was a man, and I was anxious to be alone with him. "See you all later." I hugged a few necks and said my good-byes.

"I'll call you tomorrow. You and I have to talk, honey," Michael whispered in my ear as I bid him adieu. The way he was staring at Doran's ass told me exactly what he wanted to talk about. "Tomorrow." He smiled.

In the foyer, I said goodnight to Toni. "He's really nice, Paige." She swallowed the rest of whatever was in her glass. "Where are you guys going?"

"I think he's dropping me home." I tried not to blush.

"You think?"

I explained, "We talked about going dancing earlier, but I think we did enough here. Plus, it's quarter to one."

She giggled. "I know your kind. You're going to get some."

"Shh," I shushed her. "Let me get out of here."

"Call me in the morning with details," she tried to whisper. "I want length, width, circumference, coloration, and all that shit." She was dead serious.

"Bye, Toni."

"Bye, girl." She turned to walk back to her remaining guests. "Circumference," she yelled back to me.

In the doorway, as Doran and Marcus shook hands, he looked my way. "Ready?"

"Yeah." I gave Marcus a hug and a smile. "Goodnight, birthday boy."

"You guys drive safely," Marcus said as he let us out and closed the door.

"I recognize this neighborhood," Doran said as we walked to his car. "My apartment is only about five minutes from here." He paused. "How about going back to my place for a while?"

Think of something to say . . . and say it. "Sure." Damn, playing hard to get just got thrown out of the window.

We were at Doran's place in about three minutes. The apartment was nice, very nice, so nice that I had to ask, "Who did the decorating?" It looked like the works of a woman. Shit, what wasn't supposed to match was matching, there wasn't a speck of dust anywhere, and the place smelled like a rose garden.

"My roommate," he said and walked into the kitchen, leaving me on the sofa. "Would you like something to drink?"

"Yes. What do you have?" I never heard anything about a roommate.

"Apple juice, Coke," he paused as he moved things around, "orange juice and Chardonnay." I don't care what others may say. I believed that if unrelated people of the opposite sex lived under one roof, they were fucking. Even if they didn't call themselves a couple, and even if one was ugly as sin, the booty was too convenient to pass up.

"Chardonnay, please." I looked around. "So, is your roommate here?"

"Naw, he's at work," he said.

I had to hear that again. "I'm sorry, I didn't hear you."

"No, he's not here. He works nights at the hospital."

"Oh, okay." His roommate was a man. Whew! That brought much relief.

Doran soon joined me on the sofa and handed me my glass of wine. "Thank you." He sat next to me, and with the click of the remote, Kelly Price's "Married Man" was playing. "Whoa," I joked, "is that a sign?"

"I'm not married." He showed me his fingers then draped his hand over my shoulder. "Did you have a good time tonight?"

"Yes, I did." I sipped my wine nervously. "Thank you for joining me."

He looked at me intently. "It was my pleasure."

An hour, two glasses of Chardonnay and many laughs later, Doran and I were splayed out across the sofa horizontally. Though we were fully clothed, our lips and tongues were naked and in a feverish lock. His breathing turned me on more than the feel of his hands over my body. Doran was attractive enough to have a different woman every day and another one at night. However, his trembling hands and anxious actions told a different story.

In a flash, he pulled my V-cut top to the side and out popped my breast. He looked at my piercing. "That is so damn sexy." The sensation of his warm tongue on my nipple took me by surprise and I jumped up. "Shouldn't we go into your room or something?" For the past seven years, the only man to touch me was Craig.

"You want to?"

I stuttered, "I-I don't want anyone walking in on us."

"That won't happen, but," he stood up, "just give me a minute."

When Doran disappeared down the dark corridor, I thought about what I was doing. I just wanted to be touched, to feel wanted and pleasured. My last "fling" was with Craig six months ago, and I was in desperate need of a good time with someone other than my ex-husband. However, I wanted to feel something more than a dick. With Doran, I knew that I would be getting all dong and no ding. If I wanted to feel cheap, I still had Craig's number.

"Follow me," Doran said when he returned.

I tried to smile. "Actually, I think I better just have you take me home. It's already two in the morning."

He walked toward me. "Was I too forward?"

"No." I shook my head and stood up. "You've been great. I just don't know if we should do anything to ruin the evening."

"Nothing can ruin tonight." He grabbed my hand.

"To be honest with you," I continued, "we still don't know each other all that well, Doran."

"Well, let's get to know each other." He smiled. "You can ask me anything you want."

"Yeah, but it's getting late and I—"

"Shh." He quieted me. "Stop making excuses and just let it happen." With my hand in his, he gently pulled me and started walking. Right before entering the hallway, he hit a switch that left the entire apartment in darkness, all except a glow from the opened door straight ahead that led the way.

He stopped right in front of the bedroom door. "So, do

you seriously want to go home or do you want to get to know me?" He kissed my hand. "We can talk all night, and you can ask me anything you like."

As the soft light flickered on his face, I found peace in his eyes somehow. "What's your favorite color?" My choice was to stay.

"Green," he answered as we entered the room.

"Lucky number?"

He thought for a few seconds. "I'd say nine."

Tiny candles were on both nightstands, where nothing else stood. The walls were white and bare. The whole room was too plain and empty to be a room where someone lived daily. There was a full-size bed, nightstands and a dresser with a lamp on it, and a small computer desk with an older model PC on it.

"Is this your room?"

"Something like that," he said as he closed the door behind him.

"Where's all of your stuff?" I looked around again.

"In my office in one of the rooms down the hall." He sat on the bed and pulled me to stand between his legs. "I hate for things to look junky, so I keep everything in there."

"Wouldn't that make your office junky?"

"No, I have a lot of file cabinets." He laughed then moved his hand to my ass. "Any other questions?" he asked.

"Tons." I smiled.

"Ask away." He pulled me down to him. I straddled him, my legs on both sides of his.

I asked, "What's your sign?"

"Sagittarius."

"When is your birthday?"

"December eighteenth." He pulled my shirt over my head. I continued my questioning to keep myself from fainting. "What year?"

He reached behind me to unhook my bra. "Nineteen sixty-eight."

I reached over and unbuttoned his shirt and brought it over his head. I sighed with pleasure. I saw him without a shirt every time we left the gym, but never expected to get a chance to touch it. I did one better; I kissed his chest.

"What do you like about me?" I asked when I raised my head.

"I thought you'd never ask." He palmed my breasts. "These."

I slapped him playfully on the shoulder. "I'm serious, Doran."

"And so am I." He mimicked a breastfeeding infant, sucking on them. "I love piercings."

"Thank you." My sunbursts weren't as large as Janet's; they were about as round as a quarter. That was the only thing he liked about me? I was offended. What about my personality, my smile, my eyes, and the way I lit up a room when I walked in? Feeling a little unappreciated, I hopped off of his lap and sat next to him instead.

He kneeled down in front of me then pushed me backward onto the bed and rubbed me through my panties. "I love shaved pussy." He pulled my thong aside and with too much aggression, he ran his thick, dry finger into me like a car.

"Ouch." I was startled.

"You're a big girl. You can take it." He continued with his finger. "Can't you?"

"Yeah, but there is a gentle way to do things."

"I'm sorry." He stopped but started rubbing me again. "You just feel so good."

There was something wrong with the situation. I was getting no thrill from Doran's touch. However, I didn't grumble as he pulled my body to the edge of the bed and savored, licked, taunted, and pierced my fruit with his tongue. When he was done, he fought to remove his pants so that we could complete the process, but instead I heard the front door close and it was followed by a voice.

"Dori."

"Fuck." He froze.

I jumped up and asked, "Who is that?"

"Oh shit," he said and tried to pull his pants back up. "Get dressed."

I stood up. "Who is that?"

"Just get dressed."

I was terrified as I tried to find my clothes. "Who *is* that?"

"Fuck, man," he whispered with his hands on his head, then rushed over to the old computer and switched on the monitor. "It's my roommate."

"So, what's the big deal?"

"I shouldn't have company."

"Why not?" I asked.

"Dori." The voice got closer and seemed concerned. "Doran?" The hallway light was now shining under the door.

Doran didn't have the balls to answer his roommate or me. "Damn, damn, shit." He turned on the lamp, gathered my things, and threw them at me. "Get into the closet and get dressed." He opened the closet door.

"Closet? You need to tell me what's going on." I could hear my heart beat. "I thought you weren't married." I was confused.

"I'm not." He raced around the room and blew out both candles.

"Then why in the hell are you telling me to go into the fuckin' closet?"

"Doran, where in the hell are you?" The voice was angry. "And who in the fuck is Paige? Yeah, bitch, I got your purse." I had left my purse in the living room. "Doran, answer me."

"Paige, please just go in the goddamn closet." He struggled to get his shirt on. "I'll explain later."

"No, just get my purse and get me the hell outta here." I couldn't do anything, including getting my bra to hook properly, but anything that wasn't done wasn't getting done. There was a heavy thump on the door and then it swung open.

"What in the fuck is this?" A tall, thin, light-skinned man launched at Doran and slapped him in the face several times. "What in the fuck are you doing?"

"Baby, I can explain." Doran tried to grab the man's hands. "Wait."

"I cannot believe this," the man yelled and fell against the door like he would faint. "Oh my God."

Doran stood in front of him. "It's not what you think, baby."

"Get the hell out of my face." He pushed Doran to the ground. "I am so through with you." He walked toward me but stopped halfway. "Who are you?"

"Paige." I pointed to the purse in his hand. "I didn't know that he was seeing someone, or was even gay, for that matter." I was scared as hell. I wasn't about to fight a dude over another dude. "He told me that you were just a roommate."

"You have the nerve to bring a motherfucker to our place?" The man was in tears. "Get the fuck out."

"Wait a minute." Doran was back on his feet. He looked at me and winked. "She's not telling you everything." He continued. "I brought her here to work on this computer. She's a computer programmer." He paused. "We came in here to look at it, and she started stripping and touching me and shit." He added, "It all happened so quickly that I got caught up in watching her, but you know I don't want no damn woman."

I was humiliated. "So, I just knew where you kept your

candles, too, huh?" I wasn't stopping there. "The only hard drive you wanted me to look at was in your pants." I looked at his lover. "I don't know shit about computers. I work at the same school where he works, and he's been trying to sleep with me for a month."

"C'mon baby, look at her." Doran pointed at me in disdain. "Do you really think that I would sleep with her?"

Embarrassed wasn't the word for me. "You ate my pussy, Doran," I said.

"Bitch, you wish." Doran looked like he would spit on me.

"Smell his breath." I was pissed. "Smell his breath."

"You are such a liar." The crying man didn't buy Doran's version of the story, and backed him up into a corner. "You lying bastard. I move you down here, and this is what you do to me," he screamed. "Get the fuck out." He punched Doran over and over again.

During the fight, I grabbed my purse and tiptoed past them. I quickly threw on my clothing in the hallway and walked out of the apartment, still in shock. On my cell phone, I called the only person besides drunk-ass Toni who lived on that side of town. In ten minutes, the candy apple red Lincoln Navigator pulled up to the gas station I had walked to.

"What in the hell are you doing out here without your car?" Craig asked as I got into the truck.

"Just drive," I said.

He offered advice. "You gotta be careful about who you deal with."

"Yeah, someone should've told me that before I met you," I said. "I didn't call you because I needed someone to talk to. I need a ride."

We rode in silence until we arrived at my house. "Thank you." I handed him ten dollars as he pulled into the driveway. "This is for your gas."

"Don't act like that," he said. "Are you gonna be all right?"

"Yes," I answered.

"All right."

I opened the door and without looking over at him, I asked, "Would you like to come in?" He answered me by turning off the engine. Craig followed me into the house and then into the kitchen. "So," he took a deep breath, "how was your date?"

I turned on the coffeepot and pretended not to hear him. "Coffee?"

"Caffeinated?"

"Decaf."

"Yeah, I'll take a cup." He continued with caution and walked toward me. "Did someone put their hands on you tonight?"

"What do you mean?"

"Did somebody hit you or something? Were you in a fight?"

"No, I wasn't in a fight, but I think I might be feeling a little better had I kicked somebody's ass." I rested two mugs down on the counter. "Excuse me for a few minutes. I'm gonna jump in the shower."

"How would you like it?" he asked in reference to my coffee.

"Don't you remember anything about me?" I walked away. "I'll fix it myself." Once in my bedroom, I hurried into the shower. As I waited patiently for the "just right" temperature, I smiled when I thought about the Doran incident and whispered to myself, "I'm on *Candid Camera*, right?" Doran had called another *man* "baby." Standing below the water and thinking of the way things went down was funnier than it was when I was smack dab in the midst of it.

As the warm water cascaded down my body, the serene setting made me wonder how long it'd take before I was granted my wish . . . another man. Sometimes I felt that I was expecting too much, so right there in the shower, I modified the qualities that Mr. Right Now should possess. I missed having access to love on a steady basis.

. "Lord, I don't care if he doesn't have a car, the best-looking body, or perfectly aligned teeth," I said. "I'll drive him to work. Yes, he must have a job. I'll enroll him into the gym and we can workout together, and after we're married, he can use my dental coverage to straighten things out . . . I just want a man, any man." Like TLC, I wasn't too proud to beg. "Please . . . damn."

"Two teaspoons of sugar, no cream, right?" Craig's voice startled me. Through the frosted, fogged-up shower glass I saw him approaching. "Am I right?" He held out the mug.

The coffee situation wasn't serious enough for him to track me down while in the shower and he knew it. "You're right."

"You like it strong." He slid the door open a few inches and passed the mug to me. "I remembered."

I blushed. "Thank you." I turned my back to the water and allowed it to skate down my backside as I sipped from the warm cup. Through the glass, I watched Craig not leave the bathroom. He dropped the lid on the toilet seat and got comfortable. We didn't speak as he rubbed his head a few times with his left hand and brought the mug to his mouth over and over with his right hand until it was empty.

"So, what happened tonight?" he asked as he placed the mug on the ground.

"Nothing much." I couldn't decide whether to give Doran the bad name around school that he deserved.

He stood to his feet. "You think I'm stupid, Paige?"

"Yeah." I giggled.

From behind the frostiness of the glass, I witnessed him tugging on and then removing his shirt. I had ample time to protest, but instead I took a deep breath. The caramel brownness of his chest still called out to me, maybe because my name was written on it. Two weeks before our wedding, Craig went into a love-induced binge and had *Paige* tattooed above his left peck. Every time I saw the tattoo, I got giddy. Why? One, because every other woman to ever come after me *had* to have asked the question, "Who's Paige?" Two, because he could've had my name covered by a picture of a basketball or a tiger like he promised he'd do when I informed him of the divorce. Three, I knew that it was close to his heart, not just on the surface, but also within.

"Didn't you have a date tonight?" He stepped toward the glass.

"Yes," I answered.

"What did this guy do? It's not every night that I get a call from you crying and asking for my help."

"First of all, I wasn't crying."

"Whateva." He cut me off. "What did he do?"

"He didn't do anything to me. Things just didn't go right." I sighed. "But what does?" I was watching his every move and longing for him to make the right ones.

"You didn't answer my questions," he said and pulled on the drawstring to his gym shorts. "What happened?"

"Nothing happened." By the time the words left my mouth, he was completely disrobed, and I found myself more excited than I ever was when we were together. As he walked closer, I fought to contain myself.

"Stop bullshitting me, Paige." Craig giggled and stepped into the shower. The only way to avoid the inevitable was for me to liquefy and swirl down the drain.

We stood before each other, naked. "Let me ask you a few questions," he said and took the cup away from my hand, resting it on the side of the tub. "Did he do this?" He pulled me toward him and my lips found their familiar resting place on his. Craig's tongue made mine surrender. I gave into him like an alcoholic to whiskey . . . I was a falling-down, slurring, wet mess for him after just one kiss.

His slippery hands slid to my breasts and teased my nipples, flickering excitedly over them and slightly pinching them as they stiffened. Then he squeezed them as gently but as firmly as he would a cantaloupe in the produce section.

"Did he do this?" I was already too consumed, too believing that he was my husband again, and too wanting more. "Answer me, Paige," he said with my nipple between his lips. "Did he do this?"

"No," I said as he backed me up under the water like my hairstyle didn't matter. "No, he didn't do that."

"You sure?" His suction got more intense.

"Positive." I closed my eyes and quivered as his hands trekked down my stomach, my navel, and then slithered between my mute lower lips. "Did he touch my shit?" he asked as he parted *his shit* and slowly rubbed my clit.

"No." I slowly opened my legs to allow him easier access.

He kissed me. "You sure he didn't rub on my shit?"

I was breathing like an unprepared marathon runner. "If he did, I would still be there."

He rubbed me hard and his finger dipped into me, but slid back out. "Is that right?" My comment made him angry. "You're with me. So, what does that mean?"

"Oh, oh, oh," I trembled and moaned.

"What does it mean, baby?" he asked.

"Shh," I said without opening my eyes. He wasn't going to make me read too much into this.

"Have you thought about me?"

"Shh," I shushed him again. "Not now."

My silencing him turned the beauty into a beast. He quickly spun me around and positioned himself behind me, pressing my breasts against the shower door. "Have you thought about me?" he asked again as he inserted his finger.

"No," I lied with a smile.

"Liar." He grinded what he knew I thought of often against me. "Do you miss this dick?"

"No." My mouth said one thing, but the circular rotation of my lower body said another. "I can get that anywhere."

He laughed. "You think so?"

"Yep."

"Yeah, but you can get damn good dick from me." He propped my legs open, one on the railing of the tub, and rubbed what he thought I couldn't find elsewhere up against my glossy lower lips. As he applied a condom, he spoke. "If you could get this somewhere else, then you'd still be with him."

From the back, he guided and positioned himself, then slid into me. My inner walls were like his Memory Foam mattress; his throbbing thickness fell right back into all the nooks and crannies that he once knew. The shape of things would always be configured to him.

"Until you find better, this pussy is still mine." He smacked me on my bottom. "You hear me?"

"Yes." Talk about being submissive. I'd pick cotton and call him Massa right now if he asked me to. "Yes, yes, oh shit, yes." He took me higher than marijuana ever did.

"This pussy will always be mine." The wet clapping noise that our bodies made had a rhythm that was too complex for even Jay-Z to rap to. "When was the last time?" he asked.

I wanted to make up something, but I knew that telling him the truth would make the sex even better, if possible. "You."

"Me?"

"Yes," I groaned as my eyes squeezed tighter to accept his forceful hardness. "Oh, oh, yes . . . you."

"Been saving it for me?" He put both his hands under my arms and folded them back toward him, harnessing me like a rollercoaster safety guard . . . and oh, yes, I was in for a bumpy ride.

"That's right. You keep this pussy nice and tight for me." He squeezed me and ran into me with the power and wildness of a runaway train. "This is still my motherfuckin' pussy." I was his passenger, and without a seatbelt, my conductor had me wailing, screaming, and crying out for more, more, and more until our journey was complete. He placed my internally bruised body between the sheets of my bed and lay beside me.

When the sun came up and the DSS was officially done, I retreated to the same torture I put myself through each time. "Damn," I said under my breath. I was full of regret as I moved Craig's hand from my side and looked into his sleeping face. "Why?" He was the giver of diseases, lover of many, more than likely somebody's man . . . and no longer mine.

~Situation #4~

Theo

"Damn, man. Did you fart?" Before Will could answer, I let the windows down in the car.

"Sorry, dawg," Will laughed. "I thought it was going to be a mystery one."

I covered my nose. "Damn, man!" It smelled like two gorillas shit in the trunk. "Are you sick or something?" We were on our way to West Dade for the first dance of the school year.

"I'm not sick, just a little nervous."

"Nervous about what, shitting up yourself?" I joked.

Will brushed me off. "I'm nervous about dancing with Myron's sister."

"Jessica?" I asked in shock.

He took a deep breath. "Yeah, Jessica."

I frowned. "Are you for real?" I looked at him like he had just said that he wanted to dance with a dude.

"Yeah," he answered anxiously. "Why?"

"Why?" I chuckled. "She looks just like Myron."

"Don't hate." He rubbed his palms together. "She's cute, cool, and down for whateva."

"Whateva?" I couldn't help it. "She looks like whateva."

Will was proud. "Don't hate, congratulate."

"Hate?" I looked over at him. "Never that, playboy, never over her."

"Keep it real." Will was serious. "I heard you tried talking to her before."

"Yeah, in third grade," I said.

"All I know is that you better not try that shit tonight." Will checked himself out in the pull-down mirror.

"That was third grade, dickhead." I laughed. "Everybody was cute in third grade."

"Well, I better not see you talking to her," he said. "You're known for that."

"I can't talk to her," I continued. "'cause Chewbacca don't speak English."

He laughed, but stopped quickly when he realized who the joke was on. "Ah, man, that was foul."

"That was a three-pointer right there, baby." I pretended to be shooting a ball. "Nuthin' but net."

"So, who are you after tonight?"

It didn't take me long to figure it out. "A chick in one of my classes."

"Who?"

I took a deep breath. "Angela Porter."

"*The cheerleader* Angela Porter?"

"Yep," I said with the confidence of a warrior.

Will, as pessimistic as a fallen soldier, said, "Man, you can't get her."

Those were fighting words. "What?"

"You *can't* get her," he reiterated and stressed his negativity.

Since we met, I'd been trying to school Will on the game. Pursuing a woman was just like playing basketball, which was why I could have a different one every day. However, Will sucked at basketball. Therefore, he spent a lot of time home alone on the Internet, sending instant messages to strangers.

"It's just like B-ball. You have to want it, feel it, taste it, and then conquer it. First of all, practice makes perfect or damn irresistibly close to excellence." I told him that he could practice anywhere. "Turn the sidewalk into a battle-field, smile, compliment, and be polite, but quick on your feet. Third, even when you're not playing the game or sitting on the bench, you still have to look like a player. Fourth, get your name out there. Be known for something, even if it's something bad. Women like well-known men. Finally, when it's game time, focus on winning, and be the last man stand-ing, because he's the only man that matters.

"Angela is the ball and I'm the player. I'm in control . . . She'll move at my command."

"I don't even know what all of the fuss is about her." He was less than enthusiastic. "She's *all right.*"

"All right?" I turned into the already crowded school parking lot. "Man, Angela Porter is the fuckin' bomb."

"She's just another popular girl, which isn't my cup of tea."

"Why, because she doesn't have AOL?" I joked.

"No," he said. "Because she's in my homeroom and so is her man."

"Her man?"

"Yeah."

"Who is her man?"

"Johnny Taft."

"White Boy Johnny?"

"White Boy Johnny is tappin' that big, brown ass."

"What the—?" I was disappointed. "Damn."

"So who is Plan B?" he asked.

I parked the car. "I don't have one."

Will teased. "Well, you could always dance with your baby momma." He never knew how to be serious.

"Fuck you, Will." It had been two weeks since I learned Trese's news. She and I spoke shortly a few times, but never got into any real baby talk. She informed me that her decision was to keep the kid, and to keep her mother from calling mine, I promised to help her in any way that I could. I didn't know when or how I would ever tell my mother; I just didn't want Trese's ghetto-ass mother to do it for me.

"That's serious shit. That's why I don't tell you anything."

"Whateva." He waved me off. "Jessica is serious to me, and you were talking all that shit. You can't get mad now."

"This is different, though," I argued.

"Anyway," he said, "is ya baby momma gonna be here or not?"

"Fuck you, man." I knew that it was all in good fun, but Will was getting under my skin. "I hope the hell not."

"I don't know about Trese, but Angie will be here. I heard her talking about it in class, but she's coming with Johnnie." He continued, "What class do you have Angie in anyway?"

"Ms. Patrick's." Her name brought a smile to my face and a warm feeling to every limb attached to me. Since school started a month ago, I'd had detention with her six times. I wasn't complaining because it didn't feel like I was locked up or being punished. It wasn't just me, though. I could see it written all over her face that Ms. Patrick enjoyed my hour-long stay just as much as I did.

At first I thought nothing of her abandoning her desk to sit in a chair next to me, our lengthy conversations, and her flirtatious body language, but one day when another student had to stay, she flipped the script. She sat behind her desk, never cracked a smile, assigned us work from the textbook, and after that, never said another word to either of us. At the end of our sixty minutes, I was still gathering my books when the other guy turned in his work and left. As soon as the door slammed, she sighed and smiled at me.

"Don't smile at me now. You had a brotha feeling like he was in Alcatraz two minutes ago," I joked.

"If people see you getting special privileges, they'll expect the same thing."

"Yeah, but *book*work?" I complained.

"Bookwork never killed anyone." I watched the sides of her mouth turn upward.

"Well, I'll never be late again."

"Good. I was beginning to think that you do it on purpose." She was kidding, but she didn't know how right she was.

"Well, after this, I think I'll stop the supposed purpose tardiness." I laughed.

"Come on, Theo." She stood up and pressed out her skirt. "Everybody can't know that you're the teacher's pet."

"When did I become your pet?" I didn't need to ask. It all happened the morning we ran into each other at Dunkin' Donuts and I heard her order a large mocha cappuccino. The next day, I took the liberty of ordering one for her, which meant I couldn't afford what I originally went there for. Still, it was well worth it just to see how much she appreciated my effort and also to smell her freshly applied perfume before it was broken down by the terrible odor of the school by sixth period. So, at least two mornings a week I visited her classroom to deliver her mocha fix.

"You became the teacher's pet when you became my favorite student." She was still standing behind her desk.

"Your favorite student?" I laughed in my uncomfortable chair. "If I'm your favorite, then how come I get C's on almost everything?"

"I said that you're my *favorite,* not my best student."

"Okay, you have a point," I agreed. "Well, define the word *favorite.*"

She thought for a while then started walking toward me. "Something that is liked or preferred over others."

"So, I guess you're my favorite teacher."

"You guess?" she asked.

"Yeah, on days when you don't assign homework."

She asked, "What is your definition of the word *favorite*?"

"Something that is desired." I challenged her stare and watched her go from friendly to unsure if she should be having such a conversation with me.

"Desired?" She stopped dead in her tracks.

"Yeah, desired." I stood up and grabbed my bag. "It's basically the same thing that you just said. When you like something or prefer something, it is to desire it."

"Okay," she spoke slowly, "but I don't think *desire* is the appropriate word."

"Does it frighten you?"

"No." She looked away from me.

"Did I offend you?"

It almost looked like she was flattered. "No."

"So, why isn't it appropriate then?" I wanted to know.

"Well, desire is just a very strong word to use to describe . . . what . . ." She couldn't find the right words.

I whispered, "Is there something wrong with that?"

"No," she answered quickly and fumbled over her words. "No, I'm glad, I'm happy that I'm . . ." She paused. "Happy to be considered your favorite . . ."

"So, you feel the same way?" I interrupted her.

"What way?"

"Nothing." I tried to remain upbeat and continued to smile through what I felt was rejection. Maybe it was her age that made me feel more like a man than like her eighteen-year-old high school student. "Don't worry about it."

She was flustered. "I just don't know if our meanings are the same."

"I think they are," I said.

"Desire is in a whole different realm." She tried to correct me. "What I meant is to desire me would mean something outside of me being your teacher." The classroom fell awkwardly silent.

"I do." I did think of her outside of school, and it wasn't always an image of her in front of a chalkboard or with a book in her hand.

"Huh?" She had no facial expression.

I reconfirmed what I had just said. "I think about you." I knew the difference between a woman being friendly and a woman flirting with me. "So, you've never thought of me outside of this classroom?"

"Of course." I was happy with her response until she kept talking. "I have to check your papers, don't I?"

Damn, that was a blow, but I wasn't giving up. "So, when do you want me here again?" I started for the door.

"Excuse me!"

"Don't act like that," I joked. "You know your days aren't complete if we don't have our little gatherings."

"You *really* think that I don't have anything better to do with my time?"

"Yeah." I turned back toward her. "It doesn't get any better than me."

She looked me up and down slowly with a smile. "Somehow I believe that."

Though they were uttered quickly, softly, and were encoded, her words offered hope. I felt like something was accomplished and established between us. And as though she thought that I might have some doubt about what she meant, the next day when she passed back our essays, on the second page of my paper was a fuchsia Post-It note that read:

Desire is a window.

That was a week ago. I'd voluntarily detained myself a few times since then. Coach Johnson was so upset about me being late to practices that he wanted to have a talk with her to lighten up on me, but what he didn't know was that it was me who needed to ease up on her.

Because of the dance, there was no basketball practice today, but I was still purposely late to class. However, another student strolled in two minutes after me, which meant that he'd have to stay too. He fucked up my plan. So, when the bell rang, I raced home, took a shower, and hung out at Will's house until it was time to leave. I was excited about the dance. I needed something or someone to get my mind out of a place it never should've ventured to.

When I opened the door to the dark and crowded gymnasium, the music poured into me like Coca-Cola. While Jamie Foxx and Twista told me what I needed to get things up and popping, I checked out the scenery . . . tight jeans, mini skirts, one-arm shirts, tops with no sleeves.

"Looks like this will be worth the five dollars." I smiled at Will, who was already tiptoeing and panning the room for Jessica.

"Yo, I see her. Let me go holla real quick."

I waited against the wall for almost thirty minutes, and Will didn't come back *real quick*. He never came back.

I turned down a few girls who wanted to dance and promised them that I wasn't shooting them down. I put it off on being hurt during practice. Of course I wanted to put my hands on some booty and get a quick squeeze before one of the chaperones noticed. However, when you're as tall as I am, you've got to know how to move because all eyes will be on you. I could get away with slow songs or the cha-cha or electric slide, but until Usher taught me a few moves, I wouldn't even pretend that I was an expert at anything other than basketball.

The DJ had to be old because right after that new song by Missy Elliot, he mixed in "My Prerogative" by Bobby Brown. Everyone on the floor stood still and looked at each other like, "What the—?" If my mom was there she'd be jamming, but this wasn't a party for the class of nineteen eighty-nuthin'.

"Hell Naw, turn that eight track off," the guy standing next to me yelled.

I spotted a feminine silhouette across the gym, rocking to Mr. Whitney Houston's song like it was a brand new cut. She was standing alone in the darkness on the side of the bleachers and probably had no clue that anyone could see her, but Ms. Patrick had all of my attention. Suddenly, I wanted the song to play all night.

The DJ must've seen her moving, too, because he followed up with Big Boi's "I Like the Way," and he was right. I liked the way she moved. I was a big fan of the way she swung her hips with her hands in the air, until Mr. Bess walked over and started rocking with her. She stopped and stepped away from him. He took a step toward her and reached for her hand. She responded by putting a finger in his face. She said something to him then stepped back more, fading into an even darker shadow.

I was uncomfortable when he followed her into the dimness, and I made my way to the other side of the gym. I couldn't understand if I just wanted a closer look or if I wanted to do something about it, but before I could decide, she called out my name.

"Theo."

I threw a surprised glance in her direction then pretended to veer from my beaten path and strolled over. Mr. Bess seemed irritated and stepped back.

"Hey, Ms. Patrick."

She smiled at me. "What happened to you staying for detention today?"

"Oops." I knew that I was supposed to stay, but because we would've had company, I left. "I'm sorry. I was so caught up on getting back here for the dance, it slipped my mind."

"Slipped your mind?" she said. "Well, don't let it slip your mind on Monday."

"I'll be there," I said and then stood like a post between

the two of them. I could tell that she didn't want me to go. Three minutes into the silence, he approached her from the other side, thinking that the music would mask what he had to say, but I heard every word.

"Can I call you tonight?" he said.

"There is absolutely no reason for that," she said.

"I want to explain."

"No need."

He tried to explain anyway. "Everything wasn't like it seemed."

"Oh," she giggled angrily, "everything was just as it seemed."

"Just give me another—"

"I'm not giving you shit," she interrupted in a whisper. "Get the hell away from me."

"Fine." He paused a few seconds. "Have it your damn way."

She murmured. "Fuck you, Doran."

When he walked off, I was tempted to say something, ask a question, or just burst out laughing, but she was a grown-ass woman and I didn't want her cussing me out like she did him. I just continued to stand by her and bounced to the beat.

She sighed. "So, why aren't you out there shaking your stuff?"

"You want the truth?"

"I would hope that that's all you'd give me."

"I really can't dance." I was a little embarrassed.

She grinned. "You mean Mr. Basketball only has moves on the court?"

"I have moves off of the court, but they're just not on the dance floor." I couldn't tell her exactly where I did my best work. "Plus, I was busy watching you."

She blushed. "What?"

I bit my bottom lip. "I saw you over here breaking it down, until your boyfriend came over."

She rolled her eyes and grimaced. "Please."

"Please," I said. "Y'all were cool the other day."

"A lot has happened since the other day."

"Word?" I teased. "So he ain't your boy anymore?"

She laughed. "Never was."

"C'mon, the other day y'all were planning a date. What happened with that?"

She looked me square in the face. "Mind your business."

"Aw, don't tell me that the man don't have no game," I joked. "You want me to teach him some of my stuff?"

She laughed. "Your stuff?"

"That's right."

"And what makes you so sure of your stuff?" she asked.

"It makes you smile."

She smiled. "Maybe you have a *little* something."

"It may be more than you can handle."

After my comment, she took a deep breath. "So, what did I look like dancing?" She continued, "Was I not moving fast enough for you hiphopsters?"

"No, not at all." I came at her with both of my guns blazing. "Fast isn't always better."

She was surprised. "You're right."

"You looked very sexy." I sang, "I like the way you move, ta dan da." By the time I realized that I was talking to my teacher, I opened my mouth to apologize, but she was blushing again. Women don't blush when they're offended.

"Thank you." She continued with a statement that shocked me. "Had I realized that I had you for an audience, I might've done something more interesting."

"Well, it's not too late."

Instead of busting a move, she cleared her throat, looked in the direction of the crowd, and changed the subject. "I wasn't supposed to be here, but Mrs. Bailey asked me to monitor at the last minute."

She was stunning; her smile, her hair, be it a weave or natural, was long, trimmed, flowing, and sexy. The hem of her skirt was hitting her knees while the top part clung to her butt.

"Are you at least having fun?" I asked.

"Not as much as you've probably been having."

"I got here about forty-five minutes ago. I'm still trying to get into the swing of things."

"I'm sure it won't take you too long. You're *the* guy to be around these parts."

"I don't know about that."

"Are you here alone?" she asked.

I joked. "Is that your way of asking me to dance?"

Her eyes widened and shifted like a shy girl. "No, I was just asking if your girlfriend was here."

"Girlfriend?" The look I gave her was similar to the look one might receive after saying something bad about my mother. "Who said that I had one of those?"

"Well, you are Mr. Basketball."

"Please don't call me that." I hated when the school news referred to me as Mr. Basketball, Boy Wonder, or Basketballito.

"Isn't that what most people call you?"

"Yeah, but they're all in my outer circle. They're people that I don't care what they call me." I moved closer to her. "I like for people that I'm intimate with—"

"Intimate?" She shot me a look.

"Intimate, as in part of in my inner circle. I like for those people to call me Theo, and if memory serves me correctly, I asked you to call me that once before."

"Excuse me," she said. "Is this an invitation to your inner circle?"

"No." I wasn't shy. "This is an open invitation to be intimate with me."

"Well, *Theo*," she stressed my name, "is your girlfriend here tonight?"

"I just told you that I don't have a girlfriend."

"Yeah, right." She blew my answer off. "I've seen you in the halls with that one chick a whole lot."

"Have you been watching me?"

My boldness caught her off guard. "You're a trip." She giggled.

"Why, because it's the truth?"

She looked at me like I had gone mad. "Why in God's name would I be watching *you*?" She laughed hysterically.

"Because desire is a window," I reminded her of her words and then added, "and you like the view."

She laughed. "Desire is a window and I'm closing the blinds."

I was sick of getting mixed messages from her. "Are you playing a damn game with me?" I asked in an angry whisper.

"What?" My question stunned her.

"Sometimes you give off vibes like we're cool, and then the next minute you're dissin' me."

"You're my favorite student. You know that," she patronized me.

"I'm not talkin' about that." I moved a little closer to her. "You know what I'm talkin' about."

Her eyebrows flew up, just like I wanted them to. She didn't know what to say, but Alicia Keys went and said what was on my mind. *Baby, baby, baby, from the day I saw you, I really wanted to catch your eye. There's something special 'bout you . . ."*

"Oh yeah." Her fingers started snapping and her eyes closed like she would dance by herself. "I love this song."

"Is that your way of asking me to dance?"

She smiled. "I can't dance with you."

"Why, because I'm not Mr. Bess?"

"No, because you're Theo Lakewood, who just so happens to be my student." She smiled. "Plus, you said that you don't know how to dance."

"I don't dance to the fast stuff." I stepped so close to her that her breasts raked across my lower arm when she turned my way. "When it comes to taking my time, doing things slow, and doing them right, I'm your man." She was speechless. I offered her my hand and was shocked when her fingertips touched mine. "Would you like to dance?" I asked her.

She grinned and took a deep breath. "Yes."

"Cool."

I made a step toward the crowded dance floor with her in tow, but after just two steps she pulled me back. "I can't go out there," she said.

"Why not?"

"I'm supposed to be a chaperone, not your dance partner." She looked down and tried to slide her trembling hand out of mine, but I didn't let go. "The other teachers would have a fit."

"Why are you teasing me?" I asked.

"I'm not." She looked up to me with sincerity. "I really wish that I could."

"How bad?" I asked.

She replied timidly. "Real bad."

"All right, come on." I tightened my grasp on her hand and led her toward the wall and then underneath the electric bleachers.

"What are you doing?" she asked.

"Getting out of sight." It was the perfect hiding place; we were all alone. "Let's see if you're a woman of your word."

"What do you mean?" she asked as I pulled her deeper into the darkness and then finally toward me.

"You know what I mean." I could only see traces of her face. "Dance with me." I didn't have to say it twice. For the first time, she didn't question what I had to say. She obeyed me, her arms wrapped around me, and her head fell to my chest like we had been down this road before. My fingers slid down her back and then up again. I squeezed her gently a few times in order for me to believe that I was actually holding her like I was.

Even if she had never hinted at being interested, I would've known the truth because her body told me. She melted into me like she was waiting on the chance to be close to me. For that moment, we met one another's needs. She was like nothing or no one that I had ever touched. I softly ran my hands through her hair. She gave off a fragrance so sweet that I wanted to taste her. She was warm, smooth, and though almost undetectable, she was trembling. She could never convince me that she felt nothing.

Just when I thought things couldn't get better, they didn't. Everything was everything until the DJ fucked it up by playing Avant. *I know you wanna rub. I know you wanna touch. I know you wanna feel.* The words were blatantly what we both felt and it scared her. She became cautious of the impression that she was giving me, and she let go of my hand.

"Thanks for dancing," she said.

"Whoa, where are you going?" I asked. "We're not done."

"I need to get back to my post before one of the other teachers comes looking for me."

"C'mon, just one more song?" I tried to convince her.

"I really can't." She firmed up. "See you on Monday." She walked toward the opening and didn't look back.

I stood in the darkness for a few minutes trying to figure out whether I made a move on her or a fool out of myself. When I emerged from the bleachers, she wasn't there and I was glad. I walked across the gym.

"Dance with me?" I heard someone ask from behind. I spun around and saw Trese. "It's the least you can do." Trese was looking scrumptious in a low-cut shirt and tight jeans.

"Sure." I was bent on keeping her happy to avoid her threatening to tell my mother again.

"Thanks." She stepped closer.

A slow song was playing, and when I reached down toward her waist, my hands kept going until they were squeezing her ass. "Damn," I said to myself. I had been missing certain things about her, all sexual, and judging by the look she was giving me, she was thinking the same thing.

"It's Friday, right?" Trese asked.

"Yeah."

"Isn't your mom working late?" She wasn't wasting any time.

"Yep."

"Can I come over?" She ground her pelvis lustfully into me.

Over the past three days, I concocted a plan that would either rid me of Trese totally or leave me stuck with her forever. My scheme was fresh on my mind, but our body movements were making it hard to follow through.

"Come over for what?"

"For this . . ." Right there on the crowded dance floor, Trese moved her hands down my chest, unzipped my pants, fumbled into my boxers, and began stroking me. "I want this."

I felt myself expanding with every stroke of her tiny, warm hand. The harder I got, the less dancing I could do. Before long, I was standing still with my eyes closed, biting my top lip. "Shit," I mumbled, and by the end of the song, I was searching the crowd to tell Will that I was leaving. However, I learned from other friends that he left with Jessica and had been looking for me before he left.

I grabbed Trese by the hand and had one thing, a blowjob,

on my mind while walking through the parking lot; at least
until I spotted Coach Johnson leaning against his truck, and
talking to who? Ms. Patrick. I yanked my hand from Trese's
and pretended that I had to scratch my head. It looked like
Coach was laying the shit on thick because she was all smiles.

"Fuck," I murmured when I realized that we would have
to walk right by them.

"What?"

"Nothing," I said.

"What?" Trese asked again.

"Nothing, I just didn't want Coach to see me," I lied.

"Why, because you're with me?" She was getting an attitude. "Fuck him."

"Just be quiet. It has nothing to do with you."

"Whateva."

I stopped. "Don't start, Trese. This has nothing to do with
you."

"Then why did you let go of my hand?"

"No drama tonight, okay?" Getting Trese to my house
was vital. Though I didn't have things set up quite the way I
envisioned them, tonight had to be the night that I pulled this
off. "Do you wanna do this, yes or no?" I gave her a choice.
She looked away. "Yes."

This wasn't a big production, just a circus act. In other
words, this was nothing serious. "This doesn't mean that
something has changed between us or that anything ever will
change."

"Whateva, Theo. Let's just go." We started walking again.

As we approached them, both Ms. Patrick and Coach
Johnson looked our way. She stared at Trese awhile before
looking my way. Her eyes said *What a fuckin' liar*, and as I
looked at her smiling with her ex-husband, my eyes said *You
muthafuckin' fake.*

Coach laughed heavily. "All right now, make sure that you
take her straight home," he teased.

"Of course." I swerved a little and slapped palms with him. "Have a good night."

He laughed. "You too."

"Good night, Ms. Patrick," I said.

The grin was wiped clean from her face. "Good night, Mr. Basketball," she said sarcastically. "I'm sure that you get busy on the weekends. Just try not to forget your homework."

"Never that." I looked at her and then back at her ex-husband. "You two have a good evening."

Trese and I were at least twenty feet away when I heard Ms. Patrick call my name. I turned around and she was already walking toward me. I handed Trese the keys. "Go ahead to the car. Let me see what she wants."

We met halfway. "Thanks again for the dance."

"Anytime." I winked and waited for her to blush.

"Anytime?"

"Yeah," I sighed. "The way you left, I thought that I had done something wrong."

"No." She pulled a few strands of hair out of her face. "When you do something wrong, I'll be the first to let you know it." She looked away. "I was just getting a bit too wrapped up in the whole thing. I felt like *I* was doing something wrong."

"When you do something wrong, I'll be the first to tell you not to stop," I said and we both laughed.

"Well," she looked in Trese's direction, "I hope that she didn't mind our little tango."

"She didn't." I giggled.

"I see you with her a lot." She tried to mask her jealousy. "Who is she?"

"Trese," I said.

"Not her name." She juggled her words. "I meant who is she to you?"

"Yesterday's news," I said.

"Really?" She searched my eyes for the truth. "Seems like today's top story to me."

"Naw," I lied, "she asked for a ride home."

"I see."

I changed the subject to what really mattered. "I hope that Coach isn't extra hard on me in practice now after dancing with *his* girl."

She waved it off. "Oh, please, I'm nobody's girl."

"That can be changed," I had the balls enough to say.

She was floored, and struggled with what to say next. "I have extra homework for you." Her eyes wandered from mine. "There is a word that I want you to add to your vocabulary list."

"What word?"

"*Intrigue*." She blushed.

"Okay," I teased. "I think I need you to use it in a sentence."

"Let's see." Her light brown eyes shifted nervously. "I am intrigued by you."

My face lit up. "*Intrigue* just became my favorite word."

"Good." She blushed again. "Then I expect that you will be able to use it in a sentence by Monday." She turned and walked away.

As I watched her walk away, I tried to decipher if she had just given me education or flirtation. Either way, I wanted more. Once in the car, I heard nothing that Trese was complaining about.

"Why are you going here?" she asked, pointing at the drugstore.

"To get something."

She rolled her eyes. "I'm already pregnant, so why do you need to wear a condom?"

"So that we don't have twins," I joked. "Wait here. I'll be right back."

She pulled me by the shirt as I reached for the handle. "I wanna feel you, though."

I thought of the size of my "pal" and knew that there was no way around feeling it. "Like I've said before, you'll never not feel me, and you know it."

"The damage is already done, so we should take advantage of it while we can."

I pretended to think about it. "Naw." I shook my head and opened the car door. "I'll be right back."

In the store, it took me all of five minutes to find what I needed, pay for it, stick it into my pocket, and run back to the car, where I found Trese pouting. I ignored her until we were at my house. Kevin was spending the night at his friend's, so the house was officially all mine until 3 A.M. I had four free hours, but wanted Trese gone in thirty minutes or less.

"Why are you looking so sad?" I asked as I turned the light on in my room and removed my shirt.

"'cause," she sat on the bed, "you act like I have AIDS or gonorrhea or something."

"Trese, we've talked about this before." I tried not to sound frustrated. "How do you know that I don't have something?"

She rolled her eyes. "Whateva."

"I'm serious," I said. "I'm not trying to give you anything, and I damn sure don't want anything from you."

"You've already given me something." She rubbed her flat stomach. "This is the best thing you could ever give me."

As much as I wanted to protest, I couldn't let her see me sweat. I needed her to think that I was on her side. "Yeah." I reached down and rubbed her belly. It felt the same way it felt after we ate McDonalds or while I was fucking her doggie style and reached under her. "Let's do this," I said as I removed her top. "I've missed you."

"Really?"

It was all an act. "Yeah."

She unsnapped her bra. When her perky brown nipples were exposed, my boy was at attention. My fantasy was always to slide between those mounds, but she was always too horny to do *just* that. "There go my girls." I reached for her chest and brought my mouth down to service them. My tongue flicked over her nipples until they were as hard as I was below.

"Hmm," she whispered and tried to catch her breath. "I've missed you, too, Theo."

"Can I put my dick between them?"

"Yeah." She smiled. "But I want you to taste me first."

This was definitely not part of my plan. "Okay." When I took off her jeans and saw her thong buried between the lips of her fruit, I knew that it was going to be hard to get back on track.

As she was about to remove her underwear, I stopped her. There was something incredibly erotic about the royal blue silk material being stuck in the chocolate brown and baby pink folds of her flesh. I laid her back, gently parted her juicy lips with two fingers, and then gently hiked the thong upward. The material subsided, and out popped her clit. I kissed it then moved my tongue between the wetness just beneath it. I sucked and licked on her until the flavor was gone.

I'm not one of those young bucks that believe that eating pussy is shameful or nasty. I love it, and treat it like it's a delicacy. I never know if I'm going to eat it again, so I eat each one like it's my last. It's something about the warmth, the moisture, the clit stiffening, the way the woman grinds against my mouth, and the moans, groans, and sometimes screams that I evoke from her that send me on a natural high.

I imagine my tongue as a small penis. I tease her, fuck her, beat her, and control her with it. As a matter of fact, sometimes I come while in the process. It never deters me, though. By the time the chick is ready to ride, the horsy is back in the saddle again. And once I drop the big boy on her, I can guarantee that I can have it pretty much any time my little heart desires it.

When I was through with Trese, I disrobed and mounted her. She held her breasts together as I pushed my way through and landed in her mouth. Back and forth through her breasts and in and out of her mouth. After ten minutes, I couldn't hold out any longer. It felt like a warm cotton swab traveling from my shaft to the tip and *WHAM*! Trese was having herself a warm milk facial.

"Ugh!" she screamed. "Why didn't you tell me?"

"Sorry." I was, but it played into the plan. "I couldn't help it."

"Get up." She spoke with her eyes squeezed shut. "Get up off of me."

Everything was coming together. "Come on, I'll lead you to the bathroom." I grabbed her hand then the bag from my jeans pocket, and led her down the hall. When she was in front of the toilet, I sat her down.

"Hurry up, Theo. I don't want this stuff in my eyes."

Without turning on the lights, I got a towel and turned the water on full blast so that she wouldn't hear the rustling of the bag. I removed the item from the box and its wrapper then handed her the towel. "Here you go."

"Thanks." She took it, and as she wiped her face, I knelt down before her and kissed her with one hand behind my back. "Do you have to pee?"

"What?" My question threw her. "Why?"

"Because I have to," I lied. "So if you need to, you have to hurry."

Before she could say a word, I heard the sweet sound of urine hitting the toilet water and moved into action. My hand raced from behind me to under her. Her warm liquid was falling right were I needed it to.

"What are you doing?" She giggled. "You must've seen the R. Kelly tape."

"Yeah." I faked a laugh.

"Crazy ass."

When I had what I needed, I pulled my hand from under her, stood up, and turned on the light. "In a few minutes we'll see who's crazy." I held the pregnancy test out toward her, and when she grabbed for it, I already knew the answer. I ran down the hall into my room and locked the door.

"Open the door," Trese yelled.

I joked. "The box said to let it sit for three minutes, so gimme two and a half more minutes."

She yelled, "Open the fuckin' door!"

"Wait."

"Just give me my clothes. I wanna go."

"Oh, now you wanna go?" I said. "Two minutes won't kill you."

"Whateva, Theo," she screamed. "You make me sick."

I took my time getting dressed, and six minutes later, the pregnancy test proved that the baby Trese wanted me to father existed only in her imagination.

~Situation #3~

Paige

"So, you've finally decided to return my call, huh?" Toni said into the receiver before even saying hello to me.

"I'm sorry, girl. Things got a little hectic for me this weekend."

Toni whined, "I left you three messages."

I corrected her. "You left me one message."

"Well, I called three times." She didn't give me time to explain. "I could've been dying."

"Dying?" I laughed. "I heard your message. You wanted to know if I had your red shirt. That's far from dying."

"Whatever." She giggled. "Do you?"

"Do I what?"

"Have the shirt."

"No." I really wasn't sure. "I thought I gave it back to you."

"Well, I can't find it." She changed the subject. "Anyway, what was so hectic about your weekend?"

I glanced around the teachers' lounge to be certain that no one could hear me, but Mrs. Fernandez, the home economics teacher, was a few feet away, thumbing through a magazine. "We'll talk about that another time."

Toni was excited. "Is it about Doran?" She couldn't wait.

I mocked my mother. "The gay?" I grimaced. "There will never be another story about him."

"Is it Craig again?" she asked in disappointment.

"That was so two weeks ago, and that's a done deal."

"Yeah." She sighed. "That's what you say two weeks after each time you sleep with him."

I rolled my eyes. "Well, this is the time that counts," I assured her.

"So, whom are you talking about then?"

"Who said that I was talking about someone?" Let's be real. A thirty-two- year-old woman has no business, none, flirting with an eighteen-year-old to begin with, so there was no way to explain whom I was talking about, what did or didn't happen, or even what I felt or didn't feel. I wasn't sharing this borderline embarrassing revelation with a soul. It was hard for me to believe much less ask for advice about having a crush on one of my students.

My intentions were never to lose sleep thinking about Theo. However, all weekend long he fed into my brain like a blood vessel. He wasn't someone that I aimed at pursuing. I surprised myself by dancing with him, touching him, and talking to him like I did, and after each time, I promised myself never to do it again, but the sight of him always brought thoughts that couldn't be doused by anything except more of him. Even though he approached me like a man ten years his senior, that would still make him four years younger than I was. I was going to hell.

Theo's interest in me heightened my curiosity about who he was, and I acted like it. Whenever we were alone, Theo worked hard to turn the fourteen years between us into a bridge. He'd cross it and take me back over to the other side where I felt eighteen again. However, as soon as I was alone, I'd realized that I wasn't Demi Moore and he wasn't Ashton Kutcher. Shit, Ashton is twenty-six . . . and rich.

I was fourteen years old when Theo was born. He was drinking milk from his mother's breast, and I had been seeing my period for over three years. I could be his mother. When he was in his "terrible twos," I was planning for the senior prom. Theo had naptime in kindergarten while I crammed for final exams in college. Despite all I'd done to not see him as a man, my conclusion was that he was the mold every other man should've been cut from.

"Hello?" Toni said. "You there?"

"Sorry, I was looking over a memo," I lied. "What did you say?"

"I was asking what was so damn great about your weekend."

"I didn't say anything about having a great weekend." I reiterated, "I said that it was hectic." I never hid anything from Toni, but this Theo thing wasn't anything to share. She would just assume that I reached a new height of desperation if I allowed an eighteen-year-old to infiltrate my mind.

"What did you do?" she asked.

"Nothing."

"You're confusing me."

"What?" I was sorry that I called her right before I would be seeing Theo. I couldn't get my mind right. "All I did was clean. That's what made it so hectic," I said. "I finally got around to getting rid of that stuff in the garage." I was mad at myself. "That's it. That's what made it so hectic."

"Ah shit." She sounded disappointed. "I thought you were really about to tell me something."

"You're the one gettin' it on the regular." I laughed. "You have a husband. Tell me something." Right then, the class bell rang and scared a tiny bit of the devil out of me. "Oh well, there's the bell. You'll have to tell me later."

"Nothing to tell. Marcus is out of town," she joked. "Unless you want to hear about my threesome with Mr. Duracell and Ms. Energizer."

"I'd rather not." I frowned. "Talk to you later."

"Bye," Toni said as she laughed and hung up.

Within five minutes, I'd be seeing Theo for the first time since saying good-bye to him in the parking lot on Friday after the school dance. I gathered my things with anxiety and fear, not knowing what to expect, what to say, or even what to teach. I apprehensively left the lounge.

I sauntered into my classroom a full minute before the bell and was shocked to see Theo already in his seat. I nervously avoided looking his way and nearly screamed at the sight of the single long-stemmed rose lying on my desk. I controlled my facial expressions as I opened the card atop it. It read: Intrigued by its beauty, smell, and elegance, I wanted it to belong to me. The word *intrigued* was underlined. It was the sentence that I had asked him for. Like it didn't faze me, I threw the card down, turned to the chalkboard, and scribbled the day's assignment, a pop quiz. "Aw, man." I heard the students grumbling behind me.

"Good day," I said with a smile in response to their displeasure.

"Ms. Patrick, is the grade for the quiz going to count?" a student asked.

"Every grade counts," I said as the moans and groans continued to make their way around the classroom.

"We need an incentive for doing good," Angie mumbled.

"I think an A is a great incentive," I said.

Richard Jenkins spoke. "How about if as a class we average a C or better on the quiz we get to have a party?"

I thought about it. "Okay," I agreed. "A pizza party never hurts."

"Naw, we want a pool party at your crib."

"What?"

"Yeah." The idea caught on like wildfire through the classroom, just as the negativity had earlier. "Yeah, a pool party," a female voice said loudly.

"There's no way we can all leave school and go to my house."

"True," Richard continued, "but on the weekend we can."

I laughed. "You guys don't even know what the quiz is on, and if you all lose, then what do I get?"

Theo spoke up. "Every weekend we'll take turns washing your car."

"And you will be the first one, right?" I said, half joking.

"Nope. I plan on being the first one at the pool party." He laughed and was joined by his comrades.

"Okay," I said. "You guys have a deal."

The five-question quiz was based on the first act of *The Taming of the Shrew*. In ten minutes, I was done grading them, then stood before the class with an unbelievable announcement. "Pool party this Saturday at four." The students erupted in cheers. "Wait, wait a minute." I tried to quiet them. "In order to come, I need either a phone call from your parents or written letter of consent with a home phone number on it by Thursday." I wrote my cell phone number on the board. "Let's try to keep this between us. This isn't something that the school would recommend that I do."

"So, we know our Shakespeare, huh?" Richard asked.

"No, I just have nothing to do this weekend," I joked. "Turn to chapter three in your books. There is still work to be done."

When the bell rang, Theo seemed relieved. He sat in his seat, and when the last bookbag passed the threshold, he stared at me, making me melt.

"How did I do on my vocabulary quiz?" he asked.

"Huh?"

"I used *intrigued* in a sentence." He pointed at the rose. "How did I do?"

"You did good." I picked up the flower and smelled it. "Better than I expected."

He shifted in his seat. "You look very, very nice today," he commented and when I stood up, I felt his eyes on me like fingertips.

"Thank you." I blushed.

"You had me thinking over the weekend."

"Really?" I asked. "What about?"

"Us dancing, talking, just about us being together." He wasn't shy at all. "So, what thoughts of me did you have?"

"Who said that I had thoughts of you?" I tried to pretend that I had it all together.

"I thought we were past this bullshit."

"What?" I swung around and saw him standing from his seat. "Watch your language."

"Why?"

"Because this is my classroom."

"Fuck this classroom." He grabbed his things. "It's like you're playing games with me. I guess you think I'm just some stupid kid."

I locked the door to the class, not wanting anyone to just walk in. "What are you talking about?" I whispered, hoping that my tone would encourage him to lower his voice.

"One day you tell me that I intrigue you, then the next day you're all different."

"What did I do?" I asked.

"You won't keep it real. You won't be honest with me or yourself." He continued. "I asked you a simple question, and you act as though this whole thing exists only in my mind." Theo's voice got a little louder. "You've been on me just as much as I've been on you."

"Shh," I quieted him.

"No." He refused. "I know that you have some interest in me. You tell me that with your body, but then you open your mouth and change the whole story." Those eyes of his were ripping off my flesh. "Are you interested in me or not?"

"Theo, I just can't go around—"

"Just answer the question," he interrupted.

I hesitated. "Yes," I spoke softly. "Yes, I'll admit that there is some interest, but that doesn't make it right."

He said, "It doesn't make it wrong, either."

I tried to explain. "I know, but my intentions weren't—"

He interrupted me again. "What did you expect?"

"Not this!"

"So, you were just out to fuck with my head?"

"No." I should've stopped while I was ahead. "It was just all in fun."

"All in fun?" he asked. "After a month of us talking, laughing, you dancing with me on Friday, you stopped me in the parking lot to tell me that this is all in fun." He shook his head. "I guess that answers my question."

"What question?"

"Forget it." He had his books in his hand and tried walking by me to get to the door. I couldn't believe that this boy was handling me . . . a student . . . a man. I was pissed. I pulled him back by the arm.

"Just ask me the muthafuckin' question," I said and watched his eyes fill with shock hearing his English teacher use the very word others were scolded for. "Well, ask me."

He stared at me and then let out a heavy sigh. "Did you think of me this weekend?" With eyes I wouldn't lie to, power I couldn't fight, and lips I couldn't speak to, I simply moved my head up and down slowly. He smiled and took a deep breath as well as a step back, and rested his books on the closest desk to him.

"Did you enjoy it?" he asked. I just continued to shake my head up and down as his hands made their way around my waist like we were dancing again. He was curious. "What did you think about?"

"Everything." The word came out so softly that I didn't think he heard me. He lowered himself to meet me and pulled me into him so gently that I didn't know that I was moving until I was pressed up against him. Our lips moved toward each other, the warmth of his breath covered my upper lip, and then I heard the doorknob turn.

When the person on the other side realized that it was locked, they began knocking. They knocked us back to reality.

I smiled at him. "I have to get that."

"All right," he said and quickly sat at a desk and practiced looking like the poor detained student he was supposed to be.

I walked over to the door, opened it, and Craig stormed in. "All right now, enough is enough."

"What?" I was confused.

Craig pointed over at Theo. "What's going on here?"

"What are you talking about?"

"Are you trying to kill the season?" he asked me. "You keep him here several times a week just for being a few minutes late to your class. This has to stop." For the first time, I was glad that he was talking about basketball. "He's missing out on a lot of practice because of your rules."

"Rules are rules, Craig."

"Isn't there a way around this?"

"No, because what I do for him, I'll have to do for others."

"Then can't you just take the stick out of—"

I interrupted him. "I'm in charge here. This is not the basketball court. I'm his teacher, and I call the shots in this classroom."

Craig was frustrated. "We have our first game next week."

"Anytime he is late to my class, you can find him here. His detention time should never run into the first quarter, but if it does, then that's just too bad." As I spoke, I made my way over to my desk.

"This is about you and me, isn't it?"

"What?" My neck almost snapped out of place to look back at him. "What is that supposed to mean?"

"Is this about what happened the other—"

"Hold it." I stopped Craig in mid-sentence. "Theo, you're dismissed." He stood up, and it hurt me to watch him gather his things and leave without saying good-bye, but there were things I had to say to Craig. "What in the fuck do you mean does this have something to do with the other night?" I gave him no room to speak. "Don't get it twisted. This has nothing to do with you. This even has nothing to do with me. When Theo is late, then it has everything to do with him."

"Whatever, Paige," he said. "It seems like whenever I let you have some, you go to actin' like a fuckin' lunatic."

"Whenever you let me?" I was shocked. I felt my mouth dragging on the floor. "What the—?"

"What?" He laughed like he had just stumped me. Oh no . . . I was just getting started.

"Do you know the definition of the word *let?*" I walked back toward him. "To let is to allow, or to give permission to do something. Whenever I *let,* whenever I allow, whenever I give myself permission to fuck you, it's all about *me*. It's all about when I want it, where I want it, how I want it, and it's when I choose to *give* it to you." I was in his face. "Your dick calls no shots in my life, so it seems like whenever *I* let *you* get a li'l bit, you go to actin' like a muthafuckin' lunatic." Could you tell that I was mad? "If Theo is late to my class, that's his problem. If he misses practice, that's his problem, and if it somehow becomes your problem, then deal with it and don't bring your ass to my class." I opened the door. "Have a nice day." Once again, can you tell that I was mad?

"All I meant was—"

"Have a nice day, Coach Johnson."

* * *

I put all of the energy I wanted to use boxing, kicking, and strangling Craig into two hours at the gym. I stepped on that treadmill with the vengeance of twenty people, and nearly burned up the motor. It was just what I needed, to sweat, not think, and get my heart pumping.

I got home and ate leftover spaghetti and sipped on Remy Red as I ran my bath water. I poured so much peaches and cream bubble bath into the tub that if you closed your eyes, you might think you were at a Georgia peach stand. This pampering was required due to my elevated blood pressure from Craig's comments. "I can't believe that idiot."

I took a sip from my glass then strolled into the bathroom. "Just what the doctor ordered," I whispered to myself and looked around at the candlelit room. I had created the perfect setting, but as soon as my big toe hit the warm, peach-scented water, my cell phone was ringing. I grabbed it from the counter.

"Hello, Ms. Patrick?"

"Yes," I said to the unfamiliar male voice. "Whom am I speaking with?"

"Hi, this is Ian Porter. My daughter Angela is in your class."

"Oh, okay." I smiled, remembering him from open house. He was handsome, smart, smooth, and wore no wedding band. "How are you?"

"I can't complain." He was polite. "How are you?"

"I'm fine. Thank you for asking."

"Were you busy?" he asked.

"Not really, but hold a minute for me, please." I turned off the faucet, sat down in the tub, and took a deep breath. "Okay."

"Are you sure I didn't catch you at a bad time?" he asked.

"No, I was just running my bathwater." I felt the too-much-information sensation come over me.

"Aw." He continued. "You shouldn't have to do that."

"You're right," I paused, "but for right now I do."

"Well, let me know if you ever need any help."

Whoa! We both giggled at the same time. "I will." I blushed.

He cleared his throat. "I'm leaving town tomorrow on business, and Angie said that I needed to call you before Thursday regarding permission for her to attend a pool party this weekend."

"Yes."

"All right, she'll be there. She has my permission. I won't get back in town until Saturday morning." He added, "I'm sure she'll find a way there, but I'll pick her up that night."

"Oh, okay. Thank you for calling, and have a safe trip."

"Does she need to bring anything?"

"Just a beach towel and her appetite."

"Sounds good." He carried on. "I'll have an appetite too. Will you have anything there for me to eat?"

I smiled. "Sure, I'll save you a plate."

"Will you be on it?" he asked.

Was this a freakish dream? "Mr. Porter, I—"

"Ian," he interrupted. "Just call me Ian."

I wasn't blushing anymore. "Ian, it's not that type of party."

His bluntness was a turnoff. "Well, maybe we can have that type of party after the kids are gone?"

"I'll be pretty drained." I faked a giggle. "I'll see you on Saturday when you come for Angie."

"You sure will," he whispered.

"Have a safe trip." I hung up and ripped into my Remy like there was a shortage. I moved to rest the phone on the toilet top, and it was ringing again. "Hello?"

"Are you too busy to call your own mother?"

"Ma, I spoke to you on Friday," I clarified.

"That was three days ago." Oh, Lord! Let her tell it, I was in Russia and she was in Antarctica versus me being in Florida and her in Minnesota.

"How are you, Momma?"

"I'm fine," she sighed, "but we have bad news."

"What?" I sat up in the tub, awaiting the devastating blow. "What happened?"

"Well," she spoke slowly, "Mr. Marshall passed."

"Who?" I hated when she got me all worked up for nothing. "Who is that?"

"Mr. Marshall from Arthur Street," she tried explaining. "He stayed on the corner in the yellow house."

"Oh, him?" I laughed. "I thought he died a long time ago."

She gasped. "That's not a nice thing to say."

"What? I just thought he was dead already." I giggled. "He was ninety-nine when I was young."

"Forgive her, Jesus," she exclaimed. "Stop talking like that. Mr. Marshall was the one that got the buses to start running through this area back in the sixties."

So what? The bus was always late. I let her win. "I'm sorry to hear about Mr. Marshall."

"Yeah, I still can't believe Marshall is gone, Lord have mercy." She was acting like he was a ten-year-old kid shot to death by the police. "The funeral is on Saturday."

I changed the subject. "How's Dad?"

"Albert is fine. He just got through cutting the grass, so he's in the shower now."

"Give him my love." My phone beeped; I had a second call waiting. "Momma, hold on, please." I clicked over and found Shelly Weinberg's mother on the line, phoning to be certain that I owned no guns and would have no alcohol or drugs at the party. She couldn't think that I would share my hard-earned liquor with a bunch of kids.

Momma never complained when I placed her on hold three other times to talk to parents. The fourth time my line beeped, "Ma, I have another call," she was frustrated.

"Well *damn,* Paige." Where did all that Holy Ghost go?

I wanted to laugh. "I can call you back."

"No, go ahead. I'll hold." She sighed.

"But it's free from my cell phone."

She said, "Just hurry up."

I clicked over to the other line. "Hello?" No one said anything. "Hello," I sang.

"I can't ever come that close to kissing you again," Theo said. "Not unless I can complete the mission."

My grin was something else. "Hi."

"What's up?"

"Nothing much." I sank into the not-as-warm-as-it-was water. "What's going on?"

"Chillin'." He hesitated. "What are you doing?"

"Taking a bubble bath."

"Hmmm," he snickered. "No comment."

"How did things go at practice?"

"Well, Coach J. got on me." He added, "If I miss practice again I won't be starting in the first game."

"Ooh, we can't have that," I said.

"Naw." He sounded serious. "Not at all."

"Well, you know what time my class starts. Just be there on time."

"I don't have a choice now." Theo continued. "He even called my mom."

"He did?" I guessed that Craig wasn't playing.

"Yeah." He laughed. "He knows just how much I can't stand to hear her go on and on about anything."

"I'm sorry to cause you all of this trouble," I said jokingly, but continued in a more serious tone. "I'm also sorry for making you feel the way you were feeling earlier." I paused.

"I'm not playing a game." However, things did, for me, start out all in fun.

"I'm sorry too. I didn't mean to come at you like I did." He seemed nervous. "I just wanted to know where you stood."

Lord, I hoped this wasn't a high school prank. "I'm standing in the same place you are." Honesty was the best policy. "I think you're . . ." Less was always more. "Well, your personality is . . ." Then I remembered. "Oh my God, I have my mom on the other line. May I call you back at this number?"

"Of course. Do your thing."

I smiled. "Thank you. Bye." I pressed the button. "Mom?"

"Lord have mercy, Paige. You must be sending me some money for these charges."

"I asked you if you'd like for me to call you back and you said no."

"Jesus." She called His name in vain. "I don't have that AT&T One Rate shit."

"Ma, it's not that serious." We talked for another forty-five minutes, discussing everything from bingo to recipes then made our way back to Mr. Marshall again. "So, are you flying up for the funeral?"

"Flying? Funeral? For what?" I asked. "Even with glasses, contacts, and a magnifying glass, he never knew who I was."

"Don't talk bad about the dead," she fussed. "Mr. Marshall will come and scare your ass right up out of bed tonight."

"Ma, I just refuse to spend four hundred dollars on a plane ticket to go to the funeral of a man who I saw about three times, and two out of those three times he cussed me out for touching his gate."

"He didn't mean that. He lost his mind back in the eighties."

"Well, the only way I'm flying in is if I lose my mind." I added, "You're probably just going to get a plate at the repast anyway."

She couldn't contain her laughter. "Bye-bye, silly girl."

"Love you, Ma."

"Love you too." She hung up and I'm sure raced to tell my father what I said, but as ridiculous as it sounded, she knew that I wasn't telling a lie. At most black funerals, there'd be fifty people at the service, twenty at the gravesite, and seventy-seven at Auntie So-and-So's house for the repast, many with enough nerves to ask somebody to fix a plate for their lazy son, girlfriend, or husband who couldn't make it. "To Mr. Marshall." I raised my glass, took a sip for my mother's outlandish homey, and laughed.

What started out as a nice warm bath left me a cold prune. I washed myself thoroughly and stepped out of the water quickly. I dried off, walked into my room, and heard the roar of a crowd from a basketball game on TV and thought of Theo. It was a little after ten, but I took the chance of calling.

"Hello?" a female answered.

Oh Shit!

"Hello," I said.

"Yes?"

"Hi." I had to improvise. "Ms. Lakewood?"

"Yes," she said. "Whom am I speaking with?"

"Ms. Patrick, Theodore's English teacher."

"Oh, hi." She was very pleasant. "How are you?"

"I'm doing fine, thanks. And you?"

"A little tired. I'm just getting in from work."

"Wow!" I added. "Overtime?"

"No. I'm a pediatric nurse at South Miami General Children's Hospital."

"Oh, I'm sorry. I can call you back tomorrow if you're getting settled."

"No, no," she insisted. "We can talk. Is this about Theo being late to your class? His coach called me earlier at work."

I couldn't believe that Craig was tacky enough to use this lady's work number for something so trivial. "Oh, no," I said. "I've actually already spoken to Theo regarding his tardiness, and he has promised to improve." What a crock of shit. "My sixth period class is doing so well that I decided to have a gathering at my house this Saturday to reward them. I'm calling around to get permission from the parents of the students who are interested in attending."

"Well, that's certainly nice of you, but before I grant him permission, there are some things that I must know." She paused. "Open house was on the same evening of that school bus accident, and I couldn't attend because all of the injured kids were brought to my hospital. So, I have a few questions for you now, if that's all right."

Damn! "Yes, that's fine."

"How are Theo's grades in your class up to now?"

"Well," I stuttered, "Theo's grades are good. Right now he has a B average." It wasn't a complete lie. He actually had a C-plus, but I could find something for him to do to work his way into a B.

"How is his overall focus in class?"

"He has tremendous focus." *That's right; he won't take his eyes off of me.* "He's very attentive, and extremely structured." Theo's extremely structured body demanded most of my attention in class is what I meant.

"What about his participation?"

"Well, he never volunteers, but if I call on him, he knows the answer." Before she started to worry, I continued. "Most male students are that way, though. You won't know what they know until you ask them."

"What about his conduct?"

The rose that he gave to me earlier that day came to mind. "He is an absolute, perfect gentleman."

"I should know that just by the number of girls calling this house all hours of the night." She giggled. "I thought you were one of them."

I was let down. "He's a popular guy," I faked enthusiasm.

"Oh my God, tell me about it," she exclaimed. "These little girls won't stop. They won't leave him alone. They will do whatever it takes, honey."

I felt stupid. "Really?"

"Yes, and that is exactly why I stay on top of him about his education and basketball." She continued. "Education first, basketball second. They should be his main focus. Women will be around forever, but this opportunity is something that is given once in a lifetime. If he messes this up, he'll regret it for the rest of his life."

"That's true."

She giggled. "Well, I'm happy to hear that he's doing all right in your class." I was glad that the interrogation was done. "He has my consent to attend your get-together, but knowing him, he may be hanging with his friends this weekend, so he'll have to let you know."

"Oh, well, thank you so much."

"Please, call me if there is ever a problem or just to let me know that he's doing all right."

"I will," I said.

"Have a good night."

"You do the same." I hung up and sighed. "Damn."

Mr. Popular had girls calling all the time. What was I thinking? Depressed, I got into bed and wrapped myself up tightly like a taco. With the television remote control, I flipped through channels until I saw the ending of the local news. Then it was on to infomercials, and then on to an outrageously gay guy on one of those shopping channels selling women's shoes.

I turned off the TV, hoping to fall asleep, but I wasn't tired. Lustful thoughts were plaguing me. Ten minutes later, I reached into my nightstand and pulled out that familiar yellow sock. I untied it, and out fell Mr. Bumpy, my six-inch, lime green, glow-in-the-dark, soft-studded vibrator. Yes, I was among the millions of women who wouldn't dare confess to having one, yet I couldn't imagine my life without one.

I turned it on and watched it glow. The batteries were new, so this was going to be a great night. There was nothing worse that a dildo with half-dead batteries . . . that was enough to make a grown woman cry. Years ago, it was all right for a woman to walk into a convenience store and purchase a single battery. Maybe she had a pager. Nowadays, if a woman buys a single battery or even a packet of four, a vibrator is the first thing that goes through the clerk's mind, and more than half the time, he's probably right.

I reached down and placed its head on my chief knob, the headquarters of all of my pleasure, my epicenter. "Mmmm." I closed my eyes and pressed down a little harder. Though I couldn't stand Craig, during these moments, he was useful. It was always good to think of our sex. The thought of it, along with Mr. Bumpy, drove me crazy. "Mmm." My breathing picked up as I pictured Craig on top of me with my thighs bent toward my breasts and my feet on his shoulders. When that thick, spit-shined chocolate pole traveled the walls of my cave, I was guaranteed to feel everything he was born with, his pulsation, every vein, bump, and bruise. Shit, even his skin packed weight.

"Fuck me," I whispered in the darkness when my imagination shifted from Craig to Theo. My clit bulged and trembled when I thought of his tall and firm frame over me. "Oh, yes, yes, yeah," I mumbled and fantasized about his sexy brown eyes rolling back into his head . . . he couldn't handle the thirty-two years behind this good pussy. "Oh, oh shit," I cried as he bit into his bottom lip, now masking his smile.

Still in my mind, sweat poured from Theo's brow, not from the basketball court, but from running the length of my body.

"Fuck me." My pussy was the kind he'd thought about when he masturbated, never thinking it could truly exist. "Oh my God." I pushed Mr. Bumpy into me harder. "Yesssssss." My breathing escalated as Theo, in my mind, kissed me and drilled deeper into me, filling me, and I could hold back no longer. I ground into him and groaned so loudly that I didn't hear the phone ringing until it was already on the third ring and the answering machine was about to activate.

"Hello?" I picked up, exhausted and incoherent.

"Hey."

"Hey."

Theo asked, "Were you sleeping?"

"No." I lay helpless. My lower lips were still humping air and my stomach was heaving. "No, I wasn't asleep."

"Are you okay?" he asked, guarded.

"Yeah, I'm just a little out of breath," I lied. "I ran from the kitchen to answer the phone."

"I know that you called back earlier," he chuckled. "Sorry for the interference."

"No problem."

"Thanks for the accolades with my mom." He then asked, "What do I owe you?"

I joked, "You could never pay me what all of that was worth."

"I'll try, though."

I was still trying to get myself together, and wasn't sure of what to say to him. "Are you done with your homework?"

"Whoa, slow your roll. That's not your job. I have someone who asks those types of questions already."

"Okay, so what types of questions should I ask?"

"Questions you'd ask a friend."

"Well," I changed my approach, "how was your day?"

"It was a rough day at the office," he joked. "Naw, my day was cool until I got to my last class."

"Oh yeah? What happened?"

"Well, there's this chick in my class that I'm trying to figure out." He paused. "She's a little intimidating, but approachable."

"What makes her approachable?"

It took him a while to continue. "The way her eyes always say yes to me."

I haven't heard that before. "What do you mean?"

"She's not completely comfortable with me or the idea of us maybe, somehow, someday being more than just friends, so she throws me curve balls, grenades, anything she can get her hands on." He laughed. "But her eyes always say what's really on her mind."

"And what's that?" I had to see if he really knew what he was talking about.

"Well, in her mind she's asking, 'Why or how can I be attracted to his guy? How could I show him that I'm interested without going overboard, without others knowing, and how do I know to take him seriously?' She contemplates, 'I wonder if he'd be good to me?' Then her eyes reveal the answer, which is always yes."

"Interesting."

"Am I right?" he asked with a smile in his voice.

"Just a little."

"Just a little, huh?"

"Yep," I lied.

"Just keep saying yes," Theo said. "I promise you won't regret it."

Theo and I talked for hours. When we hung up, my clock read 4:12 A.M. During our conversation, I learned that there was more to him than just the star basketball player we knew and loved at school. Theo had to be from another planet; he wasn't like any other eighteen-year-old that I knew. He had his future mapped out and was doing whatever he could to

make it possible. I knew many forty-year-old men who were still confused about their futures or didn't realize that they were already living the lives they would lead forever.

Because of his local notoriety, Theo was already a role model, speaking to young people at various churches and community functions about finding, becoming a part of, and being passionate about something, anything that would make them feel complete.

Whenever he had free time, Theo went to middle school basketball practices and games. He did this because he remembered being that age and not having anyone rooting for him. His mother had to work and his father was MIA—a Muthafuckin' Inconsiderate Asshole was Theo's definition of the acronym. Though in denial, Theo was still in a lot of pain over his father's exit.

He shared so many notable things about himself that by the end of our conversation, he felt the need to prove to me that he wasn't an angel. He told me about some perilous adventures he survived earlier in life, and also admitted to a few not so bad things, including drinking occasionally. But he had never thought of experimenting with any drugs. I learned more than I expected to ever know about him, and was already hungry for more.

~Situation #2~

Theo

En route to my locker, I saw Trese standing in front of it. I paused for a second but continued anyhow. I had nothing to fear. The clock had stopped, and the game was over.

"What's up?" I asked.

"Can we talk for a minute?"

"About what?" I asked.

She hung her head. "'bout why I did what I did."

"You don't have to explain." I didn't want to hear what was sure to be a sob story.

"I want to."

I took a deep breath and began dialing the combination to the lock. "I'm listening."

"Well, in the beginning, I really thought that I was," she paused, "and when I found out that I wasn't, I didn't know how to tell you."

I interjected. "I wasn't exactly thrilled about the situation, so you should've jumped hurdles to come and let me know."

"I know," she sighed, "I know, but as long as you thought that I was, I felt that we'd have to be associated in some way." Her voice lowered. "I knew that if I told you, things would really be over."

I asked, "Didn't you think I deserved to know, though?" Trese needed to see a psychiatrist.

"Yeah, I thought that." She wouldn't look directly at me. "But you are the best thing to ever happen to me. I didn't want to lose you."

I didn't know what to say. "What?"

"Theo, I've never met anyone like you. You respected me, took me out, and talked to me." I saw a tear slide down her cheek. "Guys are normally just trying to get me in bed." She said, "I mean, we did it pretty early, but that wasn't you . . . it was me. It was what I was used to." She wiped the tear away. "So, it was me who fucked up. I thought as long as you thought I was pregnant, we could work on having something together."

"Naw." I felt sorry for her, and decided to take the blame. "Naw, it's not you, it's me. At this point in my life, I can't do this. You're a great girl, Trese, but I have a lot on my plate, and I need to stay focused."

"Is it that you don't want a girlfriend or you don't want *me* as a girlfriend?"

I thought about her question, and didn't know how to answer her without crushing her feelings. "I don't have the time or energy it would take for us to be in a relationship."

"So it *is* me." She was embarrassed.

"No, it's just that I have no time to be in a relationship with you."

"But you have the time for sex?" she asked and then regretted it. "You don't have to answer that." She paused. "I just wanted to say that I was sorry."

"All right."

"Do you forgive me?"

"I don't know, Trese." I searched my locker for my English book.

She frowned. "I was gonna tell you the truth."

"When?" I asked.

"I don't know." I believed her. She didn't know because she hadn't planned on telling me. She was still on a mission to have my child. Trese wanted to benefit through what she thought my future would be like. She wanted to live a ghetto fabulous lifestyle through child support checks from a ball player. Her intentions were probably to drown herself in Gucci, Prada, and Versace outfits while the kid was suffering from WFS, Wal-Mart Fashion Syndrome.

"Well, what's done is done." I wanted our little talk to be done.

"True." She smiled. "So, from here on out, I promise that we will only do it with condoms."

"Whoa!" I couldn't have heard her right. "What?"

"Condoms," she said. "We won't mess around without them."

"No." I had to knock the ball out of the park. "No more. We're not messing around anymore."

"Why?"

"Why?" I asked and then continued. "I just told you that we're not going to be a couple, so you should want more for yourself." I paused and closed my locker. "You shouldn't want to sleep with me or any dude that tells you that he has no plans of being in a relationship with you."

She rolled her eyes. "I understand what you're saying, but I'm a big girl, and if you say that we can still do it and just be friends, then I can handle it."

"That's exactly what I *don't* want." I wanted someone who would never compromise her morals for me.

"That's what you said you wanted when we met."

"Well, that's not what I want anymore." I had to say something; she wouldn't go away. "Plus, I met somebody."

"When?" She got louder. "Who?"

"It doesn't matter when or who."

"Yes, it does."

"Why does it matter?"

She calculated. "Because it's Wednesday, and I was just at your house on Friday after the dance."

"So?"

"So you had me at your house."

"Yeah, but I took you to my crib for one reason."

"I know." She snatched her bag from the ground. "You're a fuckin' dog."

"I took you to my house to find out if you were pregnant or not." I looked her up and down and said, "And you're not."

"Yeah, but more than just that happened, though."

I cringed. "We didn't do anything."

"Yes, we did," she said. "You ate my pussy, in case you forgot."

"That doesn't mean we did it."

"Whateva!" She was upset. "Who is she?"

"Why?" I asked.

"Fuck you!" she screamed and began walking away. "Fuck her, too."

I tried to select my words carefully, but decided that whatever came out was what she deserved. "Fuck you, too, and don't say shit else to me after this."

"Whateva!"

"Whateva my ass. I'm serious." I looked at my watch and realized that though I still had three minutes to make it to English, I needed to hurry. I started running up the stairs, but there was no way I could be late to class and then practice again.

"Theo." I heard someone yelling my name. "Theo, wait up."

I turned around and saw Angela Porter in her purple-gold-and-white cheerleading uniform running a few paces behind me. She caught up with me and stayed with me.

"Trying not to be late, huh?" I asked.

"You know it." She laughed and trotted alongside me. "I can't get a detention."

I joked, "True, 'cause you're a good girl."

"At times." She winked at me and we continued jogging. With every strut, Angie's breasts jumped, jingled, and jangled. They seemed soft, full, and ripe. I was tempted to hold them up for her.

She asked, "Are you going to the pool party?"

"Yeah. You?"

"Yeah." The classroom was in sight, so we transformed our then slow run to a fast walk. "Can I catch a ride with you?"

"Huh?" I didn't see that coming.

"Can I ride with you to the party on Saturday?"

I smiled. "White Boy Johnny can't take you?"

"Of course," she blushed, "but I'm asking you."

"It's like that?"

"Yeah, unless you're bringing Trese."

"Trese?" I was offended. "Don't even try me like that."

"Isn't that your girl?"

"Naw, we were just friends." I felt compelled to go on. "But now we're not even cool no more."

"So, can I ride?" she asked.

"It depends." My mind went into "man mode." When anything slightly sexual is introduced in conversation, a man can't be held responsible for what he says. "I might be driving something else."

It turns out that Angie wasn't Ms. Innocent U.S.A., like I thought. "I'll ride anything," she said.

"Well, I think I have just the thing for you." I lagged behind so that I could get a better view of her ass in that short skirt. "Yeah, you can ride with me."

"What time should I expect you?" Angie asked as she opened the door to the classroom. Immediately, I saw Paige, and it seemed as if my conversation with Angie had happened months ago. She was stunning. Leaning against the front wall in a sophisticated black pants suit, her long black mane was draped over her shoulders, and even if I were blind, I'd know she was there . . . I could smell her fragrance.

"What time are you going to pick me up?" Angie asked again.

I looked away from Paige and tried to whisper, "I'll let you know later."

"Okay." Angie was talking way too loud. "You want my number?" With those words, Paige shot me an I-knew-you-were-a-liar look.

"Um, on Saturday." I had to fix the situation quickly. "The party starts at four." I spoke loudly on purpose. "I'll pick you up at three-thirty. Just give me your address and the directions."

"Cool." She smiled. "Is that all you want?"

Damn! I couldn't look like I was excited or encouraging her. "That'll do the trick."

"I'll give it to you after class then." Angie walked away to her desk.

After the bell rang, Paige didn't look my way. She stood up from the desk and addressed the class. "Good afternoon." Everything was business as usual.

At the end of class when the room was noisy with the hustle and bustle of some students exiting and others still packing up to leave, Angie approached my desk and handed me a piece of paper that included her name, phone number, and address, along with the word *whenever*.

"This is a lot of info," I joked.

"Well, this is a lot of woman." She pointed to her physique. "Call me tonight. My father is out of town until Saturday."

"Okay." I kept my voice low and smiled as I watched her walk off. The short skirt of her uniform allowed me to again see a hint of her ass cheeks. They rose and fell from left to right, right to left, left to right, then that purple-and-gold splendor disappeared through the door.

"You don't have a detention today." I was snapped back to reality with the sound of Paige's voice.

"I know." I stood up

"You're free to go." She smiled. "I don't want your coach running in here again."

"Me neither." I walked over to her, hoping that she didn't see me watching Angie's rear end. "I enjoyed talking to you last night." I did; it was incredible.

"Yeah, I did too. It's been a while since I've done that." She blushed. "I was almost late today messing around with you."

Jokingly, I asked, "Does that mean that we won't talk at night anymore?"

"No." She brushed some lint from my shirt, or at least she pretended to. "It means that I'll be running late a lot."

"Word?" I was excited.

"Word." She smiled. "Get going before you get in trouble about practice."

"True." I tightened my grip on my bookbag. "What time can I call you?"

"After nine."

"Cool." I stared at her lips as she did the same to mine. I reminisced about how close we came to kissing yesterday, but with the door not locked today, I couldn't take the chance. "I need to get to the gym."

"All right," she continued sarcastically, "I'm sure that your personal cheerleader is waiting."

"It's not even like that." I smiled, but promised her with my eyes.

"I'm just kidding." She smiled. "I'm not trying to get into your business."

"Yeah, right."

"I'm not," she insisted.

"There is no business." I felt like I owed her an explanation. "Angie asked me for a ride to your house on Saturday."

"You could've fooled me," she said. "It seems like she wanted another type of ride." A woman's intuition is always right.

"Those rides are reserved."

"For whom?"

"For . . ." I winked at her, "for a more *experienced* rider."

"Really?" she asked.

My eyes never left hers. "Really." I wanted her to know that there was nothing shy or boyish about me.

"Hmm." She had no expression. I didn't know what she was thinking until she said it. "Should she bring her own saddle?"

"Yeah, because my horse bucks sometimes." I walked toward the door. "He's a bit on the wild side."

"Well, I'm sure that he can be tamed."

"I'm sure." I wore that silly smile all the way to the gym and used that giddy, crazy feeling to dominate the court. I felt power in my legs, arms, and fingertips that I couldn't testify to ever feeling before. I was slamming, guarding, stealing, and making shots that left everybody wondering what I had for lunch.

"So, what do you have planned for us tomorrow?"

She laughed. "Hot dogs and water."

"It is gonna at least be ice water?" I asked then moved the phone from one ear to the other.

"Nope, water from the pool."

"Aw, that's wrong. I'm complaining to the school board."

"Complain," she said. "The school board can't do a thing. They're not funding this."

We both laughed. It was Friday night, and I couldn't wait to get to her house the next day. Even though we wouldn't be

alone, this would be my first time, other than our brief encounter at Dunkin' Donuts, away from West Dade.

"I'm just kidding. Toni and I are going to barbeque for
you guys."

"Who is he?" I was curious.

"Who?"

"Tony."

"Oh, Toni. *She* is my best friend."

I felt dumb for assuming. "Okay." We had been on the
phone for two hours, and I was still fighting to find the right
words to form my question. "I have a question." I wanted an
answer badly, so I just asked with the best words I could put
together. "Do you and Coach J. ever still get together?"

"Get together how?"

"Intimately." I squeezed my eyes shut and prayed for the
desired response or for her to not say that the question was
too personal.

"Well," she paused, "what exactly do you mean by intimately?"

Damn, did I have to spell it out? "Sexually."

"No," she said quickly.

"When was your last experience?"

"With him?" She sounded slightly agitated. "Or someone
else?"

I changed my angle. "Someone other than him."

"Whoa." She laughed. "It's been a very, very, very, very
long time."

"Are we talking more than a year?" I asked.

"We're talking more than seven years."

"Wow." I smiled with contentment.

She never talked much about her marriage to Coach J.,
but it didn't matter because I knew enough about him to not
like him much anymore myself. I was now extremely uncomfortable around him. I tried to separate my personal life from
my existence on the court, but with him as my coach, he

brought her to the court each and every time. I felt like Judas, like I sold him out, betrayed him by almost kissing her and fantasizing about more happening someday. I avoided him. I couldn't look him in the face, and when I had to talk to him, I used the shortest words I could find then hurried off in the opposite direction.

"What about you?" she asked.

"What?"

She was shy to continue. "When was your last time?"

Should I count Friday night with Trese? Naw, nothing really happened. "A few weeks ago."

"A few weeks ago?" she repeated, as though I had said I was screwing someone right there while talking to her. "Who?"

"Huh?" Damn.

"I'm sorry." She continued. "It was a reactionary question. You don't have to answer that."

"It's cool."

"I didn't realize that you were seeing someone just a few weeks ago."

"I wasn't." I added, "It was just a thing."

"Just a thing? Interesting."

"No, it wasn't like that. We were friends at the time."

She laughed to mask her displeasure. "It was just a few weeks ago."

"I know, but we're not friends now." I dug the hole deeper. "She's just not my type."

"You should've known that before sleeping with her."

She couldn't be mad. "He without sin cast the first stone," I said.

"Oh, Lord." I laughed. "I guess you saw *The Passion of the Christ*."

"Have it on DVD." I was glad to change the topic. "That's a serious flick."

"Yeah, it was," she said.

Paige was an amazing woman. She was funny, smart, caring, and most importantly didn't handle me with kid gloves as I thought most older women did when their "friends" were younger. Paige didn't act like she knew more than I did. She never talked about seeing more of the world than me, or having more experience in most things than I did. She was a woman, and I was hoping that she'd consider me not just a man, but *the* man.

Come on, it was Friday night. Honestly, I could be anywhere, Trese's or Angie's bed, or sweet-talking my way up under somebody's daughter's sheets. However, chatting with Paige somehow satisfied me. Had she invited me over, my car wouldn't have gotten me there fast enough. There were a few times in our conversation where I thought about asking her if she wanted company, but I didn't want to be the one to initiate anything else between us. Everything to come was up to her.

"Hey, what's up?" I said to Angie as she opened her door.

"Hi, Theo," she said in a less than enthusiastic tone.

Right away the door opened wider. "Theodore Lakewood." Her father reached for my hand. "How are you?"

"I'm fine, sir. You?"

"Oh, I just can't wait to see you in that opening game next week, man."

"Thank you." I shook his hand.

"Man," he smiled, "you are on fire. Have you decided what college or NBA team it's going to be yet?"

That was the question everybody wanted an answer to. "No, sir, not yet. I'm still weighing my options."

"If you decide on college, the smart thing to do would be to stay right here." He patted me on the back. "U.M. is the place for a guy like you."

"We'll see." People, total strangers at the grocery store,

movie theatre, and restaurants always seemed to think that I needed their advice to make an informed decision. I hated discussing my future plans with people who knew nothing about me.

I looked at Angie. "Are you ready?"

"Yeah." She stepped toward me.

I shook Mr. Porter's hand again. "Nice to meet you, sir."

"Don't let this be the only time you stop by." He was eager. "Take care of my girl."

"I will." I waved him off.

"Oh, and Angie," he remembered, "I'll be picking you up."

"Why?" She had an attitude. "Theo can bring me home."

He said, "I know, but I'll be in that area later, so keep your cell phone on."

She turned her head away from him. "Yeah, all right."

"What's wrong with *you* today?" I asked as we got in the car.

"He got back earlier than he was supposed to this morning and is already getting on my nerves." She threw her purse in the backseat. "I'm mad at you too."

"About what?"

"What happened to you calling me? I was hoping you'd come over while he was gone."

"Sorry. I got tied up."

"Too tied up for me?" She ran her hand up my thigh.

"Well, you have a boyfriend," I said.

"Yeah, but—"

"But I'm not into causing problems." I shook my head. "If you were my girl, I'd want dudes to respect me, so I'm giving my man Johnny the same treatment."

She blushed. "So, what if I was single?"

"I'd be all over you." I checked out her legs with a smile.

Angie spent the entire ride trying to convince me that Johnny would never know about us messing around. Truth was, my interest in Paige was occupying every inch of me, and this was new to me. I was turning down a beautiful girl in the hopes that a woman I hadn't even kissed would take me seriously. This was a first . . . and the last. I wanted to see where we would go, and until I proved that it couldn't be done, I was willing to try.

I was incredibly impressed when I pulled up to her pale yellow, two-car garage house, complete with ivory French doors and a wooden round-top mullion directly above them. "Nice," Angie said.

While I walked to the door, I found myself curious about who cut her grass because I wanted to do it. I rang the bell and anticipated her inviting me in, but the door cracked open and two identical bighead li'l boys fought one another to push the door toward me.

"Who is it?" the little guy in the red shirt asked.

"You were supposed to ask that before you opened the door, shorty."

"You here for the party?" he asked as I walked past him.

"Yeah," I said. "Who are you guys?"

"My name is Devin Edwards."

"My name is Kevin Edwards." The second boy strained his neck to look up at me. "You're tall."

I giggled and bent down to them. "My name is Theo." Since they were in the last name business, I added, "Lakewood."

"Do you play wideo games, Theo?"

I chuckled. "Yeah, I play wideo games. What you got?"

His eyes lit up. "Over here at Auntie Paige's house we got Dragon Ball Z and Crazy Taxi."

"Oh yeah?"

"Yeah," they answered together. "You wanna play?"

"Yeah, but show me where your auntie is first." I followed them out to the patio where I saw Paige and a tall, light-skinned lady, who I assumed was Kev and Dev's mom, working the grill. I slid the glass door to the right. "Good afternoon."

Paige spun around in shock. "Hi." She looked at her watch. "Oh my God, I didn't realize that it was so late." She approached me. "You're the first one here." Because she had company, I handled her cautiously. I wanted to hold her around the waist, but elected to drape my hands over her shoulder instead.

"Mmmm, you smell nice," she whispered in my ear.

"Thanks." I stepped back after the brief hug.

"How did you get in?" she asked, puzzled.

I pointed to the boys with their mouths pressed against the glass door. "The twins."

"They opened the door?" the light-skinned lady asked.

"Yep." I laughed. "They opened it then asked, who is it?" We were all laughing when Angie walked into the patio.

"Hi, Ms. Patrick, you have a very nice home."

"Thank you, Angela," Paige said as she hugged Angie.

"Toni, these are two of my students." She pointed at us. "Theo Lakewood and Angela Porter."

Toni walked over and shook our hands. "Nice to meet you two."

Paige smiled. "Toni is my best friend."

"Do you two need help with anything? Because I promised the twins we could play video games."

Paige laughed. "No, go ahead. Just see that they don't open up the door again."

"I will." I rushed back into the house.

"You're really, really, really tall." Kevin stared at me.

"I bet you're nine hundred years old," Devin said.

"Nope, I'm a thousand years old," I said.

"Wow," they said in perfect harmony.

"Let's play." I was just as excited as they were.

We played PS2 for over an hour before I realized that music was playing and there was a lot of talking and screaming streaming in from outside. It didn't take me long to smell something I knew had to taste good. I made my way to the patio, and it was alive with my classmates.

"Let's get this party started," I yelled after kicking off my shoes, removing my shirt, and diving into the pool.

I had a blast playing water volleyball, Marco Polo, and racing. Paige never once mentioned class, homework, or West Dade at all. She was almost as goofy as we were, and when she and Toni put on their swimsuits and joined us in the pool, I wasn't the only guy saying "Holy shit." The two older ladies had the remedy for everything that could be wrong with an eighteen-year-old guy.

Angie stayed within a foot of me the entire time we were in the pool. When the sun went down, she was bold enough to nonchalantly grab my willie and lug it toward her. It shocked the hell out of me, and something told me that Paige might have noticed it. Whenever Angie was too damn close to me, Paige called her off to help with a chore, flip hamburgers, get a pan, or help with something . . . just not me.

Though I saw jealousy in her eyes, Paige kept a smile the entire day, all the way up until 10 P.M. When most of the students were gone and Angie's father showed up, the green-eyed monster made a move toward me.

"So, how did things go?" Mr. Porter asked Paige. I was talking to Angie, but my audio was tuned into her father's voice, not hers.

"Things went well." Paige smiled. "Better than expected."

"You look terrific. I bet you turned a few of these young heads."

She blushed. "Oh, stop it." She was still wearing her black bikini top. A long, black-and-yellow wrapped skirt, tied around her waist, covered the bottom.

"I should've shown up two hours ago when that skirt was still poolside." He thought he was whispering. "I would've loved to have seen that."

"Well," Paige looked uncomfortable, "I gave Angela a plate of food for you. Do you eat pork?"

He laughed and stared intently at her heaving breasts. "There's not much that I won't eat." His eyes roamed further south on her body. "Come closer and I'll bite you."

"I put some ribs on the plate." She tried to ignore his comments. "The sauce is homemade."

"So is mine." Dude wasn't ugly, but his game was nasty and tasteless. He was too old to still be charging women with such disrespect. "If you want to taste it, I can I come back in about an hour." He moved closer to her. "You know, when everybody is gone."

"I'm exhausted, Ian." She tried to be nice. "I'm going straight to bed."

Mr. Porter smiled. "That's where I want you."

Angie was talking to me, but her dad was in violation of all of my codes. I didn't ask her to hold a minute, excuse me, or anything. I just left her and moseyed on over to her father.

"Excuse me." I stared at him, took a deep breath, and made a decision not to say what I was about to say. Instead, I turned to Paige. "Did you still want me to change those spark plugs for you?"

"Um." At first she looked confused, but she quickly caught on. "Yes, as a matter of fact, I do. Thank you for reminding me. I had totally forgotten."

"Not a problem." I looked back at Mr. Ian "Ain't Gettin' None" Porter and pointed to his daughter. "I think Angie's ready."

"Oh, is she?" He smiled. "Well, Ms. Patrick, give me a call if you change your mind."

"I think I'm all set in that department, but thanks for your concern." She extended her hand to him. "Have a good night and enjoy the food."

"I will. Thank you once again." He grabbed my hand. I didn't pull back, but offered him no expression, no smile, and no words. "And you, Theo, stop by the house whenever you want. You're a cool guy, and Angie seems to like you."

Hmm, I wonder if my basketball career has anything to do with this open invitation to his home and his daughter.

"Theo, are you busy the rest of the night?" Angie chimed in.

The three of them looked at me for an answer. "Yeah, I have some stuff to do."

She wasn't giving up. "Well, give me a call tomorrow. Let's hook up."

"Okay," I agreed just to get her and her pops to keep moving. "Y'all drive safely."

Mr. Porter put his hand on his daughter's shoulder, and it was a pleasure to watch them walk away.

"Like father like daughter, I see," Paige whispered.

"For a second I thought you were going to take him up on his special sauce."

"Well, I have nothing much to do tonight," she joked, but I didn't find the statement humorous in the least.

"How about I find something to keep you busy?" I asked, but then Toni walked into the living room with Devin and Kevin in tow. Those boys had energy like they were overdosing on Prozac and Viagra.

"Everything is just about clean back there. Just pick up the few cans that I didn't get." She smiled. "It's late. The boys and I need to get going."

"Aw, so soon?" Paige reached down and rubbed the two boys' heads. "Did you guys have fun?"

"Yeah," Devin said, then Kevin finished. "We don't wanna go home." Then they asked in unison, "Can we stay?"

"Maybe next weekend," Toni said. "You two have to go to church with Grandma in the morning."

"Ugh." Kevin started pouting. "I don't wanna go to church."

"Me either. They talk too much," Devin added.

"Don't even start." Toni grabbed them by the hands. "Let me get out of here. They're going to church. Both of 'em need Jesus." She laughed and kissed Paige on the cheek. "Nice meeting you, Theo."

"Nice meeting you, too, Ms. Toni."

"Child, please, call me Toni. I'm already trippin' about getting old. Don't make it worse."

"All right, it was nice meeting you, Toni," I said. "Bye, Dev and Kev."

"Bye, Theo," they said.

"Theo, I'm going to walk Toni out," Paige said. "Before you go, please make sure that everyone who is still on the patio knows that the party is over and they should be calling their parents."

"Okay." I agreed to do the dirty work.

"I need my house back," she whispered to Toni as they started to walk away. "Shit, I'm ready to have a drink."

There were six people still on the patio, all gathering their belongings. Four rode there together, and the other two had just determined that they lived two blocks apart and could carpool, so I didn't have to say a word. While they talked about the girls in our class who should've never owned two-piece swimsuits, I just grabbed a garbage bag and picked up the soda cans that the wind was rustling around.

"T., you want us to wait on you?" Richard asked.

"Naw, y'all go ahead. I'm just trying to get all of this garbage together."

"You need help?"

"I got it."

"All right." Richard and the others exited the patio and walked into the house. "See you on Monday."

"All right, man."

There wasn't much trash lying around, the grill was already clean, and there was nothing weird floating in the pool, so I grabbed a broom and started sweeping. I moved in slow motion so that anyone still watching wouldn't suspect that I was just wasting time.

"All right, Mr. Clean, you can come in," Paige said as she opened the glass door. "Everyone is gone."

I had been sweeping for less than five minutes. "You sure?"

"Yes." She smiled and sipped from the glass in her hand.

"What are you drinking?" I leaned the broom against the fence and approached her.

"Henessey and Hypnotiq."

"H-Squared?" I expected her to be drinking wine or something a little more teacher-like. She could get down with the get down.

"Is that what they call it?" She pulled the curtains closed.

"That's what I call it." I was nervous about being alone with her.

She asked, "Have you had it before?"

"No, let me taste it." It was "need be" time. I stepped toward her, took the glass from her hand, and rested it on the table. I bent down to meet her and licked the moist residue from her supple lips.

"Tastes good," I whispered, then I gently drew her lips into me in search of more sweetness. I parted her oral gates with my tongue and surprisingly, it was welcomed by a tender yet aggressive suction. She pulled me in, and like she was awaiting ransom money, she held my tongue hostage, applying an even more seductive taunting, sliding her lips back and forth on my tongue. I flicked my tongue wildly, fighting with hers until she surrendered it to me. Then I proceeded to suck her nectar. My hands traveled down the back of her body like a train on a track, and I squeezed her firm ass.

"Whoa." She stopped.

Damn, I messed up. "Sorry."

"It's all right." She smiled. "I thought you wanted to taste my drink."

"I did." Boy, I did.

"How was it?"

I was almost out of breath. "I've never had anything like that before."

"I would offer you a glass, but then I'd be contributing to the alcohol consumption of a minor."

If ever there were a time for me to man up, it would be now. "All right, Ms. English teacher, do you know the definition of the word *minor*?" I asked.

"Of course," she answered. "Anyone under the age of twenty-one."

"Wrong." I sat down in a chair at the dining room table. "My dictionary says lesser or smaller in amount, extent, or size." With a grin on my face, I grabbed the case of dominoes that the other students and I had played with earlier. "There's nothing small in amount, extent, or size in regards to me, so go get the bottles and let's do this."

~Situation #1~

Paige

I returned to Theo with both bottles and a smile. We played dominoes. He confessed to only playing a few times before, so after winning a few times, I became cocky enough to suggest that the loser take a triple shot of Henessey. After a few bitter shots, Theo advocated a new plan, which meant that the loser would also have to remove an article of clothing. Anxious to see what lay beneath his baggy jeans, I agreed.

What a mistake. Had I used my brain, I would've suited up before agreeing because four games lost meant off with my slippers, wrap skirt, bikini top, and then the bottom. Within thirty minutes, Theo hustled me out of almost every thread that covered my skin. He lied. He was a master domino player, and I didn't find his trickery funny.

Super intoxicated and cold as hell, I sat shyly at my dining room table in only my bikini bottom. The look on his face when I exposed my pierced nipples was one I wish I could bottle and play back on insecure days. To hold on to my dignity—and my bikini bottom—for a few moments more, I accused him of cheating, but he fought me tooth and nail.

"Well, I'm not taking it off," I said stubbornly.

"Then I'll do it."

"No." I stood up and pretended to be angry, hoping he'd have mercy on me. "Because I didn't lose."

"C'mon, Paige." He stood up and towered over me. "You lost fair and square." He made a move for my waist and I stepped back. "Where are you going?" He smiled. "If you run, don't think I can't catch you."

I blushed. "Don't chase me." I used my palms to cover my exposed, hard nipples.

"Just take it off," he said.

I felt like a high school girl again. "Theo, please don't make me do this."

"I don't like doing homework, but I have to." He kept walking toward me. "So you have to."

I took a big step away from him and pointed at myself. "But then I'll be naked."

"What's wrong with being naked?"

"It's embarrassing enough that I'm topless right now."

He licked his thick, sexy brown lips. "Once again, what's wrong with being naked?"

"That's an easy question for you to ask. You're still fully clothed."

"If you want me naked, then I'll get naked." He pulled his shirt and undershirt off in one big jerk. His bulky chocolate chest and arms seemed carved from the trunk of an oak. There were no words to compliment him with. I sighed and daydreamed of kissing and biting him in places a woman my age shouldn't dream of seeing on a man his age. Eighteen years old my ass. He couldn't be.

"We'll do our bottoms at the same time." He stared at me. "All right?"

"No," I yelled. "Let's just not do it at all. Let's end the game right here." As bad as I wanted to see the junk in his trunk, I couldn't put myself out there. He had seen fifteen-, sixteen-, and seventeen-year-olds naked and I couldn't compete with them. I had to have surgery to put some things back where they used to be. I didn't think he'd view me with the same appreciation.

He said, "I thought you were into having fun tonight."

"I am," I spoke up. "I'm just not into humiliation."

"Humiliation?" he repeated. "Paige, there's nothing humiliating about your body. Shit, you got me begging to see it." He stepped closer to me, grabbed my hands, and lowered them away from my breasts. "You're beautiful, and you have nothing to be ashamed of." He let go of my hands.

"All right," I yelled and walked over to the light switch. "I'll do it if you do it, but with this light over here off." I turned off the lamp and stepped to the center of my living room.

"Cool," he said. "On the count of three."

"Okay." I took a deep breath. "One." I was about to unveil my gem to this man, this boy, my student. How many drinks did I have? I untied the right side. "Two." After this I needed to be the president of the South Florida branch of Alcoholics Anonymous because I was the poster child of "this is what alcohol might make you do." I untied the left side. "Three," I screamed and watched him lower his pants as I yanked my bikini bottom away.

Though the room was dim, I eagerly looked over to see his equipment to find that underneath his pants were boxer shorts. I was the only one naked. "That was dead wrong." I felt naked in more ways than one and quickly stormed off to my bedroom. He caught the door before it slammed.

"C'mon, it was a joke. I didn't think you were actually going to do it," he said.

"You talked me into it," I complained. "Just wait out front for me while I find something to put on."

"I'm sorry, Paige," he said. "It was just a joke."

"Hmm, I guess that's what I should've expected from a high school senior," I whispered sarcastically. "A bunch of fuckin' jokes."

"Don't go there." He laughed. "I'm sorry."

"Okay, well, now that you've seen what you came here to see, will you please wait in the living room?" I pointed at the door. "I'm going to find something to put on."

He grabbed my hand as I tried to step farther into the dark room. "Are you really mad at me?"

I was upset with myself for being so naïve. *Look at him, those sexy brown eyes, luscious lips, and creamy chocolate skin. How could I be mad at him?* A part of me was excited, a huge portion drunk, another part embarrassed, and the rest of me wanted to see him naked too.

"I'm not mad. I just wish we wouldn't have gone as far as we did." I paused and continued in a slur, "Now I'm drunk and naked. I'm your teacher. This isn't how things were supposed to happen."

"How were things supposed to happen?"

"I don't know, just not like this." I pulled away from his grip and walked around the room, lighting my jarred candles one by one instead of turning on the bright light and further exposing myself. "This isn't the way I saw things."

"Then show me," Theo said as the orange glow of the candles introduced itself to the walls of the room. "Show me the way things are supposed to be."

"What do you m—?" I stopped when I turned to see him sitting on the edge of my bed.

"Come here." He beckoned to me.

Nervous wasn't the word for me. "Give me a minute." I opened my lingerie drawer. "Let me put on so—"

"No," he interrupted, "just come here." Before I could protest, Theo grabbed me by the hand. "Things can still just happen. There's no script or pattern that we have to follow."

He gently pulled me his way. I was now standing between his legs with my knees pressed against the bed.

I trembled as his hands slid up my calves. "You feel good." His fingers traveled up the backside of my thighs, his lips landed on my stomach, giving me precious little kisses, then the shit hit the fan . . . his tongue taunted my nipples.

"Theo." I tried to stop him. "I don't know if—"

"Shh, shh," he quieted me as his powerful hands latched onto my waist. "There's no right or wrong tonight, only what feels good."

"Yeah," I fought to be logical, "but I don't think that this is—"

"I don't care what this is or isn't." He pulled me down by my hands to him. "Try not to care about anything that's not in this room." He placed my arms around his neck. "Can you do that?"

I was busy trying to be politically correct, logical, and uptight. "Yeah, but—"

"Just answer the question." He pulled me downward to him. "Can you do it or not?"

"Yes." I was now on his lap, facing him, with my legs bent at his side. The pulse beating within his muscle growing beneath my naked skin felt like a tiny drum playing my favorite tune. "Yes, I can."

"Good." His young face was all smiles. "Show me what you want."

At his command, my lips covered his like I was rendering CPR. However, it was he who was breathing life into me. Before I could gather what was right from wrong, left from right, or up from down, he had me belly up on the bed, hovering over me with a question. "Can I?"

I didn't say a word. I just shook my head up and down. I had no idea what I was consenting to, but I watched the top of his head disappear between my thighs and saw heaven fall from the sky when his tongue attacked my swollen, pinkish-brown cherry like it was a boxing bag. "Oh, oh, ooh . . ." I moaned. The sensation and suction was so powerful that my back arched away from the bed.

He inserted a thick caramel finger. "Oh, oh my goodness," I whispered and rotated my hips as his tongue dove deeper into my infinite pit. "Shit." I grabbed the sheets with so much force that I ripped them from the mattress.

"Stop," I begged him. "Stop." Pushing his head away, nearly out of breath, I asked, "Where did you learn how to do that?"

He offered a shy grin while crawling up my naked body. "In your class." In his answer, I smelled my bittersweet aroma.

I struggled to regulate my breathing. "That was never in my lesson plans." Still in shock, I said, "But that was . . ." I reached for and took a sip of the catalyst of this lunacy, my fifth glass of H-Squared, which was sitting on the nightstand. "That was unbefuckinlievable." I laughed.

His legs dangled over the end of the bed. "So," he rubbed his nose against mine, "you're the loser."

"Wait a minute," I interrupted him. "How did I get to be the loser?" I thought for a second. "I won a few times."

He tried to make me remember. "We were playing strip *and* drink dominoes. So, let's see." He paused. "You're drunk *and* you were the first one naked." He laughed. "So that constitutes me as the winner."

"Constitute?" I giggled longer than necessary. "Wasn't that a vocabulary word last week?"

"Yes." He kissed my neck. "I used it in a sentence. Do I get extra credit?"

"Nope." I blushed.

"Damn, what can a brotha do to get an A?"

"In the world today, you have to kiss ass." I added sarcastically, "Brotha."

"Ass?" He got serious. "I'm not into all of that. This brotha won't toss salad unless it's on a plate with some croutons."

"I have bread in the kitchen if it's that serious." I laughed.

When his hand touched my inner thigh, he felt me tremble. I told him that it had been a long time, though I never specified how long. He wanted to bring my wait to an end. "What's it gonna be?" He kissed my shoulder.

"Speak proper English," I teased him. "What shall it be?"

"Fuck proper English." He lay beside me then scooped his hand under me to turn me on my side. "Can I?" he asked.

I looked into his eyes, unprotected, and saw what I always thought I was too strong to see in him: a full-grown man. For weeks I thought that he was sexy, suave, seductive, and, although at times he didn't act like it, smart. However, I always had my shield up, causing his rays to bounce off of me, but tonight his brown eyes, thick coffee-colored lips, broad shoulders, and muscular arms caught me when my defense mechanisms were breached by intoxication. "Can you what?"

"Um." He tried to control his nervousness and struggled with his words. "I meant, can we?" He took a deep breath. "Now that I've shown you that I can, well, now that you see that I know how to . . ." His hand slid down the side of my body, from my shoulder to the tip of my fingers, then down to my thighs. "Can I show you what else I can do?" I'm sure that he had never asked a woman that question, but he felt he had so much to prove to me.

"No." My flirty eyes sucked him into a realm of passion he didn't know. "I can't let you outdo me." I gently pushed his long, lean body to his back. "Why don't you let me show you a few things? Do you mind?" I asked and knelt between his knees.

"Not at all." He looked at the perfect package before him and was even more aroused. I had turned the tables and he was pleased. It felt like a dream, but a dream that shouldn't be coming true. He was actually in *my* bed, his tongue was still saturated with *my* flavor, and *I* was naked before him, asking his permission to bring it.

I leaned forward and kissed him on the lips quickly. Then my tongue trailed him from the bottom of his neck to his smooth chest, then along the firmness of his abs. I lashed back and forth over his muscles, but stopped at the tip of his shorts and untied the drawstring with my teeth, then slid his boxers down, unveiling his audacious spectacle.

"Whoa," I whispered to myself. The damn thing was big enough to have a social security number. I let my fingers walk up the side of it and counted nine steps. "Damn." I was talking to myself again. Never in a million years did I predict that I would be a part of something that so many people would consider crass, asinine, and even criminal. I had no control . . . He was the right one; who he happened to be was the mistake. I was willing to take the chance, ready for any consequence, but more than anything, prepared to make room for him in my heart.

"It may be big, but it won't bite." He joked about the way and the length of time I stared at his piece. "Show me what you got." When the damp warmness of my mouth covered his skin, he muttered, "Damn," and pushed into my moisture. Within seconds, I caught his rhythm and grew to adore his feel, smell, and taste. My mouth was a well-oiled machine, and all he wanted was to add a little more grease to my engine. "Oh, oh yeah, girl." He struggled not to bite his bottom lip too hard, but ten minutes into it, he was squealing, squirming, and groaning like there was a bomb inside of him. The seconds were ticking away, and he was ready to explode.

"Mm," I hummed as I traveled upward on his dick and kissed its tip. "You like?" I licked my lips.

He could barely speak. "Yeah." He was breathing heavily and looked down at me. "Don't stop." I stroked him tightly, but when our eyes met, he saw my concern. "What's wrong?"

I licked my lips and looked away. "I'm just thinking."

"About what?"

I hesitated. "About what we're doing."

He quieted me. "Shh. You're thinking too much. I'm not thinking about it." Still on his back, he rose up onto his elbows and took my hands in his. "There's nothing wrong with what we want to do, as long as we both want to do it." He pulled me on top of him, in a straddle position, and my legs rested outward at his sides. "Don't worry so much."

"But what if people find out?"

"Fuck people."

"You can't just have a fuck-the-world attitude about this." I rested my head on his chest. "It's possible that people could find out about us."

"All right." He steadied and positioned his flaming arrow, aiming at the target. "I won't have a *fuck* attitude about this." He rubbed his arrowhead against my wet crease. "I'll have a let's-make-love attitude about this." He locked his hands on my waist and pushed upward, again giving me no time to protest.

"Oh, ooh yes. Oh yes." I took him in and realized that there was no turning back.

"Oh shit." He closed his eyes and savored the feel of my tight, wet, hot fold. "Yeah."

I was still trippin'. "Are things going to be different?"

"What?"

"Are you going to change?"

"Why would I?" he asked.

"Just answer the question." I pushed myself downward on him.

"Never." He kissed me softly and braced my back to give me more.

"Ooh shit," I moaned. "Fuck. Oh yeah."

"I'll never change," he promised me again.

I rushed down his pole like a firefighter on her way to a

four-alarm fire. I rode him like he had wheels, taking him places that even in his imagination were unreal. His toes began to curl and his sweat beaded up as large as dimes. I assumed I had taken him to school, but he put on his game face and brought it on like no other man ever had.

He found the strength to flip me under him then mounted and nailed me to the bed. "Oh, oh," I screamed. "Oh, God." I was nowhere near a church, but Theo had me calling on the name of the Lord like he was my pastor. "Jesus." I looked up at Theo's face, but couldn't find the strength to say anything except, "Oh, oh, oh, yes, yes, yes." He pulled a great deal of himself out of me, but slowly dug his way back into my grotto. "Oh, Theo, please, oh, boy."

"Boy?" He slammed into me. "I am a man." He increased his vigor. It felt like he was about to burst through my navel. "Are you gonna treat me like a man?" His thrust fell deeper into me. "Answer me."

"Yes!" I screamed through pleasure and replied to him all at once. A salty drop of sweat danced from his forehead into my mouth. "Oh, yes."

His dark brown, glistening body tightened then shivered as he pushed into me one more time. "Shit." He closed his eyes and his octave elevated three levels. "Oh yesssssss, ah, ahh, ahhhhhh, oooh." We both climbed the steep, sleek, and snowy mountain together; we reached the summit, planted our flags, and quickly fell back to the shaft of the mountain range. At the end of our journey, his eyes flew open.

"Damn," he whispered, as he lowered himself to kiss me. He fell to my side and draped his hand over my chest. "Damn." I reached for the sheets and covered our sweaty, heaving bodies and heard him mutter once again, "Damn."

I finally asked, "Are you all right?"

"Yeah."

"Well, what are all the *damns* about?" I had to know.

"You." He rubbed his fingers across my stomach. "You."

"What about me?"

"How can I put it?" After pondering awhile, he came out with it. "You're a hell of a woman."

I was flabbergasted. I had heard that my "stuff" was good, but damn. "Wow." In the midst of my blushing, I remembered who was complimenting me and came down from my cloud. Theo was eighteen years old and probably didn't have much to compare me to. He was used to getting head in the back of cars, and fuckin' and runnin' while some girl's mother was at church.

He massaged my arm. "I'm not just talking about sex when I say that." I snuggled closer to him and figured to hell with whomever he had before me. With the way he just broke me down, I was trying to have him . . . on the regular.

"Are you okay?"

"Yeah." I shook my head. "I just hope you know what you're saying."

"I know exactly what I'm saying." He kissed my shoulder. "You're a number of unbelievable things packaged into one person, and that's something that is rare, something that I thought I'd never get my hands on, especially at this age." He paused. "Paige, you're smart, cute, funny, nice, sexy, and with what just happened between us, I can now add super freak to the list." He laughed and then continued. "I've never found all of those things in one person before. It has always been something that was too much, or not enough, or something was flat out just missing." He was looking right at me. "There's nothing missing in you."

I felt the same way about him. Nothing was missing, and he felt right.

Theo pressed his lips against mine, inserted his tongue, and my sweet juice was still present. Shortly after, we were asleep, still wrapped in our warm embrace.

*   *   *

When the telephone rang, I jumped up and scanned the clock. It was after four in the morning. My heart dropped. No one would be calling me at that hour without a purpose. I reached for the phone slowly, and on the second ring, I felt Theo stretching out next to me.

"Hello?"

"Hi," the voice said. "Ms. Patrick, I'm so sorry to wake you, but your number was still in my Caller ID from the other night."

"Who is this?" I asked as Theo began rubbing my back.

"This is Ms. Lakewood." It sounded like she was crying. "Ms. Eva Lakewood, Theo's mother."

"Ms. Lakewood?" My eyes nearly popped right out of my head. "Hi."

"Theo isn't home yet," she said. "Do you remember what time he left your house?"

I sat up and faked the panicky tone I would've really had if her son had not been in my bed. "Theo's not there yet?" I nudged him.

"No." She sounded extremely concerned. "He's never done this. If he's staying at a friend's or coming in late, he normally calls. I've spoken to all of his friends, and no one has seen him except for earlier at your house."

"Well," I lied as Theo sat up and put his ear to the receiver, "he left here around eleven when the last of the kids left." I thought quickly. "But he did mention going to another party."

"Another party?"

"Yes. A few of the students were talking about going to a house party down south."

She sighed. "Theo knows that I don't play this mess. He didn't even call to let me know that."

"That's probably where he is."

"He's never done anything like this."

"Never?"

"Never."

"Wow." I smiled and thought, *That's because he never had pussy like mine.*

"He's normally more responsible than this." She paused. "At six o'clock I'll be phoning the local hospitals and hope to God that he's not admitted into any of them."

I tried to reassure her. "I'm sure he'll be home before then."

"He better be." She continued, "I hope that this has nothing to do with some girl."

I giggled. "I hope not." My girlish days were gone. "I'll call you in the morning to make sure that everything is all right."

"I'm going to kill this boy." Ms. Lakewood apologized. "Sorry about waking you."

"No problem," I said and hung up while looking over at her incredibly attractive firstborn son with a smile. "There's an APB out for you." I slipped from under the sheets and made my way to the other side of the room to blow out the candles. "I can't believe we fell asleep with these things lit." I shook my head. "I never do that."

"That's because I've never been here."

"Is that what it is?"

"Yeah," he said. "I'm all about seeing that you start doing new things."

"Like burning down the house?"

"Yep." He looked at the clock. "I didn't realize that it was so late."

"Me neither." When I approached the bed, instead of jumping up like he should've done after that phone call, Theo lay back down. I bent toward the candle on the nightstand and let a tiny bit of air escape to send the flame to rest. "So, what are you going to do?"

"I don't know." He took a deep breath. "I'm sorry, though."

I curled up next to him. "Sorry about what?" His body was warm and his skin still smelled edible, like it did when he walked through the door hours ago.

He seemed embarrassed. "I'm sure that you've never had some dude's mother calling you in the middle of the night before."

"No, actually, this happens to me all the time," I joked. "Theo, it's okay. Don't worry about it."

He was quiet for a while. "So, is this about to happen?"

"What?"

"You and I?"

"You and me?" I corrected him teasingly.

"Whatever." He tickled me. "Theo and Paige." He continued. "Are we going to do this?"

"Do what?"

He clarified, "Are we gonna be together?"

"Um, I think . . . well." I paused. "I guess we can see."

"Don't guess. If you don't want to, just say it."

Lord, I wanted nothing more than to have a man again, but Theo wasn't really a man. Okay, in biology he was considered of the male persuasion, he carried the XY chromosome, but he wasn't a *man* man, like the one I had prayed for. Theo didn't have a job, drove his mother's former car, lived with his mother, and was still in school . . . high school, to be exact. Was I desperate?

"Hello?"

"Yes," I answered.

"Tell me what you want," he said, "and not what you guess."

"What could we have, Theo?"

"A lot," he replied without hesitation. "I know that I'm young, but I'm not your average high school senior. I'm going places in life."

"What can we have, though? What can we do together? Where can we go?"

"Are you serious?" He continued. "We can have whatever we want, do whatever we like, and go where we please, but only if we both want it."

"That all sounds good, but let's keep it real." I was straight up. "We could never go anywhere in public."

"True," Theo agreed and kissed my cheek. "But privately we can do whatever we want."

"Okay," I said. "I'm willing to see where things go."

"Are you sure?"

"Yeah." Actually, I was still thinking about it. "Is that what you want?" I asked.

"No doubt." He pulled me toward him and kissed my forehead. "I ain't never scurred." We laughed. "I guess I better get going before my mom reports the ride stolen." He positioned himself over me and kissed my lips softly. "I'll call you tomorrow."

I felt like a kid on Christmas . . . I had a new toy. I hated watching him get dressed, walk out of the door, and then reverse out of my driveway. I even fixed my mouth to ask him to stay, but that just couldn't be.

I couldn't go back to sleep, so I flipped through channels until the sun came up then got the energy to get up and complete my three-mile run.

Afraid of what her attitude would be like, I reluctantly called Ms. Lakewood as I promised. She informed me that Theo arrived around five o'clock, stating that he did go to a party after leaving my house. He left the party at one, but on a long, dark road on the way home, he fell asleep at the wheel. He did just as *she* had told him many times to do if that ever happened. Instead of driving dangerously tired, he pulled over and took what was supposed to be a power nap, but lapsed into a four-hour dream.

Later, I sat at my dining room table to eat lunch and final-ize my lesson plans. However, the many black eyes of the scattered dominoes ogled me and I smiled. The smell of alco-hol and sex had long vanished from my house and me, and surprisingly, I had no regrets.

~Situation #10~

The Fly

*H*i, it's, me *Musca Domestica* again. *Surely you haven't forgotten me. What? Are you suffering from Alzheimer's or something? I'm the housefly. Remember, it was me that first brought this story to you, hence the title of the book . . . duh!*

You can clearly see why my jaws dropped when I flew into the bedroom and saw ass everywhere. Now that you're caught up and know just as much about them and their situation as I do, please tell me what this heifer is thinking. I mean Paige is an attractive, thirty-two-year-old woman. Not only has she taken back her body—at five foot nine, she is 36-27-40, and that's not the combination to my locker—the girl is fine. Hell, even Doran's "gaydar" picked up on that. I know that you stronger than strong women are thinking that homegirl is a fool to occasionally still be messing with Craig, but honey, y'all don't know what this man looks like. Imagine a combination of Rick Fox, Will Smith, and Jason Taylor . . . that's Craig. Yeah, now let me see you resist him.

Let me get your mind percolating again. Envision, if you will, that Morris Chestnut and Tyson Beckford are siblings and had a younger but taller brother. That's my man, Theo.

As you've heard, he's doing the damn thing on the basketball court, and driving people crazy with the anticipation of his decision of college or the NBA. Everybody wants Theodore Lakewood. Colleges are giving him athletic scholarship talks during the day, but at night they call back from unknown numbers, throwing out dollar amounts. His phone is constantly ringing with calls from colleges, girls, sport agents, girls, NBA representatives, more girls, and television and radio stations wanting interviews. However, all Theo wants is a basketball, a girl, and his mother to chill the hell out.

As Theo smuggled in, once again after the bell, Paige erased the board then turned to face him and the others. "Well, it's certainly great to see all of you." She smiled at her sixth period students. "Did everyone have a good time on Saturday?"

Theo partially raised his hand and spoke without being called on. "I didn't, so I say that we do it again this Saturday." The class laughed.

"Ms. Patrick, your house is beautiful." Angie was still kissing ass. "It was absolutely perfect."

"Thank you, Angela." Paige gave her nemesis a fake smile. "So everyone was satisfied?" Theo winked, and that answered her question. "By the way, Mr. Lakewood, don't think for a moment that I didn't see you scurry in late." She found it hard to communicate with him like he was just another student.

"Scurry?" He smiled. "Is that a vocabulary word this week?"

"No, but during your detention later on, I'm sure that writing thirty sentences to include the word might make you appreciate it."

"Detention?" he whined. "I have practice, though."

"Well, this will be the free-throw line."

He pretended to be upset. "Damn." Theo was actually

very anxious. All he thought about since leaving her house was the way he felt inside of her, the way she tasted, and the way she moaned.

"I need you all to break into groups of threes and turn to section C of chapter five." Underneath the teacher routine, all she could think about was the way he handled her body when he was on top of her. "If you read the story over the weekend, then this assignment shouldn't be a problem. However, if you didn't, you better hope that your neighbor did, or this will certainly be an F."

Angie attempted to walk to the other side of the room. "Work with those around you. Angela, there are plenty of people for you to work with over there." Paige pointed then explained the assignment. She spent a few minutes with each group to be sure that her instructions were clear. During her brief stop at Theo's group, she was outright astonished to hear him discuss the story in detail. He had done his homework.

"Theodore Lakewood is a true talent," the reporter said as he wrapped up his mini-interview. "He plays the perimeter, passes the ball, and has great ball handling, shooting, and passing ability. Those things, in addition to his supernatural capability to see the floor, make him a rare find." He smiled. "Back to you, Ann."

"So, Theo, any decisions yet?" asked one the of the many television reporters who ran down to the court after West Dade won their first game of the season, in which Theo scored thirty-three points.

"Decisions?" He wiped his face with his jersey and smiled. "I prefer my coffee black, no cream and no sugar."

"That's a good one." The reporter issued a live-on-TV giggle. "I should've clarified my statement." He spoke into the microphone once more. "We know that you have everyone knocking, not only *on* your door but knocking *down* your door, NBA and college teams alike. Any word on where you're leaning?"

"Well, Wes, I've spoken to several college coaches, and I'm currently weighing my options. I truly haven't made up my mind about anything yet."

Another reporter screamed out, "We have word that you were signing with the University of Connecticut."

"Really?" Theo shook his head from side to side. "The UCONN basketball program is without a doubt one of the best in the nation, but so are Duke and Kentucky. There are many schools that I would love to be a part of. Picking just one is tough."

"So, your decision is college?" a female reporter asked.

"No, I haven't made a decision yet." His charming smile was sure to project well on the eleven o'clock news. "When I make a choice, I promise not to leave you guys out."

"You'll be holding a press conference of some sort?"

"Yes, something. After I inform my family and friends, you'll be next in line." As he answered questions, he stepped slowly toward the other side of the gymnasium, but they didn't leave his side until he disappeared into the locker room.

Paige watched all of the commotion from the bleachers. She, his biggest fan, was the quietest person in the gym during the entire the game. She didn't want to stand out, be noticed, or be mistaken for overly excited when he hit a three, stole the ball, or was at the foul line.

He spent the entire first quarter trying to pick her out of the sold-out crowd. Instead of listening to Craig's advice during a time-out, he scanned the mob until he spotted her up top in a royal blue blouse. As he ran back onto the court, he blew a kiss, which sent the girls into an uproar. Every female seated in that section believed that it was meant for her, but the real recipient never flinched.

The "after-game plan" was for them to link up at Paige's

house, so after watching him fade into the locker room, she fished her keys out of her purse and exited the back of the gym to avoid the crowd. There wasn't much light in the area, so she ran instead of walked. When she reached the parking lot, she ran right into—

"Hey, where are you going?" Ian grabbed her by the arm as she rushed by.

"Hi." She caught her breath. "You enjoyed the game?"

"Oh yeah." He smiled. "That damn Lakewood packs the house, doesn't he?"

"Yeah." The mention of his name made her search the crowd for him. "He played really well tonight."

He chuckled. "That kid must shit basketballs."

She blushed and hoped it couldn't be detected. "He's awesome."

"He has a great future ahead of him. I mean he doesn't even seem like an eighteen-year-old. Talking to him last night blew me away."

Her ears tuned in. "Where did you see him last night?"

"I didn't see him. We talked on the phone when he called for Angela." He carried on. "I told her that this is one she can't fuck up. That boy is a damn treasure. Treat that mutha-fucka like a goddamn king." He went on, giggling. "I'll change her curfew for him."

"Is that so?" Paige was less than amused.

"Hell yeah. Having him for a son-in-law would make my life complete." Ian grinned. "Shit, I'd retire the day after the wedding."

Whatever temperature blood boils at, Paige had surpassed it. "So, they're dating?"

"I don't know," he shrugged his shoulders, "but there is some interest there."

"Who's interested in whom?" She had to know.

"Well, I think they're equally interested in each other." His eyes brightened and he rested his hand lightly on her arm.

"Since you have them in your class, why don't you pair them up for special projects or to be homework buddies or something?"

What the—? "I think you need to get a life, Ian." She chuckled as the words slipped out, but her level of seriousness was no laughing matter.

"Come on, encourage them." He wasn't smiling. "They need to be together."

"I think *you* need them to be together." She tried not to sound bitter.

"Relax," he said. "Damn, I was just kidding."

"Sure. So was I." She was sick to her stomach and had to stop herself from saying too much. "I need to get going."

"So soon?"

"Yeah, I have to get home. Business to take care of."

"Can I help?" He winked.

"I can handle it."

"As I've asked before, when are you going to allow someone, a man, to handle things for you?"

"Someone *is* handling things for me," she said with the same fake smile she gave his daughter daily.

"Who?" he asked.

She tried dismissing him. "It was nice seeing you again."

"How about dinner next week at your place?" He licked his lips. "I'll bring the goodies. All you have to do is let me put it in your mouth."

How tacky. She was in shock. "I can't believe you just said that."

"I'm just keeping it real."

"Yeah, real nasty." She walked away.

On the way to her car, she mingled with the students and Ms. Henry, the economics teacher. They talked about the game, the weather, and the upcoming holiday. It was mid-November, and the chill in the Florida air was to be praised.

During her conversation with another teacher, she saw

members of the basketball team slowly trickling out of the front door, of the school. Though she was quite a ways from the door she could read the numbers on their jerseys like they were on paper in a mathematic equation just an inch away. Numbers seventeen, three, sixteen, two, six, nine, twenty-two, twenty-nine, then finally number twenty-seven walked through the doors all alone.

Before Theo exited the school, several girls, one being Angela, asked him about his plans for the evening. He lied to them all, telling them that he needed to baby-sit his younger brother. Angela volunteered to assist, but he declined the offer. His evening was already arranged. His mother, who was at the game but left in the middle of the fourth quarter to start her shift on time, was under the impression that after the game he'd hang out with the team a bit then go to Will's, where he'd sleep because Will needed a ride early the next morning. Will didn't need a ride or anything else from Theo. He was too busy with Jessica; so busy that they were even holding hands throughout the basketball game.

Once he was outside, Theo looked around the crowd until he spotted her in the distance, then pointed at his car.

"Well, Ms. Henry, you drive safely. Have a good night and an even better weekend," Paige said.

Though they were walking in two different directions, they had a common goal . . . being together. Paige hopped into her car with a smile that could turn an onyx stone into a princess cut diamond. As she reversed from her spot, headlights crept up to her bumper. She pulled off, and he flashed his lights and followed suit. Other than their moments alone after class, this would be their first time together since their "first time" together.

During this boring ride to Paige's house, I'd like to vindicate myself by discussing some common fly stereotypes. All flies do not eat shit, hover over dead bodies, or find delight in buzzing dangerously close to a human ear at three in the morning. I am a fly with class. You won't find me around your crusty-ass toilet. I stay in the kitchen, and the moment you leave an uncovered pot unattended, you better believe that I act as your professional taste tester. At dinnertime, I pray that you'll let the clumsiest muthafucka in your family pour the drinks, so that through their spillage I can get my drink on. As for trying to annoy you, hell naw. I saw what the fly swatter did to my aggravating big brother, so when you sleep, I sleep.

When she turned onto her street, Paige looked in the rearview mirror and watched the headlights behind her turn too. However, when her house came into view, her eyes widened. "What in the hell . . .?"

Theo's car was in the driveway, and he was standing in front of his opened trunk with an overnight bag draped over his shoulder. As she approached, he waved her in with a smile as the car behind her stopped.

She let the passenger window down and pulled halfway into the driveway. "Who's in that car?"

He didn't hear her. "What?" He walked over.

As she looked back, the car's lights were now off and it sped, in reverse, down the street. "That car followed me here from the school. I thought it was you."

He strained his eyes to try to make out what kind of car it was, but he couldn't. It was too far gone. "Was it Coach?"

"I don't think so. I hope not. I thought it was you." She parked, sprung from the car, and stared down the street. "They followed me here from West Dade."

"Well, c'mon." Theo walked around the car and grabbed her hand. "Let's get inside."

"Wait a second." She resisted his pulling. "Whoever it was saw you."

"So?" he said.

"Here at my house." She tried to make him understand.

"And?" He brushed it off. "I could be here for a thousand different reasons."

"Yeah, but at almost eleven o'clock at night?"

"Paige, I don't give a shit."

"Well, I do." She looked back down the road. "I could lose my job."

"Come here." He pulled her into an embrace and squeezed her. "We're already here, so let's make the most of it."

"Yeah, but—"

"Shh," he silenced her. "We're here."

~Situation #11~

Theo

I was convinced that crazy-ass Trese was either in or had something to do with the car that followed Paige. If she found out something, anything, she'd set out to make our lives miserable.

Paige opened the front door, disarmed the security system, and when she flicked the light switch, I couldn't say a word. It was West Dade paradise. Purple and gold decorations and balloons were everywhere, and a large banner that read WAY TO GO THEO was posted over the sliding glass door.

"Surprise!" She smiled up at me and stepped farther into the house. On the dining room table, set for two, was a small round cake with a basketball airbrushed onto it. Metallic purple confetti shone up from both the white-tiled floor and beige-carpeted area.

"Congratulations on your win." She left my side to light the gold candles placed throughout the living room. "I knew that the game would be yours, so I planned a victory party." On her way over to me, she turned out the lights. "You're my MVP."

Here we were, back at her place, under the orange glow of candlelight again. I couldn't believe my eyes. She had done this for me . . . for me. It might not seem like much to some, but for this eighteen-year-old, it was like prom night five times over.

"Cat got your tongue?" she asked.

My tongue wanted her cat. My hands slid down her back. "I can't believe you did this."

"You like?" she asked.

I was in awe. I laughed and rubbed my head. "This is un-believable." My life was too damn sweet. I had just led my team to victory during our first game. I had Paige, an intelli-gent, beautiful, and sexy black woman in my life, and now I was walking into my own personal pep rally. There was no word to express what type of man she made me feel like.

With my hand in hers, she walked over to the stereo, and at a click of a button, the room was filled with a low trumpet, the soft, slow melody of a piano, shivering cymbals, and drums that were too elegant to be beaten harshly. We danced, and like a rain shower on a summer day, the notes sprinkled onto me but melted into my soul before I could wipe them away.

The music made its way into my mouth and I began to hum. As the vibration walked down my body, I could no longer pretend I hadn't spent the entire day wanting her. I picked her up by the waist, found her lips, and felt her legs wrapped around me. It was an open invitation. I tried to move slowly, use tact and be romantic, but as the drummer got excited, so did I, and when the piano keys got low, I did too . . . low, down, and dirty.

I backed her up against the wall and didn't have patience for all the buttons, so I ripped the blue blouse from her chest. I had missed two shots daydreaming about squeezing her big, dark brown nipples and their silver piercing between my fin-gers.

With her tongue wildly exploring my mouth and her back still up on the wall, I pulled Paige's skirt upward to her waist and barely got my basketball shorts to my thighs before I slipped into her. I palmed both of her ass cheeks and gave her so much dick that it should've come out on the other side of the wall.

"Aaah." The saxophone wailed along with her. I bent my knees and felt myself fall into an untouched valley within her. I wanted that new property to know who was its founder. I hit that exact spot again and again, harder and harder, faster and faster, until her fingernails dug into my back for blood, her eyelids squeezed shut, and she groaned like someone was stabbing her.

"Theo," she moaned.

"Yeah?"

"I have condoms," she trembled and struggled to speak, "that we were supposed to use."

"Oops." I didn't let her comment interrupt my strokes. "Do you wanna get 'em?"

"Mmmm." She moved her head up and down. "Yeah."

"You wanna stop?" My rhythm never changed. "Do you want me to stop?"

"Damn." She sighed as the song ended and the room fell silent. "No, don't stop."

"You sure?"

"Yeah, keep going, don't stop." Her body heaved between each word, which was followed by a thrust. "Don't stop."

I felt guilty about not using protection, especially after the hour-long telephone conversation we had about condoms the day after things happened the last time. We vowed to practice safe sex. In the past, I would never dip into anybody's chocolate pudding without taking the necessary precautions. I didn't know what had taken over me. Damn!

"Paige, you feel so good." I slid our bodies down the wall and onto the plush carpet beneath. I moved her legs from my waist to my shoulders as my knees sank into the rug and I into her. The loud howl that escaped her was scary, so I slowed myself.

"What happened?" She looked at me.

"That noise you made," I stuttered. "I don't want to hurt you."

"That sound meant that it was getting good." She smiled.

I smiled at her. "Oh, it was *just* getting good?"

"You know what I mean." She laughed. "It was getting better."

"It sounded like I was killin' you," I joked.

"Then kill me," she said with the naughtiest look on her face. "Kill me, Theo."

With that said, my mushroom plowed back into her creamy soup bowl and sure enough, she howled again and again. "Is that the way you want it?"

"Yes." She licked her lips. "Slaughter me." Her legs tightened around my neck and she started to move her body like a snake, slapping that pussy into me over and over again. "Fuck me." Damn!

"Oh yeah," I said and closed my eyes.

"Fuck me, Theo." Her dirty mouth took me to another level. She wailed. "Oh, oh, oh, God." I poked her rapidly, repeatedly, and raunchily, penetrating deeper each and every time until her shaking, squealing, and squeezing led me to a final thrust. I burst within her walls and trembled for what seemed like an hour before falling to her side.

"We were supposed to eat first," Paige whispered.

"I wasn't really hungry before."

"Now?"

"Now I'll eat you if you come too close."

"Let's see." She climbed on top of me and gently touched my lips with her fingers. "Eat me," she teased and giggled. "Ouch," she cried when I softly bit her fingertip and pretended to chew.

Paige jumped up and returned a few minutes later wrapped in a pink terrycloth robe, carrying a sheet, a blanket, and two pillows. She then went into the kitchen and came back with a bottle of champagne, two glasses, and two plates of Chinese food.

"That's what I'm talkin' 'bout," I screamed, and then we got down to business.

After I was stuffed with egg-foo-this and sweet-and-sour-that, I put on my shorts and took the plates and utensils to the kitchen. I was smiling like a damn fool, and the next thing I knew, I was standing in front of her sink, washing dishes. I didn't even do dishes at home. This woman had some kind of wonderful something.

I returned to the living room to a fresh glass of champagne and Paige holding out a small wrapped box toward me. "This is for you."

"What's this?" I hadn't felt this good since my twelfth birthday when Mom surprised me with a new Sega Genesis system. I tore apart the wrapping paper and opened the box to find a flip Samsung cellular phone. "Is this mine?"

"Yes."

"Are you serious?" No woman other than my mother and aunts had ever spent more than twenty dollars on me.

"Yes, I'm serious," she said as I turned it on and giggled at the cute sound that it made. "I get paranoid when you call me from home, so I got you a phone."

"Thank you." I sat next to her on the couch and pulled her to me, kissing her on the forehead. "Thank you so much."

"My number is already programmed." Paige smiled. "If I knew Angela's number, I would've put it in there too," she said under her breath, "since you have so much to call her about."

"What?"

"Nothing." She played it off.

"Come on, don't be shy now," I said. "What did you say about Angie?"

She sat up. "I said that if I knew Angela's number, I would've programmed it, since you have so much to talk to her about. I heard that you called her last night."

"Okay."

"Did you?"

"Yeah." It seemed like Paige wanted a reason from me, but I wanted one from her first. "Why?"

"Why what?" she asked.

"Why are you asking me that?"

"Well, why did you call her?"

I decided to put this foolish thing to an end so that our night could proceed. "I forgot to write down the homework assignment, and when I called you yesterday, you didn't answer."

"But . . ." she said, "we talked last night and you never asked me about the homework."

"I didn't have to. By that time I had already gotten the assignment from Angie." I laughed. "That's why I called her."

"Well," she was embarrassed, "next time you need something from me, don't turn to anyone else for it."

"Yes, ma'am." I pulled her toward me and kissed her. "I need a little something right now." We made our way to the bedroom and before long, if it ended with an –ing, we were doing it: kissing, licking, sucking, teasing, pleasing, nibbling, groping, tasting, sweating, pulling, and pushing. We were fucking it up.

At 9 A.M. Paige's phone woke us. It was her friend Toni's husband, calling from down the street. Paige forgot that she had agreed to keep the twins until Sunday so that Toni and Marcus could attend a function in West Palm Beach.

After tearing down the WAY TO GO THEO banner, Paige met Marcus outside, talked a bit, said good-bye, then brought the boys in. She did a great job keeping us separated. The twins were in the living room and I, like a prisoner, was locked in the bedroom. Her plan was to take them out for pizza so that I could leave the house without being seen. However, when she went to take the clothes out of the dryer, in ran Dev or Kev—I couldn't tell them apart.

Not expecting to see anyone, especially in Auntie Paige's bed, he took a deep breath. "Hey! I didn't know you was in here." He walked over to the bed. "What are you doing here?"

"Hey, li'l man." I held out my hand to him. "What's happening?"

"I remember your name." He slapped my hand hard. "You're Theo."

"You're right."

He looked at my legs. "Are you taller than a giraffe?"

"Well, I've never stood next to one, but I don't think so."

"Why are you in here?" He continued, "Did you sleep here?"

"Um." I wasn't prepared for his interrogation. "Yeah, but I slept in the living room."

"Then why aren't you in the living room now?"

"I got up when you guys came, so that you could play out there."

"Kevin," he yelled. "Kevin, guess who's here?"

Before Kev could make it down the hall, Paige sprung in and struck like lightning. "Oh my God." She looked like she had died and gone to a place worse than hell. She yelled, "Devin, what are you doing in here?"

"I was looking for the Gameboy."

Her hands rushed to her head. "I keep your things in the other room." She tried not to sound too mad at him. "Aren't you supposed to knock when a door is closed?"

"Yes." He pouted then hung his head sadly. "I'm sorry."

I grabbed his arm and pulled him to me. "It's cool."

"Theooooo," Kev screamed as he ran into the room and jumped into the bed. "Come play Playstation with us."

"Yeah." Dev's spirit was back up. "Come on."

"I need you guys back into the living room." Paige pointed out the door and as they left the room, she whispered, "You have to go."

"They've already seen me." I walked over to her. "I'll play with them. It'll keep them out of your way while you work around the house."

"They talk a lot."

"I don't mind. They can talk to me."

"I don't mean to you." She was still upset. "They talk. They tell their parents everything." She was nervous. "Theo, we can't do things like this."

"Things like what?"

"Like us being together in front of people."

I chuckled. "They're only kids."

"Yeah, and they know that you're my student."

I spoke matter-of-factly. "I'm also eighteen."

"Big deal!" She huffed. "You can vote!"

"Fuck it." I was getting mad. "I'll leave."

"I'm sorry." She sighed before she spoke again. "I shouldn't have said that." She wrapped her arms around me. "I just don't know if it's wise to have you stay."

"Then I'll go," I said.

"No." She smiled timidly. "Stay."

"You sure?"

"Yeah." She blushed. "I guess I can use some help around here today."

I bent down to her lips. "Oh, and by the way," I kissed her tenderly, "voting *is* a big deal, especially in the state of Florida."

~Situation #12~

Paige

It was an overcast, rainy Sunday afternoon. The sky was dark and dreary like one you'd come across in Seattle and not South Florida. Toni spent the day at my house. Marcus came up with the idea of taking the boys to see a movie, and Toni and I eagerly encouraged him. It would mean that after two months, she and I would finally have two or three child-free hours together.

"Find something for us to watch," Toni said and threw the remote control at me. For ten minutes, I gave every channel fifteen seconds to impress me. The winner was the Lifetime Movie Network. Those gullible, crying, whining-ass women in those movies always made me feel like I was the strongest and most emotionally stable woman alive.

"All right." Toni sat up in her chair during a commercial break and stared at me. "Out with it."

"Huh?" I was shocked. "Out with what?"

"It's evident that you're not gonna volunteer information, so I'll just beg for it." She groveled, "Please tell me what's going on."

"Tell you what?" I looked at her with the best confused look I had.

Toni raised her voice. "I've been holding this in for three weeks."

"Holding what in?"

"Knowing about him." She rolled her eyes. "Or not knowing the truth about him."

"About who?" I grimaced.

"C'mon, you know whom." She giggled.

"I told you what happened with Doran."

"Forget Doran!" She continued in a whisper like we weren't truly alone. "You know who I'm talkin' 'bout."

"Okay, for real, no, I don't."

Toni grabbed the bag of Doritos on the coffee table and stuffed a few in her mouth. "My babies tell me everything." She laughed. "They don't mean to. It just runs in their blood. They can't hold shit. Their daddy is a lawyer."

What in the hell? I said to myself and prayed that Theo's name wasn't about to come out of her mouth. I was trying hard not to look like a deer caught in the headlights. "Well, what exactly did your babies have to say?"

"First of all, don't be upset with my boys." She grinned. "They meant no harm."

"I'm sure," I said while my heart sank deeper into paranoia.

"I heard about Theo."

"Who?" Did I give her my best astonished face?

"Don't *who* me." She smiled. "Theo."

Ignorance is bliss. "What about Theo?" Pretending to be ignorant is just plain stupid.

"He was at your house all day that Saturday when the boys were there."

I lied. "He was fixing something. And?"

"And he spent the night on Friday?"

"Where did you get all of that from?"

"Devin."

I reached for words and when none reached back, I resorted to first grade vocabulary. "Devin's a liar."

She threw a pillow at me. "My kids don't lie."

"Yes, they do." I threw the pillow back, and for a full minute, I recalled a story that Devin, the master liar, had fabricated as a cunning ploy to blame someone else for something he actually did. Toni wasn't paying me any mind.

"Devin said that he opened the door and Mr. Theo was lying in your bed, under the covers, watching a basketball game," she added on to her opening statement, "and I know that it was before noon because Kevin mentioned that he was in the living room watching *Recess*, his favorite cartoon, which comes on at eleven."

"You believed them?" I tried a final time to be acquitted of the charge.

"Yes," she said. "What in the hell was that boy doing in your bed, Paige?"

"Shit." I sighed, which was my surrender and a weak closing argument. Toni was my best friend; sooner or later I'd have to come to her for advice or just to vent. This secret was eating me alive from the inside out. "Yeah, he slept over."

"Shut the hell up," she shouted.

"What?"

As though she didn't expect me to tell the truth, Toni stared at me with her mouth gaped open. "You're fuckin' kiddin' me."

I couldn't look at her. "We've been seeing each other for the past two months."

"Shut up! Are you crazy?" She laughed. "I mean, I know that he's tall, handsome, and fine as hell, but isn't he like sixteen or something?"

"He's eighteen."

"That's insane."

"Thanks." I was somewhat ashamed. "Thanks a lot."

"Tell me that you're not screwing him." I knew that was the last thing Toni wanted to hear, and when I didn't answer, she shrieked, "You're fucking him?"

"Shh." I looked around like someone might hear.

"You're shittin' me."

"I shit you not." I thought my answer over. "We've slept together, but it's more than just that."

"Then what is it?" she asked sarcastically.

"We're trying to see where it can go."

"Where it can go?" By this time, Toni was standing up. "Paige, you can't be serious." Her voice echoed through the large gray room, traveling from the high vaulted ceiling to the black-and-red-art deco leather furniture, then bounced from the elegant coffee table to my ear.

"I was just kidding. I thought Devin was exaggerating like always." She disappeared into the kitchen, giving me a minute to wish that I had denied the charge a little longer.

Toni resurfaced with her expensive scotch and two glasses with a few ice cubes sliding around in them. "I was fuckin' around. Never for a minute did I think that something was really going on. I know how my kids make shit up." She stared at me with a smile. "But it seems like we really do have something to drink, think, and talk about now."

"So what *did* Devin tell you?"

She mimicked her son's voice perfectly. "Mommy, Theo played Crazy Taxi with us all day. He can drive, too." She paused to get another annoying nasal statement together. "Theo was in Auntie Paige's bed, but he wasn't asleep. I didn't wake him up."

"You think I'm stupid, don't you?"

"I'm thinking he's eighteen and he's your student. Why not at least wait until graduation?"

"It just happened," I tried to explain. "I mean, I didn't set out for any of this to happen. It just happened."

"When?"

"After the party."

"So," she was shocked, "y'all just had sex, no questions asked?"

"No." I took a deep breath. "He had been flirting with me since the beginning of the school year."

"Were you flirting back?"

I didn't want to answer. "Somewhat."

"Well, were you or not?"

I confessed, "I guess I contributed. I didn't think anything would come of it, but that night, we started drinking, talking, and laughing, and before I knew what hit me, we were naked." I sighed. "Damn, I wish I could rewind everything."

"I guess you really didn't want to tell me."

I looked at her. "It's not like I was never going to. I just wanted to keep it to myself a while until I could make sense out of what I'm doing." Though I felt odd, I continued. "I just feel so fuckin' desperate."

I expected her to agree with me, but she didn't. "What is life if you don't do what makes you happy?" She smiled. "Does he make you happy?"

"Yeah, but he's still in high school, for Christ's sake."

She approached me, sat down on the sofa, and poured the scotch. "C'mon, people think back to their high school days all the time. Do you think that they're thinking about classes, books, and teachers? No way. They're thinking about high school sex. When you did it wherever you could, were almost always getting caught, and most of all how that sweaty, sexy, tight-bodied seventeen- or eighteen-year-old boy could fuck for hours at a time." We toasted to that. "To answer your question, no, I don't think you're a freak." She paused and giggled. "His momma might, though."

"Don't remind me."

"She's gonna beat your ass," Toni joked. "Hang your grown ass out to dry."

"Shut up." I went on for close to ten minutes about Theo

and the way he made me feel. I felt the need to justify my situation.

"If it makes you feel better," Toni's eyes were eager, "you are not completely alone."

I placed my glass on a coaster. "What do you mean?"

"I have this twenty-one-year-old in my microbiology class who sits right behind me." She smiled. "He has one more time to mistakenly rub my butt before I rape his ass."

"What?"

"He's too much."

I couldn't believe my ears. The difference in our situations was that I wasn't married with kids. "You're not serious?"

"I am." She continued jokingly. "I would consider disregarding my husband and kids for a few hours to be with him."

"Did you?"

"No," she looked away shyly, "I said I would."

"Whoa." Last I heard, Marcus was the best thing since the invention of the telephone. "What does he look like?"

"Tall, slim but not skinny, brown skin and brown eyes." She smiled. "He's just handsome. I think he's mixed with a little bit of something because of the texture of his goatee, and he has no naps in his new growth."

"What else?"

"His name is Derek." She blushed. "He's so much of everything."

"Like?" I wasn't about to be left hanging.

"He's one of those thugged-out looking ones, which you know I really don't go for."

"Yeah?" I was interested. "Tell me more."

"He lives in Sean Jean, FUBU, Roc-a-Wear, sneakers, boots, and all that type of stuff." She paused. "But when he opens his mouth, he makes more sense than the professor." She continued. "The university had a talent show to raise money for the tsunami victims last week, and he was in it."

"Doing what?" I chuckled.

"He rapped." She got excited. "He was so damn good."

"Really?"

She spoke intensely. "It turned me on so much."

"Him rapping?" I asked.

"Yeah, it's hard to explain."

"Well, try, because I have to hear this."

"It was the way he held the mic, the way he pronounced words, his flow, and his message."

"What was the message?" I asked.

"The song was called 'Father Figure.' It was basically about how black men should raise the bar on their own, by striving to expect more from themselves. Not just black men with kids, but all of them should work at becoming someone a child could follow. The other part of it was for women, mainly black women. When choosing a mate, she should measure more than the inches between his legs. She should measure his manhood; the qualities that would make him a good father to her children."

"All of this and I bet he has an itsy bitsy teeny weeny."

She said, "You've missed the whole damn point."

"I got the whole damn point." I laughed. "I'm just messing with you."

"What's the message then?" she asked.

"Derek doesn't have much in the meat department. However, he'll make a wonderful father." I laughed. "I'm just kidding. I got the message, Toni."

"Don't talk about my friend like that." She pretended to frown. "Apologize for that teeny weeny shit."

"Who's to say that it's not true?" I pulled her toward me. "I'm sure that your friend is working with something."

"I hope so because—"

"Excuse me?" I butted in. "You're a married woman, ma'am."

"I know this." Then she added, "But on Friday, Derek and I started working on a project together."

"Alone?"

"Yeah." She shrugged her shoulders. "Well, we were supposed to be working in groups of threes, but he and I teamed up and no one else came over, so we're the only ones in our group."

"Wow." I didn't like the sound of it. "I know that he's supposed to be good-looking and all, but I don't know if this is a good idea. You're inviting trouble to your front door."

"Relax," Toni hurried to explain. "I just need someone to talk to." She swirled her drink around and the ice clinked against the glass.

"Talk to *me*." I giggled. "What am I, chopped liver?"

"I'm not forgetting about talking to you, but I'm not talking about talking like that," she finished in a cheerless tone. "I need male companionship, a guy to talk to."

"Marcus," I reminded her. "What about Marcus?"

"Please." She swallowed what was left in her glass. "We can't agree on anything. The only times we get along is in front of folks." Toni turned to face me head-on. "Plus nowadays, all he talks about is how much he wants us to get into the swinging scene."

"What?" My mouth dropped. "I thought you all were through thinking about that."

"I thought so, too, but apparently I was wrong." She grimaced and rolled her eyes. "How in the hell is that supposed to make me feel? It's like he's not satisfied with me."

"I cannot believe him." I was truly astonished. "Why?"

"No clue."

"Well, Toni, you were wrong for entertaining the thought to begin with," I said. "He spoon fed you this bullshit, and now you're considering eating the whole enchilada."

"No," she said quickly. "This all resurfaced while we were

in Palm Beach. We ran into a couple who mentioned visiting Cancun the same weekend that Melinda and Fred went."

"So, they're swingers?"

"Have to be," she said. "Later that night, all Marcus cared to talk about was how he'd love to see me riding the guy while he has his dick in his wife's mouth."

I was in shock. "You're kidding?"

"Nope."

I frowned. "That's not normal, Toni. Black people don't do shit like that."

"That's a lie. There are a lot of black swingers out there, trust me." She poured another round and continued. "Marcus thinks that is a way to test the strength of a relationship, have fun, and keep things sexually interesting."

"Buy handcuffs, a dildo, anal beads, or edible undies to keep stuff interesting. Don't cheat."

"Doing it this way isn't cheating, so *he* says."

"Bullshit. Doing it that way is the polite way of saying that you want to have sex with other people." I added, "That's not healthy."

"Yeah," she said weakly.

"You're thinking about it, aren't you?"

"I truly don't know." Toni's puzzled look said it all. "Okay, I know that he has probably not been faithful over the years, and God knows that I've thought of messing around, so neither of us is perfect, but how am I supposed to watch him have sex with other women?"

Marcus is a handsome guy, and from the tidbits of information I gathered from Toni, he took advanced placement courses in Long, Hard, and Rough, majored in All Night Pleasure, and minored in Vaginal Buffet. With that said, if they tried the swingers' scene, any woman who got a piece of him *would* come back for more, and it might just be without Toni's knowledge.

"At first when you said that he mentioned it, I thought he

was just bringing it up to test your limits. You know how men do that shit."

"I thought so too, and that's why I played with the idea. I was actually trying to make him jealous." She smiled. "I just wanted to see what he would say."

"Surprised the mess out of you, huh?" I cracked up.

"When he told me that he had called Fred and told him that we were open to it, I nearly died, but the part that really got me was when Melinda came over to talk to me about it. I wanted to throw up."

"What did she have to say?"

"She said that years ago they never thought or talked about doing it. They actually thought, just as we do, that it was unhealthy for relationships, and that people who participated in it were just looking for an excuse to do their thing," Toni carried on. "They went to Cancun on vacation and just happened to be staying at the same hotel where the black swingers were gathering that year. She said that they were sitting in the restaurant eating when another couple, who assumed they were with the group, approached and asked if they could join them for lunch. They thought nothing of it. In the middle of the meal, right in front of Fred, the guy starts telling her how he could see that her nipples were hard through her shirt. Before Fred could comment, the man's wife was rubbing Fred's thigh and other things through his shorts. They hung out in the restaurant for a few hours, had a bunch of drinks, and went back to the couple's room."

"Wow." The story turned me on a bit . . . just a little bit. "I wish I could've been a fly on the wall in that room."

"Melinda said that she wouldn't have given it a second thought outside of the situation. As a matter of fact, she said that they had even tried to find another hotel when they first checked in and learned of it, but when the guy started flirting with her in front of Fred, it did something, flipped a switch."

"Do you think your switch can be flipped?"

"It'll flip me the hell out." She laughed and then the room fell silent. "Let's talk about something else."

"Like what?"

She looked up toward Heaven. "Lord, forgive me for asking questions about an eighteen-year-old," she paused, "but how is the sex?"

After giggling, I had only one explanation for how good Theo was. "Do you have R. Kelly's *TP-2* CD?"

"Yeah." She tried to figure out the relationship. "Why?"

"Sex with him is like song number six."

She thought a while. "'Just Like That'?"

"Just like that."

"Shit," she pouted. "I'm jealous."

"Don't be." It didn't take me any time to come up with a reason. "We can't even be in public together."

"Yeah, but at least he's not a freak that wants you to have sex with other people in front of him."

"Yeah, but other people would freak if they found out that I was having sex with him," I said.

"Yeah, 'cause his momma is going to scrub the floor with you."

I wasn't surprised when I pulled onto my street and saw Theo leaning up against the side of my house. Ever since that night when someone followed me home, he knew to park his car behind the house.

I was still in Toni's living room when my cell phone rang. "Hey, Ms. Patrick." He called me that whenever he was starved for my attention.

I greeted him. "Hi, how are you?" Toni planted her narrow butt next to mine and slammed her ear up against the phone to eavesdrop.

He flirted. "I'm cool, but I need help with my homework."

"I didn't issue any this weekend."

"I'm not talking about English. Another subject."

"Oh?" I was blushing. "What subject is it?"

"I have this problem that I just can't figure out." He went on. "I think I know how to solve it, but I'm not sure. I wanted to check it with you."

"Okay, tell me about the quandary."

"The dilemma is that I'm over here missing the hell out of you."

I grinned. "So, what's the solution?"

"That's the thing." He was smooth. "I think I can solve the problem by coming over around seven." He asked, "Will you be home?"

At this point, we had been involved for two months, and all weekend long I fought calling him. I vowed to myself that I would go forty-eight hours without. He was now like a drug in my system, and I craved him constantly. I would steal stuff from my family and friends and sell it to others for next to nothing if it meant having me a little piece of Theo. When he wasn't around for prolonged periods, I shivered, sweat, and thought about what I needed to say or do to get him there right away. Like I said, he was now like a drug in my system. I craved him constantly.

It was 6:54 P.M. when I put my car in park. I was giddy for this boy, silly for this guy, absolutely crazy about this man, and once within the confines of my house, we were all hands, lips, and tongue from the doorway to the living room to the corridor, and that's as far as we made it.

We handled business in the hallway. The frosty cold tile pressed up against my boiling skin was more erotic than an ice cube traveling from my nipples to my stomach. The thought of Fred and Melinda's first Cancun escapade snuck into my mind and sent me into convulsions quickly, but Theo sent me back there over and over again.

* * *

"Something happened today," Theo said as I sat nestled between his long legs in my bathtub, which was filled to the brim with warm water and bubbles as a lone candle flickered from the toilet top.

"Huh?" I looked back at him, worried. "Something like what?"

"I woke up this morning and mowed the lawn without being asked, just so that I could keep myself from calling you." He pulled me closer to him. "In church, my phone was on vibrate, and I kept checking it to see if I had missed calls from you." He kissed my neck. "I wanted to hear from you so badly."

I couldn't be here in the house alone without calling him. "I know. I felt the same way today." I did every day, which was how I ended up at Toni's. I wanted to prove to myself that I had our situation under control. . . . Look at me now, between his legs. "I couldn't wait to see you."

"I'm convinced." He took a deep breath. "You got roots on me."

I turned to him and piled a handful of suds atop his head and finished it off with a kiss. "It's not called roots."

"What is it then?" His wet hands ran over my stomach and down to my thighs.

"I can't tell you. You have to figure that out by yourself." I added, "That's your homework assignment."

He took a deep breath and giggled. "You got roots on a brotha."

I knew what he was feeling. "You got roots on me too." I knew just what he meant.

DING! DONG!

"That must be the pizza."

I stood up in the tub, booty all in his face. He smacked it hard. "Ouch," I whined.

"Sorry." He was such a clown. "I got excited about the pizza."

I dried off quickly. "I can't believe you got me eating this shit."

"Don't even try it. You had Papa John's number on speed dial." He stretched out as I threw on my robe and ran out of the room. "I'll be out there in a minute," he said.

"I'm coming!" I yelled while grabbing my purse and sprinting down the corridor. "One second," I said as I stood in front of the door and tied the sash of my robe. Couldn't let the pizza boy get a peek.

DING! DONG!

"Okay," I said and opened the door, still fishing through my purse for my wallet.

"Paige, we have to talk." Craig was standing on my welcome mat.

"Well, I—" I was about to pee on myself.

"Can I come in?" he asked while ushering himself into the house without me waiting for an answer. "This won't take very long. I was in the area and I just wanted to be the one to tell you this before it gets to you in the wrong way."

A woman cannot hear those words and think logically. That's the nosy part of our brain, which accounts for a third of it. The other one fourth of my brain wanted to return to the bathroom and warn Theo, but the urgency in Craig's tone told me that there was news, drama, gossip, and I wanted to know. "What?"

"Well," he paused, "Cindy is two months pregnant."

"Cindy who?" I must have needed my ears checked. "Cindy Thompson?"

"Yeah."

"Pregnant by whom?"

The look on his face said it all. "She's pregnant."

I couldn't believe this asshole. "You said that that stuff about you two was all lies, rumors . . ." Why did I believe him anyway? "You are such a—"

"I know, I know, but at the time, I didn't know any of this."

Craig was like a crack head. You had to be careful what he told you because chances were if you walked around the corner fast enough, he had already told three other people three completely different stories. Cindy Thompson was a Caucasian woman, tall, blonde, and a secretary in the main office. I saw them having lunch together a few times, but he swore on his grandfather's mother's daughter's grave that her brother had season tickets to the Miami Heat and he was just trying to see Shaq in black. He denied even being attracted to her, called her trailer trash and all.

"So, why did I *need* to know this?"

He sighed. "She was tripping about me coming in late last night. She thinks I'm up to something . . ."

"Coming in late?" I was too far gone. "You're living with her?"

"She's living with me," he clarified.

"You bastard." The words flew out of me.

Astonished, he said, "Don't call me that."

"Okay. You're not a bastard," I said sarcastically. "You're just a pathetic fuckin'—"

Craig interrupted. "She thinks that I was with you, so she's threatening to call you."

"Oh yeah?" I huffed. "I wish she would call my goddamn house."

"I just wanted to let you in on it."

"Let me in?" I looked him up and down and frowned. "Well, let her in on this. Tell her that I don't give a damn! Did you tell her that?" He seemed surprised that I wasn't crying or screaming. "If you didn't, then maybe you need to." I grimaced. "Whatever happens between you two is none of my business, and I never want it to be. I don't want her calling me, coming to my class, or coming here with any bullshit."

"Yeah, but being my ex-wife—"

"Ex-wife is right." I continued, "I'm not your wife. We have nothing. I don't care that she's pregnant." I actually did care, but I continued nevertheless. "Do you think that I owe you a month-by-month report if I got pregnant?" I was upset and hoped I didn't sound like it. "No, it's my life."

"Yeah, but we're still intimate from time to time," he explained. "I feel like I owe you at least that."

"No, no, no more," I said. "That will never happen again."

"What did you say, babe?" The words didn't come from Craig, but from Theo, walking toward us with a towel around his waist, pulling his T-shirt over his head. He struggled to get his hands through, and when he accomplished his task, he offered us one word: "Whoa."

"*Lake?*" Craig was in shock.

"Wassup, Coach?" They couldn't be the words he wanted to say, but they were the first ones that came out.

"Don't what's up me." He searched Theo with his eyes from the ground up. "What in the hell are you doing here?" Craig looked at me and I had a revenge-is-so-sweet smile on my face. "What in the hell is he doing here with no goddamn clothes on, Paige?"

"As I said a few moments ago, my personal life is off limits to you." I placed myself between them. "This is really none of your business, Craig."

"No, this *is* my business. This *is* my goddamn house. I still pay the mortgage here."

"Mortgage?" I raised my voice. "That alimony check barely keeps my cable on."

"Is this some kind of a joke?" Craig laughed and asked, "You guys plan this? 'cause I know that what I think is going on can't be fuckin' going on."

"Why not?" Theo asked.

"Why not? Why not?" Craig pushed past me and walked over to Theo. "Why not? Because I'm the one she wants to be with."

Theo didn't back down or away. "Obviously not."

"What in the hell can you do? Get the fuck out of my house." He turned his back to Theo and yelled at me. "Are you fuckin' him?" He stepped closer to me when I refused to answer. "This is what you resort to when you can't suck my dick?"

"Oh, hell naw!" Theo snatched Craig backward by his collar and pushed him against the wall. "I don't know how you talk to her when I'm not around, but you won't talk to her like that in front of me."

"You don't know shit about what happens between us when you're not around." In one big jerk, the tables turned and Craig had Theo pinned against the other wall. He brought his fist upward with a vengeance that took everything inside of him to stop. "Don't you ever put your hands on me again, you wanna-be-grown son of a bitch." He pushed Theo sharply before letting go.

"Fuck you," Theo said while sizing him up. "I'm the muthafuckin' man of this house now."

"Keep talking shit, I'll go to jail tonight." Craig stepped back. "I would beat the shit out of you right here and right now if it wasn't for my job."

"Fuck your job. This ain't school. Let's go," Theo said while going after Craig. "Let's do this."

"No, baby." I grabbed him and tried to calm him. "I can't let you do this."

"Baby?" Craig laughed. "That's right. That's all he is, a big baby." Craig then directed his attention to me. "Tell me that you're not fucking him."

"That's none of your business," Theo defended me.

"I'm talking to my wife." He spoke to Theo, but kept his eyes fixed on me. "So fuck off."

"No, you fuck off, Craig." I pointed at the door. "Get out."

"You tell your *baby* that I'm still tappin' that ass?" He was furious when he looked at Theo again. "I've fucked her all over this house and in every fuckin' hole she's got."

"Stop it!" I shouted and hit Craig on his chest with my fist. "Stop, stop it." I was in total disbelief. "Get the fuck out of my house." I pointed to the door.

Without moving in the suggested direction, Craig looked at me like I stunk of throw up and stumbled over his words. "I can't believe you."

"Just get out." I continued pointing.

Craig walked toward the door. "Just wait until Courtland finds out about this." His statement hurt more than a million fists.

"Don't do that, Craig." If one word of this leaked to Principal Courtland, it would surely cost me my job. Ever since I complained to the school board about some of his policies, he'd been hoping to catch me in the wrong, and boy, was I in the wrong. "What about you and Cindy? I'll tell him about that. You know how he feels about fraternization."

"But at least Cindy isn't thirteen." He pulled the door open. "Have a good night, kids."

"Craig, please."

"Don't beg his ass for shit." Theo tried to hold on to me, but I had to do what I had to do. I pulled away from him and ran out the door behind Craig. "Craig, please don't do that."

"Begging now, huh?" He kept walking to his truck. "Unlike you, Paige."

"Let's just keep this between us." I tried hard not to yell at him. "Think of all the wrong you've done to me, all of the ways you've hurt me." I found myself close to tears. "You cheated on me, gave me diseases and didn't care, and I stuck with you. I stuck with your sorry, low-down, filthy ass." It was true. "I didn't drag your name through the mud like I could've. I never told your friends and family the truth about you." I finished up. "Please do me this one favor because even though I could've, I never did anything to harm you."

He opened the door to the truck and looked back at me. "You're pitiful, Paige."

I guess right now I was, but I wasn't going to act like it. "Fuck you." I looked him square in the eyes and spoke slowly. "Fuck you."

"Been there, done that, and it wasn't that long ago." Craig hopped inside, closed the door, cranked the engine, and was down the street before the tears hit my cheeks. My hands fell to my sides in defeat. My feet dragged painfully on the cement as I walked back toward the house.

Theo's long, lanky body was in the doorway. I pushed past him. "I think you should go."

"I'm not letting him run me out of here."

I turned sharply toward him with my hands akimbo. "It's not about you being run out of anywhere." I paused. "This shit is out of control now."

"Fuck him."

"You don't get it." I looked at him like he was wearing a straightjacket. "If he talks to anyone about this, I will lose my job."

"So what?" He laughed. All of a sudden he was a comedian. "Teachers don't get paid shit anyway."

I got in his face—well, a foot below his face. "Well, it's paying the bills here. Can you?" I couldn't believe he was making light of the situation. "I don't want to lose my fuckin' job." I thought about having to ask my struggling parents for help. "I can't lose my damn job."

I walked into the kitchen and Theo followed me. "I'm sorry." He pulled me toward him. "I didn't mean it like that." His hand ran down the side of my face and fell to my shoulder. "What's done is done. Coach knows. He'll either talk or he won't. We can't control that, but what we can control is what we have." He smiled.

"Yeah, but what we have is—"

His fingers touched my lips, quieting me. "Let's just keep having it." He lifted my body and rested me on the kitchen counter, where my lips immediately found his. He whispered, "I swear you got roots on me."

"You got roots on me too."

~Situation #13~

Theo

My alarm clock screamed and I spent twenty minutes deciding whether to go to school. I didn't know what to expect and how to deal with the unexpected. I was set on staying in bed, until I remembered the terrified look on Paige's face after she walked back into the house from practically begging Coach to keep our secret. I couldn't leave her to cope with things all alone. I quickly jumped out of bed and into the shower.

I wandered into West Dade extra paranoid. I felt like Tupac; all eyes were on me. There was something peculiar about the day—or was it me that was busy making it weird? This was probably the way people gawked at me, the basketball star, on a daily basis, but today I wasn't ready for it. Though I don't consider my relationship with Paige wrong, I felt guilty, and was more scared for her than myself.

I wasn't twelve or thirteen years old like the boys that those teachers I had seen on the news were messing around with. I was eighteen, so technically Paige wasn't doing anything illegal, just something that most considered unethical. Also, like she said, if this all got turned inside ou, she would be left without a job. She probably wouldn't be able to teach again, but I would still be a student.

"Mr. Wallace?" a voice from the main office poured into my third period class through the intercom.

He turned into Mr. Nice Guy. "This is Mr. Wallace." Mr. Wallace always talked to the P.A. system with a smile. I don't think that he understood that they couldn't see his always grumpy ass.

"Is Theodore Lakewood in class today?" the voice asked.

"Ah," he looked around the room and into my eyes, "Yes, yes, he's here."

"Will you please allow him to go to the athletics office to see Coach Johnson?"

"Yes." He smiled and gestured to me with his frail hand. "No problem. He's on his way."

"Thank you."

Mr. Wallace frowned at me. "Theodore, if this takes the entire period, please bring paperwork tomorrow with a signature and a time stamped on it." He turned his attention back to the class as I gathered my things. "Okay, back to the Civil War era . . ."

I had butterflies. No, crows . . . no, I had eagles soaring in my stomach. However, though I was nervous, I was ready to get the shit over with, and I wasn't going down without a fight. I had enough adrenaline pumping within me to take on the Miami Heat all by myself and still win by nine points.

I stood in front of the athletic office for a few seconds before turning the knob. There weren't any school officials, principal, or counselor in there like I assumed. As always, the room was full of paper, balls, chairs, and trophies.

"I'm in the back." My heart sank as Coach's raspy voice called out. I made my way to what we called the conference room and was relieved to see him at the round table all alone.

"Close the door and have a seat."

I did as he asked. "Wassup?" I tried not to sound intimidated or nervous, but if he had screamed or made a sudden move, I might've had a big brown mark in my boxers that Tide, All, and Whisk couldn't play with.

"We need to talk."

I snapped, "Look, this whole thing is nobody's business."

He couldn't look at me. "I want to talk to you about your future."

"My future?" I asked. "What about my future?"

"Lake, if you want to go somewhere in basketball, the relationship you're carrying on can be a detriment."

"How?"

"If the media learns about it, they'll eat you up and take away any chance you have of playing in the NBA."

"What, you gonna tell 'em?" I tried to act tough. "Tell 'em. I don't give a shit."

"Don't be stupid."

I was desperate for information. "Did you tell Principal Courtland?"

"No."

"Why not? You said you would." I wanted him to believe that I wasn't afraid of his threats.

"Lake, stop all of this hardcore bullshit, okay?" He leaned back in his chair. "I was upset. You can understand that, can't you?" He looked away. "She's my ex-wife, for fuck's sake." He sighed and then manned up and stared at me. "You come out of nowhere, half-naked, with a damn towel barely covering ya dick." He shook his head and stood up. "Look, I don't like it, but it's your life. It's her life. But if you want to get into the NBA, you better fuckin' put that shit on hold until after the draft." He added, "It just doesn't sit right with me, and if anybody else gets word of it, you're toast."

"It's not illegal," I said. "I'm an adult."

"You're a high school student and a star basketball

player," Coach reminded me. "And your ass is an inch away from being a second round pick, if that."

"I'm not a second round pick and you know it."

"No, no you're not, but you can easily become one." He tried to calm down. "If not until the draft, can't you two at least put water on it until graduation?"

"Why?" I raised my voice. "The NBA is about skill, not personal life."

"But this will drown out your skills. The media will turn this relationship of yours into your only accomplishment and a goddamn circus."

"Look at Kobe, Iverson, and J. Kidd. Everybody has problems."

"Yeah, look at 'em," he said. "But they were already in the NB-fuckin'-A when the problems developed. They didn't bring the shit with them. C'mon, it's the first of February. You graduate in a little over four months. Can't you at least stop this until then?"

I thought of asking to be transferred from her class, not calling her, not seeing her, and not talking to her for almost five months, and compared it to the way I felt about basketball. The way my heart leapt when I ran down the court, it was my first love, but strangely, so was she.

"I can't." It was the first time I had put anything or anybody before that orange piece of synthetic leather.

"We have five more games, Lake," he begged. "Can you do it until then?"

"We've played twenty games this season and lost only two." I was standing on my word. "She has nothing to do with my game."

Coach went on, "We've worked too hard for this, Lake. For four years, I've busted my ass for you. If it weren't for you, I would've transferred away from here long ago. I want this for you. I want to see you go far." He continued, and things got strange real fast. "You have the opportunity I al-

ways dreamed of, the chance I wanted but didn't get. You
need to do this." Then he delivered the real jaw dropper.

"I love you. I feel like you're my boy." He paused uncomfortably. "You're like my son." I had never heard those
words from a man, before so it was hella weird. "We've
come too far together, Lake."

Who would've thought that my closest experience to having a father would be with a man who wanted to pull my
balls through my nostrils at Paige's house? This definitely
wasn't the unexpected that I expected.

"Coach." I didn't know what was about to come out of
my mouth. "I'm grateful to you for all that you've done
throughout the years to get me to where I am." I paused.
"I'm sorry about what you walked in on. I could only imagine how it made you feel, but I've never let you down in the
past. Even when you doubted me, my decision was always
right. Please trust me. This time won't be any different. I
won't let you down. I promise." I couldn't look at him when
I continued, and he knew why. "I've held onto enough of
your secrets. You owe this to me."

He looked at me with disappointment in his eyes and
threw his hands up. We both said no more words for about
four minutes. He just stared at me, and I right back at him.

"All right, Lake, all right." He sat down and then said,
"Let's get down to business . . ."

We discussed the summer months and my possible work-
outs with various teams. My decision was the NBA, and only
he and my mom knew. I was holding it from the media, just
as Bill Clinton said when asked why he had sexual relations
with Monica Lewinsky, because I could. Honestly, I enjoyed
hearing Stephen Smith and Stewart Scott go back and forth
on ESPN about what they thought I should do and where I
might go.

"No more being late to practice?"

"All right." I promised him at least that. "Deal."

At the end of what became an hour-long meeting, Coach J. and I shook hands. Nothing else needed to be said about Paige; it was a closed chapter. However, when I was free to roam the halls, she was the only person I wanted to see. I ran to her classroom and opened the door as she was writing something on the board. The room was filled with students.

"Ms. Patrick, I have a message for you from the main office."

She looked at me nervously and bit into her bottom lip. "What is it?" she asked as she walked toward me.

I stepped back so that she'd have to come outside. "Coach J. called me down to his office earlier," I whispered.

Her eyes nearly touched me from a few feet away. "What?" She closed the door behind her. "What happened?"

"Nothing," I smiled. "He actually apologized."

"Craig?" she asked in shock.

"Yeah." I continued, "I'll tell you everything later."

"Oh my goodness." Her hands rushed to her mouth and I literally watched the worry melt from her beautiful face. "I'm so relieved." She really was. "Oh, I wish I could hug you." She kept her voice low.

I stared at her lips and had to hold myself back from leaning toward her. "Get back in there. I'll see you later."

"I can't wait." Still staring at me, she hesitated a bit then pulled the door open and pointed at the board. "Okay, you all should have this copied by now, so I'll explain the assignment."

"I start a second job tomorrow," Mom said.

"What?" I didn't even know she was looking. "Where?"

"At a clinic in Kendall." She stirred her coffee. "Just on Saturdays for the extra money."

I felt bad about not being able to work because of my practices and games. "I thought we were all right financially."

"Well," she smiled, "I want to get you a publicist, a lawyer, and whatever else you need if we're going to do this thing right, baby."

"What's a publicist?" Kevin asked.

"Someone who'll make sure that everyone knows Theo's name."

My little brother never stopped. "You mean like know how to spell it?"

Mom giggled. "No, their job is to get him interviews on TV and on the radio and schedule him at different gatherings."

"Oh, like to make him famous?" he asked.

"There you go." She held her hand out to him. "Gimme five."

"Aw, Mom." I knew that a publicist would be helpful, but I didn't think I needed one. I already had all the interviews I could handle. "I'm doing fine without one."

"No." She sipped her coffee. "We want to create a more structured image of you."

"Oh boy, a more structured image." I smiled and stuffed a piece of toast in my mouth. "I didn't know that you were getting a second job to be able to get one, though."

"It won't be for long, just until you get on your feet in the industry." She smiled and touched my hand. "I want to do what I can for you now before you meet some girl that starts telling you that I'm around you too much."

"Never that." I leaned forward, pinched her cheek, and tried to change the topic. She always got depressed when she thought of me depending on someone other than her. "What are your hours?"

She seemed happy about it. "I go in at—"

My cell phone rang. "Damn," I said under my breath. I thought it was on vibrate. She shot me a mean look, the same evil stare she gave me whenever the mysterious cellular phone chimed.

"Oh, and don't think that I don't remember that you never told me where that cell phone came from."

"I told you." I jumped up from the table and ran to my room.

"No, you didn't. You said that it belonged to your friend!" she yelled. "If it belongs to a friend, then give it back to them."

"Right!" I screamed back toward the kitchen and then answered. "Hello?"

"Good morning." Paige was just like sunshine. I knew to expect her.

I sat on my bed with a goofy-ass grin on my face. "Good morning."

"Enjoying your day off?" she asked.

"Of course I am." Then I asked, "What about you?"

"It's the teacher's workday. I have to work, remember?" she complained.

"That's why they pay you the big bucks," I teased. "Would you like lunch?"

"I'd love lunch, but I can't have you buzzing around here," she joked. "You're too damn tall. You'll stick out like a giraffe in a herd of sheep."

I thought up something clever. "What about breakfast?"

She giggled. "It's a quarter to twelve right now."

"I meant tomorrow morning." She knew what I was asking, being that it was Friday.

"Sure." The phone went silent. "I'd love to see you tonight."

"How was I last night?"

"Amazing." She went on. "That last three-pointer was off the hook."

The entire game was great. "You liked that, huh?"

"Yes, I did."

"You liked anything else?" Whatever her answer was would quench my thirst.

"You know I love to watch you play." She sighed then continued. "I can't believe that it's February. There are only three more games left. I hate to see the season go."

"Me too." I thought about the previous night. "By the way, I'm sorry about after the game." Mom had, at the last minute, taken off from work to attend the game, and afterward, Coach insisted that the entire team go out for pizza, and he, of course, had his eye on me. "When we got home I was drained. I showered and fell asleep naked."

"Hmm," she whispered sexily. "Really? Sounds like I need to move in next door."

"That's still too far."

She asked, "Then where should I be?"

"Right on top of me." My most sensitive muscle quickly stiffened as the words left my mouth. I thought of how she often got on top of me and rode me like a bicycle. She would position her hands on my shoulders like they were handlebars, sit on my seat, kick the kickstand back, and begin the uphill journey. Sweating, cussing, pulling, pushing, and biting . . . she enjoyed the ride. I allowed her to handle me, or let her believe that she was handling me. She sped up, faster and faster, deeper and deeper. Then she got cocky with it and started to ask questions like, "Whose dick is this? Is it all mine? How good is this pussy?"

At precisely that time, I put her in check. I, the bicycle, came alive. I grabbed a hold of that plump, bronze ass and held her down on my dick while I ground into her, using slow and seductive circles. That's when she realized who had control all along and began to tell me, without me asking, whose dick it was, that it better be all hers, and how good I made her pussy feel. She tried hard to be a strong woman, and I respected that, but women must understand that sex is a male-dominated sport.

". . . so I told her that I couldn't do it. I don't like when people assume that I won't mind doing something." Paige had been talking, but I was wrapped up in the bicycle thought. "Anyway, I can't wait to see you," she finished up. "Anything in particular you want to eat tonight?"

I didn't answer the question the way I wanted to because nosy Eva Lakewood had walked past my door for the third time in ten minutes. "Actually, leave the food up to me." I added, "But you know ya boy ain't old enough to buy liquor, so you hook that up."

"Ain't?" She giggled, questioning my English again.

"There is no school today, so my good English is on vacation."

"That's funny, it was there yesterday, too," she said. "What time should I expect you?"

"I should be there . . ." I paused and I thought about it, "by eight."

"Great." Then I heard the short shriek her classroom door made when it was being opened.

"Good morning, Mistress Wellington." I could tell that she was giving old Mrs. Wellington a counterfeit Kool-Aid smile. "Listen, I'll call you back when I get off, all right?" she said to me.

I whispered, "Damn, I was just about to tell you how deep I wanted to go tonight."

"Oh?" She was probably shocked. "Okay, we can certainly get deep into that later."

I teased, "With my tongue or my dick?"

"Both would work just fine." She tried to uphold her innocence with company around. "The job is always handled properly."

"Let me come and have you right on top of your desk." I was enjoying myself. "I fantasize about that a lot, your legs on my shoulders and your head hanging backward over the desk."

"We can work on that arrangement," she said. "That could be done almost anywhere."

"But I wanna do it on your desk so that I can—"

She interrupted, "Wow, you are so creative. I'm very excited about being teamed up with you." She couldn't take it anymore. "I have a visitor. I'll call you later to continue brainstorming."

"Chicken," I joked.

"Thank you." She smiled into the phone. "Bye."

I mowed both of my neighbors' lawn and earned fifty dollars, just enough for me to buy dinner like I promised. Will and his little brother Lovell came over. Lovell was Kevin's age, so whenever he was over, Kevin wouldn't be so irritating and full of questions. Will, as always, was in front of my computer as I ironed my outfit for the night.

"What are you doing?" my mom asked as she walked into the room in her beige bathrobe.

"I think that's pretty evident." I gave her a hard time.

"Boy, don't screw with me." She had her hands akimbo. "Where are you going?"

"Out," I said.

She asked, "Where?"

"Just out. Why?"

"Because I'm working tonight and I start that new job in the morning. Kevin can't be here by himself."

I had forgotten all about her working tonight. "Ah, man." I was upset. "You need to hire a babysitter or something." Damn, why did I say that?

"Babysitter?" She twisted her head to the side. "I'm busting my ass to see that you get the best of everything there is, and you tell me that I need a fuckin' babysitter? I don't need this shit. He's at Julia's every day after school when you're at practice and I'm at work. I'm not bothering my sister any more than I need to when I have a grown-ass son that can watch his younger brother."

"I didn't mean it like—"

"Yes, you did. Yes, you damn did." Tears welled up in her eyes and she wasn't about to let me say anything. "I'm about to start working a second job just so you can be prepared for what's ahead. You ungrateful—" She stopped herself. "Excuse me for not being able to afford a babysitter while I shower you with two-hundred-dollar basketball shoes and shit at the same time." With that said, she walked out of my room and down the hall to hers, where she slammed the door.

"Damn." Will laughed. "You know you shouldn't have said anything like that."

"I know." I sighed. "It just came out."

"She's pissed."

"Ya think?" I asked sarcastically.

The last thing I wanted to do was hurt my mom or make her think that I was ungrateful. Especially since my sperm donor was nowhere to be found, I believed in praising her as often as I could. I moved the ironing board aside and made my way to her room. I opened the door and saw her standing in the mirror, brushing her hair into a ponytail.

"Ma, I'm sorry." I closed the door and approached her slowly. "I didn't mean to hurt you." She didn't stop brushing her hair, and as I got closer, I realized that she was crying.

"I'm only one person, Theo."

"I know, I know. It was a stupid thing to say." I continued. "It just came out."

"You'll be gone soon, then I won't have a choice about leaving him with Julia or getting a sitter, but right now," she turned to me, "you're all I have." I was extremely moved, but I wouldn't dare walk back into the room where Will was with bloodshot, watery eyes. "This basketball thing, the thing I wanted most for you, is the thing that is about to tear you away from me."

"Ma, don't you get it?" I smiled. "Because of basketball, you won't need to leave Kevin anywhere when you go to work because you won't have to work. You won't have to live in this house. Ma, you won't have to do anything that you don't want to anymore." I looked her in the eyes. "I know that I haven't been the perfect son, but you've been the perfect mother." I pulled her toward me. "I love you, and I'm going to take care of you . . . believe that."

"I love you, too, Theo." She wiped the slowing tears away. "I'm so proud of you."

"I'm sorry about what I said." I hugged her. "If I was still a shorty, I would allow you to whoop me."

She smacked me on the butt. "It can still be done."

An hour later, things were back to normal. "I get off at seven in the morning, but I have to be at the clinic at eight. It's only fifteen minutes from the hospital, so I'll just hang out in that area instead of driving back here. I leave there at two o'clock." She looked at me and begged, "Please feed Kevin." Before leaving for work she kissed Kevin, Lovell, Will, and then me.

When the front door closed, I looked at Will. "I need a favor, man."

"What?" he asked, never truly looking my way. He was in a chat room.

"Can Kevin hang out with you and Vel tonight?"

"Yeah," he said and typed something, then realized what I asked. "What?"

"Can he hang out with you and Lovell for a while?" I was gathering things to take into the shower with me. "I have to be somewhere at eight."

"Man, your moms is gonna kill you."

"Who will tell?"

Will joked, "Kevin's mouth runs like pantyhose. He'll tell."

"Not if I give him ten dollars." I smiled. "But make sure he gets something to eat with it and not no bullshit."

"Where is *my* ten bucks?"

"I'm serious." I grabbed a clean pair of boxers. "Will you or not?"

"First tell me where you're going."

That was simple. "To hang out."

His questioning continued. "With?"

"A friend."

"Male or female?"

"Why in the hell would I go through all of this to hang out with a dude?"

"I don't know. I saw the way Mike London patted you on your ass during the game last night," he joked. "Maybe *y'all* hanging out tonight."

"Ay, fuck you, man." I never liked his humor.

"I'll take him and Vel to the movies."

"Man, that's the whole ten dollars right there," I whined.

"I'll get his ticket." Will was a fool, but I could always count on him.

"Thanks, man." I picked up the phone and dialed Paige's number. "Hey."

"How could you do that to me in my classroom?" she asked instead of saying hello.

I smiled. "I wanted to get your blood boiling."

"You did." She giggled. "It's still boiling."

"Good." I had to watch what I said in Will's presence. "Ribs all right with you?"

"Yes," she said. "Is white wine all right with you?"

It sounded like a contradiction. "Barbecue ribs and wine?"

"Yep."

"I guess." I couldn't argue.

"Will you still be here at eight?"

"Yeah, but I had a little problem with my mom, so I won't be able to stay overnight." Will shot me a what-the-fuck look. "Maybe next weekend."

"No problem." I knew that she was disappointed. "You take up too much space in the bed anyway."

"And you love every inch of it." I laughed. "I'll see you at eight."

"Can't wait."

"I know." I smiled. "Bye."

Will stared anxiously at me, expecting to know everything from A to Z about the person on the phone.

"What are *you* looking at?" I asked.

He broke his silence. "Spending the night?"

"What?" I put the phone down and started gathering my things, again, for the shower. "What?"

"You can spend the night at her house?" The computer was, for now, in second place to me. "Was that Trese?" he asked.

"Hell naw." I frowned. "You know I don't play with that psycho anymore." I added, "Plus, her and her moms sleep in the same damn bed."

"Angie?"

"No."

"Yes it was." Will jumped out of his seat. "Yes it is. Her dad is out of town on business again."

"Man, whatever, man." I smiled. "That was not Angie."

"Who was it then?"

I avoided looking directly at him. "No one that you're thinking."

"Does this chick have a sister?"

I laughed. "Nope."

"Her parents on vacation or something?"

"Nope." I walked out of the room while Will went on and on about who "she" could be.

I took a long, hot shower. I was drying off when Will banged on the bathroom door. "Hey, Theo, does she make you call her ma'am?" he asked from the other side.

"What do you mean?" I stared at the door and wondered.

"She called your phone and I answered it."

I felt caught. "Shit." The feeling that ran through me sucked the water from my body inward, drying me completely. I wrapped the towel around me so tightly that it hurt to breathe. "What did you say?" I snatched the door open.

The smile on his face dissolved when he saw the anger on mine. "Your phone rang and I answered it."

"And?"

"I wasn't pretending to be you or anything. She just started talking." Will walked backward into my bedroom.

"What did she say?"

"She said that she's leaving her garage door open and for you to pull inside of it instead of parking behind the house because she's beginning to see a problem with her lawn or something."

"What else?" I reached for my deodorant.

"That was it."

"What did you mean about me calling her ma'am then?"

"Well," he joked, "I can tell that she's not our age. Shit, she has her own goddamn house."

"And that was all she said?"

"All right, all right." Will looked guilty. "She said that she wanted you to tickle her tonsil." He smiled.

That was her code phrase for a blowjob. "What did you say?"

"I told her that I needed to call her back."

I asked, "Do you know who she is?"

"No, but she wants some tonight." He cracked up. "Handle your biz, big dawg." He made a barking sound.

"You're insane." I had calmed down considerably. "Why did you pick up my phone?"

At one point, months ago, I thought of telling Will about Paige and me, but he was truly not mature enough to handle a secret of this magnitude. Thank God I trusted my instincts.

"Damn, I thought that thing you had for Oprah was just a phase." He continued. "You really do like 'em old, huh?"

"She's not *old*." I defended her. "She's thirty-two. She'll be thirty-three next month."

"She got kids?"

I answered, "No."

"Thank God." He was relieved. "Yo, how is the dungeon?"

"It's all good." I couldn't discuss her in this manner. It left me feeling wrong. "You heard that new OutKast album?"

"Yeah, I don't like it." He laughed. "It sounds like a crack head mixed it."

I overdid my laugh just to keep the conversation away from Paige, but he remembered.

"So, how is the dungeon?"

"Man, c'mon, I said it was good."

"Is it tight? Fat? Wet?"

Giving him details in the past about other girls was no problem, but this time was different. "Man, I can't talk about her like that."

"What the—?" He scoped me up and down. "You?"

"What?"

"Damn," he joked. "I see scars on your back, Kunta Kinte."

"What?"

"You whooped like a mutha, boy." He laughed. "You need some peroxide?"

"Shut up."

"I'm serious." He went on with his logic. "Whenever a man can't talk about the pussy, that means he's headlock in that bitch and whooped like a muthafucka."

"Whatever." The room fell silent and he returned to the computer and began typing away. I started getting dressed, and five minutes later Will shouted, "I gotta take a picture of this."

"What." I looked around the room. "What?"

"Your whooped ass."

He loved to keep shit going.

Before we all left the house, I gave Kevin ten dollars and told him that the money was for him to stick to the plan. The arrangement was for me to pick him up late that night from Will's, but Mom couldn't know that we hadn't been together all night. He told me that ten dollars was for his dinner, and for five dollars more he'd keep the secret.

By a quarter to eight, the aroma from the ribs and shrimp dinners I picked up from Tony Romas, had the whole car smelling like something to eat. Surprisingly, as I pulled up to the house, the garage door wasn't open like she told Will it would be. However, as I approached, it slid up slowly, and when I was all the way in, it glided back down. I turned the car off and looked around. Suddenly, the door leading to the house from the garage opened. Out walked Paige with two jarred candles in jeans and a pale yellow T-shirt.

"This woman loves candles," I whispered to myself.

"Hey." She rested one of the candles on a workbench and the other atop an old TV stand. "Don't get out."

"Huh?"

"Stay in the car and turn on some music."

"What do you wanna hear?"

She walked over to the driver's side window. "Something a little slow but with a funky beat."

I flipped through the stations in search of just that, and found Aaliyah's "Rock the Boat." "Is this good?" I looked over and she was gone. Paige was climbing up the hood of my car.

"What are you doing?" I asked then silently thanked God that she wasn't wearing shoes. The Mazda was precious cargo for right now.

She stood to her feet, still on my hood, and started dancing. She had moves in her that I didn't know about. Normally when I heard this song, I wondered exactly who Aaliyah was singing to, Damon Dash or R. Kelly, but who cared about that now? From this point on, this was Paige's anthem.

Right before the chorus, she slowly pulled her T-shirt over her head. She was wearing a burgundy lace bra that partially revealed her nipples. *Rock the boat, rock the boat, rock the boat, rock the boat.* While she did some Jamaican-style boggling, she unbuttoned her pants. *Work the middle, work the middle, work the middle, work the middle.* She slid one hand down her jeans and into her panties and started rubbing. She was working the middle, but I wanted to rock that boat. *Change positions, new positions, new positions, new positions.* She turned her back to me and was shaking her booty like it was possessed.

Stroke it for me, stroke it for me, stroke it for me, stroke it for me. Aaliyah didn't have to tell me four times. Still behind the wheel, I unzipped my pants and pulled them to my knees, and out popped the rookie of the year. It was oak tree hard. I watched her peel off her pants and almost blew the horn with my dick when I saw that thin piece of burgundy satin disappear between her ass cheeks.

She turned around and saw me behind the wheel stroking myself and smiled. She licked her lips and removed her bra. It was like the song never made this much sense to me before. Paige stared me in the face while removing her bra. "Fuck." Whenever I saw her pierced nipples I lost control. She pressed her breasts up against the windshield and it was the sexiest thing I had ever seen. Still on her knees, she leaned back from the glass and tugged on the front of her thong until the bottom section of the front vanished into the crease of her fat, wet, brown lips, then her little button plopped out.

"Fuck this," I said and reached for the door handle and got out of the car. "Come here," I said to her as I kicked off my pants. She crawled over to the edge of the hood. I didn't want head, I didn't want to eat pussy, kiss, hug, or none of that foreplay bullshit. I simply wanted to rock her boat like she had been begging me to. I wanted to bruise, batter, and split her ship into pieces like it was at sea during a category five hurricane.

"Lay down," I said as I walked toward her on the hood, wanting to waste no time. "Put your legs on my shoulders." Before she could get her feet up, I was snuggled within her folds. "Damn." The lusty smell we made mixed with the ribs and shrimp still in the backseat made me want to eat her from the outside in, all the way to her sweet spot. "What the fuck are you doing to me?" I was talking some real serious shit, and though it scared me, I said, "I'll never, ever leave you." I meant every word of it.

My lightning rod was packed full of electricity, so I forced myself out from her sunny patch of sky. Right as I did, the thundercloud burst and the rain came falling down. I was in the midst of the storm without a raincoat, so milky white raindrops formed little creamy puddles on the hood of my car, and I could give a damn about the paint job.

~Situation #14~

Paige

"I'm hungry as hell," I said to Toni after she sent the waitress away a third time, stating that she needed more time to scan the menu. "This is Applebee's, not the freakin' Melting Pot."

"I'm sorry," Toni said. "I just can't think straight."

"Well, just get chicken." I was starving. "You can never go wrong with chicken."

She looked over at me. "What are you having?"

"The grilled tilapia," I had made up my mind twenty minutes ago, "with steamed vegetables."

"Then why are you telling me to get chicken if you're having fish?"

"Toni, just get something," I complained.

"Fine." She sighed. "I'll get the honey chicken breast."

This wasn't *Who Wants to be a Millionaire?* so I wasn't asking if that was her final answer. I waved the waitress over and told her what we wanted. When our drinks arrived, I sipped my Appletini while looking out of the window, and witnessed two cars almost collide head-on. Toni, looking out of the same window, didn't even flinch.

"Are you all right?" I asked.

"Yeah." It was a lie.

"You can't think that I believe that." I continued by asking, "What's on your mind?"

"What's not on my mind?" She shifted uncomfortably and avoided eye contact of any kind.

"What's going on?"

"Everything," she hissed. "Everything is happening and happening so quickly that I feel like I'm going crazy."

I wasn't psychic. "I can't read minds. Talk to me."

When she looked up and allowed me to see her eyes, I saw a new type of damage that had been done since the last time I had seen her. "Okay, but Paige, please don't judge me." Toni took a deep breath and said, "We did it."

"Did what?" I asked. "Who did what?"

"Marcus and I," she paused, "we experimented with another couple."

"What?" I exclaimed loudly enough that the family at another table sneered at me. "Are you serious?"

"Yes." She seemed embarrassed.

"When?"

"A few nights ago."

"Who?" I asked. "Who are these people?"

"Tara and Jamal," she said. "You don't know them. Jamal is one of Marcus' frat brothers. He lives in D.C. They were here in Miami for a night after a week in Jamaica."

"How did it happen, though?" I was confused. "I thought you were at least going to wait until Cancun. I thought you didn't even want to."

"I didn't." She grimaced. "It's a long story."

"When have we ever received our food without having at least two drinks?" I didn't wait for a response. "We have time for a long story."

By the time my last piece of broccoli was chewed, I knew everything there was to know and even what I didn't want to know. Tara and Jamal Reeves were married just two years. Tara, an ex-model, was now a well-known events planner, and Jamal owned a popular D.C. area landscaping company. With over thirty-five employees, Jamal hadn't touched a lawnmower in seven years.

Mr. and Mrs. Reeves phoned Toni and Marcus from Negril, Jamaica two nights prior to the "hookup," stating that they would be in Miami for a night and wanted to meet for dinner. Marcus and Toni accepted and agreed to meet at a South Beach restaurant. Toni was attracted to Jamal, and from the way she described him, any woman would be. Standing at six foot two and 180 pounds, Jamal was dark brown, and because he ran track in high school and college, his legs were still stacked like a stallion.

They met around nine, and like most South Beach restaurants, the place was set to candlelight, and a live band was there for entertainment. Patrons normally just hopped up and danced right at their tables or wherever the rhythm hit them. When Tara excused herself to the ladies' room and the band began playing a fast-paced Latin beat, Jamal jumped up.

"Can I borrow your wife?" he asked Marcus.

"Sure," Marcus answered jovially. "I'll borrow yours when she comes back."

Jamal pulled Toni to her feet and accompanied her to the dance floor. Once there, his hands fell right above her buttocks, and with every beat of the Latino drum, his hands tightened. His friendly eyes started out on hers, but quickly traveled down her body and grew hungry as he admired her breasts. Jamal watched her waistline gyrate, jerk, and shake without missing a beat. When the song was near climax, he was licking and biting his lips and pulled her close enough to feel that he was fully aroused.

"Whoa." She backed away from him when the next song began.

"What?" He smiled.

"I didn't know that you brought all of that up here with you." Toni regretted saying it just as fast as it came out.

"I didn't bring it with me." Jamal pulled her to him again. "You gave it to me. Just like the first time we danced."

A tad flattered, she didn't back away. Instead, she softly bumped him over and over again with her thigh as they danced. He whispered in her ear, "That feels good." Toni even went as far as to turn around and brush against his equipment with her ass. "That's it, girl." After more of what seemed to others as innocent dancing and touching, Jamal turned her around to face him.

"Does Marcus go down on you?"

"What?" Toni thought sure the alcohol and loud music was playing games with her hearing. "What did you say?"

"Does he eat your pussy?" Jamal had no shame. "While we were in college, he swore that he'd never, ever do that."

Toni didn't know how to answer. "Don't you think that that's something he would've told you if he wanted you to know?"

"I guess that's a yes." He smiled. "Well, is he any good at it?"

She was even more astonished. "Jamal!"

"Sorry." He pulled her closer then mumbled, "I know why he hasn't told me."

Toni struggled to keep up with the beat. "Why?"

"Because I might fantasize about licking the sugar off of that sweet pussy too." The bass in his voice shot straight to the inner folds of her thighs and she trembled. He continued. "I saw you in that club first, and you saw me too. You gave both of us lap dances in that back room, but you allowed me to touch you."

"That was a long time ago, Jamal." Toni lost the beat and stood like a totem pole in the midst of the party.

"Why was that, though?" he asked. "You did him first and me two minutes later, but the minute he left the room, you grabbed my hands and put them on your breasts. You rubbed my dick," he paused, "and you let me finger you."

"Jamal." She tried to back away, but he pulled her back. "Right now this is inappropriate. What I did then I did for money, and it was also a long time ago."

"Okay, fine. I'll chill," he said, ushering her back into the beat. "Most women would be flattered that her man's friend was checking her out." He continued. "Just like Tara is by Marcus." He pointed. "Look at 'em."

Toni turned to see Marcus and Tara holding each other just a few feet away, dancing in a very provocative embrace. "Excuse me," Toni said and tried to get out of Jamal's grasp to approach Marcus.

"Come here." He pulled her back. "We're all just having fun." Jamal refused to let go, but the song ended, and they all returned to the table.

Toni noticed something slightly different about the taste of her Screwdriver, but put it off on it being watered down by the melting ice. She swallowed it down quickly, and suddenly the music was different. It seemed faster, louder, and snazzier. She swayed back and forth in her seat and underwent a dramatic mood change in just three minutes. She was talking nonstop, ordering two drinks at a time, and was very hands-on with everyone. The amazing smile now plastered on her face couldn't be wiped off with Windex. Her attitude had changed, and everyone loved it.

Tara and Marcus went back to the dance floor, and Jamal made his way around the table to sit next to her. "Did I offend you?"

"When?" Toni fought to remember what was said just an hour ago. "Oh, on the dance floor? Oh, no."

"Then why did you freeze up like that?" He got closer. "I mean, when we first started dancing, you felt that I was aroused and you didn't back away. So, why did a few memories from the past spook you out?"

She really couldn't think straight. "We shouldn't have been talking like that."

"Why not?"

"Because I'm married now." She looked over at him. His lips looked like two Twix sticks, and she wanted to lick the chocolate off of them.

"Fuck all that shit. Don't you think Marcus wants Tara to suck his dick?" he asked. "You don't think I wouldn't want you to do the same to me?" He trailed his hand down the side of her torso.

She looked over at Marcus, who now had one of his hands in Tara's hair, like he was priming her for a kiss. Amazingly, Toni didn't get upset. Actually, it seemed like she couldn't. She was too relaxed, almost unable and impaired.

Jamal went on. "I wanted a taste of your pussy the first night I met you in that strip club, and I told you that."

"I remember." Toni smiled shyly.

"I still want it." Jamal's hand landed on her thigh under the table. "I think about doing it all the time."

"Really?" She was *now* flattered.

"Yeah." He slid his hand back and forth. "Would you let me?"

"Gimme a minute to think that over." She giggled, and then sucked down another funny-tasting Screwdriver. Suddenly, all hell broke loose in her mind. "I . . ." She looked on the dance floor and saw Marcus' hands caressing Tara's butt. Strangely, it turned her on. "I probably would."

His hand inched up her thigh. "Would you suck my dick?"

"Maybe." She giggled like a schoolgirl. "Maybe not." Toni felt her soul drifting away and a more sinister one sneaking in. She couldn't stop it; the transaction was complete.

He asked, "Are you wet?"

"See for yourself."

In the darkness of their corner booth, Jamal slipped his hand down Toni's pants, moved her thong aside, and inserted his middle finger into her warm and succulent meat. The voyeuristic experience with Marcus so near set her on fire. "*Feeling Hot, Hot, Hot*" was playing, and he penetrated her to the beat.

"You'll let me fuck you, won't you?"

"No," she teased.

"Yes, you would." He pushed in deeper. "You wouldn't let me do this if I couldn't hit." He licked his lips. "I've always wanted this pussy."

"Then you should've taken it that night." Her eyes were tempted to roll back, but she contained herself, gyrating slowly instead. "Why didn't you?"

"My plan was to come back the following night, but something came up and I had to fly home the next day instead of on the weekend." He paused. "Then a few weeks later he tells me that you invited him over to your place for dinner."

Marcus and Tara returned, so Jamal stopped, but in remembrance of the moment, he kept "the finger" close to his nose as he talked to his wife. Fifteen minutes into their conversation, he whispered something into Tara's ear and then brought his finger to her nose. She sniffed his finger and her face lit up.

"I think we can have so much more fun back at the room," Tara said with a smile.

At the hotel, Marcus and Jamal had what most men would consider the Superbowl of sex. It started with Tara kissing Marcus, Jamal, and then Toni. However, while kissing Tara, Toni grew increasingly curious about seeing and feeling another woman's breasts, so she unbuttoned Tara's top while the men watched and encouraged them. Toni massaged then teased Tara's nipples with her tongue as though she had walked into the room with experience. It wasn't long before they were rolling around naked on the bed, locked onto each other's lips, with their fingers slipping and sliding deep into one another's creases.

Tara climbed down Toni's body and put Marcus to shame with her tongue. The pleasure was unbelievable. While his wife was handling business, Jamal, now naked, crept onto the bed with a fully erect eight-inch dick and slid it into Toni's mouth so she could suck him. Soon he pushed Tara away to get inside.

Needless to say, they switched, swapped, and sexed each other all night, girl on girl, double penetration, sucking while fucking, the whole nine yards. In fact, they didn't leave the Reeves Hotel room until checkout time the next day. Toni, still in a daze, slept until midnight that night. When she woke up from what she thought was a disgusting dream, her badly aching body revealed that what had happened was reality.

She woke Marcus, and after plenty of questioning, he claimed the evening wasn't planned but confessed to adding something, he wouldn't say exactly what, to her drink to loosen her up a little. Loosen up? That was an understatement. He turned her buck fuckin' wild and he had no regrets.

We had been sitting in Applebee's for two hours. I didn't know what type of advice to offer. This was a call for Superman. "So, what are you going to do?"

"What can I do?" She shrugged her shoulders. "What's done is done."

"Yeah, but you can at least tell Marcus how you're feeling."

"You think he gives a damn?" She rolled her eyes. "He got what he wanted. He got to fuck another woman right in front of me." She continued. "He slipped God knows what in my drink and allowed another man to fuck me. Does it sound like he gives a shit?"

"I cannot believe this." I saw her point.

She was angry. "It's all he talks about now. He loved it, but I don't see how our marriage is supposed to survive." As though our discussion weren't awkward enough, my cell phone rang. I pretended not to hear it.

"You might as well answer it," Toni said.

I looked down; it was Theo. "No, I can call him back." I had to stay devoted to my girl and her situation.

"How are things with you two anyway?"

"Crazy." I smiled. "I'm crazy about him."

"Damn," she joked. "Maybe I need to teach high school."

"Shut up." I decided that the change of topic was good for her. "There's a Valentine's Day dance at the school next week that Theo wants me to go to."

"You going?"

"You must be out of your mind." I looked at Toni. "I'm not going to a high school Valentine's Day dance with Theo, or anyone else, for that matter."

"Why not?" She laughed. "Go as a chaperone and sneak a dance under the bleachers like you did last time."

"No thanks," I said. "I told him to go. I wouldn't want him to miss out on that type of stuff because of me."

"So, he can go with a date?"

"You're trying to get him killed. I didn't say anything about a date," I joked. "I *am* his date. I'm just not going to the dance. After graduation we can dance and frolic as much as the next couple."

"So, what will you do while he's dancing the night away?"

"Nothing." I thought about it. "I might catch up on some reading."

"No, I'll come over and keep you company," Toni volunteered. "When is it?"

"Next Friday night."

"I'm there." Toni pulled her organizer from her purse to jot down our appointment.

Shortly after, it was her cellular phone buzzing. "Oh my, oh my God." Her eyes widened when she looked at it and then back at me. "I have to take this call." She grabbed the phone like it was the Florida Lottery Committee confirming that she had indeed won the $63,000,000 jackpot.

"Hello?" Then a long paused followed. "Hi, Derek." She giggled and grinned. "Yes, I got your message, but it was a little late. Sorry I couldn't call you back."

I looked around the restaurant until I found the closest TV. Why are these types of restaurants always tuned to ESPN? I mean damn, can I see a music video or two while I'm eating instead?

"You mean next Friday?" Toni looked down at her organizer and then at me with guilt written all over her face. "Hold a sec for me, please."

"I promise you that the weekend after that is yours," she whispered to me.

I frowned. "Whatever." I really wasn't disappointed. Maybe Derek was more of a gentleman than the porno king that Marcus was turning out to be.

She spoke into the phone again. "I can be there. What should I bring?"

"Where are you going?" I asked in a whisper.

"His place," she mouthed to me then placed her finger to her mouth to silence me. "I can't have you cook without bringing something." She smiled. "Okay. Wine sounds good to me." Her conversation lasted another three minutes. "I'll talk to you later."

I mocked her. "I'm there. I'll hang out with you the night of the dance."

"I'm sorry, but dick—I mean duty calls." She smiled. "He wants to start working on our project."

"Project?" I asked. "You're taking wine and he's cooking dinner. What type of project are you two working on?"

"Paige, I need to do this." Her dimple was showing.

I smiled. "I'm not mad at you, especially since Marcus is acting like an ass anyway." I reached across the table to slap hands. "Do you!"

"That's right," she said.

"Just be careful. You hear me?" She didn't hear me. "Toni, be careful."

"I will."

On my way home, my phone rang. I recognized the number, and I normally wouldn't pick up, but the alcohol had me extra mellow. "Hello?"

"Hey there!" I hadn't heard Doran's voice in months.

"How can I help you?"

"I'm surprised that you actually picked up," he said. "Normally I get sent straight to voice mail."

"It's not too late," I said.

"Ah, c'mon." He spoke like nothing ever happened. "Can't we be friends again?"

I was blatant. "No, we can't."

"Why?" He spoke in a solemn tone. "What is it that you have against me?"

"Excuse me?" I slammed on the brakes. "Are you serious?" I pulled over to the shoulder of the road. I can't drink, drive, and be a bitch at the same time.

"Yes, I'm serious." He cleared his throat. "I sincerely apologize. I tried on many occasions to give you clues about my lifestyle."

"You didn't try hard enough."

He snickered. "But if I did, you wouldn't have talked to me."

"Damn right," I said with intensity like he was in the passenger seat. "I'm not into that down-low gay bullshit."

"Bisexual," he interrupted. "I'm bisexual, not gay."

"Whatever the hell you are, you all get fucked up the ass, so it's all the same to me."

"Hold up, honey." He sounded like an angry woman. "I didn't call you to be insulted."

"Oh yeah?" I had waited months to get all this off my chest. "Well, I didn't go to your apartment that night to be insulted either, but shit happens."

"I called because I don't want us working at the same school and not being able to be cordial to one another."

"Well, we've done it this long. Why mess it up?"

"Paige," he said, "I'm sorry. It was dumb of me to take you to my place and yes, I should've made you of aware of my sexuality." He finished up. "I was selfish and wanted to have my cake and eat it too. I wasn't thinking of anyone but me. If we can't be friends, then I at least want you to know that I am truly sorry."

"Thank you, Doran." I faked a smile. "By the way, while I have you on the line, I'm working on a story for the school's paper, and I have a question for you." I did, and I dragged it up from the pits of hell. "What pleases you most about sucking dick?"

"Writing a story for the school paper, huh?" he asked, unmoved.

"You think it's *too deep* for the paper? Well, I have another idea." I was enjoying myself. "How about fliers posted around the school early one morning before the students arrive?" I was too legit to quit. "I don't accept your a-fuckin'-pology, and I don't want to be your friend."

"You inconsiderate bitch." His words shocked me, but not as much as what followed. "What pleases me about sucking a man's dick is probably what pleases you about fucking an eighteen-year-old boy."

The tables had turned faster than the speed of light. "What?" I shrieked.

"You wanna play hard ball?" he yelled. "Let's go. Let's fuckin' go."

"Making up shit? Wow, you really need to get a life." I tried to make light of it.

"No, you need to get one. I followed you home back in November after a game, hoping to apologize to you," Doran said, "and lo and behold, Mr. Three-Pointer himself was in your driveway with an overnight bag, and his car was there all night long." He then asked, "Remember that?"

"No," I lied.

"I know about you." He laughed. "What do you have to say about that?"

"I don't know what you're talking about." I denied his claims.

"Theodore Lakewood," he spelled it out more, "your student, and the collector of detentions. I know what's going on between the two of you."

"Wow, that's a pretty interesting rumor."

"Is it? Is it?" he asked. "Well, let's see how that'll do on fliers posted around the school."

I was embarrassed. "You won't—"

He interrupted me. "Paige, I honestly hadn't planned on telling anyone about you. However, the minute anything about my lifestyle leaks out, your reputation and your job are history," he said and hung up.

"Shit!" I screamed. "Shit, shit, shit!" Pissed off at the world, I pulled back onto the street and drove home as though I had road rage against the road.

Once in the house, I paced the floor, extremely worried. So far, two people, two of the last people in the world I wanted knowing my business, knew all of the gory details. I looked in the mirror in search of a solution to my problem. Was I desperate or falling in love? Was Theo really interested? For all I knew, I could be his sugar momma, the foolish older lady, so frantic for attention that she was willing to do for him like she had for no one else.

I picked up the phone and dialed.

"Are you all right?" my mother asked in a worried tone like most would after receiving a call at almost midnight.

"Not really," I answered.

"What's wrong?" She went on, "I told you not to mess around with your breasts, letting them cut you here and there. I told—"

"I'm physically fine, Ma. I just have a lot on my mind." I sighed. "I needed someone to talk to."

"Like what? What's bothering you?" She continued. "You not thinking about doing anything crazy, are you?"

"No." I laughed. "I'm not sitting here with a gun, a knife, or a bottle of pills. I'm just in a situation, and the only way to avoid it is to get out of it." I paused. "And I just can't see myself doing that."

"If it's costing you pain, sweetie, then you better."

"But it's not," I tried to explain. "The root of the problem is also the root of my happiness. At the same time, if I let go of it, all of my problems would be solved."

She asked, "You not on something, are you?"

"What?"

"Drugs? That's what it sounds like."

"Ma, I'm not on drugs." It was almost funny. "I can't believe you would think that." Getting off of drugs would be ten times easier than asking that boy not to call me or come over anymore.

"So, what are you talking about?"

I contemplated telling her. "Nothing."

"No, something is bothering you. Now, tell me what it is," she demanded.

I sighed and thought about it. "I'm seeing this guy." I confessed that much. "He's a lot different than any other man

I've ever dated, and because of that, I can't tell anyone about him."

"Is he married?"

I rolled my eyes. "Now, you know I don't play that game."

"Oh, 'cause I was about to let you have it," she said. "What? Is he white or something?"

"No." If that were my only problem, I would just take him to a tanning salon.

"Is he a hermaphrodite?"

"Hermaphro-who? No, Ma!" I shouted. "Where did you get that from?"

She giggled. "Baby, those are the only three things I wouldn't want for you." She explained, "A married man, because what God joined together, let no man put asunder." She paused. "Now, I'm no racist, but I don't want you with a white man because when you piss him off he might mistakenly call you a nigger, and I'd have to jump off in his ass, 'cause ain't nobody gon' think they better than my flesh and blood." She paused again. "Finally, I want you to hurry up and have some grandbabies, or at least one. So, although God made them, too, I can't have you with a hermaphrodite."

"Ma, you have issues." I laughed.

"I'm serious, Paige. Other than those three, you can bring anybody home to us."

"How about a crack head?"

"Yep, just call before y'all come so that I can hide all my good stuff." She chuckled heavily.

"I wish it was that easy," I said.

"Paige, you only live once. You're not living for people. It's your life. Do with it as you like. This isn't one of those stupid Hollywood movies either, where when you die you get sent back to make your wrongs right, or for a little extra time with the people you care about." She added, "If he makes you happy, then to hell with what others say."

I sat silently a while. "Thank you."

"I don't need you down there in Florida fretting about anything." She added, "This is going to worry me."

"No, Ma." I continued. "I don't need you up there in Minnesota fretting about me. I'll be fine."

"You sure?" she asked.

"Positive."

We talked more about everything from recipes to the city renaming one of the main highways after Ronald Reagan. "Child, please," was my comment. When we hung up, it was after two in the morning on the East Coast and my bed was calling me. Though I answered it by resting my head on the pillow, I really wanted to call Theo. However, so that he would believe that I had a life outside of him, I told him that I was going to a club and probably wouldn't be home until late. The last time I checked, Applebee's didn't have a dance floor, and though the music streaming out of the speaker was oftentimes too loud, they didn't have a DJ either.

The next morning, I had three missed calls on my cellular, one at 3:04 A.M., 7:36 A.M., and the last at 8:21 A.M. I played my messages.

"Hey, this is T. It's about three o'clock and I haven't heard from you. I guess you're still at the club. I hope that you're having a good time. I'm here watching a few movies that I rented for Kevin and me." He laughed. "You heard that good English? Ya boy got it going on. Anyway, give me a call when you're on your way home or when you get in so that I'll know that you made it all right."

Then later on, "Yeah, it's me again. I woke up and saw that you still haven't called. Hit me back."

The last message was a hang-up.

I smiled and looked at the clock. It was after eleven, and

before I could save the messages, my doorbell was ringing. "Oh, Lord," I grumbled as I grabbed my robe and hurried.

"Who is it?" I asked, expecting to tell off some Jehovah's Witnesses, but there wasn't a response. "Who is it?"

"Me." I knew exactly who "me" was.

I opened the door looking like yesterday. "Hi."

"Hello," Theo said without making a move to come inside. "Thanks for returning my calls."

"I'm sorry," I said. "I just heard your messages."

"I was just checking to see that you were all right."

I blushed. "Yes, I'm okay."

"How was your night?" He leaned against the doorsill.

I hated lying to him. "It was great."

"What club did you go to?"

Think fast, think quick, quick, quick, and when in doubt, just say what sounds good. "Club Quick." There was probably a club with that name somewhere, but I had certainly never set foot in it. "Come in," I beckoned.

"I can't." He pointed to his still running car. "My mom is working that second job on Saturdays and I'm being a big brother. Kevin is in the car. We're going to the mall."

"Oh," I tried to step out of view of the car. "How sweet of you."

"Yeah, right." He smiled. "There are a few other things I'd like to be doing right now."

"Like?"

"Like taking that robe off of you."

I was flattered, but a bit weary of all of the sex talk he always came ready with. "Is that all you plan on ever doing with me?"

"What do you mean?"

"Sex," I restated. "Is that all this is to you?"

He looked absolutely flustered. "Where did that come from?"

"Just answer me," I said. "Is that all you want from me?"

"No." He looked back at the car as though his brother had bionic ears. "But we can't go anywhere together to do anything right now . . ."

"So let's just have sex, huh?" I interrupted. "I guess I should've asked you this question months ago."

"Sex is not all I want from you." He continued. "I could have sex with anyone. Do you think that I would be putting my basketball career on the line to just have sex with *you* when I could get it from any girl I want?"

"Then act like you want more from me." I crossed my arms over my chest and looked away. "We don't have to always talk about it or spend every waking moment in my bed."

"No," he lightened the mood, "there is always the hood of my car." I laughed when I remembered the incident, but was a little embarrassed. He asked, "What's wrong with you today?"

I was in kill or be killed mode. In relationship terms it meant that I was looking for something to go wrong so that I could or he could get frustrated with me, because life would be so simple without having to worry that Doran or Craig would decide to blow up my spot.

"I'm sorry. I have a lot on my mind and wanted to feel like I could count on you for—"

"For whatever you want. You can count on me, baby." He stepped inside the house and touched my face, and then pulled me into a quick embrace. "You only feel this way because there's not much we can do outside of this house together without paying for it with some form of our lives." He looked down at me. "Are you listening to me?"

"Yeah."

"Paige, after graduation I'll be your man in every aspect of the word." He hugged me. "I can't wait to go out with you, take you places, and do things with you. At the same time, I enjoy the thought of us coming back here to make love after the world knows that I love you."

"What?" Did he just finally say it?

"I love you, Paige."

I nearly fainted. I never thought that he would own up to his feelings, and I most definitely wasn't going to until he did. So, now that it was out in the open, the words traveled upward in me like vomit, then it flew out.

"I, I love you."

~Situation #15~

The Fly

It's your pal, Musca Domestica again. I'm a little sick of having to introduce myself to you, so I won't. It's only been a few chapters since you've heard from me, so if you've somehow forgotten me, that is so not my damn problem. I'm back to tell the tale of this one night that changed everything. There was absolutely too much happening with everyone for just one person to tell. Therefore, I flew my ass off throughout the city to get the news to you, you nosy mother . . . shut your mouth.

Will's house . . .

"We've drunk more than half the bottle." Will returned the Cuevo Gold tequila bottle to his dad's bar in the den. "He is gonna fuckin' murder me."

"Maybe he won't notice," Theo said.

"Ya think?" Will looked at his best friend as though he was a mastermind, and then countered his expression by saying, "The bottle was new. It wasn't even opened, Boy Genius."

"Shit." Theo smiled. "Tell him I'll buy him a new one."

They were both dressed in red and white, a requirement

for the Valentine's Day dance. Theo was in a red shirt, blue jeans, and white sneakers, and Will in white jeans and a red shirt.

"Let's go." Will threw the car keys to Theo, who was standing in the living room, and then turned off the lights in the den.

The sun was setting, but there was still enough light for Theo to give Will's outfit a once-over while walking to the car. "What the—?" Theo's laughter took over the rest of the sentence.

"What?" Will somehow knew that he was the brunt of the joke.

"You, man." Theo chuckled long and hard, with the side of the car bracing his body.

"What in the hell is so funny?" Will couldn't help giggling.

Theo looked at him again and was tickled beyond sanity. After two minutes of beating on the car and laughing, he managed to get out a sentence. "Yo, why are you wearing those gay-ass white-ass jeans, man?"

"What?"

Theo struggled to talk. "Dudes don't wear white jeans no more."

Will looked down at himself and then over at Theo. "Fuck you." He came back strong. "Look at you, you tall, red-white-and-blue, Fourth of July celebrating-looking muthafucka." Will laughed as he opened the car door. "Man, let's go."

As drunk as they were, neither one of them should've even been in the passenger seat of a moving vehicle. However, they cracked on one another and made it to West Dade safely.

I don't condone nor tolerate drinking and driving. However, in order to get the story to you, I had to subject myself to such danger. I sat near the window so that if some-

thing went down, all I had to do was fly my ass up, up, and away.

Paige's humble abode . . .

"I think that you should wear pants, Toni." Paige held the phone to her ear while peeking in on her chicken breasts basking in the heat of the oven.

Toni had six outfits sprawled out on her bed. She was excited about finally being with Derek and hoped that he was feeling a fraction of what she did.

"What difference does it make if I wear pants or a skirt?"

"If you were meeting him at a restaurant, I'd say wear whatever." Paige wasn't sure if she made sense or just wanted to sound like she knew something about dating after all these years. "However, since you're going to his house, a skirt says *I want you to eat my pussy.*"

"Well, what's wrong with that?" Toni laughed. "I want him to know that in pants or a skirt."

Paige chimed in with her logic. "He doesn't have to know that tonight. Pants say *We can't play footsies underneath the table, but afterward we'll sit on the couch, sip wine, talk, and laugh.*"

With makeup already perfectly applied, Toni ran around her house with her earpiece plugged in and her cell phone sticking out of her navy blue lace bra. She adjusted the thermostat and closed the curtains.

"So, what do I have to wear to at least get rubbed on?" she joked.

"A dress, but maybe next time." Paige giggled. "So, what's exactly planned for the night?"

"A little studying as dinner is finishing, wine." She paused. "He wants to, as he puts it, *spit* this new rap to me, too." She smiled. "I think we'll have a nice evening as long as Psycho Freaky Jason doesn't come around."

"Who in the hell is Jason?"

Toni laughed. "No, that's what he calls Giselle."

"Who is that?" Paige asked.

"Didn't I tell you about Giselle?"

Paige tried to recall. "No, but who is she?"

"She's Derek's crazy, young-ass ex-girlfriend." She giggled.

"Define the word *crazy*."

"They broke up a few months ago." Toni laughed. "She's stupid. She still calls him and comes over, but he changed the locks a few weeks ago." She paused. "From what I've heard, she's a typical young girl, eighteen or something, that can't get over the fact that the relationship didn't work. He gets a lot of e-mails, hang-ups, little gifts and shit."

"That chick does sound kinda psycho-ish," Paige joked.

"I think she's just young." Toni continued. "But damn, at any age if you find a man that hits that G-spot just right, you'll do some crazy shit."

"Amen," Paige joked. "Preach it, sistah."

"She's just whooped, but Giselle is harmless."

"All right now, don't get your ass kicked by that harmless bitch," Paige said, checking the chicken again, truly famished. "You better be careful."

"Paige, you know I can't fight worth a damn, so I'm not getting into anything that I can't get out of." Then Toni added, "Derek changed the locks and she can't get in, so she doesn't bother him as much. She just e-mails the shit out of him."

"She'll e-mail you next," Paige taunted. "Or send your ass a serious computer virus. I won't be opening up anything from your infected ass."

"Giselle is the least of my worries," Toni said. "I'm just trying to get out of here before Marcus gets back."

"Where is he?"

"Taking the boys to his mother's."

"Where does he think you're going?"

"To dinner and a movie." Toni added sharply, "With you."

"Me?"

"Yes, you, so please don't call my house and don't answer any calls from here," she said. "I'll call you when I'm on my way home."

Paige was curious. "What time should that be?"

"Whenever we're done . . ." Toni finished her statement mischievously, "studying."

"You're nasty." Paige smiled.

"Oh, look who's talking, Theo's English teacher."

"Quiet, please." Paige turned the conversation around. "Back to your outfit, wear pants. Trust me on this."

Toni studied the black pants and burgundy top with a smile. "All right." She carried all of the losing outfits back to the closet. "Thanks a lot."

"Not a problem."

"All right, I need to get dressed and out of the door before this man gets back here."

"Have a good time," Paige said.

"I will." She sighed. "If you can't get good treatment at home, it's only a matter of time before you start to roam."

"I'll never forget this, the day you blew me off for a man," Paige said.

Toni was in a jovial mood. "You know I love you, Pages." She hadn't called her that in a long time. "Thanks again for everything." Toni blew a kiss into the phone. "I'll call you."

"Bye."

Toni's world . . .

Everything was going as planned until Marcus returned two minutes before she was scheduled to walk out the door.

"So, where are you two having dinner?" Marcus asked as he studied her outfit and rested his keys on the dresser.

"A restaurant in the Grove." She hadn't exchanged many words with him since the Tara and Jamal festivity.

"When will you be back?"

"Tonight," she said.

"I know that." He peeled off his shirt. "I meant what time?"

"We'll probably see a movie, too, so I don't know." She rushed around the room for whatever she was taking.

"Have a good time." Marcus wasn't happy with her curt answers. He suspected nothing, but was eager for things to get back to normal. "Which movie are you seeing?"

Toni threw a look at him that would've sliced his head clean off of his neck if he were any closer. "I don't know," Toni snapped as she stepped into her shoes. "You don't have to wait up."

"Of course I do." He approached her from behind and wrapped his cold arms around her. "It's been a while since we've—"

"It's been nine days." She pulled away from him. "Nine days and I can't even think of having sex with you after what you did to me. Whenever I see you, all I see is the top of your head between Tara's thighs," she huffed. "All I see is the way your eyes rolled back into your fuckin' head when you were on top of her." She grabbed her purse. "Don't wait up for me."

Toni started down the stairs, but he followed and grabbed her by the arm. "So, is this the way things will be from now on?" He tightened his grip. "Huh?"

"This is the way it is right now," Toni said. "I'm going out to try to get this shit off of my mind."

He complained. "I could've taken you out to dinner if that's what it takes."

"I don't want you to take me anywhere." She paused. "I'm trying to be around people who can comfort me, not just fuck me, or let their friends do it for them."

Marcus looked long and hard at her. He stared as though he felt her pain, like he finally realized what he had put her through. "So, when *will you* be ready to do it again?"

"I can't believe you. I cannot fuckin' believe you, Marcus." Toni, extremely hurt, pulled herself from his grasp and ran down the remaining stairs. She made it to the door before speaking again. "Maybe I shouldn't even come back here tonight."

"If that's how you feel then. Do you, Toni?" Marcus said. "Do you?"

"What does that mean?" she asked as she opened the door.

"Just do whatever the fuck you have to do," Marcus said without looking her way. He slowly turned and walked toward the kitchen. "Whatever it is, just do it quickly so I can move on with *my* goddamn life." He spoke in a whisper, but she heard every word.

Toni left the house with one thing on her mind, peace, and she was set on finding it, no matter the consequences.

West Dade's gymnasium . . .
The school's gym looked better than a lot of the clubs I've frequented, and I've been around. The large, dark room was littered with red, white, and pink balloons, the music was pumping, and the air smelled like strawberries . . . let me at 'em.

After two hours of dancing, the alcohol was wearing thin. However, in a private meeting in the men's room, Will extracted from his pockets four miniature jelly jars filled to the brim with tequila. Theo downed two, and the party had started all over again. Back on the hardwood floor, he decided to lean against the wall until the DJ played a song he was feeling.

"Hey, stranger." Trese walked up and posted herself in the space next to him.

"Hey! What's up?" As the disco light shined their way, he looked down into her blouse and remembered the times. "How you doing?"

"I'm fine," she said. "How are you?"

"I'm good, I'm good." The tequila took his mouth in its own direction. "You're looking good."

"Thanks." She blushed.

"Looking real good." Theo pulled her away from the wall to check her out. "Damn."

"Stop it, Theo." She playfully smacked his hand.

For one drunken moment in time, he wished that Trese was still in his life, but only in one aspect. He was horny. "Wanna dance?"

"Sorry." She looked around. "I'm here with someone."

"Daaaaamn." He was shocked. This was the first time she had ever turned him down. "It's like that?"

"You know I would," she searched the crowd, "but I'm here with Jeffery Anderson." She thought it necessary to call him by his first and last name so that Theo wouldn't mistake her man-of-the-hour for just any Jeffery. Jeffery Anderson was Theo's rival from Sunset Heights, a high school across town. With a foul move, straight from street B-ball, Jeff had almost cost Theo his knee last season. Trese knew how much Theo hated him.

"Do your thing then, li'l momma." He pretended that it didn't bother him. "There he is, over there, if you're looking for him." Theo pointed.

"Actually, we're about to leave." She smiled. "His parents are out of town."

"Did he bring you here?"

"No." She looked away.

Theo stared past the innocent face she offered and into her wicked strategy. "So, what you're saying is that he's the first guy to show you attention tonight?" He added, "So, if I had peeped you first and had somewhere to take you, you'd be leaving with me, huh?"

"No."

"Whatever, Trese. You didn't come here with Jeff," he said. "Anyone that wants a ride can get one from you."

"Fuck you, Theo."

"Naw, that's not my job anymore." He laughed. "Fuck Jeff."

"You're just jealous," Trese puffed up into his face.

Theo quickly evaluated his feelings. "I actually feel sorry for you, Trese."

"What?" She had taken a step away, but turned back. "What do you mean, you feel sorry for me? I don't need nobody feeling sorry for me."

"I feel bad for you because you don't mean anything to yourself," he paused, "and that's more dangerous than not meaning anything to someone else."

Trese lowered her voice. "What the hell are you talking about?"

"You need to get it together before it's too late." Theo shook his head. "If this is the way you're living life now, what will you be doing five years from now?"

With a blank expression, Trese backed away until she disappeared into the crowd. Out of the same darkness came Angie.

"Hey, Theo. What's going on?"

"Nothing." He leaned back against the wall.

"Would you like to dance?"

He looked down at Angie's perfect cheerleader-molded body, and for the moment, she seemed just right. She wasn't Trese, thank God, but she wasn't Paige either. "All right."

A minute into dancing, he knew exactly what Angie had on her mind. Her hands were full of jeans and dick. Her smile and the innocent way she licked her lips made him grow harder as each song played. He tried stopping her, but she was dead set on having him. He never expected this from a girl like Angie; straight A's, ass kisser, and a member of every geeky club there was. Though he considered her actions tacky, he had given up on trying to stop her. In fact, when Angie said, "Let's go somewhere," it was Theo who led her off of the dance floor.

They left the gym, sneaked past security, and scurried upstairs into the science wing. Angie had no problem finding the boys' restroom and locking them into a stall. She glanced up at him, expecting him to pounce on her. However, he thought past the tequila and realized what was about to happen.

"I think we better get out of here," Theo said nervously

"Not a chance," Angie said. "Do you know how long I've wanted to get you all alone?"

"How long?"

"Since the tenth grade." The way Angie spoke, you'd think she had said "since kindergarten."

"I'm willing to do whatever. What do you want to do?" Angie asked.

"I-I," Theo stuttered, "I don't know."

"Well, I know what I want to do," she said, pulling his shirt up out of his pants.

"I don't know if this is a good idea, Angie." He tried to get his drunken mind to follow his heart.

"Well, I have a good idea." She reached for his belt buckle.

"Whoa." He tried moving her hands, to no avail. "What are you doing?"

"Relax." Angie grinned. "I've always wanted to know how big you were."

"Well, I can tell you." He thought of Paige sitting alone at home. "It's about nine inches when it's hard."

Angie licked her lips. "I definitely have to see it now." She didn't stop until his pants were around his knees. Once she had him in her hands, she refused to let go. "I want to suck your dick."

"Look, you don't have to."

She giggled. "I know that, but I want to." Angie knelt before him, and before he could protest, he was in the warmth of her mouth.

"Damn," Theo whispered, and it wasn't due to Angie doing a good job. It was because he didn't do a good enough job being the man Paige thought he was. "Fuck." His hands flew upward to his face in disappointment.

Angie, encouraged by Theo's words, moved faster, which meant her teeth were scraping against his skin at what now felt like sixty-five miles an hour.

"Shit." He was in pain. "Damn it, Angie stop."

"What?" She was oblivious. "What did I do?"

"Everything." He continued. "You're—"

"Who's in here?" a male voice asked, accompanied by the click-clacking sound of shoes against the tile. "Is someone in here?"

"Yes." Theo sat on the toilet and pulled Angie onto his lap. "I'm on the toilet," Theo said while holding Angie's legs up so that she wouldn't be seen.

The man asked, "And who is in there with you?"

"Nobody. I'm dropping the kids off at the pool." He laughed. "I'm handling business, man."

"I thought I heard voices."

"You heard me doing number two."

"All right," he said. "If you don't mind, I'll stand here until you come out."

"Why?" He was caught. "Who are you?" Theo asked.

"A chaperone at the dance, sent to make sure that all of the other areas were vacant." He continued. "I heard a girl's voice, so you two can come out now, or I can call security to make a big deal out of this."

Theo waited, but the man refused to go away. It was like a hostage standoff. "You still there?"

"Yes," he said. "Are you all coming out?"

"Damn, man." Theo was frustrated. "We were just messing around. We're not doing anything illegal."

"I understand that, but my job is to escort you, or anyone in these parts, back down to the dance."

"We'll go back as soon as you leave."

"Fine," he whined, "I'll just call security." The noise from the man's shoes moved away from the stall door. Theo quickly thought about the untrained and unprofessional security guards spreading the news to the other faculty members. In a flash, he imagined the look on Paige's face as she learned that he was found in a restroom stall with Angela Porter, doing God knows what.

"Okay," he surrendered, "we're coming out." He put Angie's feet down, stood up, and fixed his clothing.

When the lock disengaged, Angie pushed the door open and stepped out. "Please don't call my father." She burst into tears and begged.

"This is a matter just between us," the man said, and Angie ran out of the restroom. "Okay, come on out, son." Theo stepped out slowly and stared into the face of Mr. Doran Bess.

"Well, well, well, Theodore Lakewood." Doran smiled. "I know a lot of people that would love to know about this." He paused. "No need to worry, though. You're cool by me." Without a word, Theo walked past him like the whole thing never happened.

Theo searched the gym for fifteen minutes before he found a sweaty Will dancing with a group of girls. "I'm leaving." Will didn't hear him, and he didn't care to. He was in hip-hugger heaven. "Will," Theo tapped him on the shoulder, "I'm out. I'm bouncin'."

Will strained his eyes to see his Timex. "Why?" Ten-thirty wasn't the time they agreed on. "What's up?"

"I just need to get out of here."

"Damn." Will looked at the eager girls and then back at Theo. "Please don't do this to me, man. I don't have another ride."

This was the happiest he had ever seen Will. He had no rights to ruin his night. "All right, man," Theo said reluctantly. "I'll wait in the car."

"Are you all right?"

"Yeah." Before the word was completely in the air, Theo turned and walked away.

"Thanks, man," Will screamed to his back.

During the long walk to his car, Theo didn't know what bothered him more, making the mistake with Angie or getting caught during the mistake. He had never once entertained the thought of cheating on Paige. After all, he had no real reason to. She was everything he ever wanted: sexy, smart, independent, spontaneous, patient, loving, affectionate. The list was never-ending.

"Fuck," he whispered as Angela's close-to-castration blowjob came to mind. "The shit wasn't even good."

"How did it get that far?" he asked himself. He imagined some guy with his tongue next to Paige's pussy and became sick to his stomach. For someone to get that far with her meant that she allowed it. The same stood true for him. He allowed it.

Derek's ground floor apartment . . .

"Aren't we supposed to be studying?" Toni chuckled.

"We will," Derek said as he gently pushed her naked body toward the black satin sheets of his king-sized bed. "You really thought I invited you here to study?"

"Yeah." Toni smiled. "Study and eat."

"Well, I am about to eat." He parted her thighs and began to blow delicately on her already glistening lips.

"All this time I thought you wanted me to be your study partner because you thought I was smart." Toni faked a frown.

"You weren't wrong." He tenderly kissed her lower lips. "You're smart, but you're sexy as hell too."

"Really?"

"Yeah, but I see more than just your body." Derek smiled as he looked over the hills of her breasts. "You have a lot going for yourself."

"Like what, a husband and two kids?" Her intentions weren't to think out loud, but she did. "I'm the perfect booty call, no strings attached."

Derek stopped and rose up. "It's not like that."

"Tell me about it." Toni stared up at the ceiling. "I haven't even been here for an hour." She first met Marcus as a stripper. Though he married her, he treated her like he was still paying for lap dances. In fact, all the men in her life handled her like they were paying for it. It was always tit for tat, you do me and I'll do you. "It's always like this."

"Whoa. Don't compare me to anyone," he responded sharply. "If you have something on your mind and want to talk about it, then let's talk."

"You don't seem to want to talk to me," Toni said.

He completely abandoned his post and lay beside her. "Let's talk."

"Naw." The turmoil she left at home she expected to find when she returned. The last thing she wanted to do was talk about it. "I'm all right," she lied.

"If you were really all right, you wouldn't be in my bed," Derek informed her. "I know that your husband is a lawyer, you have two boys, and a big-ass house. If everything was in order, you wouldn't jeopardize all of that to be here."

"Derek, please don't—"

"Well, talk. I don't know what's bothering you unless you say something."

"You won't understand. You're not old enough to—" She stopped herself.

"Okay, so we're moving on to me being twenty and you being nine years wiser than me now?"

"No, we're on me being twenty-nine and stuck in the worst situation any woman could ever be in." Toni didn't know how to make him understand. "All I wanted was to get away . . . Just forget it."

"Well, that's why I invited you here." He paused. "No, I didn't just want to study, and yes, I've been thinking about us doing this, but not just this. I'm open to whatever can happen."

"Yeah, right." She just couldn't get her mouth to stop.

Derek was confused. "Didn't you think that all that nasty talking on the phone would lead to this?"

"Yeah," Toni rolled her eyes, "but not after forty minutes behind closed doors."

"All right." He stood up from the bed with a fed-up face. "I'm not holding you down if you don't want to do it."

"I'm sorry, Derek." She wanted to be comforted, and right now he was all she had. "I do want to be here." He was also right about the phone sex they were having every other day for almost a month. "I really wanna be here."

"In my bed?" he asked her to confirm.

"Yes." She pulled him in with her feet.

"Are you sure?"

"Positive." She gave him puppy dog eyes. "You forgive me?"

"Yeah. You play too much, though." He laughed, and without saying another word, Derek left the room. He returned minutes later, beckoning for her with his hands. He led her to his bathroom and though it was dark, three small candles struggled to provide the room with the ideal glow.

The sound of the rustling water falling from the faucet to join the suds below was hypnotic, and the cucumber melon aroma served as an aphrodisiac.

"When you're with me, you're brand new again." He lifted her up, placed her in his bathtub, and humbled himself before her. As though she was being baptized, Derek squeezed the warm sponge over her body, and then gently applied it to her tender, honey-brown skin. He washed her worries away. She was brand new.

On his knees outside of the tub, he fed her cherries, strawberries, and grapes. However, to her, his fingertips had more flavor than any fruit that had ever graced her lips. Beneath the surface of the bubbles, he massaged her and whispered things in her ears that she hadn't heard since becoming a wife. He told her things that made her feel like a woman.

Forty-five minutes later, without drying her off, Derek picked her up and carried her back to his room. He laid her on the bed and knelt before her opened legs again.

"Toni, you're not here just because no one else wanted to come. I asked you here because I didn't want anyone else here. I wanted you here, so try to relax." With that said, Derek's tongue touched her fleshy switch and her entire body shuddered.

Toni's movements nearly seemed choreographed to match Mary J. Blige's "All That I Can Say," playing in the living room. At least Mary had something to say. Toni was now speechless. Just seconds into the process, she tried pulling away. She found Derek's suction too gratifying. He held on to her thighs and shook his head from side to side, meaning, "Where are you going? I'm not finished yet." The movement brought a wickedly stimulating sensation.

Tugging heavily on her knob and plunging into her with his tongue over and over, Derek looked like an infant sucking for the gift of life. He had a Doctorate in Pussyology and gave her another fifteen minutes of professional treatment before surfacing. He crept up her torso and repositioned their bodies. She was now atop him, with the black satin sheet to his back.

"Put me in," he said.

Toni hesitated, but after several long sighs, couldn't hold it. "Derek, I don't expect you to want me tomorrow," she paused, "but I need you to pretend that you love me tonight." She added, "Don't fuck me." She swallowed hard. "I mean, I know that that's what you probably want to do, but just please don't treat me like it."

She was desperate for the warm feeling she yearned for so long. She wanted it tonight, even if it was just make-believe. "Don't fuck me." Tears were holding on to the corners of her eyes.

He stared into her face. "That wasn't my intention." His lips met hers gently. "Put me inside and let me prove it."

Toni trembled feverishly as she reached down and affixed his shovel to the surface of her patch of moistened earth. All he had to do was muster up the energy to dig . . . and dig he did. With the sensitivity of a true gentleman, he hollowed out her tunnel slowly. She studied his facial expression and searched for the face of a man who was just glad for pussy, any pussy, but the look was absent.

In his arms, she felt like a rose petal that fell from the rose of an arrangement delivered to a queen. He was gentle, unhurried, and affectionate. He appreciated her body. Though he was eager to be with her, his intentions were never to make her feel as though that was all she was worth. Something brought this beautiful, caring, frail woman into his arms, and he felt the need to value her.

Now sweaty, moaning, biting his lips, and unable to control the way his eyes kept floating upward, Derek admitted, "I've thought about this a lot."

"Me too." She looked into his face. "I, I—" She stopped

in mid-sentence, but convinced herself that life was too short not to say what was on her mind . . . even if it wasn't right. "I think about *you* all the time."

"So do I," he panted.

"Thank you for being gentle with me." Her tears escaped.

His hands clenched her buttocks and he slowly filled her from the bottom up. "You don't ever have to tell me what to do. I know how to treat a lady." He enjoyed the way her breasts wiggled and jiggled each time she fell onto him.

"Good," she said.

He beckoned her for a kiss. "Now come here." Together they believed that they were touching heaven, but it was hell that was reaching out to them all along. Derek moaned, "Stay with me tonight." At that very moment, a deafening sound filled the air, followed by pieces of shattered glass from the window above the bed. Before either of them could respond, there was nothing, or no one, to respond to.

~Situation #16~

Theo

"Did I wake you up?" I said as she opened the door with eyes halfway closed.

"Don't worry about it," Paige groaned and assured me while her wine-colored satin robe hung half open. "Come in."

"I thought you'd still be up." After what happened at the dance, I had to see her. I felt awful. I dropped Will off and was headed home when the memory of Angela on her knees in front of me slapped me in the face. I made a U-turn straight out of the Hollywood movies and called her when I was two minutes away.

I fought with telling her about the incident, and decided that if I couldn't tell her, the least I could do was provide comfort for the unknown act that I didn't try hard enough to stop. "If you were already in bed, I'll just leave."

"It's not a problem, Theo." She closed the door as I entered, and stared into my face. "Are you all right?" It was as if she were glaring into my very essence.

"Yeah." I looked away. "Just a little tired, that's all."

She moved closer to me. "Are you sure?"

Could she smell my cheating blood? What was giving me

away? "I'm fine," I lied with a smile, but I couldn't look at her. "I just wanted to see you." To mask my guilt, I brushed my hand over the switch and turned out the lights.

She laughed. "If you want to see me, you can't do that in the dark."

"I'm a blind man tonight. Seeing, to me, is through touch, so I'll just have to feel you." I grabbed her hand and followed her to the bedroom.

"Where did you park?" she asked. We were now standing in her bedroom. "How was the dance?"

"The dance?" I thought about what would happen if I were upfront and what would happen if I weren't. I slid my arms around her and pulled her toward me slowly. "You should've been there."

"Me?" She smiled. "Why?"

"It would've changed my whole night." That was the truth. If she were at the dance, there would've been no way to get into half of the things I did. "I really wish you would've been there."

"We'll have plenty of dances together after this little thing called graduation that's coming up." She smiled and kissed my chest through my T-shirt.

"I hear you." I held her.

"I'm sleepy. Are you staying?" she asked.

"Yeah." I paused. "Yeah, I'm staying."

Eventually, we made our way to the bed, talked, and then snuggled closely next to one another. With my secret nestled uncomfortably between us, I sprinkled her neck and upper back with kisses. My conscience kept me awake, and if she weren't sleepy, I would've made love to her. I probably still could've, but I hadn't even washed Angie's dried-up saliva off of me.

An hour into staring at the closet door, Paige's cellular phone started to ring. She moaned and ignored it, but seconds later, it was chiming again. She reached for it and flipped it open, "Yeah," she said in a weary tone and went silent. "Yes." She paused. "All right, all right, no. We're not together right now." Her hand rushed to rub her eyes. "Yeah, we *were* together . . ." She continued. "Why?" She reached over and clicked on the lamp on the nightstand. "She's not there yet?" Paige looked at the clock then rolled over onto her back. "No." She paused. "I don't know . . ." She was interrupted. "Now, you wait just one minute . . ." She sat up and raised her voice. "Marcus, don't yell at me and don't call me a liar because I—" She was upset. "Why?" She paused. "Why? Why in the hell are you yelling at me and asking *me* all of these questions?" She ran her fingers through her hair. "What? What? What did they say?" She froze. "When?" Paige jumped out of bed. "No, no, that can't be right."

Right then, even though she was brown-skinned, Paige went pale, and the expression on her face went away. It looked as if she wanted to faint, vomit, and cuss someone out all in the same breath. "Oh my God . . . and they think it's her? Why would they think that?" She leaned against the wall. "Where?" She scrambled around the room, not sure of what she was looking for. "Where?" She got loud again. "No, I want to. I'll meet you there." Tears took over her voice. "No, I'm coming. I'll meet you there." She hung up.

"What's going on?" I asked as she dropped to the bed like a tattered rag doll. "Paige, are you all right?"

"It's her." She cried and paused. "It's her. That's where she told me she was going. She was going to Cutler Ridge."

"Who? Who went to Cutler Ridge?" I was confused. "What are you talking about?"

She wailed for a while and spoke a sentence of slow, slurred words that I couldn't comprehend. "I can't understand you, baby," I said as I wiped the tears from her eyes. "What are you saying?"

She struggled to compose herself and managed to spill these words. "A woman was killed . . . they think it's Toni."

"What?" I jumped up. "What happened?"

She started talking, and immediately I felt as though I was in a movie. Marcus had called from the back of a police cruiser on the way to Cutler Ridge, to a crime scene where a woman was murdered, and they suspected that it was his wife, Toni. Next, Paige and I were speeding down US-1. I followed the directions given to me by an officer because Marcus was too shaken up to tell us where he was.

During the entire ride, Paige continuously dialed Toni's cell phone number. Toni never picked up, and Paige grew angrier with each call because her voice mail was full. She couldn't leave a message to let her know how much trouble she was in.

The flashing red and blue lights from the sea of police cars surrounding it encompassed the pale yellow apartment complex. "This is it," I said to Paige as we pulled up, hoping that it was all a mistake.

Within minutes of arriving and being repeatedly asked to stay behind the yellow police ribbon, Paige spotted Toni's husband. "Marcus!" she yelled. He had his hands on his head and was being escorted out of the complex by two officers. "Marcus!" Paige yelled again. However, he didn't acknowledge her, or anyone, for that matter. He seemed in a state of shock.

"Where is she?" Paige frantically dashed under the police line, and before the officers could catch her, she had reached him. "Where? What? Tell me . . . tell me."

When he was able to speak, he confirmed her worst fears. The body in the apartment was that of her best friend. Paige stared at Marcus in disbelief and made him repeat the sad truth, and then fell onto him.

The two of them held onto one another, and I was told that I couldn't enter the restricted area. During my "standing around," I overheard three police officers having a conversation. Apparently, Toni was creeping on Marcus with a dude that lived in the apartment complex. The dude had a restraining order out on his ex-girlfriend. The ex-girl was a psycho, and police had been called to the apartment several times in the last few months. Whenever they were called, it was because he had company over and she was bitter. The ex would call and call and then wait outside to confront the man and the new girl, one time even waiting until the next morning. Toni and the dude were having sex when the deranged ex threw a concrete block through the window above his bed. It landed on Toni's head, killing her immediately.

We didn't leave for Paige's place until the coroner's van came and Toni's body was removed from the bed, which became her final resting place. They rolled her by us in a body bag atop a tall stretcher, covered with a burgundy cloth. Paige never gave up on her friend. She continued to place calls to her. She continued to receive no answer, her voice mail was full, and she still couldn't get her message to Toni.

The week went by at the speed of lightning. Paige took the entire week off from school. She spent her days with Marcus and the twins. However, at night, she wanted me by her side, even if I had to beg, steal, or kill to pull it off. When we were together, she didn't talk about Toni. I think that after being at Marcus' house and around Toni's family and children from nine in the morning until nine at night, when she was home, she tried to pretend that her life was somewhat normal, like Toni was still just a phone call away.

I attended the funeral, but sat in the back of the church. I could only watch as the woman I loved needed a man beside her. Marcus' older brother, I care not to know his name, comforted Paige. I tried not to be jealous, but he wasn't an ugly dude. He was around forty, wavy black hair, light-skinned, tall, and looked like he used the hell out of his gym membership. I heard through the grapevine that he was a martial arts instructor, but I didn't give a fuck. I had seen all of Jackie Chan's movies. I knew the moves too.

Yeah, I was hatin' on the brotha. It made me sick to my stomach to see her walk into the church with the other family members with him clutching her hand, land her leaning on him all through the service. He was wiping her tears away, and during the parting view, he had to hold her around the waist when she nearly fainted. I couldn't even get close to her.

Several news crews were across the street from the church. Ever since it happened, the story was covered extensively: *Married Woman Killed While in Bed with Her Lover, by His Former Girlfriend.* They couldn't dream up a better story than that. The reporters were lined up across the street from the church parking lot. A few of them walked onto the church grounds when they saw me and had the audacity to ask me questions about my choice, college or the NBA, as I walked to the Mazda. I was just the basketball boy to them. They didn't care that I knew Toni. A story was just a story to them. It didn't matter where they got it. I gave them a blank stare and jumped into my car. I didn't go to the gravesite. I just couldn't stand to see anymore of the Paige and Bruce Lee show.

I didn't hear from her until close to midnight. I had no reason to be upset with her but I was, so I pretended that she had woken me up when she called. As selfish as this might sound, I was hungry for her to pay more attention to me. Everything lately was Marcus, Kevin, Devin, and now, Marcus' brother. Tonight would be her first without me since the ordeal. Had she asked me over I would've jumped at it, but she didn't.

"Sorry, go back to bed," she said and hung up.

Two days later, her first day back at school, I made it to my seat in her classroom right as the bell rang. My intentions were to be late, but my feet were anxious about getting there. Even *they* wanted to be near her. She was wearing a black dress. Even in mourning she was sexy. Her smile was back, and she looked somewhat back to life. She thanked the class for all of the well wishes, cards, and phone calls over the past week, and took it easy on us by talking about her friendship with Toni for the entire period.

The bell rang and she dismissed us and began to gather her things. Angie walked over to my desk.

"Theo, what are you doing after school?"

"Why?" I looked past her at Paige; I hoped she wasn't listening. "What's up?"

"My dad is away on business until Wednesday. Wanna come over?"

"I'm meeting with the coach from Southern Kentucky State." It was the truth.

She was persistent. "What about after that?"

I tried to keep my voice down. "Angie, I'm sorry about what happened."

"It's cool. At first I was freaked out about getting caught," she smiled, "but I still want to finish."

"I don't want you to." By then the classroom was almost empty and anything not said in an extreme whisper would be heard. "Look, Angie." I paused. "I'm seeing someone."

Angie looked upset. "Who?"

"Why should that matter?"

"Because obviously she isn't doing something right," she said in a whisper.

I shook my head and stood up. "She has nothing to do with what happened. That was all my fault."

"Theo." Angie was embarrassed. "You let me su—"

"Mr. Lakewood, were you late to class today?" Paige asked from across the room.

I was relieved. "Yes," I lied, "but can I get a break? I'm having a meeting with a college coach today."

"There's no such thing as a break between you and me."
She smiled. "The coach will have to wait." She turned her attention to Angie. "Were you late, too, Angela?"

"No," Angie said. "We were just talking about something that's going on later." Angie turned back to me and tried to be nice. "Give me your cell number. We'll talk later."

I watched Paige cross her arms over her chest and wait on a response from me.

"It's my girl's phone. I can't."

She stared at me a while, no doubt regretting sucking my dick. "You are so fuckin' wrong for this," she murmured and then walked away.

Paige giggled as she locked the door and slowly strutted back to her desk. "So, what happened between you two last week?" she asked.

"Huh?" I almost cracked. "What do you mean?"

"It seems like I always have to save you from her. How did you deal with her while I was out?" She sat on her desk.

"I wasn't dealing with her." I breathed a sigh of reprieve. "And for the record," I smiled, "I can handle myself."

Still atop her desk, Paige let her hair loose, and as she crossed her legs, I watched her dress crawl up her thighs. "Did you give the substitute a hard time?"

"No." I was already stiffening. "But I'm ready to give you one."

During her week of mourning, though I spent each night with her, I never touched her sexually. I figured it would not only be tacky of me to expect sex from her during such a difficult time, but it would also show a lack of respect for her friendship with Toni. However, I wanted it. Each night I was physically ready, willing, and able. So, this sitting on her desk and flirting business, I was going to milk.

"What is it that you're ready to give me?"

I walked toward her. "A hard time," I said and continued, "a very, very hard time."

"How hard?"

"It's rock candy, baby." I slid my hands up her thighs.

"What time do you have to meet the coach?" she asked.

"At three-thirty."

"Where?"

I couldn't have cared less about the coach then. "He's meeting me at my house."

"That means we don't have much time," she whispered and pulled her dress up, revealing her light blue underwear. "It's already two thirty-six."

"I have fifty-four minutes," without looking at the clock I finished, "but I can give you ten of them."

"Ten?" Her tone was seductive. "What can you give me in ten minutes?"

"The question is what *can't* I give you in ten minutes?"

Her eyes shuddered then closed as my fingers snuck into her panties and rubbed against her silky moist spot. She reached down, unbuckled my belt, and gravity sent my pants toward the ground. Through the peephole in my boxers, she massaged me. I was standing there with veins protruding and throbbing like one more stroke would send me into convulsions. I pulled away from her grasp because I wanted dinner. I couldn't fill myself up on appetizers. Just as she had in my fantasies, she jumped down from the desk and leaned over it, letting me hit that sweet spot from the back.

I bit into my bottom lip. "Damn." I could still hear lockers slamming, kids shouting, feet running, beating on the wall, and air brakes of school buses in a distance. The combination of people being just a few feet away sent me to another level. Not that I have experienced all of these, but I had to believe that this feeling was better than smoking, drinking, shooting up, or snorting anything. I was high on pussy, and though I promised her ten minutes, I was only good for about four; the mood was too powerful.

Suddenly, a voice from the main office streamed into the

classroom through the intercom. "Ms. Patrick, are you still in your classroom?"

"Shit," she whispered and froze up for a second until I jabbed her back into what we were doing. "Oh, yes," she said to me and then answered them. "Yes, yes, I'm here."

"Do you remember if Joshua Bates was in your homeroom today?"

"Um." She reached over to the other side of the desk to get her attendance book and I took advantage of the extra depth. "Oh God," she said and looked back at me to suggest that I would get us caught if I continued to give it to her so damn good. And I didn't stop. As she tried to reach the book again, I tried reaching her rib cage. "Oh Lord," she exclaimed.

The office personnel interrupted. "I'm sorry, did you say something?"

"No," Paige lied. "Just, just give me a minute. I'm checking the book."

"Oh, okay."

Checking the book? Paige backed that thang all up on me like it was nobody's business, and it really wasn't. She grinded, shook, and squeezed me within her juicy walls, all while the office lady waited on a response. It was almost like being watched. Unable to utter a sound, our facial expressions said it all. We experienced the highest height of ecstasy we ever had. I gathered the bottom of my shirt and stuck it into my mouth to contain myself vocally as I prematurely freed my passion into her.

"Ms. Patrick, are you still there?"

"Yes, yes, one second. Things are kind of crazy. This is my first day back," she panted as I pulled out of her.

"Yes, I know," the voice said. "How are you feeling?"

"Oh, I'm feeling all right." She looked back at me. "A lot better than I ever expected."

"Good for you," the voice said happily. "Just take things one day at a time and things will continue to get better."

"Thank you." Paige quickly grabbed the book and flipped through the pages. "Okay, here we go, yes, Josh was in class this morning."

"Okay, thank you so much," the lady said. "Keep your head up."

"I will," Paige answered, and we watched the green light, indicating an open communication, disappear. She walked over to where I had collapsed on the floor and knelt to kiss me. "I've been missing that," she whispered.

I pulled her closer. "I've missed that too."

"Get up." She looked at the clock. "You have to go."

I had already forgotten the meeting. "Damn." I jumped up, fixed my clothes, and grabbed my bookbag. "Thanks."

"No." She smiled. "Thank you."

"I'll call you later." I hated to leave, but I couldn't stay a moment longer. The coach was coming all the way from Kentucky just to talk to me.

"Damn, I love you," I said right before opening the door to leave.

"Well, damn, I love you too." She smiled. "Bye."

Though my decision was to play professional ball, it was still unknown to many. Had I chosen college, it wouldn't have been Southern Kentucky State; however, I didn't want to be rude when Coach Stiller called and requested to meet with me while he was in Miami. Rumor had it that I was his only reason for being in Miami.

Coach Ronald Stiller, the tall, thin man I had seen on ESPN countless times, walked into my house with two things that never left his grasp, a smile and a hunter green and pale yellow SKSU duffel bag. My mom always thought that he was one of the sexiest white men alive. For two hours, she cleaned our house in preparation of his presence. Weeks prior, she insisted that I not meet with him alone. She made him schedule the meeting time around her work schedule, and even wore a new hip-hugging outfit that I had never seen.

Coach Stiller made some sweet promises, and I smiled all the way through the two-long-hour talk and homemade meal, but I wasn't swayed. Though he was interested in me as a player, I noticed his interest in my mother as a woman, and I didn't like that one bit. He complimented her clothing, hair, and even her "athletic" physique.

When he was about to leave, he gave her his cellular phone number, stating, "If there is anything that I haven't covered, please call me." He was supposed to give me that number, not her. He stared her down like he had already caught the now very contagious jungle fever. When he remembered that I was standing right next to her, he looked over at me.

"Well, I sure hope that I've convinced you to consider Southern Kentucky," he said while opening the driver's side door of his rental car.

"Definitely," I lied. "You've given me something to think about."

"I hope so." He went on, "I truly hope so because we—"

"Mom, telephone. It's the hospital," Kevin yelled out the window.

"Oh." She sighed. "Mr. Stiller, please excuse me. I have to take that."

"Not a problem, Ms. Lakewood. It's been a pleasure meeting you. Please call me . . ." Then he added, "If you have any questions or concerns about the school."

"I will," she said and returned to the house. He smiled and watched her ass until it disappeared behind the door.

"I bought this for you." He handed over the SKSU bag. "I didn't want to give it to you in front of your mother. I didn't want her to think that we were trying to bribe you with SKSU gym shorts, T-shirts, and other shit." He laughed and handed over the bag.

"Thanks." I accepted it. "As soon as I review all of the information, I'll be in contact with you."

"Alrighty." He lowered himself into the car. "I can't wait to see you in green and yellow, son."

"Okay." I offered him a bogus smile. Green and yellow? Hell no.

He reversed out of the yard, tooted the horn, and disappeared down the road, probably on his way to the airport to board a plane to give the same "we want you" speech to the next guy the following day.

I slung the bag over my shoulder, and once in the house, threw it into Kevin's room like I had done with all the other ones from the other schools. Kevin would soon find something to do with its contents. At the rate he was growing, soon he'd be able to wear the stuff.

"Mmm." Mom walked into my room. "That Coach Stiller is something else."

"I can't believe how you two were acting," I said.

"What do you mean?" She blushed.

"Oh, please." I was grossed out. "All the flirting, the compliments, and the phone number exchange? That was nasty."

"How is that nasty when you can do only God knows what with whomever this girl is you're seeing?"

"Yeah, but I'm not trying to get my freak on in front of you, though. Y'all were just straight gross." I jokingly showed her the door to exit my room. "Out of my room, freak."

"You sure you don't want to go to college?" she joked.

"Nope." I sat on my bed and looked over at her. "I'm NBA bound, baby."

"All jokes aside." She got serious. "I'm your mother, so it's my duty to ask you questions like that." She walked closer to the bed. "If you change your mind about the NBA, I'll still support you. I will support whatever decision you make."

"I know, Ma." I smiled. "Thanks."

"All right." She smiled and continued. "Now, how would you feel about Coach Stiller being your stepfather?"

I jumped off of the bed and she ran away. I chased her all the way to her room and tickled her until she screamed uncle and apologized for the borderline vulgar statement. She laughed, kicked and screamed, and somewhere in the middle of it all, I managed to rip a huge hole in my pants. The frustrating part of it all was trying to find a clean pair. Everything needed to be washed.

"Damn yellow and green bullshit," I said as I walked into Kevin's room. "Where is that bag I just put in here, squirt?"

"What bag?" Kevin's eyes never left his video game.

"The Southern Kentucky yellow and green bag," I said.

"Under the bed."

He still wasn't really paying me any attention. "Can you get it?" I asked when I realized that he expected me to find it.

"Dawg, man, I just started on a new level." He pressed pause and fished underneath his bed until he surfaced with the bag. "Here."

"Thanks." Once in my room, I closed and locked my door, fearing my mother's retaliation. I searched the bag and found a new pair of shorts, but continued to go through it. There were shirts, sweat pants, gym shorts, flags for cars, hats, whistles, even a face painting kit, but all the way at the bottom of the bag was a white envelope. I grabbed it and expected to find SKSU information. However, the green in the envelope was a different shade than the green in the school colors. The envelope was full of money.

I counted it over four times before I believed that it was real. One hundred one hundred dollar bills. Ten thousand dollars along with a note that read: *We'll take care of you.* I stayed in my room for over an hour trying to find a hiding place for it. Finally, I decided to stuff it into the smelliest shoe I owned, the ones I called my "lucky ladies." I couldn't fit into them anymore, but they were on the sideline at every game. Mom hated them because they smelled. She wouldn't touch them because they smelled, but she wouldn't throw them out because she knew that they smelled like winners to me.

After the money was secure, I dialed Paige's number. Why? Because she never once complained when my needy ass asked for lunch, gas, or spending money. She had always given to me unselfishly, so I couldn't wait to do something, anything, and everything I could for her.

"Hello?" Paige answered.

"What's up?"

"Nothing. I was just thinking about your detention." She smiled into the phone.

Yeah, it was still on my mind too. "I know that it's just Monday, but what do you have planned for the weekend?"

"Not much." She then asked cautiously, "Why?"

I was anxious. "Pack your bags. We're going to Key West on Friday after school."

"What?" she asked. "Theo, that sounds great. I would love to take a vacation, but right now, that's not within my budget."

"Fuck your budget," I interrupted with a smile. "*I'm* taking *you* to Key West."

"How?" She laughed.

"Just make sure you pack. I'll explain everything tomorrow."

The next day, I told her all about the money, and she didn't seem to mind where it was from, just as long as we were going to be together and away from the norm.

The week dragged by like it was on a snail's back. Friday final arrived, and after the last bell, I sat in a restaurant down the street from the school until she returned with the rental car.

On US-1 southbound, away from everyone we knew, she said that she felt like screaming, and she did. We both turned into two blissful kids just looking to have a good time . . . together.

We checked into our suite at the Hilton Resort and Marina around 8 P.M. It was massive; a dining room table set for eight, a full living room with a sofa, coffee table, and loveseat. The bathroom was equipped with a stand-alone shower and a Jacuzzi on the other side. My favorite room, however, was the bedroom. Coming out of the wall over the bed was a bamboo frame covered in beige sheers. The sheers encased the bed romantically.

We showered and were in a restaurant called Six by ten o'clock. It was a very nice place, crisp white linen tablecloths, beautiful live flowers, and candlelight. Paige was all smiles as the waiter left to get our drinks.

"I guess this is our first date."

"It is." Then I flirted, "Do you kiss on the first date?"

She blushed. "No, I'm not that kind of girl."

I reached under the table and ran my hand up her thigh. "What kind of girl are you?"

She smacked my hand. "Not that kind either." She proceeded to tell me that she was a respectable girl who would never dream of giving out more than a handshake on the night of a first date. Suddenly, her face lit up. "Let's play around."

"Play around how?"

"Role play," she said. "Let's be strangers tonight. Let's pretend that the restaurant was full and I, hungry and just wanting a seat anywhere, asked the waiter to ask you if you'd mind sharing a table."

I thought she had lost her mind. "Are you serious?" I guess she was, because when she spoke again, she was someone else.

"Thank you for allowing me to join you. I just couldn't

wait a minute more to get something into my stomach." She reached her hand out to me across the table. "My name is Paige."

I giggled. "Nice to meet you, Paige." I couldn't believe we were going to do this. "I'm Theodore." I always used my full name when I wanted to give off a little sophistication.

"I won't bother you with conversation." She grabbed her menu and scanned it.

"Actually, conversation is just what I was hoping for tonight." I smiled.

We role-played throughout dinner, treating each other like strangers, yet we flirted just enough to let the other know that an after-dinner rendezvous was possible. Boy, was it possible.

A little after midnight, we were strolling down Key West's tiny cobblestone streets, the ocean breeze rustled past us, and we were still locked into our game of pretending to be foreign.

"So, what hotel are you staying at?" I asked.

"Um." She faked a struggle to remember. "I think the Hilton, or is it the Hyatt or the Hampton?" Paige giggled. "Something that starts with an H. I'll know it when I see it."

"I can't have you roaming around all alone not knowing where you're going."

"No, no, you've done enough for the night, picking up the check and all. You don't have to walk me there," she insisted. "I'll be fine. Thank you for the kind gesture, though."

"It's not a problem." I thought of something quickly. "My hotel is in the same direction."

"Is it?"

"Yes."

"You know what? I just remembered my hotel is this way." She made a quick right into an alley. "So, we're not going in the same direction." She waved me off as if to get rid of me. "Nice meeting you."

"Nice meeting you too." I stared at her as she walked down the dimly lit path. The red rayon skirt continuously slapped the back of her thighs. Watching her hips switch back and forth was like looking at a tennis match; you had to follow the bouncin' ball. Her high-heeled sandals raised her up, seemingly right to where she needed to be for me to just grab her and ram into her from the back.

I wanted her badly and was in a rush to get back to the room. "Paige," I called out to her as she was about to disappear into the darkness, but she didn't look back, so I followed her. "Paige." I ran to catch up with her.

"What are you doing?" She looked back at me like she was afraid and began walking faster. When I didn't answer, the look of pure horror took over her face. "Are you following me?"

She was still playing the game. Though I wanted to hurry up and get her in the Jacuzzi where our wet bodies could slip and slide into each other, this would do. "I paid for your dinner."

"And?" She began trotting.

"And now I want what I *really* paid for."

She made a left, thinking she'd escape me behind a dark building, but it was a dead-end with no lights. "Please," she panted. "I can pay you for my portion of the check." She fought to open up her purse, but when I reached her, she held it out to me instead. "Take it. I have money, credit cards, and jewelry in there. Just take it."

I grabbed the purse and threw it to the ground. "Thanks, but that's not what I want." I slowly backed her into the wall.

"Please." She looked frightened for real. "Please don't do this to me."

"If you stay quiet, I won't hurt you." When I lifted her skirt, my hand fell into her wet fold. "I won't hurt you." I loved the way she felt. "Just let me put my finger in it."

"Please." She shivered and it looked like she wanted to cry. "I, I won't report you to the police. Just take the money."

"I don't want the money." I tightened my grip on her hand. "Shh." I roughly kissed her lips. "Open up your legs a little bit more." She did. I rubbed her bottom and wanted to see just how long she could pretend not to want me. "You came out without any panties. You were looking for this." I allowed one finger to ease its way into her. "You like that?"

"Please." Her tone was slowly changing. "Please stop."

"Not before I give you something else."

She squirmed and moaned a little. "You said that you just wanted to put your finger in it," she cried. "You did, so let me go."

"I am going to finger you." I undid my belt buckle with my free hand. "I'm going to finger you with my biggest finger." I laughed as I pulled my pants down. "What kind of woman runs around without panties?" I got harsh with her. "Sounds like you're looking for trouble, so I'll give you what you came for."

"Please," she whimpered. "Don't do—"

"Shut up." I launched my finger deeper into her and the look of enjoyment was written all over her face, but she tried to keep the act going.

"Please stop. Stop now and I won't tell the police."

I brought her hand down to my weapon and made her stroke it. My dick was hard enough to backhand somebody if I turned around quickly. I pulled my finger from her and rubbed her fleshiest part.

"I'll scream if you keep doing that," she groaned.

"Go ahead and scream." The sound my fingers made on her wet flesh drove me crazy. "I'll give you something to scream for." I lifted her up, fixed her legs around my waist, backed her into the filthy wall of the old museum, and pushed myself up into her. "Scream, Paige. Let me hear you scream rape." Her juices welcomed me. "Yell for the muthafuckin' cops." Her hands clinched me around my neck. "Don't hold onto me. You're supposed to be trying to get away." I pounded her again and again, and suddenly she was giving me that pussy like she was raping *me*. "I knew you wanted this dick."

The next night, our last night in Key West, we went to a club called Locos. I slipped the doorman a fifty-dollar bill to pretend that he looked at my ID when he looked at hers. He passed me a smile and allowed us in. I had tried the same stunt at two other places and failed miserably. I guess this guy had mouths to feed, thank God.

The atmosphere in the club was very relaxed, and as with most establishments in Key West, everything was open. The club had a roof but no real walls, just three or four long, horizontal pieces of wood separating us from the people on the sidewalk.

After about three shots of tequila each, Paige and I were on the dance floor. She was a raging bull and my lips were the red flag that provoked her. She couldn't stay away from them. We were dancing to a fast song, but to our own slow beat. I pulled her into me and kissed her so passionately that it felt as though I pulled her soul out and right into mine.

There were people talking, dancing, and bumping into us. We ignored them all until one voice just wouldn't go away. "Theodore Lakewood, is that you?" The voice was about 250 miles south of where it was supposed to be. I opened my eyes and stared into the round, pink face of Principal Michael Courtland, whose jaws nearly hit the floor when the woman I was kissing turned to see who had called her lover's name.

He smiled. "Oh, and Ms. Patrick." He cleared his throat. "What a pleasant surprise."

~Situation #17~

Paige

"**M**r.—" The innocent facial expression I thought of issuing ran away. "I mean Principal Courtland." I didn't know what to say, how to say it, and most of all, I didn't know what he would have to say. I gasped. "What brings you here?"

He looked at me strangely and continued sarcastically. "Well, I heard that you could see everything down here." He glared at Theo. "I guess they were right, huh?"

Theo hesitated a bit before answering. "Depends on what you're looking for."

The music stopped and the uncomfortable silence between the three of us filled the air as the DJ gave birthday shout-outs to people in the crowd. We stared at one another until not saying anything meant that someone was on the verge of saying something dumb.

"Okay." Mr. Courtland disturbed the peace. "Ms. Patrick, may I speak with you alone?" He pointed toward the side-walk. "Outside?"

Theo saw the uneasiness on my face. "What's to say that I can't hear?" he asked.

"Mr. Lakewood," Courtland shot Theo a shut-the-hell-up

look, "this is an official Miami-Dade County Public School matter."

"Whatever, man," Theo interjected. "There's nothing you—"

"Theo, I'll be right back." I patted his chest. "It'll just take a minute." I smiled.

Mr. Courtland was already making his way toward the sidewalk. I didn't know how I was going to defend myself. Surely he wasn't blind. He saw us. He saw *us*.

"Well, Ms. Patrick," he paused, "I'm quite surprised at you." His smirk said just how much he was going to enjoy this. "You, of all people, the upholder of every rule, the angel amongst the faculty." He went on. "I wish I could just pretend that I didn't see what I saw, but doing that would mean breaking the rules." He looked away but quickly found me again. "This will *have* to be brought before the school board officers."

"Mr. Courtland," I tried to reason with him, "school will be out in a few months and Theo will be a graduate. Can't we just be adults about this?"

"Be adults?" he asked. "You're here lip-locking with a child, Ms. Patrick. So, I ask you, who is it that isn't acting like an adult?"

"He's not a child," I defended him and hoped to make a difference. "He's eighteen years old."

"Eighteen, nineteen, or twenty," Mr. Courtland stated loudly, "he's still a student at West Dade." He was agitated. "Ms. Patrick, you know the policies." He continued sarcastically. "After all, you defended them so well when you complained to the school board about how I wasn't following a few of them."

"That was a different situation, Mr. Courtland. Most of the things I brought up were safety concerns."

"Yeah, well, so is this." He chuckled derisively. "Most parents won't feel safe with a teacher like you in the school."

Immediately, the urge to spit in his face became over-whelming. I didn't do it, but I probably should've, because either way, I wouldn't have a job come Monday. "This is not illegal, Mr. Courtland. Theo is not a minor."

"He isn't a minor, but he is a student. He is your student, it is unethical, and you know that we don't stand for that."

"You don't stand for anything." I had had it with him, and also with trying to stay polite. "Take me to the school board, the superintendent. Take me to the fuckin' board of directors. Take me to the President of the goddamn United States." I put my hands akimbo and let him have it. "I don't give a fuck what you do, what you say, or who you say it to." My bluntness shocked me. "If I never set foot in West Dade again that'll be damn fine with me."

He looked down at me with an antagonizing grin. "Don't take it personal." They were the same words I used on him after the school board told him to shape up or ship out. He smiled and had the nerve to throw open his arms. "Since you're already here, join me and Mr. Bess for a cocktail later." He continued smiling. "No hard feelings, huh?"

Mr. Bess. What the—? "You're here with Doran?"

"Yes, in search of a—"

". . . a *gay* ole time, I presume." I finished his sentence with words I'm sure he wouldn't have used. "That's interesting."

"False accusations don't travel far."

"Well, West Dade isn't that far."

"I'm not doing anything illegal or against policy." He smiled. "I'm simply hanging out with a comrade."

"Does your wife know that your comrade is gay?" I finished. "Down low brothas are crossing the color lines, I see."

He laughed. "Once again, you and your falsehoods."

"Falsehood?" I returned his chuckle. "I had an encounter of the worst kind with Doran and his boyfriend, and if I remember correctly, his name wasn't Falsehood." I turned and walked away.

"Sleep in on Monday, Ms. Patrick, because as of this moment, you are suspended. I will have a substitute in your classroom indefinitely, and the board will contact you regarding their decision about your return."

I felt my body do a *Matrix Reloaded* turn to look back at him. "I don't need their decision." The last thing I wanted was this foolishness spinning into a public forum to humiliate me and make me out to be a child-molesting teacher like Mary Kay Letourneau or Debra Lafave.

"I quit." The words flew out of my mouth. "I'll deliver my resignation letter to you personally, and then you can let the goddamn board know what *my* decision is about returning."

I walked back into the club and Theo was standing by the bar, without a drink, just a blank gaze. "Let's go," I said and grabbed my purse and other things he had placed on the bar.

"What happened?"

I was pissed beyond the normal level. I had Mike Tyson's intensity. I wanted to bite somebody somewhere. "Let's just go."

"Tell me what went down." Theo tried holding my hand.

"Please . . ." I pulled away. "You won't understand, and even if you could, I don't feel like talking about it right now." I rolled my eyes. "Let's go."

He wasn't budging. "I wanna know what he said. I am involved in this fuckin' shit too."

"Oh, it's fuckin' shit, huh?" I snapped. "Just how fuckin' involved are you in this, this *shit*?" I didn't give him room to answer. "Because I'm up to my hairline in this *shit*. I just had to quit my damn job just so that no one will find out about this, this relationship that you now call shit."

"I didn't mean it like—"

"You know what you were saying." I tried to keep my

voice below the embarrassing raging-woman level. "You meant it just like fuckin' that."

"No, I didn't." He raised his voice and boy, did I not appreciate it that. "Stop jumping to conclusions. I wasn't even finished saying what I was saying." He got even louder, and people started to look over at us. "Learn to listen some fuckin' time. You're not always right."

"I'm done." I could hardly breathe. "I am so fuckin' done with this right now." With my belongings, I dashed out of the club and hailed a cab. I was humiliated because of the way Theo felt he could talk to me. Hurt because of the way Courtland tried to degrade me, and wanted to scream because I just had to, not wanted to or could afford to, I *had* to quit my job. When the cab ride was over, I rushed up to the hotel room and while weeping like I had scraped the skin off of both knees and elbows, I began packing my bags.

Courtland would probably see that I wouldn't get another teaching job within the tri-county area, so if I wanted to stay in the public school arena, I would probably have to move to Central Florida or teach at a private school. "Shit," I said to myself while folding up my pants and tossing them into the suitcase.

I heard the door open and close, and then through the corner of my eyes I saw Theo's towering presence in the doorway. Pretending not to see him, I continued with my tears, pouting, and packing.

"Where are you going?" he asked, and I refused to answer. He walked over and snatched the shirt I was folding out of my hand. "Where are you going?"

I looked at him like I would anyone who was challenging me, and picked up the shirt to fold it again, but he tore it from my grasp once again.

"What is your problem, Theo?"

"You." He threw the shirt across the room. "You are my problem, Paige."

He wasn't doing or saying anything to make things any better. He twisted the knife in my back. I asked, "When and how did I become a problem to you?"

"When you won't let me be your man. You keep flipping the damn switch." He was serious. "Sometimes I'm your student, your friend, or your boy, but for once let me be your fuckin' man without having to beg you."

I started to speak. "I don't—"

"I'm talking." He shut me up and continued. "I'm sick of you treating me like a boy, or like the lesser of the two of us, like I don't know anything." He looked into my eyes. "You know what I meant down at the club, when I said that I was involved in the fuckin' shit. I was saying that we're a team. When you hurt, I fuckin' hurt. I was concerned. As your man, I wanted to know what happened, what was said, what the next step is."

"That's it," I barged in. "I don't know what the next step is."

"That's okay. That's why we're together. We're supposed to figure these things out together." He walked closer to me and slowly grabbed my hands. He took them up to his lips. "Allow me to be your man, Paige. I can do it."

He was right. Many times I didn't discuss things with him because I just didn't expect him to "get it." I dealt with problems alone that women normally shared with their mates. I figured that at eighteen years old he would never understand my "real world" situations. I hadn't allowed him to fully be my "man" outside of sex. I sheltered him from my world so that he wouldn't feel inferior, but I had succeeded in doing just that. I made him feel less of a man by being my man.

"I'll tell you what happened." I walked out to the balcony and he followed. "I quit to avoid them firing me and dragging our names through the mud of the school system. If they suspend me, everything would have to be brought up, documented, and discussed by the board. I can't handle that." I focused on the street four stories below and the water adjacent to it.

"I'm sorry, Paige." His facial expression said that he really was. "You don't have to ever handle anything alone," he promised.

I forced a chuckle. "That's easy for you to say. You don't have anything to lose."

"I do." He ran his hand down my back. "I stand to lose you, and losing you would mean losing me."

I didn't allow his words to roll off of me. I let them melt, penetrate, and soak into my soul. "Thank you." We leaned over the balcony railing with the whistling sea breeze in our faces and heard the occasional conversation of people passing beneath us at two in the morning. Theo was staring at me.

"I've never been so in love with anyone before." He paused. "I want to spend the rest of my life with you. I want you to be my—"

"Don't." I had to stop him. "Don't say something that you'll regret tomorrow."

"See, that's what I mean." He was frustrated. "Let me talk, let be a man, Paige." He said sharply, "I know what I'm saying and what I'm doing."

"Okay." I brushed him off. "Talk."

He changed his tone and the subject, and then stood up. "I'm controlling the rest of the night."

"Why?" I had to know.

"No room or time for questions." He continued. "Just be submissive to me."

"Submissive?" It was already after two, so what harm could it be to let him have some fun until the sun came up? "Fine. The night is yours."

"Great," he said. "From this moment on, there will be no second-guessing me. Just do as I ask." He smiled.

"Yes, master." I bowed to him jokingly.

Still looking down at the drunkards staggering to their various hotels, and listening to the waves splash against the docks, Theo stood behind me. Within a few minutes, I felt a difference in his wand. It was now hard.

"Take off your clothes."

"Out here?" I refused. "Are you insane?" I looked back to see him topless and stepping out of his bottoms. "Theo, what are you doing?"

"It's my night, remember?" He stroked his chocolate bar. "C'mon, let me see you."

"Are you serious?" I asked. "People are still out, and if anyone is in those boats docked right there," I pointed, "they can see us."

"And?"

"And they can see us. Plus, if guests are in these rooms next to us, they can see us if they peep around that little wall."

"So?"

"So put on your clothes."

He sat down on the patio chair. "Come ride this dick."

"You're serious?"

"Yeah. You can't say no to this." He pulled me over and lifted my shirt over my head. My nipples stood at attention as the cool ocean air rushed by them, then he kissed them and slowly removed my jeans. "You've never said no to this dick." He knew me well. Another gentle breeze brushed my nipples and sent a great sensation to my bare clit. My lower lips were all greased up.

"I want you to fuck me," Theo commanded. "If you don't do it right, then I'll fuck you."

"How do you want me to?"

"Don't be polite," he said and pulled me closer. "Be rough with this dick until it spits at you."

"It's gonna *spit* at me?" I joked as I straddled him. I wrapped my hand around his piece, steadying it, bracing it for its entrance. As I sank onto it, I felt the thickness disappear within my tight walls and I rose up off of him, all the way to the tip, and then slid back down to the shaft.

"Don't play with me, Paige. Fuck me," he said.

With voices beneath us, and eyes I believed were watching from the boats tied up not too far away, it was hard for me to get in the groove of things.

"Stop being so well-mannered," Theo said. "Ride this dick like a nasty girl." I couldn't. He was hitting my spot when I dropped down, but I didn't want to make a sound, move too fast, or get too freaky in public. "Fuck me."

"I am," I whispered.

"You're being cute with it." He smacked my ass. "If you don't fuck me then I'm gonna fuck you, and you won't like how I'm going to do it."

"I am." I was still scared of being spotted.

"Damn it." He grew impatient and pushed me off of him. "I'm not playing."

"Wait," I pleaded. I didn't know what to expect. Theo stood me up, bent me over the rail, and entered me from the back. My face and chest were dangling over the railing and could clearly be seen from the street. Theo *fucked* me. He did so hard and fast that I couldn't be the mute I started out as. I grabbed the rail and moaned loudly each time he plowed into my warm, wet, and fleshy meat.

During the ten-minute stint, there was one man in particular walking below with someone who looked up and saw me. They stopped and watched quietly. He stuck his hand into his pants. Each time I tried pushing back against Theo to get out of his view, he insisted on me staying there as punishment for not doing him right the first time . . . and I—don't tell anybody—actually liked it.

Monday morning came and I wasn't ready for it. As a matter of fact, at noon I was still in front of my computer trying to type out a resignation letter. I didn't want to mention the real reason, but I didn't want to not have a reason at all. I didn't know what to write. I searched the Internet, flipped through a book on letters, and scoured my mind again and again.

Though the possibilities for the letter were endless, none of them were quite my situation. I didn't know where to start. This was the millionth time that I found myself missing Toni. I could've called her up and said, "I need your help with this."

"My help?" she would've answered. "You're the damn English teacher."

"Toni," I envisioned myself whining into the phone, "I'm serious. I don't know what to write. Help me." I would've sighed. "At least tell me how to start."

"I've never had to write a resignation letter." Toni, ever the comedian, would laugh and continue. "You know I always get fired."

I laughed to myself as I remembered my friend and began typing. Within an hour, I was able to put together about twenty cliché sentences to form my letter. As I read it over and over to myself, the sadness railroaded me. It was unreal. I slowly sat on the sofa and couldn't believe that after all of the years I dedicated to furthering my education I would no longer have a job in my desired field, and all because I allowed my foolish heart to get the best of me.

I was now forced to wonder what Theo's next step would be. Would he run to me or away from me and into the hills? Now that the heat was out of the kitchen and spreading throughout the entire house, where would he stand? He wanted to be a man, my man, so let's see if he'd be manly under pressure.

Theo came over that night with a black shoebox with a red ribbon tied around it. Before handing it to me, he said, "I

feel horrible about you being without a job, all because of
me." He paused. "This is all that I can do to help you right
now."

"What is this?" I shook the box. Its contents clunked
around a bit. "What's in here?"

"If I was just going to tell you, I wouldn't have spent ten
hours trying to tie that bow," he joked. "Just open it."

I pulled the bow until it turned into a long red ribbon, and
yanked the top from the box. "What is that sm—" Funk of
two million years ran into my nostrils and I nearly gagged.
"Yuck." I pushed the box toward him but he pushed it back.

"Just take it out."

I hurriedly rummaged through the red tissue paper and
saw the dirtiest, smelliest, nastiest gym shoe I had ever seen.

"It's one of my lucky sneakers."

"Yeah?" I frowned at the stench and held my nose. "What
am I supposed to do with it?" I pointed at the shoe.

He smiled. "It's symbolic of something."

"What?" I looked at him, puzzled, still holding my nose.

Theo smiled. "It's symbolic of me and what you've done
to me. You saw past the things that said that we shouldn't be
together, and found something within me that you decided to
make a part of you." He took my hand away from my nose
and brought it down to the shoe. "Look beyond the dried-up
dirt, the smell, and the scuffs of this shoe, and you'll find
something that I'd like for you to make a part of your life."

"What?" I thought I would faint, not because of the smell,
but because of what I felt was waiting inside. Was he about
to pop the question? *This is too much,* I thought nervously.
He guided my hand into the shoe and my fingers brushed up
against something tightly wrapped in plastic. I grabbed it and
pulled it out.

"Open it," he said.

I tore open the white plastic bag and saw greenbacks,
dinero, bills; it was money. "What's this?"

"It's seven thousand five-hundred dollars," Theo said. "It's the rest of the money that that coach gave to me. I know that when you resign tomorrow you won't be eligible for unemployment or anything, so I wanted you to have this money, and I hope that it'll last until you get another job, or until I can provide for you."

"Provide for me?" His demeanor was shocking. "Are you serious?" I asked.

"Yes." He kissed me on the forehead. "I don't want you to suffer because of me."

"But this is all the money you have."

"Yeah, but I don't have a mortgage, phone, light, water, cable, and other bills." He smiled. "You need it more than I do right now."

This was no time to cry, but a few tears managed to run out on me anyway. "Thank you." I embraced him. I didn't know how long it would be before I would be up and running again. He had come through for me. Now I was convinced that he wasn't running to the hills, but running into my arms. "Thank you so much."

Theo was the first eighteen-year-old I knew with sense, sensibility, compassion, and consideration for others. When I was his age, if it wasn't my mother or father, I didn't care what someone was going through. To give them my last possessions, they'd have to have a gun to my head.

"I love you," I whispered, not so much for him to hear or know, but because the feeling was overwhelming within me.

"I love you too."

In a very professional blue pants suit, I drove to West Dade, parked in the visitor's parking area, and walked into the school with my head held high. I sauntered into the main office with a smile and an envelope containing my resignation letter. "Good morning," I said, as I marched up to the desk.

"Hello." I could tell that something was up. Mrs. Jacobs, the head secretary, was acting brand new with me. "How can I help you?" The entire office fell silent.

I wanted to say, "Damn nosy bitches," but instead I asked, "Is Mr. Courtland in?"

"Ah, yes." She swallowed. "Yes, he's here."

"May I visit with him?" I asked.

"Um." She looked around like it was her first day on the job. "I don't know. I'll have to check his appointment book." She stared me down as far as the counter and back up to my eyes again. "Have a seat, please."

"Thank you," I said as she walked away. "Let him know that I, Ms. Paige Patrick, in case you forgot my name, would only need a few minutes of his time."

Instead of sitting like Mrs. Jacobs suggested, I continued standing in front of the desk and observed the office employees surfacing from a back room one by one to get a glimpse of the teacher that had done whatever the rumor had me now doing.

I pretended to look through my cell phone for a number, and then pretended to have a short talk with a friend. After that, I listened to the fat steel clock tick away the seconds. With every passing tick and tock, the constant stares turned my confident approach into insecurity. There were steady whispers.

"Is that her?"

"Oh, that's who it is?"

"There she is!"

"I can't believe she actually did that."

They were all hypocrites, though. Had Theo, the star high school basketball player and round draft pick in the NBA, d paid them any mind, they'd be happy to lie in the same bed of nails I had made for myself. Girls, don't hate, emulate.

"I'm sorry." Mrs. Jacobs returned. "He's not seeing anyone without an appointment."

"What?" I was too busy trying to hear the distant murmurs. "Can you repeat that?"

"Mr. Courtland isn't seeing anyone without an appointment."

"Is that so?" I snickered. "When is the next available time?"

"Let me check." Mrs. Jacobs grabbed the book again. This time she sighed. "Tomorrow at ten."

"Then I'll be here tomorrow at nine fifty-five." I continued. "You can tell him that my resignation letter is only two paragraphs, so our meeting won't even last until ten."

"All right." She was dumbfounded.

Without a good-bye, I snatched my envelope from the counter and felt their eyes on my back until I was out of sight.

Ten minutes after school was out for the day, my phone was ringing. "Hello?" I tried to make my voice sound as though it was the second day of a gloriously long vacation.

"'Sup baby?" Theo asked.

"Nothing."

"Enjoying your day?"

"Yeah." I pretended not to have a care in the world.

"How did the meeting go?"

"There was no meeting," I said. "I had to schedule an appointment with him for tomorrow at nine fifty-five."

"Damn."

"How was school?" I asked.

"Same thing, different day." He added, "different teacher, too."

"Poor baby." I frowned.

"No one can take your place." He paused. "I miss you."

"Yeah, right. You can probably get away with everything now."

"No, I really can't," said Theo. "Knowing that you're not gonna be here anymore is driving me crazy."

"Well, it's almost the end of March. You graduate in June, so you have less than two months." I tried to encourage him. "The school year will be over before you know it."

"True, but . . ." Silence filled the connection. "I noticed a few teachers looking at me kinda strange today, staring at me and shit."

"You're Theodore Lakewood." I giggled. "They always stare at you."

"Naw," he said, "today was different. All eyes were on me today. I mean I got stares from every-fuckin'-body; the janitors, the cafeteria ladies, the office workers, even the people that cut the damn trees. Man, it felt like everybody was saying something about me." Then there was the dreaded confirmation. "And Mrs. Greene, the guidance counselor, stopped me in the hallway by her office and handed me a card with her office hours on it." He finished up. "She said if I needed to talk, her office was always open."

"Damn," the word escaped me.

"That's what I felt like saying."

The next day, different day, different suit, same resignation letter in the same envelope, I drove to the school and was surprised to see all of the local news station vans parked there. I was glad that West Dade had something going on. I hoped that it would take the focus off of me for the five minutes I planned on being there.

I cleared security at the gate and parked in the visitor parking again. I checked myself out in the mirror, reapplied my lipstick, and opened the car door. As I stepped out, I noticed the six or seven reporters that were conversing all looked my way. I faintly heard one of them say, "There's our girl." I looked behind me and all around to see whom "their girl" was. There was no one else around.

"Ms. Patrick, is it true that you are involved in a romantic relationship with a student?" the female reporter asked and shoved her microphone in my face.

"Ms. Patrick, who is the student and how old is he?" a male asked.

A third reporter queried, "Is the student a male or female?"

I shouted, "What?" They weren't trying to let me get away without some type of response.

"Who is the student?"

"How long has the affair been going on?"

I began walking toward the school and tried to shield my face from the cameras with the envelope. However, the reporters were relentless. They surrounded me so I had to pretty much walk in circles to shake them individually. I tried running, but they ran after me.

"Ms. Patrick, are the accusations true?"

"Leave her alone," A voice yelled. "Don't you guys have respect for anyone?" Theo's hand pulled me out of the vulture pit. "Why do you do this to people?" He held onto me. I could almost feel the zoom lenses tightening in on our fingertips.

"Theodore Lakewood?" a reporter gasped. "Are you the student in question?"

They all held their microphones up extra high to hear whatever he would say. I squeezed his hand, a hint for him not to say anything, but before his brain picked up on my clue, he was speaking.

"Yes," he said, "I am the student, and I'm also eighteen years old. If I can vote on who the next man to lead this country should be, then I can make decisions regarding my personal life as well. We are doing nothing wrong." I nudged him and we walked into the school side by side.

"Why in the hell would you say that?" I was angry.

"They're going to put that on the news, in the paper, every-where."

"So what?" he said. "They can't tell me what to fuckin' do."

"Yeah, but you have to think of consequences before you open your mouth."

"I did."

"You did?" I struggled to regain my composure. "What were you thinking?"

"Don't start that." He looked down at me. "I was think-ing that I don't want you to go through this alone, which is why I'm here." I could continue to bicker with him about re-vealing too much to the public or I could be grateful that he was still standing by my side. He wasn't running, he wasn't hiding, and he wasn't a coward. He could take it and was showing me, once again, that he was a man.

"Thank you," I said.

He walked with me to the main office but waited outside.

"Those reporters didn't bite you, did they?" Courtland asked as he closed the door to his office. The entire process took about twenty minutes. I handed him my letter and he handed me some papers to sign. He informed me that the process still wouldn't be complete until I went to Downtown Miami to the county office to complete an exit interview and sign even more papers.

"I'll do that tomorrow," I said as I stood.

"I hate to see you go." He reached his hand out to me with a smile.

"Go to hell." I looked down at his hand and willed it to drop off.

I walked out of his office and once again, all eyes were on me. When I met Theo in the hall, I hugged him so that the cu-rious eyes sneaking a peek would be satisfied. We walked out of the building together.

"Did you resign so that you could continue a relationship with Theodore Lakewood?" a reporter asked.

"No." I stopped walking. "I resigned so that I could continue on with my life." I tried to smile. "Speaking of relationships, you guys should wait out here until Principal Courtland comes out and ask him about his relationship with Mr. Doran Bess, the new math teacher here. *Their* love story should be even more interesting than mine." With that said, Theo and I walked to my car and had our first lunch, in town, together.

That evening, we returned to my house and made love with an unheard-of passion. It was as though we had been imprisoned and suddenly set free. My response to his touch, his words, to the feel of him was amazing. Things seemed new, better, and ten times more powerful.

As we finished and lay side-by-side panting, sweating, and dehydrated, my cell phone lit up and vibrated itself off of the dresser.

"I think you use that to play with when I'm not here," Theo joked as he got up to go to the bathroom.

"I do." I laughed and reached down to the ground for the phone. "Hello?"

"I guess you thought you were really doing something when you said that shit to those reporters," Doran said.

"Yeah, as a matter of fact I did," I said, smiling.

"Don't fuck with me."

"Sorry." I tried to calm him. "I truly didn't mean to get you involved. It was personal and had nothing to do with you."

"Well, it sure as hell sounded like it. You said my god-damn first and last name."

"Yeah, but it was about Courtland. He and I are even now."

"Even?" he asked. "Even? What in the hell did I have to do with you getting even with him?"

"It was the only thing I had."

"Oh yeah?" He went silent. "Well, I've got a little getting even to do with you."

I giggled. "Everything is out in the open now. I have nothing to hide."

"You don't, but your man does," Doran said. "Ask your little boyfriend about being in a bathroom stall with Angela Porter on the night of the Valentine's Day dance."

My smile dropped. "What?" I sat up in bed.

"I caught them fuckin'." He gave a sinister laugh. "I caught them. Ask him about it. I know that he's right there. I'll hold the line if you want me to."

"Fuck you, Doran." I hung up the phone and Marion Jones couldn't get to the bathroom faster than me. I opened the door as Theo was washing his hands. I stared at him and tried to make myself believe that things weren't about to end right here and now after all that I had given up. Doran had to be just making things up to make my life miserable. Theo wouldn't, he couldn't, he didn't. Shit, I would kill him if I found out it was true. He noticed the blank look on my face. "What's up?"

I walked toward him. "That's what I want to know."

"Who was on the phone?" He cupped some water and brought it up to freshen his face.

I proudly said, "That was Doran Bess."

"Oh." His eyes left mine immediately. "Oh, okay."

I would make a terrible detective. I had to get right to the core. "What happened between you and Angela at the dance?"

"What do you mean?" His eyes suddenly widened and he couldn't close his mouth as he grabbed a towel and dried his hands and face. "What?"

"You heard me." I got loud. "What happened at the fuckin' dance?"

He threw the towel into the sink forcefully. "Man, fuck that punk-ass muthafucka." He tried to walk past me.

"Why, because that punk-ass muthafucka is telling the truth?" I leaned against the wall to frame him in the room. "Isn't he?" I shouted. "Is it true?"

He stared at the wall. "Is what true?"

"Did you do it?"

"Do what?" He angrily pushed his way past me.

Never in a million years did I expect this. Me, a grown woman, enraged about my eighteen-year-old boyfriend sleeping with a teenage girl. What happened to my life?

"Did you fuck Angela?" I asked. When I turned and walked into the room, he was sitting on the bed with his head in his hands. "All I want to know is, is it true?"

"Nothing really happened." He wouldn't look up at me.

"What does that mean?" I pushed his head back. I needed to see his eyes. "What do you mean by nothing really happened? Did you have sex with her or not?"

"No. There was no sex, Paige." He jumped up from the bed and held my hands. "We didn't have sex, Paige. I'm not lying to you. We did not have sex."

"Then why were you in a stall with her?" I couldn't understand. "*Were* you in a stall with her?"

"Yes."

"Why?" I asked and he looked away again. "Why, Theo?"

"'cause she wanted to." He took a deep breath. "Damn."

"She wanted to what?" I asked.

"She wanted to go down on me," he answered and stood up.

"Did she?" I yanked my hands away from him and found myself banging on his chest. "Did she?" He said nothing, but Theo's silence said everything that I didn't want to know.

"And you came here." The tears fell heavily onto my bare

breasts. "You came here to my house, to my fuckin' bed after you let her do it." I don't know when I stopped hitting him, but I found myself beating on the bed. The pain from Craig and every other person who had ever let me down returned, and I let out a cry that came from the very bottom of my soul. It surfaced in one word. "Why?"

"Paige, it's not like what you're thinking."

I asked, "Did she do it or not?"

He hesitated. "Yeah, but she—"

"Get out."

"Wait!"

"Get the fuck out of my house." I grabbed his pants, shirt, anything that belonged to him and tossed them at him. "Get the fuck out."

"Paige, just listen to me."

"Listen to you?" I was disgusted with him. "Listen to you? After all I've been through. After all of this bullshit I've been through, I don't have time to listen to anything. You just wasted six months of my life."

"I'm telling you the truth," he yelled. "At least I'm being a man about it."

"A man?" I almost laughed. "That's exactly what your sorry ass is not."

"I am."

"You're not!" I yelled. "You are so not."

"Just let me talk!" he shouted angrily at me. "Let me explain."

"No!" I shouted back. "Who in the hell do you think you are, Usher, with your late-ass confession?" I threw his underwear at him. "Save it! If you had something you wanted me to know, you would've told me. No one should have to call me to tell me what the fuck you did."

He was frustrated. "I'm trying to be a man!"

"No, a *man* wouldn't have gotten caught." I thought about what I had said. "No, actually, if this relationship, or whatever it is, meant anything to you, then you wouldn't have let the bitch suck your dick." I was hurting. "Get out of my house."

"You ain't even letting me t—"

"Get out!" I shouted and backed away.

"Paige." He walked toward me, but before he could say a word, I was sobbing.

"Please, just get out," I said and walked into the bath-room, slammed and locked the door behind me. "When I'm done, I don't want you here." I turned the shower on full blast so that I wouldn't hear anything that he had to say. I sat on the toilet seat and poured my tears into a large green towel.

~Situation #18~

The Fly

They say eatin' ain't cheatin', and suckin' ain't fuckin', but you can't tell that to a woman scorned, especially not a black woman. I don't blame Paige, "get your punk-ass out, bitch." Don't feel sorry for Theo. He ain't no damn saint. Angela didn't happen upon his dick in a package of hot dogs. He put it in her mouth.

Hell no! Ladies, imagine a woman on her knees in front of your man with his dick in between her fingers. She looks up and smiles at him and the bastard smiles back, never thinking about the times you've gone without just so he could have, or the good times you two shared. Then her soft, eyeliner- outlined lips, stacked with layers of dollar store glitter-gloss, squeeze around him. Her clammy tongue flicks him gently and his eyes turn over into the back of his head, more so than when you perform. Not only does your man allow it, the muthafucka enjoys it.

Eva Lakewood paced the area in front of the door inside her house with the cordless phone in hand. It had been ringing ever since the five o'clock news, when she, and the rest of South Florida, learned of her son's involvement with his

English teacher. Though she heard her son's voice, saw him on the screen, and understood what he had to say, Eva needed to see him for herself. Reporters seemed comfortable waiting in front of the house for someone, anyone, to come in or go out.

She dialed Theo's cell phone number every ten minutes, but received no answer. She left him countless messages and before long, his voice mail was full to capacity. Eva was angry, embarrassed, shocked, and disappointed in her son. She hadn't even taken off her uniform. She continuously peered out of the window hoping that he would show up and say that it was all a joke.

He pulled into the driveway a few minutes before eleven. She would finally make some sense of it all. The reporters crowded around Theo's car.

"Theodore, can we get a comment from you?"

"Is it true that you two were caught together in Key West?"

"What does your coach, her ex-husband, have to say about this?"

"Were you two sexually involved?"

Theo ignored them and pushed through the sea of reporters just like he did when they asked him stupid questions after losing a game. He marched into the house and closed the door in their faces.

"Well, hello *Mr.* Lakewood," Eva said as she turned and stared him down from the crown of his head to his size seventeen shoes. "I've been calling you for the past five hours."

"Oh, yeah, I had my phone off." He walked past her. "What's up?"

She followed him into his room. "Well, I guess I know who bought you the damn cell phone now."

"Oh God." Theo threw his hands up. "Ma, please."

"Ma, please?" she shouted. "Ma, please my ass. Theo, what in the hell do you think you're doing?"

He didn't know what she knew. "What?"

"What?" she said sarcastically. "Messing around with your teacher."

"Look, I can make my own decisions." Theo added, "It's my life."

"No!" Eva yelled. "It's not your life. It's your damn future that you're fuckin' up." She grabbed the remote and powered on the television. "They're already talking about how this shit may change your standing in the draft."

"I don't think that this has anything to do with my game."

She threw the remote on the bed. "Well, apparently somebody thinks so."

He felt the weight of the world atop his head. "Ma, they just want something to talk about."

"Oh yeah?" she asked. "Well, you sure gave them a lot."

"Whatever. I don't wanna discuss this right now." All Theo could think about was waiting an hour and a half for Paige to come out of the bathroom, and she never did. Each time he screamed or banged on the door, she turned the water up louder. He pretended to leave, but she found him out by calling his phone and hearing it ring in her bedroom. When he answered, she simply said, "Please leave," and hung up. He then turned off his phone and forfeited. He left her alone in her house, her tears, and her pain. Now he walked into turmoil at his own house.

"Ma, I need some time to myself. Please, let's talk about this in the morning."

"In the morning?" she said. "No, Theo, I want to know what's going on. Are you really involved with Ms. Patrick?"

"Yes." He was short and sweet. "Yes."

"Yes?" She couldn't believe what her son was saying. "She is your teacher, old enough to be your mother," she paused, "and your coach's wife."

"Ex-wife," he corrected her. "They're divorced."

"Whatever," she snapped. "When did all of this start?"

Theo forcefully closed the drawer he was looking in for something to change into after his shower. "Do we *have* to have this conversation?" He was annoyed.

"You are my son; You were on the goddamn five o'clock news, about to be on again at eleven, and the fuckin' phone has been ringing off of the goddamn hook." She pointed up into his face. "Yes, we have to have this conversation *right* now."

"Damn, Ma."

She was sick of the runaround. "Look, if you don't want to talk, then I'll call her. I still have her number, ya know."

"Man." He thought long and hard then turned to look at her. "It started during the first month of school . . ."

She folded her arms across her chest, sat on his bed, and listened. Theo didn't bother with details, just what she needed to know, along with the fact that he thought their relationship was over because of the mistake he made with Angela. In six minutes, he summed up their entire relationship. "And that's it."

Eva was speechless and jealous. She couldn't believe that her baby was in love. The things he had done and was willing to do for Paige and the things that she had done for him were incredible. Had Theo told her the same story about a girl his age, she would've called him an idiot for messing up and urged him to make things right, but instead she said, "I can't believe that she is so desperate for a fuckin' man."

Eva stood up angrily and couldn't determine if her bitterness was because she wanted someone to care about her half as much, because she herself was desperate, or because her son loved someone other than her.

"I cannot believe what some women would do to get a man." She realized that she envied Paige.

"Well, I'm just glad that it's all over." She paused. "Maybe you should tell that to the reporters."

"I'm not telling them shit."

"Watch your mouth."

"Whatever." He blew her comment off. "So *she's* the bad person in this. Is that how you see it?"

"I didn't say that she was a bad person." She rolled her eyes. "But she's certainly needy. To be in a relationship with a child, she has to be."

"Needy?" Theo had something that he had been holding in for three years. "Maybe she *was* needy. She *needed* me. I wonder why she was needy, though." Theo pretended to really think about it. "Hmm, I wonder why she was craving love from somebody, anybody, even a quote-unquote child." He added as he stood in his mother's face, "I wonder if it had anything to do with you fuckin' her husband."

"What?" Eva's neck nearly snapped to look sharply up at her son.

"Don't play stupid with me. I knew about it." Theo had never spoken to his mother this way. "I knew about it for the entire time you were doing it. That motherfucka came here late at night and you snuck him into your room. His cell phone number was in the caller ID all the time. He never called here for me."

"That was a long time ago."

Theo yelled, "He was married and you were fuckin' him. So, who is really the *needy* one here?"

She hesitated. "All of that ended years ago." Eva embarrassingly stood up and tried to leave.

Theo blocked her in the room. "Here you are talking about her being desperate. What about all that shit you did when Coach Stiller came here? Cleaning the house, cooking dinner, and wearing the tightest muthafuckin' thing you could find? That wasn't years ago."

"Shut up."

"No." He raised his voice. "I call that desperate. If I wasn't here that day, he could've and would've probably fucked you, and that's all he would've wanted, just like Coach J." Theo paused. "I love Paige. *I* went after *her*. She was always concerned about my age and what people would think about our relationship. I begged her to give *me* a chance." Focusing in on his mother's eyes, Theo added, "She wasn't looking to just get fucked like you."

He knew it was coming, and braced himself for the slap that his mother laid on his face. Eva was out of his room before the sting went away, but he had even more to say.

"I know about the abortion you had for him, too. I found those pills and looked them up on the Internet." Her room door slammed.

Spoken words are irreversible. Once in the shower, Theo felt horrible about the things he said. He didn't so much regret what he said, just how he said it. He wanted to apologize, but was sick of always being the one to ease her pain. He was hurting too.

He walked back into his room, turned on his phone, and within minutes it was ringing. He was excited.

"Hello?" He didn't bother to look at who was calling.

"Damn, boy." It was Will. "How much does it cost to be like you?"

"What's up?"

"You, man," giggled Will. "How could you keep that from me?"

Theo wasn't in the mood. "Lemme call you back."

"Naw, man," Will insisted. "We gotta talk about this shit now."

"I can't, man." He was agitated. "I have to go." He hung up the phone and then the house phone chimed.

He answered the line. "Hello?"

There was a bit of silence then, "Hey, Theo," Trese said.

"I can't talk now."

"What, you got homework?" She paused. "Oops, I forgot. You're the teacher's pet; you don't get homework. You just eat that bitch's old, stale-ass pussy."

"Fuck you, Trese. The only stale pussy I ever had was your wide as the Grand Canyon shit."

"Nigga, you wish!" Trese shouted. "I can't fuckin' believe that you dropped me for an old, fat muthafucka."

"First of all, she's nowhere near fat or old, and if she was, I wanted her, I still want her, and that's that." He paused. "Ain't nobody *dropped* you because you can't drop what has already fallen down in the muthafuckin' gutter." Theo's anger escalated. "We never had anything. I didn't want you; I never wanted you. I fucked you just like all them other cats did." He wanted to call her something outside of her name. "Fuck you, and don't call this goddamn number again."

He immediately dialed Paige's numbers. The house phone was off the hook, and her cell phone was turned off. He sat on his bed and remembered the horrible look on her face when she rushed into the bathroom, the pitiful way she wept, and the way she struggled to breathe. Paige made it clear that she never wanted to see or talk to him again.

Never in his life did he imagine he could care so much about anyone, and even more about the way he made her feel. "Shit," he whispered, and before he knew what hit him, he was in tears.

At three in the morning, Paige was still pacing the floors of her house. She needed something to do so that she wouldn't do something foolish. She cooked, cleaned, organized, and cooked again. The pain of being betrayed was a wicked one. It was different than the feeling that came with being cut off by someone in traffic or having the power company disconnect your lights. This feeling was next to insanity.

Finally retiring to her room, she sat on the bed and put the receiver on the hook. Instantaneously, it was ringing. The Caller ID spat out the name of someone that wasn't Theo, so she answered. "Yeah?"

"Are you all right?" Craig asked.

"Ah . . ." She wanted to lie, but the words wouldn't come out. "Ah."

"I saw the news," he said. "I just want you to know that it wasn't me. I didn't say a word to anyone."

"I know." Her voice was weak.

"Paige, are you all right?"

"No."

The dick in shining armor said, "I'm on my way."

She hung up the phone and tried to relax. In bed, she turned on the television, but the audio on every show, movie, or news became the argument she had with Theo earlier. *Get the fuck out . . . We didn't have sex . . . Fuck you . . . I am a man . . . She wanted to go down on me . . .*

It took all of the good sense she had left not to pick up the phone and call Ian to tell him that he had gotten his wish. His daughter had fucked a future NBA star, which was the first step in his get-rich scheme. He could probably retire early if Angie did a good enough job, especially without a condom. Pregnancy meant a guaranteed paycheck.

The phone rang; Craig again. "You need anything?"

"No." She tried to hinder him. "You don't have to—"

"I'm almost there. I'll call you when I'm at the door." Craig hung up.

Five minutes later, the phone lit up again. "Are you at the door?" she answered.

"No, and you better be glad that I'm not." As the female voice spoke, Paige looked at the caller ID. It was Theo's house number. "How could you do this?"

Paige pretended not to know who was on the other line. "Who is this?"

"This is your boyfriend's mother," Eva said in the harshest tone Paige had heard in a long while. "What kind of woman are you?"

"Ms. Lakewood, I know that you're pretty upset right

now, and so am I. I am in no mood to have this conversation with you." She tried to be civil.

"You don't have to talk," she said. "I'll do *all* of the talking."

"Sorry, I just don't—"

Eva interrupted. "Why would you want to ruin my son's life?"

"Ruin his life?" Paige asked. "I'm the one without a job now." She paused. "Maybe this is a conversation you should have with your son."

"Why, because he found someone younger than you? Or is it because he found someone better than you?" She finished off with, "He's eighteen. What the fuck is your problem?"

"Wait a fuckin' minute." Paige sat up. "You are not calling my house at three in the goddamn morning with this shit." Paige recalled all of the things Theo had said about his mother. "Your lonely ass needs to get a life, always walking around crying about not having a man. Don't hate me because mine just happened to be your son. You just can't stand the thought of him caring for anyone if it's not you."

"He always had girls here," Eva lied. "You couldn't think for one moment that my son was serious about you." Eva snickered. "After all, you couldn't even please your own fuckin' husband."

Paige pulled the phone from her ear and shouted, "Don't you *ever* fuckin' call my house again, bitch."

Since Theo's mother had reminded her of who Craig really was, Paige was further enraged when he arrived. Craig's agenda was always pussy. His plan tonight was to give her some sympathy dick to ease the pain of her frustration. He was going to let her cry on his shoulder, talk it all out, but the forecast was, before morning, to be deep in her pussy. He really didn't give a shit about her problem.

She met Craig outside and didn't allow him in, telling him

that she really needed to be alone. After twenty lines similar
to, "I just want you to know that someone cares," "you
shouldn't be alone right now," and "I'm here for you," Paige
stood her ground and sent him away. There would be no
more sympathy sex in her house.

~Chapter #19~

Paige

"I have so much going on this time that I decided to write you a letter," I said and spread my blanket next to Toni's tombstone. "I know how nosy you are, and I didn't want to forget to tell you anything."

It was eight o'clock on a sunny Saturday morning in June, but it was so hot it felt like it was one in the afternoon on an August day. I found comfort in the lush green grass that cushioned me. Someone, probably Derek, had recently put fresh flowers on Toni's grave. As though she could really hear me, I described each sunflower, orange rose, blue delphinium, red carnation, and yellow daisy to her. "It's beautiful, girl."

After sitting in silence, tracing her name with my fingertip over and over again, I looked at my watch. It was 9:30. My appointment was at 10:30, but I couldn't leave without telling Toni what was what in my life.

"Let's get started." I pulled the long letter out of my purse.

"Dear Antoniqua." I burst out laughing. I frequently joked that her name had to be short for something, so I made up names for her. It always brought us joy. I continued to chuckle and started over.

"Dear Toni, it may seem foolish and almost ungrateful to

say this, but at times I feel that you're the lucky one. You have no more worries, fears, or pains. You've crossed over and . . . left me behind. You have escaped what we, still here, have to deal with . . . all of the regular bullshit of being alive." I paused awhile and scanned what I had just read. It made so much sense when I wrote it, but now it just sounded like drivel. I skipped most of it.

"Well," I took a deep breath, "a lot has happened since the last time I visited. I figured you would enjoy knowing that Marcus is still single." I looked away from the paper. "You used to kid about something happening to you and said that Marcus would have someone else before rigor mortis fully set in, but he still talks about you." *Yeah, every day when he, ever the lawyer and loving husband, calls me with updates on the wrongful death lawsuit that he is filing against Derek.*

"Marcus misses you, and is doing a wonderful job with Kevin and Devin. By the way, I saw them yesterday, and I didn't think it was possible, but they're more handsome than ever before."

"They miss you. I miss you. You've been here for four months, and I will never get used to coming here to be close to you." I looked around. "Toni, I feel somewhat guilty about what happened to you. I don't think that I did enough to stop you from going there that night. For some reason, I feel that I could've said or done something to keep you from ending up here."

Tears crawled downward. "I still pick up the phone and dial your number. I call when I know that no one is there, just to hear your voice on the answering machine." I shook my head from side to side. "I miss you so much.

"I managed to look at your cell phone bill. I have Derek's number, and have been fighting the urge to call him and ask about your final moments. I want to know, and then I don't want to know. I'm not sure if I'm ready to deal with whatever he may say." My heart ached. "I don't want to think that you felt anything or that you struggled. I find peace in thinking that you just slipped away."

I couldn't believe that our friendship was reduced to me reading to a block of grass in hopes that my words would sink seventy-two inches below.

"By the way, I'm single again, and also unemployed." I tried to smile. "The Theo thing didn't work out. We broke up about two months ago." I paused.

"I know that you want the whole story, so I'll give you as much as I can. Here you go. Courtland, who I learned was screwing Doran, saw us together in Key West, and threatened to fire me, so I just quit." I paused and looked away from the note.

"Well, his plan was also to humiliate me, and that he did. The bastard had reporters waiting for me at the school the day I went to resign. I refused to answer any of their questions. However, Mr. Theo comes out and reveals the entire thing with cameras rolling and all." I stopped to breathe and giggle. "And I told the reporters about Courtland and Doran.

"Believe it or not, it gets worse." I sighed. "That same night, Theo and I were at my house and Doran called. He informed me that Theo had cheated on me with Angela, the girl from the pool party that I couldn't stand." I sighed again. "I kicked him out, cussed his ass out, and haven't seen him since. I've spoken to him a few times, though. He calls every so often to ask if he left this or that at my place or to ask how I am. I keep the conversation short, very short, but I haven't heard *anything* from him in about three weeks, so I guess he got the picture." I thought for a second. Did I get the picture?

"I miss him, though. I'd be lying if I said anything different, but I meant what I said about not allowing another man to hurt me twice." I was nervous. My fingertips traced the letters of her name again as the wind rustled my shirt and hair.

"I have one more thing to tell you." What I had to say wasn't on paper, and until that moment I hadn't planned on telling her. "Since the day that I met you, you always had one wish for me, and you died without that wish coming true." The tears flowed faster. "Toni, I am two months pregnant." I stopped to let her soul rejoice a bit. "But when I leave you today, I'm going to an abortion clinic. I'm not keeping the baby." I cried.

"They already made me out to be a pedophile on the news. Thank God he's eighteen or I would be in jail." I wiped my tears. "I can only imagine how people would treat me if I had this baby. It wouldn't be fair to either me or the child, especially the child." I stood up before Toni could whisper words to make me reconsider.

"Please forgive me." The sun became hotter. "I just cannot put myself through this." I struggled to fold my blanket as fast as I could, but it was like she was tugging on it, asking me to stay, to think it over a little more. I couldn't. "Watch over him or her when they get there today." I blew a kiss in the wind and tried to make myself smile. "I'll see you in a few weeks."

The reporters seemed to have lost interest in me, especially since Theo couldn't be seen coming to or leaving my house. However, as a precaution, in a Marlins baseball cap and the darkest shades money could buy, I pulled into a parking spot at the clinic and scoped out the front of it before scurrying toward the door. I had gone to extreme measures to see that no one learned of my "appointment." I rented a car two days prior and had been staying in a hotel under an assumed name ever since. The last thing I needed was my "procedure" on the five o'clock news.

"Ms. Black?" A lady in pink scrubs opened the door and looked into our faces, each of us more nervous than the woman to her right. "Ms. Michelle Black?" the nurse called

again, and then I quickly remembered that it was the name I
had given them since my intention was to pay in cash.

"Right here." I stood up.

She smiled. "Come with me, please."

As I walked away, I wondered what the women I left behind in the waiting room thought of me. Did they speculate
as to what my reason for being here was? If they knew my
situation, would they deem it worthy? Or was I just selfish?
After all, I wasn't raped and carrying the child of a violent
stranger. I hadn't been beaten by an aggressive lover after
which I had not felt my baby move for days. I wasn't fourteen and scared to death of my father. I was simply a woman
who hadn't used protection. I had no story to tell, and I had
no good reason. I *was* being selfish.

"Right in here, Ms. Black." The lady pointed into the
small room.

I was nervous. "Thank you." Were thanks appropriate? I
mean I was about to have an abortion in the damn room.
Why would I say thanks? I was trippin'.

"The nurse will be with you shortly. She'll prepare you for
Dr. Roth."

"Oh, I thought you were the nurse." I was worried about
meeting too many people in this place.

"No, I'm just a receptionist." She smiled. "But I am in
nursing school, though. I graduate in a month."

"Good for you." I forced a smile.

Ushering me into the room, she said, "Just change into the
hospital gown behind the curtain, then get comfortable. The
nurse will be with you shortly." She closed the door and left
me all alone.

I didn't want to look around the small, gray room. I didn't
want to see something that would scare the shit out of me. It
would serve me better not to see or focus on all of the pointy
metal instruments seemingly glaring at me. I purposely
looked down at the green-tiled floor, stepped behind the cur-

tain, rested my purse on the floor, and began removing my clothing.

I heard the door open and felt a bit of a breeze hit my back. "Ms. Black?"

"Yes?"

"How are you feeling?"

"Oh, I'm fine," I lied from behind the curtain. "How are you?"

"Well, it's my first day back at work."

"Are you the nurse?"

"Yes, ma'am." I heard the door close.

"Were you on vacation?"

"No, just a short leave."

I struggled with my jeans. "Okay."

"Do you mind if I ask you a few questions while you're changing?"

"No." I finally got out of the stubborn pants. "Go ahead."

"Thank you." She rustled some paper. "What is your age?"

I joked, "You want the truth?"

"I'm afraid so." She giggled.

"I'm thirty-two."

"Thank you." She continued. "Have you had one of these procedures before?"

"No." I frowned. "No, I haven't." Who would or could do this more than once?

"Okay," she said. "Do you, or any immediate member of your family, have a history of any of the following illnesses . . . ?" She read off a long list of sicknesses that to my knowledge had as much to do with abortions as, ahem, George W. Bush has with honesty.

"Did you say insanity?" I asked.

"No."

"Okay. Well, no, I'm all clear then." We both laughed.

"You requested the twilight anesthesia, correct?"

"Yes." I put on the hospital gown and tried to tie the annoying strings in the back. It was like a cat chasing its tail. I reached to the left and they swung to the right. I reached to the right and they swung to the left.

"Who did you bring with you?"

"Huh?" Her question threw me off.

"Who will be driving you home after the procedure?"

They told me over the phone that I needed someone to drive me back, but I didn't think that they would actually ask. "My husband is at a coffee shop a few blocks away," I lied. "I'll call him when I'm ready."

"He could've been in here with you."

"No," I said adamantly. "No, I'd prefer doing this part on my own."

"All right." She continued. "Just to verify information, you are under twelve weeks, correct?"

"Yes." I finally tied the strings. "I am two months pregn—" I stopped myself. Saying the word *pregnant* just didn't seem right. "I am two months into this." I stepped out from behind the curtain and suddenly felt too unsure of myself, and my decision, to hold my head up.

"Do you know if—" The nurse stopped talking, but I felt her staring at me. "Paige?" Did she call my name? "Paige Patrick?" How did she know me?

"I'm Michelle Black." My heart sped up as I looked into her face without knowing who she was. "Who are you?"

"You are *not* Michelle anything." She was a tall, thin black woman with long, straight hair. She looked to be about forty, but not a year older. She was light brown, with a narrow face and full lips. The white uniform, stockings, and shoes actually looked like a fashion statement on her.

"I am Eva Lakewood."

"Shit." I rolled my eyes. "What a clinic I picked." I

grunted and made a move to walk back behind the curtain, but she grabbed me by the arm and looked down at my stomach region.

"Is that Theo's baby?"

I pulled away from her. "No, it's *my* baby."

"Did you tell him?"

"The only person that needs to know found out two weeks ago, and if there was an appointment available at that time, I wouldn't have run into you." I added, "Therefore, no one needs to know about this."

She followed me behind the curtain. "You should've told him."

"What for?" I looked up at her angrily. "Can I have some privacy, please?"

She stepped away from the curtain. "It's his right to know."

"What the hell do you care about what I'm doing? I thought you'd be glad."

"A lot has changed."

"Well, I didn't get the newsletter," I huffed then I continued talking and putting on my clothes. "Wasn't it you that called me and cussed me out a few months back?"

"Yes," Eva spoke in a light whisper.

"Didn't you say that you were glad that he cheated on me?"

"Yes, but—"

"Thank you," I interrupted. "So, why give a shit about me being pregnant or having an abortion?" I pulled my shirt over my head. "You have me out of your hair and your son's life."

"I'm sorry about the things I said to you that night, Paige." She paused. "The truth is, Theo and I had a terrible argument that night. He said some upsetting things to me in order to defend you and," I heard grief in her voice, "instead of hurting him back, I decided to hurt you." Without saying another word, I pulled up my jeans, grabbed my purse, and bolted around her.

"Paige, please don't get rid of that baby," Eva said as my hand reached for the doorknob.

"Why? So that you can really make my life a living hell?" I asked. "C'mon. Give me one good reason I should have this kid."

"Don't you have *any* sympathy for me?"

"Sympathy for you?" I asked with a snicker. "For what?"

In a whispered cry, she fell into the chair behind her. "My son only died three weeks ago."

"What?" I felt gravity on me like never before, pulling me downward, yanking my chains. "What?" She couldn't have been serious, but she would be demented to make up something so drastic. "What did you say?" I stared at her.

"He's dead," she said from the chair next to the "termination" table. "But I guess you don't give a damn."

"He's dead?" My back hit the door and stopped me from falling.

"Yeah." Eva's eyes were already red. "I thought you knew."

My body shook as I raised my head to look into her face. It seemed to take ten years, and on my journey I reminisced, remembering the first day Theo walked into my classroom, his first detention, the first time we kissed, the day I saw him fully nude, the day he nearly caught the kitchen on fire trying to imitate Emeril, and all of the times we made love. "No, oh my God, no." My head was spinning, my body was falling, and my heart felt like it was failing. The next thing I remembered, I was lying on the table of doom with Eva checking my pulse.

"There you go." She smiled. "Sit up and drink some water."

I did, but quickly got back to the matter at hand. "When did this happen and why didn't anyone call me?"

"I thought you knew, but after the way I talked to you, I didn't expect you to voluntarily come around."

My breathing was still irregular. Actually, it felt like I wasn't breathing at all, so I drank more water. "I would've come." The tears made their way from my heart to my eyes and kissed my skin. "I would've come," I repeated a half dozen times. "I would've."

"I'm sorry," Eva said as she helped me to my feet. "I wanted to call you back that night and apologize, but pride got in the way. I didn't want to admit that I was wrong." She wrapped her arms around me. "It's terrible that it takes something like death to put things in perspective. I am truly sorry, Paige."

"I'm sorry too." We both cried and held onto each other for a few minutes. "This can't be real."

"Believe me, it feels like a nightmare. This is my first day back to work," Eva spoke as she rubbed my back, "but I don't even think that I can do this anymore." She sighed. "I can't watch women throw their babies away when I would give my life to have my own son back."

"What happened?" I needed to know.

"He and some friends went to the beach, and a riptide carried him out. They say that he struggled, he tried, and he fought all he could to get back in, but he couldn't make it. He went under and never resurfaced." It was hard for her to go on. "At least not until the rescue team pulled him out like an hour later."

I regretted the way I treated him on our last night together, but I figured that somewhere down the line we would both mature and end up properly discussing the matter. I should've listened or cried and allowed him to comfort me that night. However, I wanted to hurt him back. I turned my ringer off, didn't return his calls, and pretended not to be interested when I *did* decide to pick up the phone. I was play-

ing the angry woman role, but I wanted him more than anything and I still loved him . . . but I was three weeks late and
five dollars short.

I wanted him to show up at my door uninvited and *make*
me hear him out. I didn't want to ask him to come over; I
wanted love to bring him back. I even kept the house spotless
awaiting such a day, but he was such a gentleman that he did
what I asked and respected the facade I presented and
stopped calling *three weeks ago* . . . now I knew why. These
foolish games we play in life . . . no one ever really wins.

"I loved him so much." I sighed painfully as I hugged her.
"I can't—" All I was left with were memories, memories of
this and memories of that, but in time they, too, would fade.

"Oh my God." It was then that I realized that Theo had
left me with the ultimate memory, something that would only
age to remind me more and more of him, something that
meant that he'd exist throughout my lifetime. Theo had left
me with a child, his child. "I can't get rid of this baby."

"It seemed like just yesterday when Kevin was a baby."
She smiled. "Now he's gone."

"What? Who?"

"Kevin? My son." She looked at me peculiarly, realizing
the mistake. "Oh, oh no. I'm so sorry. I didn't say. I should've
clarified that it was my younger son, Kevin."

"It's Kevin that died?" Lord, the pressure lifted and I felt
as though I could dance a jig, but all in all, she had still lost a
son. It didn't matter which one. I still felt her pain—well,
kind of—but it would be inappropriate for me to express
how happy I felt that Theo was still breathing.

"I'm still sorry."

"Thank you." She wiped her face.

"Wow." I wiped my tears away.

"You thought it was Theo," she said. "Still in love, huh?"

I sighed. "Still in pain, too, though."

"I used to date a married man who was in and out of my house, back and forth between me, his wife, and only God knows who else. He walked around with his head held high, like he did no wrong, like he wasn't sorry for anything or anyone." She stopped. "That's the kind of man that you leave and don't look back at." Eva continued. "However, Theo has shown me what a man who should be forgiven and deserves a second chance is supposed to look like. I see him every day, Paige. Everything he says and does tells me that he still loves you." She paused. "Although it hurt him badly when you didn't show up to the funeral or call, all he wanted was you."

"Really?" I felt giddy.

"Really." She shook her head up and down. "I can't have any more children, and even if I could, they could never replace Kevin. But a grandchild would sure bring some light back into my life." She grabbed my hand. "But it's your decision to make." She turned her back to me and walked behind the curtain to pick up and fold the gown I left on the floor. "By the way, I never saw you here, Michelle."

"Thank you, nurse." I walked out of the room and left the clinic with my baseball cap and shades in my hand. I had nothing to hide.

I didn't need a map. I had dropped him off and screeched out of his neighborhood plenty of times to remember the street and the house well. I pulled into his driveway and parked next to his car. As I walked toward the house, I imagined him not being able to contain his happiness and sprinting out of the door to greet me. That didn't happen. Instead, I rang the doorbell six times and was walking back to the car before I heard the lock click.

I turned around and saw his sweet, young, and handsome face. "Hi," I said and slowly walked back toward the house.

"What's up?" he said without a smile, and closed the door behind him.

"Nothing much." I did need a map now, to guide this conversation. "How are you?"

"Good."

"Um . . ." I didn't know where to begin. "I just heard about Kevin and thought I would come by to offer my condolences."

"Okay," he said, gazing across the street.

"Okay?" I asked. "Okay, is that all you're going to say?"

"Yeah, to someone who is three weeks late."

I took a deep breath. "I just heard about it less than an hour ago. I would've came sooner if you—"

"I called you that night." He raised his voice.

"I probably wasn't home."

"You were," he said.

I tried to defend myself. "How do you know?"

"Because I called from my cell, right outside of your house. Your car was there, and I even watched you walk by the window a few times."

"I'm sorry." I was caught. "I didn't know why you were calling."

"Well, now you know why," he said and started to turn away.

"Theo," I said, "I'm sorry about not being there for you, especially since you never left my side when I needed you after what happened to Toni." I couldn't believe that I was actually in his presence again.

"It's cool. I'm over it." He paused. "I just figured that that was my punishment."

"No." I stepped closer to him. "I'm not that cruel of a person. Had I known, I would've been at your side night and day, regardless of what people would've said." I wanted to touch him. "So, how are you *really* doing?"

"Better," he said and shook his head. "I can't wait to move out of this house, though. I see him everywhere and it's driving me crazy."

"I know how you feel. I feel that way whenever I go to Toni's house. It's comforting yet creepy at the same time." He glanced down and looked at me, and it was like the first time all over again. I couldn't hold back.

"I miss you, Theo." I grabbed his hand and he didn't pull away, so I continued. "There is a lot that we need to talk about." I squeezed his hand gently. "I'm hoping that—"

"Pookie." The house door opened. "Pookie, is that the pizza?" A tall, slim, light-skinned young girl pulled the door back. She was wearing the tightest, shortest pink shorts I had ever seen, and she was staring right into my face. She had the balls to ask, "Who is she?"

"Not the pizza guy," Theo said to her. "They'll probably be here soon, though."

"Okay." She studied me and closed the door slowly.

I sighed and quickly pulled my hand away from his. "Well, *Pookie*," I said with as much disdain as I could without crying. "I won't take up any more of your time." I was already walking back to my car. "I was just stopping by to see that all was well with you."

"All is well with me," he said mockingly. "What about you?"

I opened my car door. "Couldn't be better." I looked over at him. "Nice seeing you again." Before I could put the car in reverse, *Pookie* was already in the house. I was waiting for Ashton Kutcher to spring from the bushes with the camera crew, 'cause I had just been *Punk'd*.

"I cannot believe this shit," I said as I turned into the drive-thru of my favorite ice cream parlor. "Let me have two scoops of chocolate on a large waffle cone, heavy on the Hershey's syrup, please." All I kept seeing were those tight pink shorts. She was pretty, had a nice body, long hair, and long legs. She would look great standing next to him at the NBA draft. "Bitch," I whispered when I thought of him making love to her.

On the drive home, I cried and cried until salty tears got in the way of my sweet, velvety chocolate ice cream. I got frustrated trying to manage them both and ended up tossing the cone out of the window a few blocks from home.

I turned onto my street and almost went into cardiac arrest when I saw Theo's car next to mine in the driveway. My heart jumped, leaped, and skipped, until I noticed that he *and* Ms. Pink Shorts were waiting outside. "What in the hell is this?" I asked myself. "He's bringing this bitch to my house?" Oh, hell Naw!

I honked my horn and down rolled my window down. "Please get out of my space." She jumped into the driver's seat and reversed, onto the street.

I parked and Theo approached me. "Didn't you say that we needed to talk?"

"Theo, I'm not into drama." I walked past him and up to the door.

"Auntie," he shouted at Ms. Pink Shorts, "I'll call your cell when I need you to come pick me up."

"All right, Pook," I heard her say in the distance.

"Stop calling me that, man," he yelled.

Auntie? Oh, damn!

"That's your aunt?" I asked. "She looks so young."

"My mom and grandma were pregnant at the same time. She's a few months older than I am," he said. "She came down from Atlanta for the funeral and acts like she can't leave."

"I'm sorry." I covered my face. "I thought that she—"

"I know." He smiled. "Everybody thinks the same thing."

"Why didn't you say something?"

"For the same reason you stopped answering my calls."
He giggled. "I wanted to see how much you wanted me," he
walked up to me, "and I see that you do."

I blushed. "You don't know."

He bent slowly toward my lips until his touched mine. His
arms, those arms that I loved so much, found their way
around my waist. His tongue was sweeter, longer, and
quicker. He smelled just as I remembered. My hands rushed
to his back and he felt my body surrender.

He held me tightly. "I never stopped caring for you, and I
never will."

We moved from the porch into the living room, and as to
cleanse ourselves of the past, we ended up in the shower. I
stood beneath the showerhead, remembering the day with a
smile as the warm droplets of water sprinkled my body. Drip
. . . drop . . . plop . . . splash. I closed my eyes and giggled as
each one kissed my breasts then sashayed slowly toward my
nipples.

It was so good to have Theo back in my house and heart.
When he entered the bathroom, my thoughts were, "There is
a God." Theo turned off the lights and allowed the glow of a
candle to soften the mood.

The shower steamed up when he stood behind me and insisted on washing my back, my breasts, and my already
washed wet pussy. I allowed him full access. However, after a
few wipes, he forgot all about the towel and caressed me
with his hands. "Ooh," I moaned, and it encouraged him to
rub a little harder, a tad bit faster, and just a smidgen deeper.

Theo enjoyed the systematic way the warm water fell from
my stomach to my pussy, mixed with my juices, and then slid
onto his fingers. His dick began to rise as the warmth of my
pussy melted onto his fingertips. He hardened and the tip of
his stick turned a pretty shade of brownish pink. It whis-

pered, *Taste me*. And as though I could draw nectar from it, I dropped to my knees and dropped my jaws. I didn't suck him right away, but allowed him to penetrate my mouth over and over again at his own pace.

Sure, as I tasted him I thought about Angela's mouth once being there, but I used the experience as therapy. If you truly want to get over something, sometimes you have to force yourself to relive it. So I did, and I had to do it with the knowledge that regardless of who had climbed the mountain before me, I was the first one to reach the summit and plant a flag.

I started sucking him, pulling every sexual thought he'd had that week right out of the tip of his dick and into me. He grew thick, thicker, and then I tasted trickles of his excitement. Over a period of five minutes, the fleshy feel of my moist tongue, lips, and meaty cheeks satisfied him so much that he couldn't hold back. "Oh, shit." He pushed down on my head until the very tip of his dick ran past my tonsils.

He was at his peak, and I knew to move quickly. Instead of racing to the bedroom, I bent over the toilet and welcomed him to pleasure me from behind. Theo stroked his dick with his wet hand and guided it into my waiting pot of honey. "Oh, yes," we said simultaneously. I felt like singing that Mase song, *Welcome back, welcome back, welcome back*.

I ground my pussy in small circles, and Theo pulled all the way out and rubbed and beat my clit with his tool, then plunged back within me. He did this several times, knowing just how crazy it made me.

"Damn, I've missed you, Paige," he said and blasted into me over and over for about four minutes before he was shooting into me. Afterward, we completed our showers like zombies and returned to the room. With his back up against the headboard, I cuddled next to him.

"I've missed you so much."

"Really?" He smiled. "Paige, you have no clue what I've been going through these last two months." He kissed my forehead. "I have a few questions to ask you."

"Okay."

"Are you . . . ?" He thought for a second and then re-worded his question. "Will you please come to my graduation?"

"Yes, of course." I smiled. "Yes."

"Great. Now, what about taking me to the airport when I leave for some interviews next month?"

"Yeah, I can do that," I joked. "Not like I have a job or anything."

"Okay, well, since you don't have nothing to do . . ."

"Anything," I corrected him, just like old times. "Well, since you don't have *anything* to do."

"Be quiet." He smiled and covered my mouth. "Since you ain't got shit else to do, how about accompanying me to the draft?"

"Me?" I was astonished.

"Yeah, you." That bright white smile of his was back. "Will you?"

"What will I wear?" It was the question any woman would ask after being asked to joined the assumed NBA number one draft pick at the actual draft.

"Is that a yes?" he asked.

"Yes, yes." I was excited. "Yes, I'll go."

"Cool." He grabbed my hand and continued. "Now, what about when I get my first check from the NBA? Will you go house shopping with me?"

"Oh my God." My right hand clenched my heart. "Yes, I'll be honored to help you select your first home."

Theo then became serious. "Will you do me the honor of living there with me?"

His question knocked the wind out of me. "You want me to—?" I stopped in mid-sentence. I couldn't believe that he wanted to share his dreams with me. And then came the tears. "Yes." He was truly amazing.

He left the bed to get me some tissues, and as he handed them to me, he said, "Well, since I got you on a roll, answering 'yes' to everything . . ." I wiped the tears from my eyes, and when I could see clearly again, he was on his knees next to the bed. He had a Kleenex tissue neatly folded and encircled by a one-carat princess cut platinum diamond ring.

"Will you marry me?"

All I could think was, *Are you serious? Are you serious? Are you serious?* but I couldn't even say it. I was shaking and smiling all at the same time.

"Is that a yes?"

"Yes, yes, yes, yes." I finally let it out, and he slipped the ring on my finger. "Oh my God, Theo! Oh my God."

"I love you, Paige." He got back in bed. "I want to spend the rest of my life with you. I never want there to be another day where we don't talk, kiss, hug, or make love. You are second nature to me, like breathing. I cannot live without you."

"I love you." I wrapped my arms around him and kissed his lips.

After the excitement of the moment minimized and I could breathe again, I stared at him. "Now I have a few questions to ask you."

"Shoot." He pulled me closer to him.

"You hungry?" I asked.

"All the time." He rubbed his stomach.

"You've missed me?"

"You know that."

"Have you thought about me every day?"

He laughed. "Yes."

I looked at him and squinted a little. "You want to live with me?"

"Of course. I just asked *you* that."

"You want to marry me, huh?"

He said, "I sure do."

"Do you want to have children some day?"

"Yeah." He kissed my shoulder. "A whole basketball team."

"Well," I grabbed his left hand and placed it on my stomach, "you'll have your first player in seven months."

"Yeah!" He quickly realized what I was saying and sat up. "Yeah?" he screamed. "Are you serious?"

"Yes, you're going to be a coach."

"Oh my God." He picked me up and sat me on his lap. "I love you." Then he bent to kiss my stomach. "And I love *you* too."